WILLIAM A. GLASS

AS GOOD AS CAN BE

A NOVEL

HP

Hawkeye Publishers

Library of Congress Control Number: 2019920052

Paperback: 978-1946005342
Hardcover: 978-1946005403
Ebook: 978-1946005410

Also by William A. Glass:

OFF
BROADWAY
A Marriage Drama

Novel by
William A. Glass

This book is dedicated to my mother,
Jacque Lansdale Glass

TABLE OF CONTENTS

CHAPTER ONE
SHEMIRAN

Dave Knight is on his toes peering through a playroom window at the snow. It fell overnight, but there are already tracks in the fresh powder. They lead to the shallow end of the swimming pool. Several servants have gathered there, and now Dave sees why. "Uh-oh, Haji fell into the pool again," he exclaims.

"Let me see," Melissa says, shoving Dave aside. Haji Baba is her donkey, and she watches with concern as two houseboys cling to his tail. The driver, Mahmoud, is partway on the ice holding the animal's neck. "Stupid donkey," Melissa says. "Now he's stuck." She allows the curtain to close and goes out.

Soon Melissa is back holding a Coca-Cola bottle. "This is for you," she says and gives the drink to Dave. He takes a swallow and immediately gags. As he regurgitates his breakfast, Dave's nurse, Farah, rushes over and looks at what's left of the drink. "You give brother soap water," she says to Melissa. "Bad girl." Farah spins Melissa around and gives her two bops on the behind. Then she takes Dave on her hip and carries him down the hall to the master bedroom.

Lieutenant Colonel David S. Knight Jr. answers Farah's knock. He belts his uniform jacket while listening to Farah describe what Melissa did. Then the officer wrinkles his nose. "What's that smell?" he asks.

"He throw up," Farah replies.

"Well, get him changed, we have to leave," Knight tells the nurse. "Stop sniveling," he barks at Dave.

"You don't have to holler at the poor child," Bobbie Knight says to her husband. She's still in bed, propped up on pillows having breakfast. "I wonder why Melissa takes such delight in tormenting him."

Farah carries Dave into the bathroom to clean up. Then she takes him to the bedroom he shares with his brother, Dan, who's sitting on the floor playing. The toddler looks up and blinks his brown eyes curiously as Farah gets Dave into a fresh set of clothes. Dan's the only one of the children to inherit Knight's dark good looks. The others all have Bobbie's fair hair, light-colored eyes, and Celtic complexion.

While Farah gets Dave ready, Knight goes downstairs to the kitchen. His youngest child, Marie, is in a high chair being spoon-fed breakfast by the family's cook, Aliya. "Where in the hell is Mahmoud?" Knight asks with an impatient glance at his watch.

"Haji fall in pool," Aliya replies.

"Not again," Knight exclaims. He stalks to the front door past Oscar, who's wagging his tail in anticipation of a pat on the head. Knight ignores the dog and goes outside, where he's momentarily stunned by the sight of the Alborz Mountains rising in front of him. With the sun just up, only the peaks are illuminated, so the icy spires appear to be floating. It's a captivating illusion, but Knight now turns his attention to the swimming pool. "Where's the goddamn rope?" he shouts after a quick assessment.

"I get," Mahmoud hollers back. He beckons a gardener to take his place holding Haji's neck.

As the driver makes his way to the stable through deep snow, Knight lights a cigarette. He watches Mahmoud return to the pool with a length of thick rope, loop it across the donkey's chest, and then organize the other servants to pull on the ends. They quickly haul the animal out. "Put Haji back in the shed and lock the gate," Knight directs. "What idiot left it open anyway?"

Flicking the cigarette away, Knight reenters the house to see Farah coming down the stairs with Dave who is once again properly attired. Melissa follows, holding the hand of her nurse. Knight shepherds both schoolchildren outside and into the backseat of the family car. Mahmoud closes the door behind his passengers then gets behind the wheel. "Don't you people ever learn?" Knight asks as the vehicle gathers speed.

"Yes, boss."

"No, you don't, or you would've got the rope right away."

"Forget rope."

"That's what I mean," Knight laughs. "You forget what worked last time and go back to what was not working last time; pulling on the poor creature's tail, for Chrissake."

Knight relaxes now that they're on the way, and soon the vehicle is passing through the outskirts of Tehran. At first, there's little traffic, but as they near downtown, the streets become congested. Wagons drawn by horses or donkeys intermingle with bicycles, pushcarts, automobiles, and trucks. Businesses housed in rudely constructed cinder block buildings line the road. In between are rubble-strewn vacant lots that shabbily dressed pedestrians cut through on their way to work.

Once past the commercial district, the neighborhood improves, and soon Mahmoud is turning onto the treelined street that leads to the United States embassy. It's in a compound that takes up an entire city block. Enclosed within the walls are the ambassador's residence, an apartment building, a dinner club, barracks for the Marines, and the multistory embassy building, which is topped with an antennae array. This electronic gear was installed by Knight and his command to spy on the Russians.

As the Knights' car approaches the embassy entrance, a crowd chants anti-American slogans. Many of the protestors carry signs while others shake their fists. They crowd around the front gate, so a squad of Marines comes out to clear the way. Then a sergeant waves the vehicle through, and now, despite all the chaos at the house this morning, Mahmoud pulls up to the embassy building right on time. He springs out of the driver's seat to open the back door, and the Knights go inside. Once past more Marine security, they approach a bank of elevators. Melissa and Dave take one down to the basement schoolroom, while their father goes up to his spacious corner office on the sixth floor.

"The demonstration was smaller this morning," Knight tells his secretary, Janice Watkins. She's a recent college grad from Kansas who's married to one of the immigration counselors.

"Yes, it looks like they're running out of steam," Janice agrees.

Downstairs, Mrs. Rhonda Harper oversees the schoolroom. She's a tall, plainly dressed woman with a dull but pleasant face who succeeds in looking middle-aged even though she's not yet thirty. Mrs. Harper majored in education at Auburn University then married an Air Force sergeant. Now her husband works as a contractor helping the Shah maintain his fleet of F-86 Sabrejets.

There are eight children in Mrs. Harper's care. Dave is the youngest; the oldest is ten. They sit at desks arranged in a circle, and every day Mrs. Harper makes up individual folders containing age-appropriate worksheets for them. Then she spends each morning in the center of the circle going from desk to desk working with each student in turn.

Today Dave is given a piece of tracing paper taped to a chart that depicts five capital letters. His task is to trace the five letters using a marker, but he makes a mess. None of the squiggly shapes he draws resemble letters, so Mrs. Harper patiently replaces the tracing paper. "You need to focus on your work," she says. "Don't just scribble."

Mrs. Harper turns to work with another child, and when she looks back, Dave is on the floor playing with a jack-in-the-box. "Dave, you're supposed to be working now; playtime is coming soon," she says. Dave ignores her, and when Mrs. Harper leaves the circle and walks toward him, the boy playfully runs around her to the other side of the room. "If you don't settle down, I'll have to put you in the corner," the teacher threatens.

"You can't catch me," Dave laughs and as Mrs. Harper again approaches, he tries to get past her. However, this time she cuts him off. So now the teacher sits Dave in a corner facing the wall. "If you behave for ten minutes, you can rejoin the group," she promises.

Soon it's playtime, and the children scatter to find toys. Dave is allowed out of the corner to join them. "Who needs to go?" Mrs. Harper asks, and several kids raise their hands. The teacher takes them out in the hall where a Marine is on guard. He walks the children to the lavatory and waits outside.

Meanwhile, Mrs. Harper returns to the classroom and finds Dave lying on the carpet fast asleep. She decides not to wake him, but when Melissa returns from the potty break and sees her brother on the floor, she kicks him. "You can't sleep now," she says.

As class resumes, Mrs. Harper gets a book and settles into her chair. "It's story time," she calls, and the students eagerly gather. They sit on the floor at the teacher's feet as she begins reading *Hansel and Gretel*.

"Leave me alone," the girl next to Dave says.

"What's going on?" Mrs. Harper asks.

"Dave's bothering me."

"No, I'm not."

"Well, come sit next to me," Mrs. Harper tells Dave. Then with the troublesome boy seated nearby, she resumes the story.

"I want *Snow White*," Dave interrupts.

"We read that yesterday," Mrs. Harper says.

"Snow White!"

"Not today," the teacher replies. "We can read *Snow White* tomorrow." Mrs. Harper continues reading, and all is peaceful for a time. Then she hears Dave humming under his breath. She ignores him at first, but the sound gets louder. "Dave, be quiet," the teacher orders. However, Dave leaps up and begins marching around the room.

"Heigh-ho, heigh-ho, it's off to work we go," he sings, swinging his arms.

"OK, back to the corner with you," Mrs. Harper snaps, and immediately Dave is running again with Mrs. Harper in pursuit. The other kids watch, mouths agape, until the teacher gets Dave by the ear and, using that appendage, drags him toward the corner. On the way, Dave collapses, and the teacher loses her grip. She stands over him breathing heavily. Then turning to the circle of children, Mrs. Harper says, "OK, playtime."

"We already had playtime," Melissa complains.

"We'll finish the story later, now go play."

Mrs. Harper turns to Dave. The child is whimpering and holding his ear. "Get in that chair right now," she orders, "or I'm calling your father."

Dave doesn't want any trouble at home, so he goes back to the corner, and for now, just sits and quietly daydreams. Someday he'd like to have a donkey of his own, and Dave pictures himself riding one that's even bigger than Haji

Baba. As he rides his donkey down the driveway, the servants all admire him. But then Mrs. Harper intrudes on his fantasy. "Go get your lunch and come back," she says.

Dave goes to his cubby, gets his lunch box, and looks inside. Aliya knows peanut butter is his favorite and, sure enough, she packed him a peanut butter and jelly sandwich, a thermos full of juice, and two cookies. He sits in the corner to eat, and when he's finished, Dave gets up to return the lunch pail. "Get back in the chair," Mrs. Harper orders. "You have ten more minutes."

As lunch hour winds down, kids that need to go are again accompanied to the lavatory. Then it's time for the afternoon class, and Mrs. Harper releases Dave from the corner. She places more worksheets on each child's desk then goes around helping the students get started. Melissa is doing subtraction, so the teacher pauses to help her with a problem.

"Need to pee-pee," Dave whines.

"We just had a bathroom break," Mrs. Harper says. "Next one's at two." She goes back to working with Melissa, but when Mrs. Harper looks up again, she sees Dave has left his desk and is now at the door. "OK, back in the corner," she snaps.

"Pee-pee," Dave cries, and as Mrs. Harper comes for him, Dave again runs away. But this time the teacher quickly catches the child. As she drags him toward the corner, Mrs. Harper notices Dave is leaving a trail on the carpet. She sees a dark stain on his pants and releases the sobbing boy who slumps to the floor. The teacher looks down at the freckle-faced, green-eyed five-year-old and wonders for the hundredth time how such a cherubic-looking kid could be such a terror.

The other children have been watching Dave's go-round with Mrs. Harper, and now one shouts, "Dave pee." Soon all of them are laughing and pointing at the front of Dave's pants.

"Get back to your work," Mrs. Harper yells. "Do you want to sit in the corner too?" The teacher goes out in the hall and comes back with the guard. "Corporal Hernandez will stay with you while I'm gone," she tells the students. "He will make sure you do your assignments." The children gaze solemnly at the lance corporal who is immaculate in his dress blues. Then they get back to work.

Now Mrs. Harper speaks softly to Dave: "Come on, sweetheart, we'll get you cleaned up." She takes him to her apartment and washes his underwear and pants. After twenty minutes in the dryer, the garments are ready, so she gets Dave back into his clothes and returns to the classroom. The remainder of the school day passes without incident then parents start streaming in to pick up their children. When Knight arrives, Melissa immediately rushes over. "Dave peed his pants," she announces.

"Yes, we had a little accident," Mrs. Harper says and looks imploringly at Dave who stares morosely at the floor.

"Sorry to hear it," Knight says, but he has become accustomed to getting bad news about his oldest son. Nevertheless, he needs a drink, so Knight takes his children to the Alborz Club next door. It's an attractively furnished watering hole with a bandstand, dance floor, tables and chairs for diners, and a long, well-stocked mahogany bar. Knight sits Dave and Melissa at a table then approaches the bartender. "Let me have the coloring stuff," he demands.

Once Knight has his children set up with a coloring book and crayons, he returns to the bar and orders a rum and Coke. Several embassy staffers are seated nearby enjoying happy hour. "India was better off with the Brits," one of them is saying.

"Yeah, they kept things under control," an immigration counselor agrees.

"That country is basically ungovernable," a Marine officer suggests. "It's just a collection of warring tribes each with its own language. The British were able to play one off against another. That's how they kept the lid on."

"Now look at it," the first man says, "riots, turmoil, killing."

Knight half-listens to the conversation while gazing at his reflection in the bar mirror. People often say he looks like Humphrey Bogart, and in this light, the resemblance is there. He lets his cigarette dangle from the corner of his mouth. "Can I get you another?" the bartender interrupts.

"Sure," Knight replies, and shortly a fresh rum and Coke appears. He squeezes a slice of lime into the drink and lights another smoke. There's a pause in the bar talk and Knight seizes the opportunity to weigh in. "The greatest mistake the British made in India was introducing modern sanitary methods," he opines. "Before that, diseases like cholera, diphtheria, dysentery, and so on kept the native population in check. Now look at the mess they've left behind; a motley rabble half a billion strong and growing."

The other barflies nod their heads in agreement with Knight's Malthusian views. Some have heard this rant from him before but don't let on. They hope he'll put a round of drinks on his tab. However, Knight now looks at his watch and gives a start. "Got to go," he says. "The cook will have dinner on the table soon, and if I'm not back with the kids, my life won't be worth living."

After tossing back his drink, Knight pulls on his overcoat and goes to the children. "Show me what you've done," he says, feigning interest. Melissa holds up a neatly colored drawing of Donald Duck then Dave displays his paper. It's supposed to be Huey, Dewey, and Louie but looks like Oscar's breakfast. "Very nice," Knight comments after a cursory glance. "Let's take them home and show Mama. Now button up, we're going outside."

When Knight and his offspring arrive home, an irate Aliya reheats the now cold dinner and then sulks as the family eats. Afterward, the nurses take charge of the children while their parents repair to the master bedroom. Bobbie changes into a nightgown while her husband showers. She's at the vanity brushing her hair when Knight comes out of the bathroom. "There were fewer demonstrators this morning," he says while putting on his pajamas.

"That doesn't mean anything," Bobbie replies. "They'll be back in force on Friday after prayers."

"You're probably right. Maybe we should just get out of Dodge. That's what everyone says."

"And leave all this?!" Bobbie puts the hairbrush down and turns to face her husband.

"You take a big risk going to Sharia court," he says.

"Why? The accident wasn't my fault. That man pushed his cart out of the alley right in front of the car. I couldn't avoid him."

Knight sits on the bed and takes a *Newsweek* off the nightstand. "It's the mullahs," he says idly flipping through the magazine. "They don't approve of women driving, so now they're out to get you."

"Well, too bad," Bobbie retorts. "No one's running me off."

"I think I'll have a nightcap. Care to join me?"

"You already had two drinks at dinner."

"You have no idea what my day was like."

"No, and you can't tell me, can you?"

"It's secret, other than the problem with Dave."

"Poor child."

"He's backward."

"Don't say that!"

Abruptly, Knight stands up. "Well, I'm going to get a drink. Sure you don't want one?"

"If you're determined to drink, take a blanket and pillow downstairs with you," Bobbie insists. "I know how you get, and I'm not in the mood."

"You're never in the mood," Knight says bitterly. "Maybe if you'd drink a little you wouldn't be so damn frigid." He snatches his pillow off the bed and goes out. As the door slams, Bobbie wearily rubs her temples. A headache is building behind her eyes, so she reaches for a box of pills and swallows three. Then she goes to the door and locks it.

It's a bleak wintry morning in downtown Tehran. Snow crunches under the feet of people waiting to enter Sharia court. Women in the queue are covered from head to toe by burkas while most of the men are in peasant attire consisting of baggy pants, long, voluminously sleeved shirts, and knee-length woolen vests. They look on impassively as three four-door Chevrolets pull up. Bobbie and Lt. Col. Knight are in the middle car while the other two are occupied by Marine embassy guards who, like Knight, are wearing civilian attire.

The Marines leap from their vehicles and escort Bobbie and her husband into the ornate red-brick courthouse. Inside, ancient brass chandeliers hang from the rafters. Below them rows of benches are rapidly filling with spectators. At the front of the hall, a raised dais supports three throne-like chairs and a podium, set off to one side. No one is on the stage at present.

As the Knights look around, Davash Barzani, an interpreter from the embassy, comes in accompanied by another professionally attired Iranian. "Good morning, Colonel," Davash says as he approaches the Knights. "Allow me to introduce Mr. Eghbali, who will be representing us today." The lawyer shakes hands with Knight and nods to Bobbie. Then he escorts them down the center aisle to the first row. The dead man's family occupies the front bench on the opposite side.

After a wait, three men wearing white turbans and black robes come into court from a side door and stand on the dais facing the crowd. Slowly the hubbub dies down in deference to these clerics. In the silence, one of the mullahs launches into what even the non-Farsi-speaking Knights can tell is an invocation. Cries of "Allahu Akbar" end the prayer and the lead mullah summons the lawyers for each side to the dais. When Mr. Eghbali returns, he speaks to Davash. "The victim's family will present their case first," is the translation.

At a signal from one of the clerics, the opening witness for the family steps to the podium and delivers an impassioned eulogy with much crying, shouting, and waving of the arms. The speech sets off a sympathetic reaction among the spectators, and soon the courtroom is in bedlam. Men stand moaning, weeping, and pulling at their clothes while on the dais the three clerics calmly finger their beads.

An hour later, the first speaker finishes and then a woman in a burka takes the stand. She commences wailing in a heartrending manner. Immediately, the women in the crowd join in the display of grief. As the courtroom once again erupts, Mr. Eghbali takes advantage of the chaos to move to the other side of the building where he sits next to the man who was the first witness. "This doesn't look good," Knight fumes. "The rats are deserting the sinking ship."

"That's the brother of the wife of the dead man Mr. Eghbali is speaking with," Davash explains. "He's trying to arrange a settlement. The woman up there now is the widow."

After the widow concludes her lamentations, one more witness appears, and then the morning session is over. Once the building empties, the Knights and their escorts go back to the embassy to eat a nervous meal. Afterward, they return to Sharia court and as they wait for the trial to resume the benches again fill with excited spectators. Soon the courtroom is full, and people must be turned away at the door. Instead of departing, these latecomers remain outside.

Inside the courtroom, the crowd noise ebbs as the judges return to the stage. Then the plaintiff's attorney calls his next witness. He's a bearded, robed, and turbaned man who approaches the podium then begins to rhythmically bash himself on the chest first with one open palm and then the other. The men in the courtroom rise and join in. Meanwhile, Mr. Eghbali returns to the Knights' bench and sits next to Davash. He talks at length with the interpreter as thunderclaps reverberate off the exposed brick walls.

Having been briefed on developments in the case, Davash now turns to the Knights. "The family has one more witness, then it'll be our turn," he explains. "But God be praised, Mr. Eghbali feasted the brother at lunch and got a settlement."

"How much?" Knight asks.

"Five million to the family and one million for their lawyer. You also owe Mr. Eghbali a million."

"What?" Knight exclaims. "That's much more than usual."

"The brother says he's sticking his neck way out on this," Davash replies. "His sister will do what he says, so we either make this deal or else."

"Or else what?"

"Sharia law says 'an eye for an eye,'" Davash explains. "That means the punishment for your wife would be death. The family can choose the method. They could elect to have her tied to a stake, and one of them run her over with a car. That would be considered appropriate; however, they will probably choose stoning. It would be simpler since none of them have a car. They stone women who have been convicted in the vacant lot next door. Everyone participates. It's what passes for entertainment around here."

"Guess we'll have to pay, in that case," Knight says laconically. "How much is that in dollars?"

"One hundred and fifty should do it."

Knight takes out his wallet and hands Davash some bills. "Good that I brought enough," he says. "Even though I thought it would be less."

"I'll go to the bazaar and be back in half an hour with the rials."

"There's no rush; we aren't going anywhere."

The last witness for the family is wrapping up when Davash returns with the settlement money. He gives the bag to Mr. Eghbali who goes off to meet his counterpart. Meanwhile, the defense is called to make its case, so Bobbie goes to the podium accompanied by Davash. She's wearing a navy blue suit with an ankle-length skirt. Sunglasses and a maroon scarf obscure her face. Still, Bobbie looks glamorous; like a movie star traveling incognito.

At the podium, Bobbie launches into her speech, expressing regret, remorse, sorrow, despair, and every other emotion she thinks might help the situation. She fervently wishes none of this had happened. The dead man was a pushcart peddler bringing bundles of twigs from the country to sell as kindling. Bobbie pities his impoverished family; they have now lost their breadwinner.

As Bobbie drones on, frequently pausing for Davash's interpretation, the spectators grow increasingly restless. The tension rises when at the conclusion of Bobbie's speech, the lawyer for the family stands and addresses the mullahs. Immediately he is summoned to the dais where a heated argument breaks out. As the purport of the discussion becomes known, the crowd seethes. Shouting erupts in the back of the hall as white-helmeted club-wielding members of the Imperial Guard force their way inside. They take up positions along the aisle, and the crowd grows more agitated. Angry muttering fills the air.

Eventually, the clergymen on the dais give up the argument and send the family's attorney back to his bench. Then the lead mullah takes center stage and makes an announcement that instantly transforms the spectators into a raging mob. As shoes fly through the air pelting the plaintiffs, protestors hold their benches aloft and hurl them at the Imperial Guards who swing their truncheons wildly. The Marines use their hand-to-hand combat skills to protect the Knights.

Slowly the Imperial Guards drive the mob from the building. In the suddenly quiet courtroom, Knight turns to Davash. "What did the judge say to kick off the fun and games?"

"He said that the infidels paid blood money and according to the law the case is dismissed."

An Iranian officer dressed in elegant, white uniform enters the courtroom and approaches the Knights. "Allow me to introduce myself; I am Colonel Radzwilli of the Imperial Guard. Please accept my apologies for this slight unpleasantness." The officer dismissively waves his arm to indicate the demolished interior and the scores of prone figures bleeding on the floor.

"Nothing your boys couldn't handle, I see," Knight grins.

"It is an honor to be of service," the Iranian officer replies with a slight bow. "Now come, and I will see you safely on your way."

Outside, the Shah's forces are still pursuing protestors up the icy street. Darkness has fallen but the night is lit up by blazing vehicles that were overturned and torched by the mob. Cries of wounded demonstrators fill the smoky air. "Here is your transportation," Colonel Radzwilli announces as the embassy cars come around the corner then pull up in front of the courthouse.

"Once again, Colonel, your men were magnificent!" Knight says with a salute.

"God willing, it will always be so," Radzwilli replies, touching the brim of his headgear.

It's a short ride back to the American compound. Once they're inside the embassy gate the Knights can relax. "Let's go to the club," Knight suggests.

"Yes, I could use a drink," Bobbie agrees.

"Come on," Knight says to the Marine officers. "I'm buying."

As the Knights enter the Alborz Club, they find that news of the acquittal has preceded them. "Three cheers for Bobbie," someone shouts and after a roar of approval a queue forms of those eager to shake her hand. "You've got more balls than ten men," a contractor tells her. Knight gives the man a withering glare for his crassness.

After the impromptu receiving line peters out, excitement in the room ebbs and the club settles back into its familiar routine. In the corner, several officers gather around a piano as an embassy staffer picks out a tune. At the bar, Bobbie is the object of attention from a semicircle of homesick expats. Her husband stands nearby, drink in hand, surrounded by his usual coterie. Tonight, Lieutenant Blankenship, one of the Marine officers, joins the circle. The young man unthinkingly unzips his jacket, revealing a shoulder holster with a Colt .45.

"Good thing they took the money today," Knight comments with a glance at the handgun.

"Yes, sir, could've gotten ugly," Blankenship says regretfully.

"So, they were really going to stone Bobbie," an immigration counselor exclaims. "I don't understand this country."

"You should read Curzon if you want to understand Iran," Knight declares. "Anyone who hasn't read *Persia and the Persian Question* has no business here." The other men in the group nod their heads sagely, though none have read the book. Neither has Knight, but that doesn't deter him. "Nothing good has come out of Persia since Alexander defeated Darius at Gaugamela," he continues.

Before Knight can launch into a blow-by-blow description of the battle, Blankenship interrupts. "Why is that?" the Marine asks.

Knight is irritated but has no problem changing tack. "It's simple, Lieutenant," he says condescendingly. "In Darius's time, the Persians practiced a progressive religion called Zoroastrianism, but later, Islam took over."

"What was so great about Zoroastrianism?" Blankenship persists.

"Zoroastrianism took in any gods that wanted to join," Knight replies. "So, when the ancient Persians conquered a new province, the deities of the defeated tribe would simply be added to the ones the Persians already worshiped. In this manner, they gained acceptance of their rule and built a mighty empire. You see, Zoroastrianism was inclusive. It fostered consensus. Contrast that with the 'my way or the highway' approach of Islam that supplanted it. Mohammedans conquer territory to spread their faith, offering new subjects a stark choice: convert or perish. Not a great way to win hearts and minds. That's why the Persian Empire failed and why the Middle East stagnated after Mohammedanism took root." Knight gives his admirers a self-satisfied smile and finishes what's left of his drink. Then he deftly extracts a fag from his pack of Chesterfields and tamps it down on his lighter. The bartender brings another round.

"Hey, Knight, cut the bull over there and come sing a song," Ambassador Davenport bellows from across the room.

"Sorry, my master calls," Knight says importantly. He carries his fresh drink over to the piano.

"Do the one about that Arab, whatever," Davenport demands.

"You mean 'Abdul Abulbul,'" Knight replies.

"Yeah, Abdul," Davenport nods.

"Not that again," Bobbie shouts from the bar. But Knight ignores his wife and begins singing:

Oh, the sons of the Prophet are brave men and bold
And quite unaccustomed to fear,
But the bravest by far in the ranks of the Shah,
Was Abdul Abulbul Amir.
If you wanted a man
To encourage the van
Or harass the foe from the rear
Storm fort or redoubt you had only to shout
For Abdul Abulbul Amir . . .

Knight carries on singing the many more rousing verses of the old music-hall number then brings the ballad to its dramatic conclusion. As he holds the final note, the room erupts in applause and cheering. Several voices shout, "Give us another." However, Bobbie disagrees. "That's quite enough," she declares, and with purse and coat, she heads for the exit. Her husband hastily follows.

All is quiet in the Knight household early Sunday morning because the servants have the day off. Dave loves Sundays because it's the one day of the week when he is free from Farah and can get some attention from his parents. So now he tiptoes down the hall and quietly opens their door. Sure enough, they are awake and relaxing in bed. A tray of dirty breakfast dishes is nearby.

"I suppose you want to be read to," Knight says, putting down a magazine. He likes reading to the children, though with Dave it can get tiresome. That's because Dave gets stuck on one book, and for weeks at a time that will be the only one he wants. Lately, it's been *Grey Squirrel's Party*.

Dave climbs onto the bed, but before his father can begin reading, Dave interrupts. "Today I will read," he says.

Knight laughs, "Maybe in a couple of years."

"I can read," Dave insists and tries to wrest the thin volume from his father.

"Stop that."

"Why don't you let him try?" Bobbie asks. "What can it hurt?"

Knight gives his son the book. "Sure, go ahead, read," he says.

Dave delightedly looks at the first page and recites the text: "Grey Squirrel wanted to have a party. 'Little Duck,' said Grey Squirrel, 'will you come to my party?'" Then he slowly turns the pages, delivering the lines spoken by Grey Squirrel and each of his friends including Red Fox, Wise Owl, Yellow Bird, and so on. In the story, Grey Squirrel invites each of them, and they all come to the party, which turns out to be a roaring success. "The end," Dave says and smiles at his parents proudly.

"How in the hell did he do that?" Knight asks his wife.

"I'm not sure," Bobbie replies. "Honey, come over here by Mama," she says to Dave. "I want to look at the book this time while you read."

Dave eagerly scrambles over and settles next to her. "Put your finger on each word as you read it," Bobbie says reassuringly. "Can you do that for me?"

The child starts "reading" again, but it soon becomes apparent that he can't do as his mother asks. Dave keeps "reading" one word but putting his finger somewhere else.

"He memorized the damn book," Knight exclaims. "He can't read."

"No, he can't read, but what child this age memorizes a seventeen-page book?" Bobbie replies. "Let's start over," she tells Dave. "I'll read and point at each word." She begins reading, then when she gets to the phrase "have a party" Bobbie leaves her finger on the "a." "Do you know what letter this is?"

"Yes, Mama, it's an 'a,'" Dave says.

"That's right," Bobbie replies. "Now you see 'a' is also a word." She continues reading *Grey Squirrel's Party*, pointing out other short words that Dave can recognize. Now he really can read. It's exciting, but soon the lesson ends. Nevertheless, Dave takes the book downstairs and continues picking out words while eating breakfast. That evening before dinner, Dave studies *Grey Squirrel's Party* while his parents have cocktails. Later, after his bath, Dave takes the book to bed with him.

The next day the servants are back at work and so is Knight. He's in his office at the embassy having a slow morning until Davenport summons him. The ambassador is a good-natured heir to a Midwestern meatpacking fortune. He's an unassuming man who wears a perpetually rumpled look, which goes well with his jowly face and the stogies he smokes. "Hi, Roger, how's your morning going?" Knight asks once they're alone.

"It was OK until I got a call from Mullah Asfandara."

"That can't have gone well."

"You're right," Davenport agrees. "He told me that Ayatolla Hazmajhani wants Bobbie out of the country."

"I'll speak to her," Knight promises. "But you know how stubborn she can be."

"Asfandara says if she's still here Friday, the ayatollah's gonna drop a fatwa on her at prayers."

"That's not good."

"Right again," Davenport agrees. "Bobbie wouldn't be safe anywhere in the world."

"Can't the government do anything?"

"They can arrest Hazmajhani," Davenport says dryly, "and have revolution in the streets."

"Guess I'll have to put my foot down then," Knight sighs. "No two ways about it."

"There's a Pan Am flight to Frankfurt Friday morning," Davenport says. "That gives you the rest of the week to pack."

"We've done it in less."

"I'm sure."

Knight spends the next several hours working the phone. By the close of day, he has orders to return to the States and travel reservations. When he gets home, Knight breaks the news to Bobbie, and they start packing. Two days later the movers come to put the furniture and anything not needed short-term into wooden shipping crates. Knight sells the car that evening, then on Thursday Bobbie canvasses the neighborhood and at the last minute finds a new home for Oscar. After that, it's time to say goodbye to the servants. They assemble in the foyer, and Knight goes down the line speaking to each one while handing out wads of rials. The children and their nurses cry, but Mahmoud is happy. He's lost his job but gained a donkey. The driver rides off into the sunset on Haji Baba.

Early the next morning, an embassy car comes to take the family to the airport. It's snowing, and Knight's last view from the porch is of a monochromatic landscape where the whiteness is only relieved by the dark trunks of the skeletal trees that line the driveway. Just a faint outline of the mountains is visible through a veil of snowflakes.

Three days later Knight is at Fort Monmouth, New Jersey, for a meeting with General James Gaston, commandant of the US Army Signal Corps. Gaston's office occupies a suite on the third floor of Russell Hall. It's the largest building on the post and arguably the ugliest. The massive brick edifice would look like a Bronx tenement if not for a bit of white marble façade slapped onto the center of the building.

When Knight gets upstairs, he finds two sergeants and a captain working in the commandant's outer office. They leap to their feet and salute. A few minutes later, Knight's shown in and finds his boss sitting behind a brightly polished mahogany desk. Light shining through a series of floor-to-ceiling windows reflects off the general's bald dome as Knight strides across the room and comes to attention. "Sir, Lieutenant Colonel Knight, reporting as ordered."

Gaston rises from his chair, casually returns Knight's salute, then comes around the desk to grasp his subordinate's hand. "How was your trip?" the general asks.

"Sir, it was tedious."

"Then you could probably use a drink."

"Yes, sir."

Gaston slides open the door of a cabinet to reveal a well-stocked bar. "Still drinking rum?" he asks.

"Yes, sir, rum and Coke."

As the general tends bar, Knight looks out the window where a garrison flag ripples in the sturdy breeze. The front lawn of the headquarters leads onto the parade ground, which is surrounded by signal school buildings. Beyond that is the four-story base hospital where Dan was born. Knight has spent a lot of time at Fort Monmouth and has many good memories of the post.

Gaston comes over with the drinks. "Sink the Navy," he toasts.

"Hear, hear," Knight seconds and they drink to it. Then the two men settle down to talk.

"How's Bobbie?" Gaston asks.

"She's mad we had to give up the house in Shemiran, but she'll get over it."

"Well, you did a great job over there," Gaston comments. "Our friends at the NSA love the product; they say it's absolutely essential."

"Glad to hear it."

"I don't have to tell you what that means for us when budget time rolls around."

"No, sir."

"But now I guess we have to find something else for you to do."

"That's right."

"I don't have anything that's hot right now," Gaston says. "But we can always send you back to Leavenworth until something turns up. They love you there."

"Sir, that would be great."

"Let's seal the deal with another drink."

"Yes, sir."

After the meeting Knight returns to the hotel in New York where his family is recuperating from the trip. "We're going to Kansas," he announces.

"Wonderful," Bobbie exclaims. She likes Fort Leavenworth, and it's within driving distance of her hometown in Texas.

"When do we leave?" Melissa asks.

"Not till we get a new car," Knight answers.

So that evening Knight goes out, kicks some tires, and buys a Plymouth station wagon. Early the next morning the family packs up and heads west. Marie rides between the two adults in the front seat while Melissa, Dave, and Dan sit in back. The roof rack holds their suitcases and trunks.

Bobbie has purchased a good supply of coloring books, toys, and Golden readers for the trip, and this keeps the children busy while their father drives. He makes good time and doesn't stop until they're clear across Pennsylvania.

The next morning, after breakfast, the family hits the road again. Late in the day when the children get restless, Knight entertains them with Irish drinking songs. The singing continues until they stop for dinner. Afterward, Knight puts the backseat down, and Bobbie uses pillows and quilts to make a bed. There's room for all four kids to stretch out.

The journey resumes as the Knights roll across the rich farmland of Indiana into the setting sun. It's the time of day when local radio stations go off the air so city-based clear-channel stations can broadcast without interference. Bobbie twists the dial until she picks up a Chicago station playing "A String of Pearls."

"You can't beat Glenn Miller," Knight says approvingly.

A little later Bobbie asks for a bathroom break, and Knight stops at a filling station. Before they leave, he buys two bottles of Coca-Cola, each in a little paper sack. He pours half the contents of each on the ground then fills the bottles back up with Bacardi. When the couple resumes the journey, both have damp, brown sacks tucked between their knees.

With the children asleep, Bobbie and her husband enjoy driving along, listening to nostalgic music, and sipping their drinks. After a while, the Plymouth stops again, and Knight invests a dime in a couple more Coca-Colas. In this manner, they travel deep into the night until finally stopping at a motor court. Knight goes in to register then parks outside their room. After taking a few things inside, he and Bobbie come back out for the children. "Look," Knight says, "they're completely zonked out."

"I can take Marie," Bobbie offers.

"Don't you think we should just let them sleep?" Knight asks, slipping an arm around Bobbie's waist.

"But I don't want them waking up and wondering where we are."

"I'll come out and get them before too long, I promise."

"Oh, OK then."

The next day, the family arrives at Fort Leavenworth. Roughly nine months later, Perle Jenkins Knight is born at the post hospital.

CHAPTER TWO
THE SHORT COURSE

Lt. Col. Knight is addressing a cohort of army officers packed into a lecture hall at the Command and General Staff College (CGSC). "It's always great to welcome another class to Fort Leavenworth," he intones. "I'm sure you're happy to be here for the short course and not the long course." A ripple of laughter greets this opening. The audience knows that those doing "the long course" are incarcerated on the other side of Fort Leavenworth at the military prison. "The short course" is the ten-month-long graduate-level program they are attending at the CGSC. It's a by-invitation-only program for favored field-grade officers.

"My job here is to instruct you gentlemen on the role of the Army Signal Corps," Knight continues. "Many of you are from the infantry, and the motto of the infantry is 'Follow Me.' Well, the motto of the Signal Corps is 'Call Us When You Get There.'" More laughter greets this joke, and General Daniel Snyder chuckles along with the rest. He's the commandant of the CGSC and is seated in the back of the hall observing.

After Knight's last class of the day is over, he goes to the Fort Leavenworth officers' club bar. "I need a drink," he tells a group of lower-ranking instructors. "God love the infantry, but they are dense."

"Maybe they just aren't interested in the Signal Corps," a mustachioed artillery major suggests.

"Just as I have no interest in the Field Artillery," Knight smiles. "But I had to take a gunnery class for the Officer Basic Course anyway. It was terrible.

We were in the bars outside Fort Sill every night then had to be back in the bleachers at dawn the next day hungover to beat the band. I never knew what the instructor was going on about. Something to do with azimuths, throw weights, Willy Peter, trajectories, bags of powder, counterbattery, it was all a jumble. Somehow, I was skipped over for two weeks and spared the embarrassment of being selected to solve a problem at the big board. Then on the second-to-last day, I got called up front. As the instructor was writing out the problem, I saw a Kappa Sigma ring from the University of Georgia on his finger. So, when my turn on the board came, I placed my hand flat, showing him my Kappa Sig ring from Florida. 'I have no idea how to solve this,' I whispered. The instructor, of course, walked me through the solution, and that is how I got my artillery certification."

"Last call for happy hour," the bartender announces, and now his customers hasten to order one more. Several, Knight included, order two drinks at once to take advantage of the reduced price.

Once things settle down, the bar conversation turns to football. Knight's not interested in sports, so after finishing his drinks, he waits for a pause in the conversation then announces his departure. "Why leave now?" one of the men asks. "Let's have a song."

"Not tonight. I've got to stop by the PX and get my wife something," Knight says. "Then we have to get ready for the reception."

"What reception?" one of the instructors asks.

"General Snyder's having a shindig for the foreign officers and wants me there," Knight says importantly. "So, Bobbie and I will have to make an appearance."

"How's she doing, anyway?" another instructor inquires.

"Oh, she's back in the ball game," Knight lies. In fact, Bobbie is still recuperating from her latest trip to the delivery room.

"How did you come to have so many kids, anyway?" the artillery major asks.

"Too many cocktail parties," Knight answers with a grin.

At the PX, Knight purchases a box of assorted chocolates for his wife. Today is their wedding anniversary, and he hopes the gift plus a few drinks at General Snyder's will get Bobbie in an amorous mood. She has not been at all responsive since the baby came.

Knight leaves the PX and drives toward the residential section of the base. He finds a parking spot not far from the two-story, red-brick row house the family now calls home. Knight switches off the engine and gazes distastefully at the scene in front of him. A dented metal trash can sits beside the concrete steps that lead to his front door. It's aligned with the beat-up garbage cans of the neighbor houses. On the opposite side of the street is a facing row of similar dwellings, each with its garbage-can sentinel.

Knight climbs the steps to his stoop and opens the door. He walks through the tiny living room, past a steep flight of stairs, and finds Bobbie in the kitchen. Perle's in a high chair while the older children are seated around the table. They seem unenthusiastic about the liver-and-onions dinner.

At the high chair, Bobbie is trying to interest Perle in a spoonful of Beech-Nut split peas, vegetables, and bacon, but the infant is having none of it. So, Bobbie pretends to eat some. "Yum yum," she says, holding the spoon to her lips. Then she passes it over to Perle who takes a dubious nibble then pushes the spoon away. Bobbie looks toward heaven for deliverance but only finds her husband standing in the kitchen doorway. "Happy anniversary," he says, handing over the chocolates. Then Knight bends to kiss his wife, but at the last instant, he sees a glop of something on her lip. It's the color of pigeon droppings, so he hastily redirects his affection to her cheek.

"Thanks for the chocolates, honey. I completely forgot. I mean, today has just been crazy."

"How so?"

"Well, first there was that officers' wives' thing with Mrs. Snyder," Bobbie says. "Then Dave's teacher called; she wants to meet with us tomorrow."

"Again?"

"This time with the principal."

"Well, I have class most of the day."

"I told her that," Bobbie replies. "She agreed to meet during lunch."

"Oh, all right," Knight agrees. "So when's Mrs. Murphy getting here?"

"Not till seven."

"Then how are we supposed to get ready?"

"You go ahead," Bobbie says. "Then you can take over here."

By the time Knight comes back down, the sitter has arrived. Brianna Murphy is a middle-aged lady with children of her own. Her husband is watching them tonight while she earns extra money babysitting. Now Mrs. Murphy takes charge of the Knight children so Bobbie can go upstairs. Meanwhile, Knight makes himself a drink and relaxes in the living room.

An hour later, Bobbie comes downstairs in a turquoise and white cocktail dress with a single strand of pearls. "You look fabulous," Knight says as they walk out to the car.

"Thanks, honey."

General Snyder's house is a red-brick, five-bedroom Victorian set on a rise of ground in the center of Fort Leavenworth. Upon arrival, the Knights find the house crowded with international officers in a wide array of uniforms. Soon several are vying with each other to get Bobbie a drink. Meanwhile, Knight helps himself to a canapé from a tray carried by one of the white-jacketed waiters. Then he gets a rum and Coke from a makeshift bar and is soon deep in conversation with several Iranian officers. "The Shah is trying to drag the country kicking and screaming into the twentieth century," one of them proclaims.

"He better not get too far out over his skis," Knight says wisely.

"The presence of so many foreigners is indeed a problem," the Iranian concedes.

"By foreigners, you mean infidels," Knight laughs.

"That's what the clergy calls them and worse," another Iranian officer comments. "In the summer, foreign women go to the bazaar wearing shorts. The mullahs say they are harlots."

"It's the contractors," Knight observes. "The Shah bought the F-86, now you need trained people to service them. Unfortunately, our technicians bring their families."

The Iranian officers are sipping soft drinks or juice, but Knight prefers something stronger. He excuses himself to get another drink then looks around for Bobbie and sees that she's on the porch with a group of officers' wives. So, Knight's free to go into the den where a group of American officers has gathered around a piano. Soon he's leading them in an old standby: "The Man on the Flying Trapeze." He sings the first couple of stanzas solo:

> *Once I was happy, but now I'm forlorn,*
> *Like an old coat that is tattered and torn;*
> *Left in this wide world to weep and to mourn,*
> *Betrayed by a maid in her teens.*
> *Now this girl that I loved, she was handsome,*
> *And I tried all I knew, her to please,*
> *But I never could please her one quarter so well*
> *As the man on the flying trapeze.*

At this juncture, the group, which includes General Snyder, all join in the rousing chorus:

> *Oh, he floats through the air with the greatest of ease,*
> *This daring young man on the flying trapeze;*
> *His actions are graceful, all girls he does please,*
> *My love he has purloined away.*

The men around the piano enthusiastically continue the song with Knight singing the verses and the others coming back with the chorus. At the end, the den erupts in cheers and Knight is eager for another number. So, he's chagrined to see his wife in the doorway emphatically giving the signal for "no more."

With the songfest now over, Knight wanders back into the living room and circulates among the guests. Later, he finds General Snyder in line at a bar. After getting fresh drinks, the two men fall into conversation. "MacArthur had it right all along," Snyder says. "It's terrible the way he was treated."

"Truman will go down in infamy," Knight concurs.

"Not just for that, but also for losing China."

"He left the nationalists in the lurch, that's for sure."

"Problem is the state department is riddled with communists."

"The rot goes all the way to the top if you ask me."

Bobbie comes over and waits for a pause to interrupt. "It's late hon," she tells her husband. "We've got to get home."

"Let's just have one more for the road," Snyder suggests.

Bobbie goes to find her coat and purse while the men knock back a final highball. Meanwhile, Mrs. Snyder is at the front door saying farewell to several guests. After they go, she remains where she is, gazing expectantly at the few hangers-on that remain. Finally, the Knights leave.

"You'll never get promoted if you can't act more mature," Bobbie tells her husband once they're in the car.

"But Snyder was singing just as loud as everyone else."

"He already has his stars. What have you got?"

When the Knights get home, they go upstairs and find Melissa in their bedroom tending to Perle who's in her crib. "Why aren't you in bed?" Knight asks his oldest daughter.

"Perle was crying," Melissa explains. "I gave her a bottle and changed the diaper. Now she's sleeping again."

"When did the babysitter leave?"

"I don't know. I was asleep."

Bobbie comes out of the bathroom brushing her hair. She goes to her vanity and sees that the box of chocolates she left there is open. Several pieces are missing, and the black paper wrappers are scattered on the floor. "Who got into my candy?" Bobbie asks.

Knight whirls around, sees the mess, stalks over to Melissa, and seizes her by the arm. "You've been sitting here eating your mother's candy," Knight hollers. "Goddamn."

"No, no, I didn't, I swear," Melissa cries. She tries to jerk her arm away.

"Well, who did?" Knight snarls.

"I don't know who ate it," Melissa pleads.

"Well, we'll just see."

Knight goes down the short hall and bursts into the room Dan and Dave share. He throws the light on and shouts, "Get up."

Dan is slow to react, so Knight snatches the covers off the child and drags him onto the floor. Dave leaps to his feet. His father reeks of tobacco smoke and when he hollers a sickening sweet mist fills the air.

"Get downstairs," Knight orders. "Now." Then he goes to get Marie.

The center of the living room floor is covered by a Persian carpet, while the periphery is bare parquet. Knight seats each child in a corner on the wood. Then he leaves to fix a drink. Returning, the officer settles into his chair and lights a cigarette. "OK, kids," he says calmly, "we need to find out who ate Mama's chocolates. Now the best thing would be for whoever did it just to speak up." Knight looks meaningfully at Melissa, who boldly meets his gaze. Then he turns to Dave, who quickly looks away. Marie plays with the hem of her nightgown oblivious to the goings-on while Dan stares off into space. No one fesses up.

Knight mashes the cigarette out while exhaling the last drag. "All right," he says, "I'll ask each of you one at a time."

"Melissa, did you eat Mama's anniversary candy?"

"No, I did not."

"Dave?"

"No, sir."

"Dan?"

"I was asleep."

"Did you eat the candy?"

"No."

"Marie?"

The little girl looks solemn. "No, Daddy," she swears.

"This is truly sad," Knight comments. But he doesn't seem sad as smoke spirals from a freshly lit Chesterfield and ice cubes clink gaily in his drink. The officer's demeanor is that of a man who has an unpleasant but necessary duty to perform. A job that he's uniquely qualified to handle. "One of my kids is a goddamn liar," Knight declares, "and I'm going to find out who. You are all going to sit right where you are until the one who ate Mama's anniversary candy confesses. I don't care if it takes the rest of tonight and all day tomorrow." After this speech, Knight settles back into his chair with a copy of *Newsweek*.

As the wall clock ticks away the minutes, Dave becomes increasingly restless. Just the thought that he cannot get up makes it imperative for him to get up. So, it's a struggle to sit still in the quiet room. The only sound other than the clock is the rustle of magazine pages. After a while, Knight goes out to get another drink.

"Why don't you confess so we can all go to bed?" Melissa asks Dave.

"Why don't you?"

"Because I didn't do it."

"Then who did?"

"You."

Knight returns to his chair, and once again the room quiets. But presently, a thumping sound is heard. It's Dave bumping the back of his head against the living room wall. At first, the sounds he makes are faint, but gradually Dave increases the force, and soon the thumps are readily discernable. Melissa smiles wickedly. Then Knight stubs his cigarette out and looks at his oldest son expectantly. "Do you have something you want to tell me?" he asks.

"I did it," Dave blurts. "I ate the chocolates."

"So, you lied," Knight says bitterly. "On top of everything else, you're a goddamn liar."

Dave responds by pounding his head into the wall even harder, and Knight rushes over to grab him. "Stop that," he seethes, spraying Dave with spittle. "You'll wake your mother."

"Can I go to bed now?" Melissa asks.

"Yes, and take Marie and Dan upstairs with you," Knight says. Then he too goes up only to return moments later with his leather belt.

The next day during lunch, Knight leaves work and picks Bobbie up for their meeting at Fort Leavenworth Elementary School. Mrs. Fitzgerald, the principal, along with Dave's teacher, Mrs. Bell, are waiting in the principal's office when they get there. The teacher is a stout older woman with salt-and-pepper hair and a stern expression. She wears a navy-blue sweater, gray skirt, sensible shoes, and support hose. The principal is much younger and is fashionably dressed. "We have some concerns about Dave," she says to kick off the meeting.

"That's right," Mrs. Bell exclaims. "He doesn't belong at this school."

"Why in the world not?" Bobbie inquires.

"They have a special school in town for kids like him," Mrs. Bell explains.

"I don't understand," Knight says.

"He's slow," Mrs. Bell elaborates, "retarded."

"How can he be retarded?" Knight asks. "Dave has a phenomenal memory."

"Then he will fit right in at the special school," Mrs. Bell says. "They have kids there who memorize the calendar. You can give them a date that's fifty years from now, and they will tell you what day of the week it falls on."

"Retarded children often have special abilities that we don't understand," Mrs. Fitzgerald explains. "But like Dave, they can't play nicely with others, do simple math, or write their names neatly. They require special attention."

"Makes sense," Knight agrees. "I've had nothing but problems with Dave."

"Absolutely not," Bobbie interjects. "This is ridiculous. Sure, Dave is a handful, but he's not stupid. How many six-year-olds can read as well as he does? He's way beyond the first grade in reading."

"That's part of the problem," Mrs. Bell responds. "He refuses to cooperate and read along with the rest of the class. Dave's always reading ahead in the story and never knows the place when it's his turn."

"So, he's retarded because he reads too fast?" Bobbie asks sarcastically.

"No, that's only one example," Mrs. Bell snaps. "When we have nap time, and everyone is supposed to be on their mat, Dave's up running around. Later, when he gets tired, he sleeps even if nap time is over. When we're doing arithmetic, he has his nose in a storybook. Dave only does what he wants."

"Sure, he's difficult," Bobbie replies. "I understand. But Dave is not retarded, and he's not going to that school."

"Well, something's got to give," Mrs. Bell says heatedly. "Either he goes, or I do."

"Thanks for sharing your concerns, Mrs. Bell," the principal says soothingly. "Now if you don't mind, I'd like to speak with the Knights alone."

The teacher departs in a huff. Then, with only the three of them in the room, Mrs. Fitzgerald broaches an idea. "Let me see about transferring Dave to another first-grade class," she suggests. "Please excuse me for a few minutes."

Mrs. Fitzgerald returns five minutes later with a slender young woman she introduces as Carolyn Curtis. "I want to explore the idea of transferring Dave to Carolyn's class," the principal announces.

"I understand that Dave has some exceptional abilities," Carolyn says pleasantly.

"He also has some issues," the principal replies.

"What issues?"

"He won't sit still unless he's reading," Mrs. Fitzgerald says. "So, he's behind in math, writing, and spelling. Also, he's rarely ready for his nap when the other kids are."

"Well, my approach would be to let him nap whenever he wants and allow him to read when he needs to calm down. That would solve a couple of these problems. About math, writing, and spelling, I'll just have to see what I can do."

"That's all we can ask," Bobbie smiles.

Knight drives Bobbie home after the meeting. "Why can't Dave be like Melissa?" he wonders. "She makes straight A's and her teachers love her."

"No two peas in a pod are alike," Bobbie replies.

"I just wonder if Farah didn't drop him on his head one day when we weren't looking," Knight says.

"Don't even joke like that," Bobbie replies heatedly.

Dave spends the rest of the year in Mrs. Curtis's class and seems to make progress, but in the fall, he begins second grade with a new teacher named Frances Barnes. Soon Dave is again taking notes home complaining about his behavior. When the quarterly report cards come out, his grades are terrible. "You'll never get into West Point at this rate," Knight warns.

★

"How's Bobbie?" General Gaston asks Lt. Col. Knight. They are seated in Knight's office at the CGSC. The general flew out from Fort Monmouth specifically for this meeting.

"She's thriving," Knight replies. "'Keep 'em barefoot and pregnant if you want 'em to be happy.'"

"Can't say you haven't done that," Gaston laughs.

"And what about Gracie? How's she coping with having both Ann and Steve away?"

"Oh, she's fine," General Gaston replies. "Grace takes out her maternal instincts on the Scotties now, so she's happy."

"That's good."

"Of course, you and Bobbie will have a full house for a long time to come," Gaston says. "What's Melissa now, eight? Nine?"

"She's ten," Knight replies. "Just finishing fifth grade."

"Well, she and the others may be going to a different school this fall," Gaston says. "An opportunity has come up that should interest you."

"I'm all ears," Knight replies.

"It's US Army Europe," General Gaston elaborates. "Courtney Hodges and I talked. He told me the Russkies are up to no good and he wants to beef up USAREUR's intel shop. I said we have just the man."

"Sir, I appreciate your confidence," Knight responds. "Sounds like a great opportunity."

"You won't be officially reporting to Courtney," Gaston explains. "I have a brigadier assigned to him who'll be your boss, but you'll get plenty of exposure."

"So, when do I start?"

"July 1st," Gaston answers. "They're working on your orders now. In the meantime, you're to take a pre-deployment leave after the current class here graduates."

"Yes, sir."

"I'm supposed to ask," Gaston says. "Would you prefer to go by air or sea?"

"Air; it's faster."

"Then you won't be able to take a car."

"Then make it ship, sir, we'll need the Plymouth."

"Done."

"Sir, this calls for a drink," Knight exclaims.

"Guess you could twist my arm."

After General Gaston leaves for the airport, Knight goes straight home. "We're moving," he announces.

"Where?" Bobbie asks.

"Heidelberg."

"Wonderful," Bobbie exclaims.

"Where's that?" Dan asks.

"Germany," Knight replies.

"What's Germany?"

"It's a country, stupid," Melissa says.

"Let's celebrate," Bobbie suggests.

"It's happy hour at the club," Knight responds.

"I'll get ready."

Knight changes into casual clothes while Bobbie gets into a frilly cocktail dress. By the time they get to the club, a lively crowd of officers and wives have already gathered. Most are seated at tables outside on the patio. It's a beautiful early summer evening, the pool is open, and many have brought children. The older ones congregate in the main swimming pool while several toddlers make use of the wading pool.

While Knight wanders from table to table chatting with colleagues, Bobbie removes her sandals and takes Perle into the wading pool. Then Dan stubs his toe. Bobbie holds him on her lap as he cries it out. Then the boy rushes back to the pool.

Bobbie has barely touched her drink, but now with Perle asleep in the stroller, she picks up her rum and Coke. Just as quickly, she sets it back down. To the consternation of the happy hour crowd, Bobbie leaps fully dressed into the swimming pool. She kicks her way across to Marie, who has flipped her swim ring over. All that can be seen of the child is her kicking feet.

After Bobbie turns Marie right side up, she pats her back until the child coughs up water. Then, with her dress billowing around her, Bobbie carries Marie to the shallow end of the pool. Knight comes over and helps Bobbie climb out. She dries off while Knight gathers up their things and gets the kids into the car. Before leaving, Bobbie stops by the lifeguard station for a few choice words with the young man there.

The following Friday is the last day of school. That afternoon, Bobbie looks at the reports brought home by Melissa, Dave, and Dan then calls Fort Leavenworth Elementary and makes an appointment for Monday. Later, when Knight arrives, she gets him comfortably settled then shows him the report cards. Melissa has straight A's and glowing comments from her fifth-grade teacher. Dan has average marks, and the teacher has commended him for diligence. Dave's report shows that he failed English, math, writing, and spelling. He will have to repeat the grade.

"Whoever heard of a child failing second grade?" Bobbie asks.

"Mrs. Barnes has been warning us all year," Knight replies.

"She never said anything about putting him back," Bobbie declares. "I'm going to have it out with them."

Bobbie has every intention of going to the school on Monday, but that morning when she opens her eyes the light stabs into her brain like a pitchfork. The migraine is so vicious it's all she can do to make it to the sink before throwing up. Then she swallows several pills, lies down, and puts a damp washcloth over her eyes.

So, Knight goes to the meeting with Mrs. Fitzgerald and Frances Barnes by himself. "Whoever heard of a child failing second grade?" he pleads. "This will scar him for life."

"On the contrary, it will do Dave good to be older than the other kids in his class next year," Mrs. Fitzgerald replies. "The added maturity will give him self-confidence."

"That's nonsense," Knight snaps.

"Well, Dave simply isn't ready for the third grade," Mrs. Barnes insists. "He doesn't get along with the other students, won't sit still, fails every math test, and never writes a letter the same way twice."

"Have you thought about taking him to a psychiatrist?" Mrs. Fitzgerald piles on.

Knight abruptly stands. "Thanks for your time," he says.

A couple of days later, Knight attends the graduation ceremony for the latest CGSC class, then bids farewell to General Snyder and his acquaintances from this stint at Fort Leavenworth. The next morning the Knights load into the Plymouth and depart. They are going to visit Bobbie's mother, who lives in Oakwood, Texas where they will spend Knight's leave.

Soon the Knight family is south of Fort Leavenworth, traveling through a sparsely populated agricultural region. There's nothing to see out of the car windows except acres of immature wheat wavering in the breeze. It's a sunshiny day, and prairie flowers splash the roadsides with color. The farther they get from the miserable street they lived on at Fort Leavenworth, the happier Knight becomes. "I'm thinking of a person that all of you should know," he declares. It's the beginning of a car game they often play.

"Me first," Melissa hollers. "Is this person a man?"

"Yes."

"Is he alive?"

"No."

"I'm next," Dave declares. "Was he in the movies?"

"No."

It's Dan's turn. "Come on, Dan," Melissa prompts.

"I don't want to play," Dan complains.

"Come on," Melissa pleads.

"Oh, all right," Dan says. "Is it Abraham Lincoln?"

"No," Knight replies.

After several rounds of the game, the children get bored, and none want to play anymore. They sit staring out the window while Knight listens to a ball game on the radio. Later, as they're passing through Tulsa, Melissa sees a Tastee Freez on the next block. "Ice cream," she pleads, "please, please, pretty please." Now Dave and Dan pick up the cry, and Marie shares the excitement. Knight slows down as he approaches the Tastee Freez and makes as if to turn in while the children squeal in anticipation. But then Knight presses down on the accelerator and keeps driving. Melissa moans piteously, and the young ones follow suit.

"That's not funny," Bobbie admonishes her husband, but he finds it amusing, so this game is played again as they pass through other towns. However, settlements are few on the prairie, and during the long stretches in between, the children begin to fight. Melissa starts by pinching Dave, who lets out a blood-curdling scream. Knight reaches back and swings his free arm hoping to swat the troublemaker. The children dodge, and this too becomes a game. Then they come to a medium-sized town with a Dairy Queen and the kids all shriek like crazy for ice cream.

"If I pull over and stop this car, you'll be sorry," Knight promises.

"He means it," Bobbie declares. "Dave, get your book. Melissa, Dan, do some coloring. You need to behave."

Bobbie's intervention results in a few moments of peace, but then Melissa uses her pinching technique on Dan. She latches onto his leg, takes a fold of skin between her thumb and forefinger, and twists. As Dan screams, Dave comes to the rescue by driving an elbow into Melissa's ribs. She lets go of Dan and digs her nails into Dave's arm. He emits a shrill wail while Knight again swings his free arm behind him, hoping to clobber one or another of his children. But it's Perle, sitting innocently in the front seat next to her father, who catches an elbow. Now she commences bawling, and Knight's had enough.

The sun is lying low on the prairie as the Plymouth comes to a halt next to a fallow field. A family of crows pecking at the remnants of last year's crop pauses to watch as Knight lines his children up and takes off his belt. "Put your hands on the car," the officer orders. "If you move them, you'll be sorry." He swings the leather, and soon the miscreants are repenting. They hop, twist, turn, cry, and promise to behave. Meanwhile, Bobbie puts the backseat down and makes the bed. When the family resumes the trip, it's quiet in the back other than some sniffles and a few muffled sobs.

Three hours later they arrive in Oakwood where the main street is the two-lane state highway they come in on. No traffic signals impede those passing through the town, and the lighted sign on a decrepit gas station is the only indication of commercial activity. At one time, Oakwood boasted a bank, cotton gin, and general store all owned by Bobbie's grandfather, Sam Gorman. The businesses were supposed to be taken over by his son, but he died at Château-Thierry. Now the bank is under new ownership, the cotton has played out, and all that's left of the store are some dusty merchandise displays stored in a garage.

When the Knights get to the sprawling wooden house where Bobbie grew up, her mother, Ethel Gorman, is waiting. "Mama," Bobbie cries, and Ethel stiffly allows herself to be hugged and kissed. "I didn't expect you until much later," she says upon breaking free.

"We made good time," Knight explains.

"Where are the children?" Ethel inquires.

"Come, I'll show you," Bobbie replies.

Ethel peers into the back window of the Plymouth. "Oh, they look like angels," she exclaims.

"Yes, my children are remarkably well behaved when asleep," Knight quips.

"Well, let's get them into bed," Ethel suggests.

After the children are all tucked in, Knight takes a drink out on the porch while Bobbie sits at the kitchen table with her mother. Ethel's a stern-faced, gray-haired retired school teacher with a well-upholstered figure. Bobbie is her only child, and she hasn't seen her husband, Edwin, for twenty years. He's a gold prospector who was rarely home in the best of times. The last occasion when Edwin did stop by, he gave Ethel a dose of the clap. After her doctor made the embarrassing diagnosis, Ethel went home and told her husband to leave and not come back. Now the elderly woman looks across the table at her daughter. "Honey, you're down to just skin and bones," she says.

"'You can never be too rich or too thin," Bobbie shrugs.

"That's hooey," Ethel replies. "You look downright sickly. We've got to fatten you up."

"All right, Mother, whatever you say."

"Is he at least treating you right?" Ethel asks worriedly.

"He treats me fine."

"That's good," Ethel says dubiously.

Early the next morning Knight goes outside to smoke a cigarette and look around. Ethel's yard features two beautiful magnolias and a large pecan tree that shades the house. In the back, a wooden garage opens onto a dirt side street. The road in front of the house is also unpaved. Several run-down houses are nearby. A dog is barking in one of the yards.

Inside, Ethel is cooking bacon and eggs. The smell entices Melissa and Dave into the kitchen. Then Bobbie brings Dan, Marie, and Perle. "This is your grandma," she tells them. They stare at the iron-haired woman bashfully.

"My, look how big you are," Ethel says to Dan. "You were just a tiny baby last time I saw you."

"Not so tiny," Bobbie protests. Dan weighed in at eleven pounds on the day he was born.

Ethel picks Marie up. "I don't believe we've met," she says. "What's your name?"

"Marie Elizabeth," the child smiles.

"What a lovely name."

Melissa is spreading butter on her toast. "Grandma, have you got any jelly?" she asks.

"Why, of course," Ethel says. "And you can call me Gram. That's what I called my grandmother."

"OK, Gram," Melissa says brightly.

After breakfast, Bobbie carries Perle down the hall for a diaper change. Meanwhile, the other children get dressed then go outside to explore. First, they use the rocking chairs on the porch. Later, they look in the garage and find the merchandise racks from the closed store. Some of the fixtures still hold products including work gloves, fly paper, mouse traps, and multicolored spools of thread. The children use these to play store. Melissa gets to be the shopkeeper and uses an antique brass cash register to ring up sales. Dave, Dan, and Marie are customers.

After lunch, Bobbie insists on some quiet time, so Perle is put in her playpen while Marie and Dan nap on their beds. Melissa spends the time coloring while Dave reads. Later, as the afternoon heat fades, Ethel prevails on a neighbor, Mr. Anderson, to give the children horseback rides. He brings a docile mare named Molly to the house, and the Knight children ride her up and down the dirt road until it gets dark.

The next day another neighbor, Garrett Lawson, invites the children to his house and offers to demonstrate making butter. Melissa and Dave are permitted to go with the old man. He lives on a nearby farm in a weathered, clapboard two-story house. It has a front porch reached by a steep flight of rickety stairs. Mr. Lawson has wrinkled skin, white hair, and a long beard stained with tobacco juice. He wears denim coveralls and a red and white checkered long-sleeve shirt. His scarred and calloused hands are burnt brown by the sun.

After showing Melissa and Dave how to milk his cow, Mr. Lawson works the churn on the porch. Then he invites the children inside and offers them buttermilk. Melissa tries a sip and immediately wrinkles her nose. It tastes spoiled, but she's too polite to say so. Dave doesn't like the buttermilk either.

Mr. Lawson's living room is sparsely furnished. There's a wooden table and some chairs in the middle while a spinning wheel gathers dust in a corner. Two rocking chairs are arranged in front of the fireplace. On the mantle is a signed photograph of General Nathan Bedford Forrest. Mr. Lawson takes the picture down and shows it to Dave. "My pappy rode with Forrest," the old man says. "He killed a lot of Yankees, you know, in the war." Mr. Lawson looks at Dave expectantly but is disappointed by the uncomprehending expression on the child's face. Carefully he places his prized possession back over the fireplace.

Dave and Melissa return to Gram's house in time for lunch. After eating, the Knight children have another quiet time. Then Ethel comes up with an idea. "Let's take a ride out to the river," she suggests.

"What for?" Knight asks.

"I want to see if the rain the other day caused it to rise."

"Who cares?"

"Come on, it's something to do," Bobbie says impatiently.

The family piles into the Plymouth and rides a short distance to where the Trinity River flows. Knight parks on the shoulder of the highway, and they all go onto the bridge to peer at the muddy water. It's an evil-looking stream, full of snags and home to alligators, cottonmouths, gars, and snapping turtles. No one in their right mind would go swimming in the Trinity, so all the natives can do is look, check the water level, or maybe drop a line in to see what manner of creature takes the bait. "Can we go now?" Marie asks.

"Hush. Gram wants to look," Bobbie says.

"At what?" Dan asks.

"Oh, OK," Ethel snaps. "We can go, but I want to stop by the cemetery."

The Oakwood Cemetery is on a desolate stretch of dirt road near town. When they get there, Ethel goes to the Gorman enclosure while the others follow. "That's mine," Ethel says, pointing to a patch of bare red clay. Like the other plots, hers shows signs of severe erosion.

That evening after dinner, Bobbie is at the sink washing dishes while her husband smokes a cigarette at the kitchen table. "Isn't there anything to do around here?" he asks.

"Mildred's going to a party in Waco tomorrow night," Bobbie says. "I'm sure we could tag along." Mildred Zimmermann is Bobbie's best friend. They attended Palestine High School together.

"Hell yes," Knight says. "We've got to get out of here."

"I'll talk to Mother," Bobbie promises.

After much persuasion, Ethel agrees to babysit, and late the next afternoon Mildred and her husband stop by to pick up the Knights. The children wave as the Zimmermanns' Caddy rumbles away. It kicks up a cloud of red dust that takes a long time to dissipate in the hot still air.

After their parents leave, Dan and Marie go back into the house while Dave and Melissa stay outside. Dave climbs a tree while his sister sits by the hedge picking green berries. "Leave those alone," Ethel tells her. "They're poisonous."

Ethel goes inside and makes each child a snack of ginger snaps and apple slices. She puts Perle in her high chair and seats Dan and Marie at the table. Then she goes outside to get the other two and finds Melissa sitting on Dave's chest trying to push one of the green berries into his mouth. She's got it past his lips, but Dave is gritting his teeth. Try as she might, Melissa can't push the thing through.

Ethel grabs Melissa and drags her to the side of the yard. She breaks a branch off a bush, trims it, then uses the switch on Melissa's legs. Soon the child is crying, so Ethel lets go. Melissa runs inside to her room. She throws herself onto the bed sobbing.

Meanwhile, Dave goes in to have his snack at the kitchen table. Afterward, he straps on his gun and holster. Out in the yard, Dave plays cowboys and Indians, emptying his six-shooter at foes that look like trees and bushes to ordinary people but appear to him as warriors, medicine men, and chiefs. Eventually, he tires of the game and goes inside where Dan is playing with a fire truck. Dave grabs the toy and runs into the yard while Dan gives chase hollering furiously.

Hearing the commotion, Ethel goes outside. "Stop it, Dave," she hollers. "Give Dan back the truck." But Dave runs off with the toy as his grandmother angrily follows. It takes a while, but she finally corners the boy. Then Gram gets her switch and applies it to his bare legs. Though Dave cries and begs her to stop, there's little mercy in the exasperated woman. She leaves the child crumpled on the ground weeping.

Dan takes the fire truck back inside and sits on the floor next to Marie, who's playing with lettered blocks. Ethel wants to get on with her chores, so she goes into the kitchen to string beans for dinner. All is peaceful for a while but then she hears a ruckus in the living room. Dave and Dan are fighting over the fire truck again.

This time Ethel collars Dave before he can run, then thrusts him into the hall closet. "You can stay in there till you agree to behave," she says. Dave bangs on the door, hollering and screaming in the darkness. He jumps up and down hysterically then lands on a row of building nails that protrude from the floor in the back of the closet. Ethel opens the door when she hears Dave shriek and finds him lying on the bloody floor. She goes to the phone and cranks the handle until Mr. Anderson comes on the line. He hurries over in his pickup and takes Dave to a doctor while Ethel stays at the house to watch the other children.

Hours later, Mr. Anderson returns with Dave, and even though dinner has been set aside for him, all the boy wants to do now is sleep. After tucking him in, Ethel puts the other children to bed as well. As the house quiets, she sits in her room and listens to the radio for a spell. Then Ethel changes into her nightgown and gets under the covers. Sometime during the night, a car pulls up, and she hears voices, laughter, and the slamming of doors. There's a crunch of gravel as the vehicle accelerates away.

CHAPTER THREE
THE PLACE UNDER THE BRIDGE

The Neckar River has frozen solid, and hundreds of people are taking advantage of the rare occurrence to go out on the ice. Among them are Lt. Col. Knight and his five children. They're walking toward the orange-colored roofs of Heidelberg and an Old Town restaurant the family calls "the place under the bridge." It's a cozy bistro off a cobblestone plaza next to an eighteenth-century stone bridge.

When they get to the restaurant, the Knights are seated at a corner table next to a tile oven. Gradually the stove thaws their feet while a platter of Wiener schnitzel warms their bellies. Then the family walks back across the river to where the Plymouth is parked. This time they use the bridge.

"Did you get something to eat?" Bobbie asks when Knight and the children arrive home.

"Yes, we went to the place under the bridge," Melissa answers.

"Good, then I don't need to fix anything," Bobbie says.

"What did you eat, Mom?" Dan asks.

"Oh, I just had soup and a salad; it was plenty for me."

"You kids need to get ready for bed now," Knight orders. "Tomorrow's a school day."

While Bobbie takes the children upstairs, Knight relaxes in the living room of the house the family has called home for the last two years. It's a handsome prewar four-bedroom located in the prosperous Heidelberg suburb of Handschuhsheim. The only problem is that it's too far from the American schools at the army base where Knight works. So now Melissa, Dave, and Dan are attending nearby German schools.

Dave often plays hooky, but it's bitter cold the next morning, so he goes to school. At first, he tries to understand what the teacher is saying, then he gives up and gets out a comic book. It's one he's read several times before and doesn't hold his attention. He's happy later when the class is sent outside for recess.

On the playground, a game of tag gets underway, and Dave joins in. It's fun at first, but as he's pausing to catch his breath, another boy comes over and spits at him. "*Ami*," the kid exclaims then turns to walk away. But Dave tackles the German from behind, and instantly the antagonists are surrounded by a yelling crowd of schoolmates. When Dave manages to get on top of his adversary, some of the spectators begin aiming kicks at his head. One lands on Dave's cheek, so forgetting his current opponent, he grabs the next boot that comes sailing in, then stands and twists the German's foot, bringing him to the ground. Dave's on the kid in an instant, but before he can land a punch, the bell rings signifying the end of recess. That ends the melee.

On his way back to class, Dave brushes some of the dirt off his clothes. He has bruised knuckles, a swollen cheek, and the coppery taste of blood in his mouth. The injuries are not unexpected. Fighting is a regular feature of Dave's school day.

Back in the classroom, it's time for *diktat*, which means that the teacher will spend the next half hour reading from a book while the students write down what she says. Dave used to try and write down what he heard during *diktat*, but after almost two years of getting his notebook returned with big red X's covering every page, he has stopped making any effort. The teacher has not said anything about this. She is no doubt relieved not to have to look at Dave's illegible gobbledygook anymore.

As the teacher drones on, Dave idly puts a hand over his eyes to block the light. Then he separates his fingers to create a gap, and he can see the teacher sitting at her desk. She has her head down reading. Dave tries this with his other hand, first covering his eyes, then peeking through a gap. Next, he makes a fist and holds it up to one eye while shutting the other. With his fingers clenched, Dave cannot see the teacher, but when he opens them, his hand becomes a telescope, and he can see her. Now Dave uses two fists to block both eyes then slowly opens his fingers to make a pair of binoculars. He sees the teacher staring at him incredulously. "Dave, *raus*," she shouts. The boy knows this means "get out," so he quickly gathers up his coat and satchel then walks shamefaced to the door.

The next morning Dave walks past the school and keeps going. Eventually, he reaches the outskirts of town where the land is divided into small plots. Apartment dwellers rent these to use as gardens, and in the summer, they are full of life. But now the icy plots are desolate. All that's left of summer is the withered stalks of long-dead plants that poke up through the snow. Dave wanders the area until it's time for him to go home.

The family's housekeeper is in the kitchen when Dave gets home. Rosa is a cheerful lady, but there's an air of desperation about her. The maid's bright red hair doesn't go with her gray eyebrows, and she chain-smokes.

Rosa glances at Dave and notices his bruised cheek and the ugly scabs on his chin. There's a bluish tinge to the child's lips, so she puts milk on the stove and makes hot chocolate for him. Then Rosa sits at the table with her coffee and a cigarette while Dave warms up. A little later, Dan and Melissa come in. Rosa makes them snacks while Dave goes upstairs to lie on his bed. Soon he's asleep, but then his father comes in. "What are you doing in bed?" Knight asks, pulling the covers back. "You should be doing your homework."

"I don't have any homework."

"That's funny; both Melissa and Dan are studying."

"I already did mine."

"Then go outside and play."

Dave puts on his coat and mittens then goes into the yard. For a while, he entertains himself throwing snowballs, but suddenly he's shoved to the ground and Melissa is on his back. She pushes Dave's face into the snow. When he manages to raise his head, she grasps a handful of the white stuff and rubs it over his nose and mouth. "How do you like it?" she asks rhetorically.

At twelve, Melissa is much bigger than her nine-year-old brother, so all Dave can do is wait her out. Finally, she gets off, driving a knee into Dave's back for good measure. He warily gets to his feet and goes inside to the bathroom. Looking into the mirror, Dave sees that the scabs on his chin have been scrubbed off. Pink fluid oozes out as he gingerly blots the wounds with toilet paper. Dave's been getting these painful sores on his lips and chin ever since he can remember.

Once Dave's finished in the bathroom, he takes a book and goes into the kitchen. It's always the warmest room in the house, especially when the oven is on, as it is now. He peeks inside and sees they're having chicken pot pies for dinner; that's one of his favorites.

While Dave is waiting for supper, Knight comes in and opens the refrigerator. He takes out a bottle of Coca-Cola with a twisted-up paper napkin stuck in it, Molotov cocktail style. The plug is supposed to keep the mixer from losing its fizz, but it doesn't work. Nevertheless, Knight pours some of the flat Coke into his glass then tops it off with rum. "It's Melissa's turn for KP tonight," he tells his son before going out. Dave envies Melissa. Cleaning the kitchen is easy when the family has these frozen dinners, much harder when pots and pans are involved.

When they finish eating, Melissa clears the table while the rest of the children go upstairs. After they're bathed and in pajamas, their father reads them a story. Then they go to their rooms and wait to be tucked in.

Knight spends some time with Marie and Perle, and then goes down the hall to the boys' room to gently tuck the covers around each of them. Once that's done, Knight sits on the edge of Dan's bed and quietly sings:

> *Sure a little bit of Heaven fell from out the sky one day*
> *and it nestled in the ocean in a place so far away*
> *and when the angels found it sure it looked so sweet and fair*
> *they said suppose we leave it for it looks so peaceful there*
> *So they sprinkled it with stardust just to make the shamrocks grow*
> *it's the only place you'll find them no matter where you go*
> *then they darted it with silver just to make the lakes look grand*
> *and when they had it finished sure they called it Ireland.*

After the song, Knight kisses each of his sons and then goes out. As soon as the door closes, Dave retrieves a book and flashlight from beneath the bed. As he reads, Dave occasionally hears his father yelling at Melissa downstairs.

The next morning, Knight prepares breakfast for everyone then sees Melissa, Dave, and Dan off to school. Afterward, he goes to his office at USAREUR headquarters and begins the day by reading a news summary. Then it's time for his weekly staff meeting, so Knight goes to a conference room where the men who report to him have gathered. One by one, each intelligence officer submits an update on his area of responsibility (AOR).

Knight is bored as the officers responsible for Northern Europe, Western Europe, the Baltics, and the Mediterranean conduct their briefings. But he perks up when Captain Fernandez, the officer with the Eastern Europe desk, begins. Fernandez has noticed significant changes in Soviet radio traffic picked up by antennas Knight had installed along the border. He props a map of Eastern Europe on an easel then overlays an acetate pinpointing locations where enemy radio traffic is originating. Using a pointer, Fernandez indicates areas in East Germany, Poland, and the Baltics where radio traffic has decreased. Then the officer points to places in Romania, Eastern Ukraine, and Southern Czechoslovakia where it has increased. Next, Fernandez displays a chart with USAREUR's consensus view of the Soviet order of battle two weeks ago. After that, he puts up his estimate of the current Communist dispositions based on his analysis of the signals intelligence. The captain's conclusion is that fifteen Russian armored divisions have recently moved into new positions.

"We need to get to the bottom of this," Knight exclaims. "I want to immediately increase staffing for Eastern Europe by temporarily reassigning our best men from the slower AORs. We'll create a task force. I need to see a detailed plan by 1600 hours." Knight rises, then strides importantly out of the conference room. He's in the hallway waiting when Fernandez comes out. "Do we have any recent U-2 images that might corroborate your findings?" Knight asks.

"Yes, sir," Fernandez replies, "we got some material in this morning."

"I need those aerials," Knight orders. "I also want the charts you used in the meeting just now."

"Yes, sir."

Knight has lunch at his desk, and while he's eating, a sergeant arrives with the U-2 photographs. After studying the spy plane images and Captain Fernandez's presentation, Knight abruptly gets up and goes down the hall to a bank of elevators. He steps into one and finds his boss, General William Sandifer, along with USAREUR Commandant General Courtney Hodges inside. "It's great running into you this way," Knight says to Sandifer. "We need to talk."

"Sounds important," Sandifer replies.

"Yes, sir."

The elevator reaches the top floor, and the three men step out. "Can you give me an idea of what it's about?" Sandifer asks.

"The Russians are poised to invade Hungary," Knight blurts out. "They have over five hundred tanks assembled on the Romanian side of the border and an equal number in position to invade from Czechoslovakia."

"How confident are you in this information?" Hodges asks sharply.

Knight hesitates for a moment then pushes all his chips in. "Very confident, sir," he declares. "My conclusions are based on geospatial analysis of Soviet radio traffic confirmed by aerial surveillance."

"Then I better call Ike," Hodges says. The four-star turns and strides briskly toward his corner office.

"Good going, Knight," Sandifer exclaims after the commandant leaves. "Prepare to conduct a briefing on this as soon as I can get on the old man's calendar."

"Yes, sir."

Two days later, Russian tanks roll into Hungary. This turn of events, while tragic, is nevertheless a boon to Knight's career. In recognition of his excellent work, General Hodges invites Knight to his office. General Sandifer joins them.

"Care for a martini?" Hodges asks his subordinates. He's already pouring gin into a shaker, so both guests nod enthusiastically. Once the cocktails are distributed, the gloating begins. "We kicked the shit out of the agency on this one," Sandifer chortles.

"Dulles is having a conniption," Hodges agrees.

"The NSA gets a black eye as well," Sandifer throws in.

"They should have looked a little closer at the SIGINT we gave them," Knight points out. "They had the same data as us."

"I told Ike we got to get you on the promotion list," Hodges tells Knight. "It's way past time. Why, you got more brains than any of these infantry full birds we got around here. Hate to admit it 'cause I'm a grunt myself."

"No comment," General Sandifer smirks. Everyone knows you have to be smart to get into the Signal Corps.

"Ike asked my advice on what to do about the damn Russkies," Hodges confides. "I told him we can either nuke 'em or let it be. They got twice as many tanks as we have in Europe, four times as many men, and eight times more artillery."

"We've relied too much on the nuclear deterrent," Sandifer says, "and have drawn our forces down to a dangerous level."

"You're right," Hodges agrees. "But those decisions are above my pay grade."

A little later the meeting breaks up, and the workday is over. Knight goes to the base commissary to get groceries then stops by the Class VI store for a bottle of rum. Once home, he looks for Melissa and Dave and finds them in their rooms. "I went to the commissary," Knight tells them. "Go and unload the car." Then he goes down the hall to check on Bobbie. She's lying in bed with a damp washcloth over her eyes, so he quietly shuts the door then goes back downstairs.

As the groceries are brought in, Knight puts them away. Afterward, he makes a drink then goes into the living room to enjoy the surroundings. Unlike their house in Kansas, this one is big enough to hold the Knights' eclectic assortment of furnishings. Persian carpets cover the wooden floors, antique clocks stand in corners or tick on the walls, and a massive Iranian brass tray depicting scenes from the life of the Prophet hangs over the fireplace.

It's been a good day, so after his drink Knight goes into the kitchen and gets all the ingredients together for his world-famous spaghetti sauce. Less than an hour later, everything is ready, and he calls the children to the table. As always, Knight's spaghetti is a smashing success, even with Dan, who eats everything except the mushrooms. While they wait for him to finish, Knight relaxes at the head of the table with a fresh drink. "I'm sure you all know that the Russians are invading a nearby country right now, spreading terror as they go," he tells the children. "Communist goons are torturing and murdering Hungarian patriots at this very moment. They may come here next, so we have to be ready to evacuate."

Dave is excited by the news. He wants the Russians to come so he can get out of school. But Marie and Perle are fearful. They look nervously at the door, expecting to see Communists breaking through any minute. "What's evacuate?" Perle asks.

Now Knight realizes he may have gone too far. "Don't worry, kids," he says. "We'll get plenty of notice if we have to bug out. Now, Dave, you have KP. Dan, you can sit there until you eat your mushrooms. Girls, get ready for bed, I'll be up shortly to tuck you in."

Knight puts his cigarette out, takes the ashtray into the kitchen, and dumps it. Then he makes a bowl of milk toast for Bobbie and carries it upstairs. While his father's gone, Dan removes all but one of the mushrooms from his plate, wraps them in a paper napkin, then crams the wadded-up food into the front pocket of his jeans. When Knight comes back, Dan spears the remaining fungus with his fork, holding it up for his father to see. "Almost finished," the child announces then pops the thing into his mouth gulping it down whole. Dan shudders then smiles at his father mirthlessly. "May I be excused?" he asks.

"Yes, you may," Knight replies. "Go brush your teeth."

Dave has meanwhile cleared the table, and now he drags a dining room chair into the kitchen, stands on it, and fills the sink with soapy water. As he scrubs the pots and pans, Dave can faintly hear his father singing upstairs.

After finishing with the cookware, Dave washes the dishes, glasses, and silver. Then he uses a sponge to wipe the stove top and kitchen counters. He's sweeping the floor when his father comes back downstairs. "How's it going?" Knight asks.

"Almost finished, sir."

"Let me know when you're ready for inspection."

"Yes, sir."

Dave dries the dishes then goes into the living room to get his father. "Kitchen is ready for inspection, sir," he says hopefully.

"Stand by," Knight orders.

Dave returns to the kitchen, and after a while Knight strolls in. The officer bends over the stove top looking closely at the surface. Then he examines the sink. Next Knight reaches out with the flat of his hand and runs it over the back of a counter. "What's this?" he asks, turning his hand over and opening it so that Dave can look.

"Crumbs, sir."

"Yes, goddamn it, crumbs," Knight snaps. "You're wasting my time." He gets his glass and, after mixing a drink, goes out.

For the next thirty minutes, Dave works on the counters. Then he asks his father to do another inspection, and again, Knight examines the kitchen. He looks inside the oven then runs his hand over the top of the refrigerator. After that, Knight gets a broom and digs into a corner. Not finding anything he tries another corner of the room and comes up with some dust. "What's this?" Knight seethes. "Why, a goddamn nigger maid could clean this kitchen better. You need to get back to work."

So, Dave sweeps the floor again then carefully examines every part of the kitchen, paying close attention to places his father has caught him out before on other KP nights. Afterward, he tries again.

"Sir, the kitchen is ready for inspection."

"Can't you see I'm busy," Knight says, lowering a *Time* magazine. "I'll check it later; you can go brush your teeth and turn in."

Dave quickly ascends the stairs and prepares for bed. He's tired and soon falls asleep. It seems only moments later that his father shakes him awake. "Get up," Knight hisses, and an alcoholic mist fills the air.

Once father and son are back in the kitchen, Knight points to a spot where he found more dust. "I'm ashamed to call you my son," he spews. "This kitchen wouldn't pass inspection in the Italian Army, let alone the United States Army. I'm giving you one hour to correct all the deficiencies."

Around 2:00 a.m., Dave is once again sweeping when his father comes into the kitchen holding an empty glass. "What are you doing here?" Knight slurs. So, Dave goes back upstairs.

A few hours later, Dave is up and dressed for the day. He walks past his school and plays hooky again. When he gets home that afternoon, Rosa puts a bowl of soup and some bread out. After he's eaten, Dave wanders into the den in search of something to read. He's always been intimidated by the dusty books in his father's library, but today Dave's desperate. All the comics and storybooks in his little collection have been read and reread. He pulls a thin volume off his father's bookshelf entitled *Principles of War*.

The sentences in von Clausewitz's treatise are short, and Dave can read most of the words, but he quickly grows bored because there's no story. So, he reshelves the book and gets down another volume. This one is entitled *History of the German General Staff*. Dave leafs through it, looking for pictures and finds a rogue's gallery of grim-faced Prussians in ornate uniforms. He tries to read the text but quickly runs into unfamiliar words and place names.

Next, Dave spots a book on the shelf entitled *Berlin Diary*. It's about a subject that fascinates him—the Nazis. Ever since coming to Germany, Dave has been learning about them. After the war, many Nazis were put on trial and then hanged. Some escaped the noose by shooting themselves or swallowing poison.

Dave sits cross-legged on the floor and reads the diary until he's interrupted by Melissa, who sneaks up from behind and gets him in a headlock. Melissa's forearm slips under Dave's chin and cuts off his air supply. He tries to pull her arm away but fails, so in desperation Dave clenches his fist and hooks it into his sister's face. When the arm around his throat goes limp, Dave leaps up and runs for the stairs. He almost makes it to the top before Melissa catches him. She drags Dave back down the steps by one foot, bumpety-bump.

Attracted by the noise, Rosa comes out in the hall and forcibly separates the two children. Dave runs out the front door and takes off up the street. Once he's well away from the house, the boy slows to a purposeful walk.

It's after dark by the time Dave comes to the riverbank where barges are tied up along the quay. Lights glow in the cabins of the vessels, bespeaking home and warmth for the families who live aboard. As he walks, Dave fantasizes about stowing away and riding a barge downriver until he can transfer to an ocean liner bound for the States. But the idea is impractical. He comes to the Old Bridge and goes across it into Heidelberg. In the darkened plaza, reality sets in as it always eventually does when Dave runs away. He's cold and hungry.

A kiosk with a pay phone is nearby and Dave waits by it for someone to come along. After a while, a lady bundled up in a coat and scarf walks toward him. *"Entschuldigung bitte, haben Sie Kleingeld für das Apparat?"* Dave asks.

The woman looks at Dave askance, but she gets out a change purse and gives him some coins. *"Danke,"* Dave says.

"*Gern geschehen*," the woman replies as she hurries away.

Dave dials home, and his father picks up midway through the first ring. "Where have you been?" he asks.

"Walking."

"OK, so where are you now?"

"The place under the bridge."

"Don't go anywhere. I'll be there in ten minutes."

On the way home, Knight admonishes his son. "I don't know what to do with you," he says. "You've run off before but never this long."

"Can I go live with Gram?" Dave asks. "I wouldn't be any trouble for her."

"Absolutely not," Knight growls.

Bobbie is sitting at the kitchen table wearing a bathrobe when they come in. Her face looks drawn in the harsh light, and she exudes a profound world-weariness. Dave wonders what became of his glamorous mom. As if reading his thoughts, Knight says, "You put your mother through hell tonight."

"Oh, hush," Bobbie says, putting a bowl of chicken noodle soup on the table. She waits as Dave slurps his dinner. When he's finished, she takes him upstairs for a warm bath and bed.

It snows on and off the rest of the week, then late Saturday afternoon with his parents downstairs, Dave enters their bedroom, gets his father's belt, and takes it into the bathroom. After locking the door, he drags the clothes hamper over to it and gets on top. Standing, he pushes the belt end through the buckle to form a loop. Then Dave fastens the end of the belt to a hook on the back of the door, pulls the loop over his head and clenches it around his neck. Without a thought, he kicks the hamper over. After a jolt, he's hanging.

Looking down Dave sees that his toes are only three or four inches from the floor. It doesn't seem like much, but now everything within view takes on a pink tint, which gradually darkens into an opaque red. An explosion of heat fills his head.

Dave wakes up on the cold, white-tiled bathroom floor. He tugs at the belt then pulls it off. The end is attached to a pie-shaped chunk of wood and, looking up, Dave sees that the door has splintered. He worries about getting blamed for this, so he climbs back on the hamper and pushes the wood piece back into the crack. After replacing the belt, he goes into his room to wait for the shaking to stop. "Never again," he mutters.

CHAPTER FOUR
PURGATORY

At Paul Revere Village, near Karlsruhe, Germany, senior army officers live in two-story, four-bedroom houses in a secluded enclave known as "snob hill." That's where David S. Knight Jr. and his family have resided since Knight's promotion to full colonel. From Paul Revere, it's an easy commute to the 516th Signal Group where Knight is now the commanding officer.

Aside from "snob hill," the rest of Paul Revere Village is a slum consisting of five-story tenements for GIs with families. It's not very attractive, but for the Knight children, living in the housing complex has one significant advantage— now they can attend American schools.

This morning, at Paul Revere Elementary, Mr. Black's fifth-grade class is studying geography. Dave Knight has the textbook propped open in front of him, so to all outward appearances he's focused on Central America, the subject at hand. But tucked inside the geography book is a paperback, *The Hound of the Baskervilles*. So, while Mr. Black drones on about the banana business, Dave tries to follow Sir Arthur Conan Doyle's devious plot. Then the bell rings, and it's time for lunch. Dave goes to the cafeteria, gets a tray of food, finds a seat at an empty table, and eagerly picks up reading where he left off.

In the afternoon when class resumes, Mr. Black passes out *Weekly Readers* and calls on a student in the first row to read aloud from an article about the St. Lawrence Seaway. Then after a couple of paragraphs, the teacher has another kid take over. Meanwhile, Dave has read the article, so he skips ahead to one about Nikita Khrushchev visiting Disneyland. After a while, he dimly hears Mr. Black say: "Dave, please pick up reading where Danny left off."

Dave looks blankly at the teacher, and Mr. Black is not surprised. "We're on page one at the bottom of the third column on the left," he prompts. Dave finds the place and begins confidently reading the passage. After several paragraphs, Mr. Black interrupts, and another student picks up the dry recitation.

School lets out at 3:00 p.m., and some students immediately set out for home. Others gather outside the building, talking and laughing. Abruptly, a circle of excited children forms around two kids who are fighting. Dave sees that his sister Marie is one of the combatants; the other is a Negro boy named Adam who's in Dave's class. Marie's only in third grade, so it's not surprising that the older boy is beating her up. Without thinking, Dave breaks through the circle of spectators and steps between the pugilists. "Hey," Adam protests and wings a punch at the interloper. Dave ducks and circles away. Then Adam throws another wild punch and when that too misses, he grabs Dave, and the two begin wrestling.

"Watch out, Mr. Wiley's coming," someone in the crowd hollers.

"I'll let go if you do," Dave tells the other boy.

"Deal," Adam says, and both run off before the principal can get there.

"What happened?" Dave asks Marie on the walk home.

"He offered to swap his boulder for my cleary," she explains. "But when I gave him mine, he wouldn't give me his."

"You should have come got me," Dave says.

"I can take care of myself," Marie snaps.

At lunch the next day, Dave is at a table by himself when Adam comes over with his tray and sits. Neither says anything, but now they have buried the hatchet. So, once school is over, the two boys go to a nearby playground and shoot marbles. Afterward, Dave walks home, has a snack, and then settles into his father's easy chair with Sherlock Holmes. A few minutes later, Dan comes into the living room with a school book and plops down on the sofa. "I have to study for a social studies test," he says.

Both boys read quietly for a while then Dave gets up to pee. He returns to find Dan has taken his seat. "You get up, you lose it," Dan smirks. As the brothers prepare for battle, the front door opens, and Knight comes in. "Boxing match tonight," he tells his sons. "You're going."

"Can't," Dan whines. "I've got too much homework."

"Well, you're going," Knight says to Dave. "I'm not making the trip by myself."

"Yes, sir," Dave happily agrees.

Soon father and son are on the autobahn heading for Mannheim. "Where were we in the poem?" Knight asks.

"'The uniform he wore was nothin' much before, an' rather less than 'arf o' that behind,'" Dave quotes Kipling.

"OK, here's the next line," Knight says. "'For a twisty piece of rag, and a goatskin water-bag was all the field-equipment he could find.'" Dave repeats the new line several times, and then his father gives him another. By the time they get to the outskirts of Mannheim, he knows another verse of "Gunga Din." This will be the third poem he has learned during trips to sports events with his father. The 516th Signal Group fields basketball, baseball, and boxing teams. Knight supports them all.

Now Knight turns his attention to finding Turley Barracks, the venue for this evening's entertainment. To get there, he and Dave go through the center of Mannheim, past block after block of bombed-out apartment buildings. Some are only partially destroyed and people still live in the intact portions. Their lights can be seen winking through the rubble.

At Turley Barracks, Knight shows his ID to the gate guard and is directed to the gym. Inside, two or three hundred animated troops are drinking beer in the stands. Knight looks for Captain Connor, manager of the 516th's boxing team, and finds him down by the ring.

"They have a good lightweight, but the rest of the lineup is very average," Connor tells his boss.

"That's too bad," Knight replies. "Moreno needs work."

"Well, he ain't gonna get it tonight," Connor predicts.

Soon the first fight is underway and, as expected, the Signal Corps lightweight is outclassed. "Watch the way the Turley fighter moves," Knight tells Dave. "Notice that he never comes straight in or backs straight out but is always circling one way or the other. Our boy cannot get his feet set; he has no idea where the next punch is coming from."

The next bout is another one-sided contest. Miguel Moreno is one of the top welterweights in the army and soon the Turley Barracks boxer is flat on his back. The man unsteadily rises to his feet and wants to continue, but the referee signals an end. A chorus of boos greets this decision.

In between fights, Knight goes to the concession stand and comes back with a beer for himself and a soda for Dave. Then they watch the remaining bouts with Knight providing a running commentary. When the last one ends with a favorable decision, Knight congratulates Captain Connor, grabs Dave's hand, and rushes for the exit. He wants to get a head start on the inebriated infantry.

The next day, once school is over, Dave goes home with Adam. After giving them some cookies and milk, Adam's mom sends the two boys out to the playground. They swing, do the teeter-totter, and push each other on a roundabout. Then Dave and Adam get out their marbles, make a circle in the dirt, and play knockout. As Dave is lining up a shot, Marie walks by with some friends. "Can I play?" she asks, holding up her bag of marbles.

"No," Dave replies. "Go play with kids your own age."

It's almost dark when Dave gets home just in time for dinner. Ingrid, the family's current housekeeper, has made chicken and dumplings. Everybody likes this meal except Dan who won't eat his dumplings. "If you don't clean your plate, you won't get dessert," Bobbie threatens. "And Ingrid made a strudel."

"Did you hear that?" Knight asks. "Now eat up."

"I'll eat half," Dan offers.

"All right," Knight agrees then everyone watches as Dan takes a delicate bite of dumpling and swallows it. Meanwhile, Bobbie goes into the kitchen, gets the dessert, and sets it on the table near Dan. "Only three more," she says encouragingly.

"Guess what?" Marie blurts out. "Dave has a new friend. He's a Negro."

"Surely not," Knight scowls.

"Just a kid I shoot marbles with," Dave mumbles.

"I saw them eating together in the school cafeteria," Marie pipes up again.

"Now, honey, I'm sure you weren't sitting at the same table with a Negro at lunch," Bobbie exclaims.

"Yes, he was, I saw them," Marie says.

"He's my friend," Dave declares.

"You don't eat with Negroes," Knight insists.

"I asked him over to play Friday."

"If you bring him into this house, I'll throw both of you out," Knight promises.

Dave looks longingly at the strudel then turns to his father. "May I be excused?" he asks.

"Hell yes," his father agrees.

Instead of going to school the next morning, Dave exits the housing complex, walks into town, and waits at a streetcar stop. He has to jostle with adults when the tram comes, and there are no open seats once he's aboard. He stands and looks out the window as one block of drab, postwar apartment buildings after another flashes past. Finally, a seat opens, so Dave settles in, takes out a paperback, and begins reading.

Ingrid's still at the house when Dave gets home that afternoon. He's happy to see her because she often brings stamps for him. Dave recently took up collecting, and Ingrid's been helping. Today she has brought a stamp with a drawing of a locomotive, one with a portrait of Konrad Adenauer, and another that depicts the Atomium from the Brussels World's Fair. "*Danke*," Dave says excitedly. He runs to his room to mount the stamps then looks through his growing collection.

That evening Knight and Bobbie are dressing for a cocktail party when the phone rings. "Hello," Bobbie answers then listens for a moment. "Sorry to hear that," she says. "Let us know if you need anything."

"Who was that?" Knight asks.

"Mrs. Dimsdale," Bobbie replies. "Her five-year-old came down with measles. She won't be able to sit tonight."

"Oh no."

"I'll talk to Ingrid," Bobbie says. "Maybe she can help out."

Ingrid has her own family. Nevertheless, she agrees to stay an hour or two extra and promises not to leave until the children are in bed. So, the Knights depart, leaving their housekeeper in charge. She prepares dinner for the kids then makes sure each has a bath. Once they are all in pajamas, Ingrid puts them to bed and then leaves. The moment the door shuts, Dan jumps out of bed. "Hide-and-seek," he hollers, and the others rush to join in.

Hide-and-seek in the dark is the Knight children's favorite game, and now they have the entire house to themselves. Eagerly they gather and use "rock, paper, scissors" to determine who will be "it." Melissa loses and starts counting while her siblings scatter.

The Knight children play happily for over an hour, but the game breaks down when Dan gets tired of waiting to be found and starts jumping up and down on his parents' king-sized bed. When Marie and Perle hear the commotion, they leave their hiding places to join in. Melissa tries to intervene. "You're all going to be in big trouble," she threatens.

"Says who?" yells Dan.

Just then, Perle misses her descent, crashes onto the floor, and begins wailing.

"I told you something would happen," Melissa shouts angrily. She kneels to tend to the baby of the family then takes Perle to her room.

Now Dan leaps off the bed, landing on his feet with a thud. He grabs a pillow and swings it at Marie. "Pillow fight," he shouts. Marie happily drags another pillow off the bed and whips it around, catching Dan on the side. Soon they are swinging at each other with wild abandon, but Dan quickly pounds his little sister into submission. She holds her hands up to protect her head yelling, "I give, I give."

"Stop it," Dave hollers.

"Make me," Dan replies.

Dave grabs Dan's pillow, and they have a tug-of-war until it splits open and a cloud of feathers fly out. "Now look what you've done," Dan hollers. He throws a looping punch that Dave dodges, then Dave gets Dan in a headlock and starts punching him with his free hand. Marie grabs Dave's arm from behind. "You're hurting him," she cries. With Dave immobilized, the fight fizzles out.

They're all tired now, so Marie and Dan go back to their beds while Dave returns to his parents' room, sweeps up the feathers, and straightens the bedcovers.

Then he picks up a novel from his mother's bedside table and settles into a chair. After a while, Melissa comes in. "Get to bed," she orders.

"Mind your own business," Dave replies. Then before he can react, Melissa snatches the book out of his hands.

"You're supposed to be in bed," she insists.

Incensed, Dave tries to get the book back, but his sister holds it away with one hand and stiff-arms him with the other. Dave angrily stomps on Melissa's foot, and with that, she drops the novel. Dave snatches it up and heads down the hall for the stairs going down them three and four at a time. But fury provides Melissa with the impetus to catch up. As Dave reaches the bottom and turns, Melissa reaches over the banister and grabs a handful of his pajama shirt. She jerks Dave back, then grasps his head and smashes it into the octagonal newel post. Dave slumps to the floor, and for a moment Melissa is quite pleased with herself. But as Dave unsteadily rises to a sitting position, blood flows from the side of his head. His pajama top is quickly saturated, and now Melissa is scared. She picks up the hall phone and dials 0. "We have an emergency at 47 MacArthur Circle," Melissa says. "It's my brother; he fell down the stairs."

Soon a patrol car pulls up, and Melissa opens the door for the Military Police. Dave squints as a flashlight shines into his eyes. "Fell down the stairs, huh?" an MP asks, glancing at Melissa dubiously. Then an ambulance arrives, and the attendants strap Dave to a stretcher for the short ride to the post hospital. Later, Knight and Bobbie come. They sit with Dave until he's released.

The next afternoon, Knight calls a meeting with Melissa and Dave, who now sports a white bandage wrapped turban-like around his head. The three sit at the kitchen table to talk. "It's a real shame your mother and I can't go to a party without all hell breaking loose," Knight begins. "Everyone says I have the worst-behaved kids on base. What do you think that does to my chances for promotion? People say if I can't discipline my children, how can I lead troops?"

"I can't help it if Dave fell down the stairs," Melissa replies.

"Stop that nonsense," Knight snorts. "I hate liars worst of all. Anyway, my year with the 516th will soon be over, and I have orders for my next duty assignment. We'll be moving to Georgia soon and can make a fresh start there. However, this misbehavior has got to stop, so I've decided on the appropriate punishment. Neither of you will have a birthday this year."

"You can't do that," Melissa gasps.

"Oh yes, I can," Knight says, getting up to leave. "There will be no presents, no party, nothing for either of you. Your birthdays this year will be just like any other day."

The two children sit stunned after their father goes out and it's quiet for a moment. Then Melissa glares at Dave. "Everything was perfect until you came along," she says spitefully. "I wish you were dead."

It's Friday afternoon, and Mrs. Reid has a special treat for her students at Forest Hills Elementary School in Augusta, Georgia. "We're going to watch the World Series," she announces. "Line up." Then Mrs. Reid leads the class into the lunchroom where a TV has been set up in front of several rows of folding chairs. Soon they are joined by the school's other two sixth-grade classes.

Once the students take their seats, Mrs. Reid turns on the TV. The game is about to start, but first, there's a commercial. A beautiful young lady appears on the screen and holds up a Gillette Lady Blue Starburst Long Handle Safety Razor. The model is wearing a white terrycloth bathrobe that covers her modestly from neck to toe. But as she extols the virtues of the product, the spokeswoman gracefully sits and allows the lower portion of one shapely leg to appear. Then she applies lather and begins shaving while continuing her spiel. Unfortunately, at this point, no one in the lunchroom can hear her. That's because the sixth-grade boys have gone wild. Some are howling while others moan; a few are whistling and cheering. Simultaneously, three teachers jump up and head for the TV. Mrs. Reid gets there first, pulls the plug, then turns to face the assembled students. "Back to class," she shouts angrily. "Line up."

Now instead of watching baseball, the sixth-grade boys get to sit at their desks and write a sentence that Mrs. Reid scrawls on the blackboard: "I will learn to behave like a gentleman." Each must write this sentence one hundred times. Some finish the task early, but Dave Knight takes until the bell rings. Then he turns in his paper, goes outside, and is waiting for the bus when a loud argument breaks out among the throng of students still exiting the building. Turning, Dave sees his sister exchanging punches with a boy. Quickly Marie gets the better of it, and the kid covers his face and cries. Marie walks away triumphantly and joins the other army brats boarding the bus to Fort Gordon.

The ride to the post takes a little over half an hour. Once there, the Knights and several other officers' dependents get off at the stop for Maglin Terrace. Quickly Dave and Dan change clothes then go to the playground where some boys are already throwing a football around. Soon more kids arrive, and a touch game starts. Although Dave and Dan are not any good at football, they can at least block. The contest goes on until dark then the Knight boys go home to rustle up something to eat.

The next morning, Knight takes his children grocery shopping in the yellow Opel station wagon he bought in Germany. When the family arrives at the commissary, it's mobbed with soldiers who are either assigned to Fort Gordon's Southeastern Signal School or the Military Police School. The Knights fill their shopping buggy with a week's worth of food and then go through the checkout. Afterward, they drive to the post hospital to pick up a supply of pills for Bobbie. "Everyone out," Knight orders.

"What for?" Dan asks.

"Because I said so," Knight snaps. He knows that if he leaves his offspring in the car, a fight will likely start, so now he leads the children across the parking lot. As usual, Knight is in uniform with his silver eagles flapping on his shoulders. He strides along, shoulders back, head erect, arms swinging, while the children sullenly straggle behind. They approach some deuce-and-a-half trucks loaded with troops on sick call. The GIs grin and whisper among themselves as the small parade passes. Then Perle, who is bringing up the rear, pipes up.

"Daddy, what happened to that man?" she asks, pointing to a soldier on one of the trucks who has a fresh white cast on his arm.

Knight glances in the soldier's direction. "Oh, he probably sprained his wrist shooting craps behind the barracks," he says loudly.

At that, the soldiers whoop with laughter. "You got that right, Colonel," one of them calls.

When Knight and the children get home, they unpack the car and put the groceries away. After a dinner of fish sticks, frozen vegetables, and powdered mashed potatoes, they gather around the dining room table to play poker.

Knight has been teaching his children the game, and by now they are reasonably adept. But that doesn't stop him from critiquing each hand after it's played. "Perle, why did you stay in with nothing when Melissa was showing two tens?" he asks after one hand. "Dave, you have kings wired back to back and come out with a quarter right off," he says later. "You scared everyone out of the pot; a dime would have kept them in." It's almost midnight when Knight announces, "Once around to the dealer." A little later when the game ends, Marie has the most chips.

Bobbie takes the children to Augusta the next day to an Episcopal church she likes. However, the children don't have the patience for it. To them, the service seems to drag on endlessly as the sun backlights the stained-glass windows beckoning them outside. So, it's like a jailbreak when the family finally gets home. The kids rush to change and go to the playground. They stay there until dinnertime, then the weekend is over, and it's time to get ready for school.

In the morning, Knight sees his children off to school, then PFC Dwight Miller arrives in a staff car to take him to work. Miller is a tall, ruggedly-built man from Arkansas. With his dark hair, dark eyes, and long black eyelashes, the driver bears an uncanny resemblance to Elvis Presley. He takes Knight to the Signals Intelligence Building, which is located just off the parade ground in the center of the post. Inside, rows of cheap government desks and chairs fill the workspace while dented green metal filing cabinets line the walls. The floors are of dark linoleum polished to a dull glow by the never-ending supply of draftees available for such work.

At one end of the sprawling building, a mahogany door with gleaming brass hardware opens into Knight's elegantly furnished office. The walls are paneled and the floor richly carpeted. Two easy chairs, a sofa, and table occupy the center of the room while Knight's desk is in back. Outside Knight's office are desks for his aide, Captain Lance Kinsey, his secretary, Sue Brandt, and the office manager, Sergeant Major Reynier. "Good morning," Knight says as he walks past them into his office.

After a short interval, Sue comes in with a cup of coffee and the newspaper. She's a slightly built elderly lady who lives in the nearby town of Grovetown. Sue has been working at Fort Gordon since it opened in 1941.

For the next hour, Knight sits at his desk reading the news while frequently glancing at his watch. Then he strolls out to where Sergeant Major Reynier is seated, and the non-commissioned officer (NCO) leaps to his feet. He's young for a sergeant major, but prematurely graying hair, intelligent eyes, and a cynical expression provide the gravitas necessary for his rank.

"At ease," Knight says. "Is everything ready for the general?"

"Yes, sir."

"Where's Captain Kinsey?"

"In the data center, sir, just going over everything one more time."

"All right, then, get me Miller."

"Yes, sir."

PFC Miller drives Knight to the airstrip where they meet General Sandifer who has been promoted to major general and is now commandant of the Signal Corps. Then Miller takes the two officers out to the hinterlands of Fort Gordon. They inspect several electromagnetic antennae arrays that can gobble up radio waves emanating from anywhere in the world. Afterward, Miller takes them to the Signals Intelligence Building, and Knight shows the general an air-conditioned annex filled with computers. The machines are being fed punch cards by white-coated technicians causing myriad red and blue lights to blink and reels of magnetic tape to jerkily spin first one way then another. "This is where the data is stored," Knight tells Sandifer. "Satellite, U-2, and radio. We can search thousands of pages of intercepts in mere minutes."

"Very impressive," Sandifer replies. "You know the NSA is relying on us more and more. General Busby says that without this he'd be flying blind."

"Sir, it's always nice to be appreciated," Knight says.

PFC Miller drives General Sandifer back to the airfield and then returns to the office to take Knight home. When they get to Maglin Terrace, Dave and Dan are in the front yard tossing a football. Melissa is inside, and she accosts her father when he comes in the front door. "Mom had to go to an officers' wives' thing and took the car," she says. "I badly need to go to the PX."

"What for?"

"I need glitter, colored markers, and other stuff to make a Thanksgiving poster for school."

"Well, you'll just have to wait until your mother gets home."

"Then I'll be up all night." Melissa pouts. "It's a big project; I need to start now."

"Oh, come on, then," Knight says. They go outside where PFC Miller is showing Dave how to hold the football.

"Your thumb should be underneath," Miller instructs. "When you release the ball, keep your fingers on the laces." Dave throws a dying duck to Dan; it wobbles all the way.

"Take the ball straight back next time then come over the top and let it roll off your fingers," Miller says. He demonstrates with a tight spiral to Dan that's too hot for him to handle. Dan picks the ball up and heaves it back. Then Dave tries another throw, and this time the ball rotates as it wobbles. "That's it," Miller says excitedly.

"Hey, I have something important," Melissa interrupts.

"Miller, take Melissa to the PX," Knight orders. "Afterward, you'll be done for the day."

"Yes, sir."

Dave and Dan stay outside throwing the football and enjoying the autumn weather until dark. But over the next several weeks, Indian summer gives way to winter. Knight has leave coming, and now he firms up plans to take the family to Florida for the holidays. That's where Knight is from, and his father and sister still live there. Neither has a big enough house to host his large family, however, so they'll stay with Barbara Rice, a close family friend. She has plenty of room.

The day after school lets out for Christmas, the Knights load into the Opel and drive south. Every time they stop for a bathroom break or to refuel, the weather is nicer. On the last stretch, Knight rolls the windows down to let in the balmy, ocean-scented breeze. He's now on familiar ground, and even though it's dark, he unerringly finds his way to the Rices' house in Coral Gables.

The Knights find Barbara waiting up for them. She's a vivacious dark-haired beauty in her early forties married to a geriatric bon vivant named Robert Rice who's forty years her senior. Robert made a vast fortune developing South Florida real estate and the Rices live in a magnificent Venetian-style home with a huge ground floor perfect for entertaining. Aside from the six bedrooms upstairs, the property has two guest cottages out back next to the tennis courts.

Barbara has these ready for the Knights, and she gets them settled there before leaving so they can unpack.

The next day, the Knight children are eager to meet their grandfather. So, after breakfast, the family gets back into the car and drives over to the Spanish-style hacienda where David S. Knight Sr. lives. His wife, Violet, opens the door. She's a diminutive, curly-haired brunette who was Knight Sr.'s secretary for many years then married him after his first wife died. Knight greets Violet effusively. "You look great," he exclaims and kisses her cheek.

Then Knight cordially shakes hands with his father, a tall, white-haired, bespectacled gentleman. "Who wants lemonade?" Knight Sr. asks, to break the ice. Dave and Dan immediately raise their hands then go into the kitchen with their father and grandfather. "I'm retired now," Knight Sr. tells the boys as they sit at the kitchen table with their drinks, "but I used to work as an engineer."

"On a train?" Dan asks.

"No, I worked building things."

"You have to be strong for that."

"I'm still strong," Knight Sr. says. "Watch this." The old man goes to the corner, kneels in front of a kitchen stool, takes hold of one of the legs, then stands and lifts it straight out. He holds the stool there with his arm muscles knotted up, then kneels and replaces it. A sheen of perspiration gleams on his forehead.

"That's nothing," Dan says. "I could do that." The boy grabs a leg of the stool, but it barely moves. "Well, Dad could do it," Dan says, looking at his father.

Knight throws up both hands. "Not me," he says.

"What did you build?" Dave asks his grandfather.

"First I built railroads, then the waterworks."

"He was chairman of the Miami-Dade Water and Sewer Department," Knight brags.

"Oh, I tried to quit several times, but they wouldn't let me," Knight Sr. laughs.

"Why not?" Dan asks.

"I was the only one who knew where everything was."

"Everything what?"

"Oh, valves, pumps, drains, stuff like that."

"Wasn't there a map showing where those were?" Dave inquires.

"I was too busy during the years we were putting it all in to make one."

"So, you had to stay."

"Yes, I had to stay and train my replacement," Knight Sr. says. "Together we ran the department plus did the schematics. I was finally able to retire five years ago."

"You must be rich from all the money you got," Dan exclaims.

"That's funny," Knight Sr. laughs. "Let me give you a piece of advice. If you want to get rich, don't work for the government. That's what I told your father, and look at him, same deal as me, working for the government and poor as a church mouse."

"How can you be poor living in a big house like this?" Dan asks.

"Oh, I'm not going to tell you what I paid to build this house back in the twenties, but it wasn't much," Knight Sr. says. "No one wanted to live here then. It was a mosquito-infested swamp before the canals and no air conditioning. Robert Rice is the one who came up with the name 'Coral Gables.' I guess he thought it sounded better than 'Alligator Hell.'"

Violet bustles into the kitchen. "What's this?" she complains. "For men only? We've been waiting for you. Now come join the rest of us."

In the living room, Violet is determined to be the center of attention. She prattles on inconsequentially while the other adults feign interest. But the young ones are bored and become increasingly fractious. Soon Violet grows weary of the children and announces that Grandpa needs his afternoon nap. So, the Georgia branch of the Knight family returns to the Rices'.

That evening, Knight takes Bobbie and the children to his sister Elizabeth's house. She's a distinguished-looking woman with the same black hair as her brother. Elizabeth was among the first group of women to graduate from Duke University then married a pediatrician named Wilbur Hughes. He was once highly thought of in his field, but at this point, Wilbur's career has stalled.

The problem is that children hate him. He's a jowly, cigar-chomping toad of a man who goes out of his way to be obnoxious.

The Hugheses have three lovely daughters. The oldest, Mindy, was named Orange Bowl Queen just out of high school then dropped out of college to marry the owner of several Burger Kings. The middle daughter Phyliss is a stunning redhead who skipped college and is currently crewing on an ocean sailing yacht. The youngest Hughes daughter, Hailey, is home from Florida State University and answers the door when the Knight clan arrives. She's a tall, well-proportioned girl with a mass of honey-blond hair framing her photogenic face. "Hi, Aunt Bobbie," she says. "Uncle Dave."

"You can't be Hailey," Knight exclaims, eyes widening.

"In the flesh," Hailey smiles. "Let me show you where Mom and Dad are."

Hailey graciously walks the Knights through the house to a screen-enclosed pool out back. Elizabeth and Wilbur are at the patio bar. "Well, there you are," Elizabeth exclaims when she sees her brother for the first time in six years.

"Hi, sis," Knight says, and the two siblings share a hug and peck each other's cheek.

"Are all those legitimate?" Wilbur asks, indicating the children.

"Why, of course," Bobbie laughs.

"Honey, why don't you make a couple rum and Cokes?" Elizabeth suggests.

Wilbur tends bar for the visitors while the Knight children rush off to change into bathing suits. Hailey is not interested in swimming, so she goes back to the living room to watch TV.

"So how does Dad look?" Elizabeth asks. She doesn't get along with Violet and consequently sees little of her father.

"Much older," Knight replies.

"Well, you haven't seen him for so long."

"That's right; he was still working the last time."

"Now you'll be able to come more often," Elizabeth says. "Thank God they didn't send you back to Kansas."

"Yep, this is a reasonable drive."

"So, was she drinking?" Elizabeth asks.

"At 1:00 p.m., come on."

"Oh, we had them over here once right after the marriage," Elizabeth says. "You should have seen her throwing back the Scotch."

There's a commotion as the Knight children return and enter the pool. First Melissa executes a lovely jackknife then Dave opts for a cannonball. Perle is in a swim ring and delightedly kicks her feet while paddling with her arms. Meanwhile, Dan and Marie get into a vicious splash fight in the shallow end, and Dan quickly overwhelms his sister. Even though she surrenders, Dan won't quit. When Marie puts her hands over her eyes and turns around, Dan circles her, swinging his arms wildly. Finally, Marie exits the pool and cries her way to Bobbie. "Please make him stop," she pleads.

Knight goes over to the pool. "Stop pestering your sister," he tells Dan.

"Why don't you make me?" is the cool reply.

Knight flushes. "Get out of the pool this minute, or else."

Dan is now in the deep end, treading water. "Or else what?" he mocks. "You gonna come in and get me?"

"OK then, I'll take care of you when we get back," Knight threatens. "I have my belt." As his father goes back to the bar, Dan quickly swims to the side of the pool and pulls himself out.

"OK, OK, I was just kidding," he says.

"Ten-minute time out," Knight snaps. "Go sit."

The next couple of minutes are quiet, but the peace is shattered when Marie goes to where Dan is serving his time. "Na-nan-a-nana," she taunts. "I can swim but you can't." Marie sticks her tongue out, and Dan slaps her. She retaliates using her fingernails to claw Dan's bare chest. Infuriated, he grabs Marie's arm and flings her into a set of patio furniture. Knight rushes over to grab Dan, while Bobbie comforts Marie who is wailing. "We're leaving," Knight announces.

Once back at the Rices', Knight forgoes the belt and settles for another favorite punishment. "We'll have a nice long time out," he says, then puts Marie in one corner of the small living room of the cottage and Dan in the other. Then Knight makes himself a drink and settles down on the sofa with a magazine.

The debacle at the Hugheses' ends Knight's effort to introduce his children to the Florida side of the family. The next day, Barbara Rice retains a strong-arm babysitter, and that allows her guests to go out at night to enjoy the Coral Gables holiday party whirl. The children spend the rest of their vacation under house arrest. Then the Knights return to Georgia, school resumes, and the family falls back into its familiar routine.

On the Maglin Terrace playground, as the short winter gives way to spring, gloves, balls, and bats appear while football goes on hiatus. Dave and Dan are just as inept on the softball diamond as they were playing football, but PFC Miller tries to help. He's often at the house waiting to drive Knight somewhere and likes to coach his boss's sons. "Use both hands when catching," Miller instructs. "Don't copy those fancy pants you see on TV using only one hand."

"We play softball at school during PE," Dave tells the driver. "The other boys laugh when I drop fly balls."

"Tell you what," Miller says. "Come out early tomorrow morning, and I'll hit you a few before the school bus comes."

Dave is excited the next morning and goes outside as soon as it's light. He throws a ball up in the air and catches it until Miller arrives. They go to the softball field, and the soldier puts Dave in the outfield, then hits a ball to him from home plate. Dave misses it. "Get in line with the direction of the ball as soon as you see it come off the bat," Miller coaches. He hits another fly that drops short. "Next time try and judge the flight of the ball so you can tell where it's going to come down," he explains. "If it's a pop-up, you come in; if a long ball, you have to back up." They keep practicing and Dave begins to make some catches. Then it's time for the school bus.

Miller walks back to the housing complex with Dave. They find Perle and Dan waiting at the bus stop. "Where's Melissa?" Miller asks.

"She's not going to school today," Dan replies.

"Why not?"

"She has a black eye."

"What happened?"

"Marie hit her."

"They fought?"

"Oh yeah, the MPs had to come."

"What about Marie?"

"She got her nose broke. The MPs took her to the emergency room. Now her face is all taped up."

"Where were your parents?"

"At a party," Dan says. He turns to get on the school bus, which has pulled up behind him.

All spring, Bobbie sees Dan and Dave going back and forth to the playground with their gloves and bats. Often, they are out in the yard throwing a ball. So, at the end of the school year, she signs them up to play in Fort Gordon's Little League. Then Bobbie looks for something her daughters can do. She finds a summer camp the army has for dependents at a nearby reservoir. The primary activity there is water-skiing, and the Knight girls all fall in love with the sport. They are at the camp off and on all summer. When the baseball season ends, Dave and Dan also get a week of camp. Then it's time to return to school.

On the first day back, Melissa stays on the bus when it drops her siblings off at Forest Hills and doesn't get off until the vehicle reaches the Academy of Richmond County (ARC). It's a historic high school that has served Augusta for over a hundred years. The building's white staircases and window casements stand out dramatically against its red-brick façade. Melissa is nervous looking up at the imposing structure, but then she spots some friends from junior high. Soon she's in a crowd of happily chattering girls on their way up the stairs to the second-floor main entrance. She finds her homeroom then takes a seat at one of the antique wrought iron desks. Generations of students have carved their initials into its wooden surface, which has a hole for an inkwell. Melissa gets out a notebook and pencil then eagerly awaits the teacher.

Meanwhile, at Forest Hills, it's more of the same for Perle, Marie, Dan, and Dave. For them, grammar school is like purgatory. It seems to go on forever, and there's no escape. They even look wistfully toward Langford, the miserable little junior high school next door. That's where Melissa went, and where they will go to school after the seventh grade.

On school days, Knight always makes breakfast for his children. He read that it's the most important meal of the day, but his kids never have time to sit down for it. Instead, Knight stands by the door and hands each child something to eat every morning as they run out. One fall morning, the officer is perturbed to see he has a meal left over after the bus pulls away. A few minutes later, Melissa comes out of the bathroom. "Dammit, you missed the bus again," Knight complains.

"Sorry," Melissa says nonchalantly. "Guess I lost track of the time."

"Well, come on, let's get you to school."

PFC Miller is leaning against the staff car, working a toothpick, when Knight and Melissa come out. "Hi, Dwight," Melissa says.

"Hi."

"Miller, you need to take Melissa to school again," Knight orders. "Come straight back."

"Yes, sir," Miller says as he opens the car door.

"Wait one," Knight tells the driver. He hastens back into the house only to come out moments later holding a paper plate with two pancakes. Melissa reluctantly takes the food. Then she and Miller leave while Knight returns to the kitchen and makes some flapjacks for himself. He now has plenty of time to eat.

That afternoon Knight is sitting in his office with nothing to do. It's not yet three o'clock and happy hour isn't until five. He decides to jump the gun. Knight goes down the hall to the Coca-Cola machine and, after depositing a coin, pulls the lever. Down the chute rattles a sexy little green bottle full of his favorite mixer. He takes it back to the office and pours half down the sink in his private lavatory. Then he gets a bottle of Bacardi out of a desk drawer. At that moment Sergeant Major Reynier comes on the intercom and interrupts his boss. "Sir, may I have a word with you?"

"Can't it wait?" Knight growls.

"No, sir."

"Oh, OK then," Knight says and puts the bottle away.

Two knocks and the door swings open a couple of inches. "Permission to enter?" Sergeant Major Reynier asks.

"Come," Knight replies.

The soldier marches to Knight's desk, snaps to attention, and executes a crisp salute.

Knight tosses a salute back. "What is it, Sergeant Major?"

"Sir, permission to speak freely?"

"Of course," Knight says impatiently.

"Sir, we have a problem with PFC Miller."

"Oh?"

"He's been telling nasty stories about him and Melissa."

"What?!"

"Yes, sir, I'm afraid so," Reynier says. "His squad leader relayed this to me."

"Goddamn, so it's all over the barracks by now."

"Yes, sir."

Knight sits silently for a moment. "Well, check back with me tomorrow," he finally says.

That evening Knight has a chat with Melissa. "I'm getting you up at five thirty tomorrow morning instead of six."

"Why?"

"I'm tired of you missing the bus."

"I won't miss it again, I promise."

"That's correct, because you're getting up early."

The next day, Melissa tries another tack. "I have to write a book report on *The Last of the Mohicans*," she tells her father when he gets home from work. "But I left the book in my locker."

"That wasn't very smart."

"I could get a copy from the post library, but Mom is gone."

"We can go after she gets back."

"What about the staff car?"

"No."

On Friday night, Bobbie and her husband must make an appearance at a reception, but they are free of social obligations the rest of the weekend. So after dinner on Saturday, Knight convenes his card-playing buddies for a friendly game. At first, Melissa and Dan don't want to play, but the others eventually talk them into it. "Come on," Marie urges, "there's nothing else to do."

As the evening progresses, the players take turns dealing, then sometime after eleven, Knight calls the last round. After expertly shuffling, he allows Perle to cut. Then Knight deals everyone a down card and one up. Dan's hole card is an ace, so he tries to shield it from the prying eyes of Marie by holding the card under the table. Knight calls him on it. "If this was a real game," he tells his son, "someone might think you were cheating, and you would get shot." Knight points his finger at Dan, holding his thumb back like the hammer of a pistol. Then he drops the thumb. "Bang," he shouts. Dan flinches.

Knight has had several rum and Cokes and is enjoying himself. As Marie shuffles the cards for the next hand, he decides to break some news. "We're getting a new driver," he announces.

"What do you mean?" Melissa gasps. "What about Dwight?"

"Damnedest thing," Knight chortles. "He got transferred to a signal station in the Aleutians. Sergeant Major Reynier put him on the plane yesterday."

Melissa leaps to her feet, sending her chips flying. "You bastard," she cries. "You did it." Melissa runs wildly down the hall to her room and slams the door. The rest of the family can hear her in there throwing things, sobbing, and cursing.

"Let's make this the last hand," Knight says affably.

CHAPTER FIVE
DOUBLE PLAY

After a dreary winter, it's nearing the time of year when Augusta's dogwoods and azaleas burst forth. The big news in town is that ex-President Eisenhower is coming for a visit. Ike's primary interest is golf, but on the off chance he might stop by Fort Gordon, a horde of draftees is sprucing up the base. Meanwhile, at post headquarters, Knight is having one of his frequent meetings with General Clifton, the commandant of Fort Gordon. Late last year Knight was appointed deputy commandant, so Clifton is now his boss. "The Pentagon is worried about juvenile delinquency," Clifton is saying. "The high schools are rife with it, you know, drinking, fighting, car racing, vandalism, and so on. I need to tell higher-higher what we're doing to keep it off the base. Can you put something together?"

"Yes, sir," Knight replies.

"It's the damnedest thing," Clifton exclaims.

"Sir, it's that rock 'n' roll," Knight opines. "We should just ban it from the base."

"How're you going to do that?" Clifton asks. "We can't confiscate every radio."

"No, sir, guess not."

That evening when he gets home, Knight tells Bobbie about his latest assignment. "I swear, Clifton must think I have nothing but time," he complains.

"Oh, come on," Bobbie replies. "Something needs to be done. There's nothing for the older kids to do on base."

"We have movies, swimming pools, bowling, gyms, ball fields, what more do they want?"

"They certainly don't want to associate with that crowd of beer-guzzling GIs at the bowling alley," Bobbie replies, "or dive into a pool full of horny soldiers. They want to be with other teens. They need activities."

So, the next morning, Knight meets with Sergeant Major Reynier and Captain Kinsey. "General Clifton wants us to come up with some activities for the older dependents," he tells them.

"Sir, I could teach a jujitsu class," Kinsey offers. He's a tall, athletic man with black belts in several martial arts.

"You wouldn't have many takers for jujitsu," Knight replies.

"Sir, kids love to swim," Reynier interjects. "Why not reserve the indoor pool for dependents one night a week?"

"That's right," Kinsey agrees. "Teens could have open swimming and activities."

"Like what?" Knight demands.

"We could ask the Red Cross to give a lifesaving course."

"That's more like it."

Now the ideas come fast and furious, and at the end of an hour, the men have enough to fill a report. That afternoon General Clifton is suitably impressed when Knight briefs him on the plan. "This is excellent," he declares. "Just what I need to keep the Pentagon off my back. Now you need to make it happen, Colonel."

"Yes, sir," Knight replies. Then he returns to his office and delegates implementation of the youth program to Kinsey.

Another of Knight's duties as deputy commandant is vendor relations, and this has led to a marked improvement in his social standing. That's because many of Augusta's finest families have been forced into crass commercialism thanks to the late unpleasantness among the States. By necessity, these folks now find themselves entertaining people with whom they would not otherwise associate. Tonight, for example, Colonel and Mrs. Knight will be attending a dinner party at the home of Blake and Nancy Beaufort. Their Edwardian mansion was built by Blake's grandfather, a cotton broker. Nowadays, the

Beauforts' income derives from Coca-Cola—they own the bottling rights for the Central Savannah River Area.

When the Knights arrive, they find several impressive cars already parked in front of the Beauforts'. These belong to the other dinner guests: Richard and Zeena Greyson, Howard and Abigail Houston, and Phil and Denise Coleman. Zeena is a highly successful author of romance novels, Howard is a cardiologist, and the Colemans own Augusta's Chevrolet dealership.

After a convivial meal, the Beauforts escort their friends for the evening into the living room for after-dinner drinks. While Nancy pours, Blake makes sure everyone is comfortably seated in front of the stone fireplace. The lights are turned low, but from time to time a log flares and briefly illuminates the oil portrait of Button Gwinnett that hangs over the mantle.

The blaze died down some during dinner, so Blake rests his brandy snifter, opens the fireplace screen, and pokes at the embers. Then the host selects a log and places it where it will do the most good. Afterward, he turns and addresses Knight. "I envy you," Blake says. "Your job has taken you all over the world to live, but when I go abroad, it's as a tourist."

"Some places you don't want to live," Knight observes.

"What about Germany?" Nancy asks. "That must have been wonderful."

"We loved Germany," Bobbie gushes. She sips crème de cacao against doctor's orders.

"I'm thinking of Korea," Knight elaborates.

"You were in the war?" Zeena asks.

"No, I was there in '45."

"What for?"

"To take over from the Japs," Knight explains. "MacArthur sent me there from Okinawa. I virtually ran South Korea for a year."

"What was the country like?" Denise inquires.

"Very primitive."

"How does an army colonel get to be in charge of a country?" Howard wonders.

"Good question," Knight answers. "And I was just a lieutenant colonel at the time. Anyway, MacArthur was the titular head of state, not me. What happened is that after processing the Japs out of South Korea we had to keep things going, and at the time all the utilities, railroads, coal mines, steel mills, and other industries belonged to one conglomerate. It was called the New Korea Company, and MacArthur put me in charge of it. So I ran the economy."

"That's what I mean," Blake interjects. "You've had all these fantastic experiences around the world while I've been stuck here running the family business."

"A funny thing happened after I'd been at the New Korea Company a year," Knight says. "Congress sent some accountants to audit us."

"Why?" Zeena asks.

"Guess they thought I might be tapping the till."

"Were you?" Howard inquires.

"You'd have to be a real deadbeat to steal from those people," Knight laughs. "I've never seen such poverty."

"So how did the audit come out?" Phil asks impatiently.

"Price Waterhouse sent a team from New York. They came to my office in Seoul, all of them wearing dark pinstripe suits, white shirts, and red ties. Introductions were made and I offered them a drink. 'We're here to work, not drink,' the leader said. 'We intend to spend the next month going over your books, now let's proceed.' So, I called Mr. Cho, our finance officer. 'Please bring up the ledgers for the Chonju Railway Company,' I told him. Shortly, Mr. Cho and his staff came in carrying stacks of ledgers, which they plopped down on my conference table. The Price Waterhouse team pounced on them, throwing open first one and then another. Finally, one of them said, 'What's with all these Japanese characters? We can't read these. Don't you have any books in English?' I told them, 'Guys, these ledgers have been kept in Japanese since 1912. I don't have the budget for translating them, so I've left Mr. Cho in charge. He was here with the Japs, now he's here with us, and he'll still be here long after we're gone.'"

"So, what happened?" Zeena asks.

"Well, the Price Waterhouse boys stood around scratching their heads for a minute before the leader said, 'Well, Colonel, guess we'll have that drink now. We're done.'"

Polite laughter greets this punch line. "You should write a book," Zeena comments. "You have all these great stories."

"Oh, I could never do what you do," Knight replies. "I'm not creative."

"What's this I hear about the infantry coming?" Blake asks Knight. The infantry is known to drink a lot of Coca-Cola.

"All I know is we continue to get occasional units coming through on rotation," Knight says. "Mainly airborne; they use the parade ground for drops."

"Some construction guys from Kellogg, Brown & Root stayed at the Holiday Inn a couple of weeks ago," Phil says. "Rumor is they're bidding on a project to build an airborne training course."

"There have been no announcements about that," Knight says cautiously.

The dinner party breaks up a little before midnight. When the Knights get home, a patrol car is in front of their house. Two MPs are in the front yard with Dave and Dan. Both boys are disheveled, and Dan is holding the bloody hem of his pajama shirt up to his nose. Marie and Perle are nearby in their nightgowns.

"What's the problem, Sergeant?" Knight asks the senior MP.

"Sir, we got calls from the neighbors," the soldier says, "and found these two in the yard trading punches."

"OK, Sergeant, I'll take it from here."

"Yes, sir."

After the MPs leave, Bobbie hustles Marie and Perle back to bed while Knight takes Dave and Dan into the living room for a time out. He keeps them up most of the night, so it's no surprise when neither of them wants to go to school in the morning. "I've got a headache," Dave pleads when his father comes in to cut on the light.

"I don't want to hear it," Knight replies. "You're going."

Dave and Dan make it out to the bus on time, then sleep uncomfortably in their seats until it's time to get off the vehicle and go to class. Later that morning, on the Forest Hills playground, the students talk about the upcoming Masters golf tournament. "Tommy Bolt is staying at my house again this year," a boy announces. "Last year he got so drunk one night we found him the next morning passed out in the yard."

"Mike Souchak always stays with us," another kid brags. "One time he and Doug Sanders were drinking beer in the living room, and Mike bet Doug he wouldn't eat one of our goldfish. Mike had to pay up."

Dave has been standing on the fringe of the group listening, and now he laughs. "What's so funny, scab face?" one of the kids asks him.

"Nothing," Dave replies and quickly walks away.

Once Masters week is over, the end of the school year is in sight, so people in Augusta turn their attention to vacation plans. For Bobbie, this means finding activities for her children so they're not underfoot all summer. She again signs Marie and Perle up for several weeks of summer camp, but Melissa has outgrown camp. She's old enough to work now, so Knight finds her a summer job at the PX. As for the boys, they're easy to keep occupied; Bobbie enrolls them in Fort Gordon's new Pony League.

On the first day of baseball, Dave and Dan discover that their father's aide will be the coach of their team, which is called the Tigers. At practice, it's hot, and the gnats are swarming, but Captain Kinsey is determined to get the team into shape. "See that light pole?" he says pointing. "When I say 'go,' run to the pole, go around it, and come back. Last one does it again." Dan is among the first to finish, but Dave struggles, barely managing to beat a red-faced kid who wheezes a few steps behind.

"OK, outfielders play 500 over by the fence," Kinsey tells the panting boys. "Infielders stay with me, and I want the pitchers and catchers to go to the bullpen." So, Dave, Dan, and the other outfielders hit balls to each other while the pitchers throw to the catchers and Kinsey conducts infield practice with the remaining players. After an hour the coach calls the boys in to run some more before the session ends.

The Tigers' first game is a week later, on a Saturday morning. Dave and Dan are excited the night before, then Knight shares some news that makes all his children happy. "Captain Kinsey has invited us to his lake house to go water-skiing this weekend," he says. "We leave after the baseball game in the morning."

The next day, despite their best efforts, the Tigers get hammered 11-2 in the season opener. Kinsey isn't happy. He comes over to Dave after the game and grasps his shoulder, kneading it like an angry masseuse. "You need to work on your bunts," he snarls. "What did we say in practice? Get the bat on the top part of the ball to force it down. What did you do? Popped it up. Right to the first baseman." Kinsey emphasizes his disgust by digging a beefy thumb behind Dave's clavicle. It hits the nerve, and Dave feels an electric jolt of pain. As the coach stalks off, Dave sees the fully loaded Opel pull into the parking lot. He and Dan climb into the back.

It's a long drive to the lake, but the Knights are in a holiday mood, so the time passes peacefully. They play car games, sing, and look out the window so it doesn't seem that long before they're turning onto the winding dirt driveway that leads to Kinsey's place. The captain has beaten them there and is waiting outside looking very fit in red swim trunks, hairy chest, and dark tan. "Come on," he calls to the Knights. "I'll show you where to bunk."

The cottage only has three bedrooms, so once inside, Kinsey shows Dave and Dan the cots they will sleep on in the living room. The Kinseys' seventeen-year-old son, Tim, is giving up his room so Melissa, Marie, and Perle can have it. He will be on the living room sofa while Knight and Bobbie take the guest bedroom.

After they unpack, the Knight children change into swimsuits, then rush down to the dock where Kinsey's boat waits. "Ladies first," Kinsey announces as he helps Melissa into a lifebelt. At sixteen, she has blossomed, and the floral-patterned one-piece bathing suit she wears does little to disguise her budding figure.

Melissa stuffs her blond hair under a swim cap, picks up a ski, and jumps into the water. As the boat drifts away from the pier, Kinsey tosses her the towrope. Then the powerful outboard roars and Melissa comes out of the water on one ski. She's the picture of grace, slaloming back and forth behind the boat as Kinsey makes several circuits of the broad cove that fronts the cottage.

Knight and Bobbie watch proudly as each of their children has a turn water-skiing. Dave is the last then after he wears his arms out hanging onto the towrope, there's time for Tim. He's a tall, rangy kid with his father's good looks and dark tan. Now he and Kinsey execute a nifty trick. Tim puts on a ski and grasps the handle of the towrope while standing at the end of the dock. Then his father pushes the boat's throttle forward, and as the slack disappears, Tim leaps. They time it so the towrope tightens just as the boy's ski hits the water. Tim takes off without getting wet.

After Tim finishes his turn, the young people return to the house chattering happily. While they take turns in the shower, the adults relax on the patio. It's delightful outside with the sunset fading on the horizon and fireflies flickering among the trees. The remoteness of the cottage and the lapping water inspire a castaway feeling. In the distance, the outline of the North Georgia Mountains is faintly visible against the darkening sky. "How in the world do you persuade yourself to leave here every Sunday and return to Fort Gordon?" Bobbie asks Kinsey.

"It ain't easy, especially during the summer when Tim and Phyllis stay here," Kinsey says while affectionately patting his wife's knee. Phyllis Kinsey is a pert bleached blonde from nearby Athens. She wears flip-flops, frayed khaki shorts, and a shocking pink blouse. With her short tomboyish haircut and golden tan, she looks younger than she is. "This is my favorite time of year," Phyllis proclaims. "Don't have to put up with this big galoot but three days a week." They all laugh while Kinsey leaves his hand on his wife's knee. This is the second marriage for both.

As darkness falls, Kinsey gets up to start a charcoal fire while Phyllis and Bobbie go inside to make preparations for dinner. It's a simple affair featuring hot dogs, hamburgers, baked beans, and corn on the cob. After eating, the children gather in front of the TV while the adults freshen their drinks and begin a game of hearts. Everyone is tired, however, and no one stays up late. In the morning the kids all have another round of water-skiing before the Knights must leave for home.

Reality sets in Monday morning when Knight returns to work and finds Sergeant Major Reynier waiting. "Sir, Major Glimp called. He's requesting an appointment."

"Who's Major Glimp?"

"Sir, he's the post housing officer."

"What does he want?"

"Sir, I asked, but he said that he'd prefer to meet privately with you."

"OK," Knight says. "Set it up for sometime tomorrow."

"Yes, sir."

The next day, Major Glimp shows up early for the meeting. He's a tall, thin officer with sharp features. "Care for a cup of coffee?" Knight offers.

"No, sir," the major replies. "I'll just get right to business, if that's OK."

"Sure."

"Sir, we've come up with a housing alternative I think you'll like."

"I doubt it," Knight replies curtly. "We're fine where we are."

"Sir, several of your neighbors disagree."

Knight flushes. "Who might that be?"

"Sir, that's beside the point," Glimp replies. "Suffice to say we've received several complaints. It appears that things get rambunctious at your house. The noise doesn't comport with the tight proximity of the units at Maglin."

"So, what's the alternative?"

"Colonel Felts is transferring to the Pentagon. You can move to Boardman Lake."

Boardman Lake is the most attractive neighborhood on post. The commandant's house is there, and five smaller houses are widely spaced around a drive that circles the pond. Full colonels always occupy these. "I'll consider it," Knight concedes. "And call you in the morning."

After work Knight rushes home to tell Bobbie. "Honey, we've been offered one of the nicest houses at Fort Gordon."

"Hell no," Bobbie erupts. "Why move?"

"Now, baby," Knight pleads. "Why don't we have a look before saying no? It'll take no more than five minutes."

"Oh, all right," Bobbie sighs.

It's a short drive from Maglin Terrace down a steep hill to Boardman Lake. Once there, the road forks to circle the pond. Knight goes left past the commandant's quarters then stops in front of Colonel Felts's house. It's an attractive old-fashioned, two-story wooden home with a fieldstone walkway that leads up to the broad porch. "Hey, Dave," Felts calls from a side garden where he's pruning roses. "Are you thinking about moving in?"

"Bobbie doesn't want to budge," Knight replies out of the car window.

"You'd be crazy not to take this," Felts exclaims, coming over. "Why don't you park and have a look."

Inside the house, Miriam Felts politely offers to show the visitors around. First, she leads them down a hallway into the kitchen. "It's an old house," she says, "but all the appliances are new." Then Miriam opens the back door, which leads into the garage. "We mainly go in and out this way," she says. "Comes in handy when unloading groceries."

The two couples go back up the hallway into the living room, which is separated from the dining area by a foyer and a staircase that lead to the four bedrooms upstairs. "Nice fireplace," Knight exclaims, admiring the raised fieldstone hearth.

"Yes, but we haven't used it much," Felts says. "The winters are so mild."

"Here's what we use a lot," Miriam declares. She flips a wall switch, and as a low rumbling noise fills the house, the curtains bow in, and a breeze begins to swirl.

"Attic fan," Felts crows. "Who needs air conditioning?"

"It's wonderful," Bobbie exclaims. "I'm sold."

"How 'bout a drink?" Felts inquires.

"Thought you'd never ask," Knight replies.

Once the highballs are ready, the two couples go onto the front porch to enjoy the view. It's less than a quarter mile down to the lakeshore across a grassy field past a stand of tall pines. A water wheel turns lazily behind the dam at the end of the lake while towering oaks, maples, and poplars rise from the hillside across the way.

"This is lovely," Bobbie says.

"Yes, we're going to miss it," Miriam sighs.

"Oh, you'll love Washington," Knight exclaims. "Everyone who's been there raves about it."

"I'm sure we will," Miriam says hopefully.

"Do you know where you're going to live?" Bobbie asks.

"McLean," Miriam replies. "They have the best schools."

"The house is costing us an arm and a leg," Felts complains. "My housing allowance won't begin to touch it."

"There's no help for it," Miriam says. "When you're at the Pentagon you have to find your own housing."

"Can I get you another?" Felts offers.

"Thanks, but we've got mouths to feed," Bobbie says, standing up.

"Good luck with the move," Knight says as he and Felts shake hands.

"You too," Felts grins.

Knight goes onto the front porch to look for the school bus and sees it halfway down the hill at the far end of Boardman Lake. The vehicle is the same color as the fall leaves on the poplars that line the shore. Their reflections dance like flames in the choppy waters of the pond.

Back inside the house, Knight goes to the foot of the stairs. "It's almost at the Durhams'," he shouts. "Hurry." But upstairs all is pandemonium. Dan is furiously pounding on the bathroom door while inside Marie stares into the mirror applying eyeliner. She's in the seventh grade now and has discovered that boys aren't just for beating up. Meanwhile, Dave's in the basement ironing a shirt. He gives it a couple finishing touches then slips it on while running up the stairs.

"Have you seen my book bag?" Melissa asks.

"Isn't that it next to the door?" Dave replies.

The bus pulls up in front of the house, and Melissa grabs the book bag. Knight hands her a bacon-and-egg sandwich as she goes out. "Tell the driver to wait," he asks. Then one by one the other Knight children rush out while the driver insistently honks his horn. Finally, Marie comes downstairs, gets her sandwich, and strolls down the front walk, arms full of accoutrements. As she climbs aboard, the enlisted men's dependents in back sarcastically applaud. Marie ignores them, and once seated she uses a can of hairspray to laminate her teased tresses. She pays no heed to mounting protests from others on the bus who object to being gassed this early in the morning.

After dropping the younger kids at Forest Hills and Langford, the bus continues to ARC where Melissa gets off. She goes to her homeroom, now decorated for Halloween with spider webs, witches, ghosts, and goblins. The bell rings, and the intercom crackles as school Principal Lester Oldman's voice comes into the classroom. "Welcome back," he says. "I hope you had a nice weekend." Then Mr. Oldman leads the students in the Lord's Prayer and the Pledge of Allegiance. Afterward, he turns the mic over to Steve Walsh, President of the student government.

"Good morning, ARC!" Steve says enthusiastically. "We have a busy week starting with a pep rally in the cafeteria today at noon. Make sure you're there. The bus to the Benedictine game leaves right after lunch on Friday. Cost is three dollars. Also, we have a car wash to benefit Key Club after school Wednesday, so bring your ride and make a donation. Oh, and this is a GMB week."

GMB is student code for "get Miss Ballantine," the overly strict school librarian. So, after Melissa finishes her morning classes, she goes to the library and randomly picks out five books. Then she joins the crowd of students at the checkout counter where Miss Ballantine is frantically working to keep up with demand. There's an unnatural hush in the high-ceilinged room, though it's packed full of smiling teenagers. They're afraid to so much as whisper.

After a long wait, Melissa gets to the head of the line and checks out. Then she takes the books to her locker where they will remain until Friday when she and all the other students who withdrew unneeded books during the week will return them. At that point, the library shelves will be empty, but the counters and tables will hold stacks of unread tomes needing to be reshelved.

In the cafeteria, Melissa goes through the line, pays for her selections, then finds her place at a table reserved for college-bound seniors. Suddenly a gaggle of cheerleaders bursts in waving pom-poms and shouting: "Here we go,

Richmond, here we go." Students pick up the chant as the school's marching band files into the cafeteria with drummers drumming. Then the first bars of the ARC Musketeers' fight song ring out, and the students leap to their feet singing:

> *Richmond will shine tonight, Richmond will shine.*
> *She'll shine in beauty bright all down the line,*
> *She's all dressed up tonight, that's one good sign.*
> *When the sun goes down, and the moon comes up,*
> *Richmond will shine.*

At the end of the song, Steve Walsh leaps onto one of the dining tables. "Are we gonna beat Benedictine?" he shouts, and the students holler back: "Hell yeah."

"I can't hear you," Steve yells. "Are we going to beat Benedictine?"

"Hell yeah!!!!"

This colloquy is repeated numerous times. Then the band strikes up "Dixie." The students don't sing along with this tune; instead, they punctuate it with a wide variety of efforts to replicate the rebel yell.

Meanwhile, at Langford Junior High, Dave is outside the lunchroom killing time with several other boys while waiting for afternoon classes to begin. "Pussy is good but so is honey," one of the kids recites. "Fuck your fist and save your money." The boy grins at the others idiotically and pantomimes jerking off. His father owns a disreputable roadhouse just up the hill from the school and he, as well as the other students in the group, are at the nadir of Langford's social hierarchy.

The bell rings, and now it's time for Dave to go to algebra class. The teacher is Mrs. Jason, and every day she reviews the homework from the day before then goes to the board and demonstrates how to solve the problems that come next. But Dave ignores her. He sits at a desk in the back row and reads a paperback.

After school, on the bus home, Dave tries to get up a football game. "Hey, who's gonna come out and play?" he asks.

"Can't, I have too much homework," Patrick Spilling says.

"Oh, come on, you can join in for one hour," Dave pleads.

"OK, but I leave at five," Patrick says. "That's it."

"All right," Dave agrees happily. If Patrick plays, then so will his younger brother, Dwayne. Soon Dave has commitments from seven boys and Becky Clifton. She's one of the best players.

After changing out of their school clothes, Dave and Dan grab their bikes to go up to Maglin Terrace. The hill is steep, and neither can ride all the way up it. They try standing on the pedals and zigzagging, but eventually, both must get off and push. Then General Clifton's staff car goes by, and Becky laughs at them through the rear window. She's waiting at the field when Dan and Dave get there.

As one of the older kids, Dave now calls the plays in the huddle. "Becky, set up on the right, go out five yards, fake inside, then cut back toward the sideline; you'll be the primary," he instructs. "Dan, you be wide left, go out ten yards, stop, fake a button hook, then take off. Look over your right shoulder; you'll be the secondary. Ben, center the ball on the third hut and block. Gary, be the halfback and block. Everyone got it? OK, break."

Dave finds Becky on the out pattern, and she manages to turn upfield for a nice gain before getting tagged. "OK. Now, everybody, same thing," Dave says once they're back in the huddle. "Only this time Dan will keep coming back on the button hook, and I'll hit him."

After completing the short pass to his brother, Dave calls the next play. He has Dan fake the button hook again then do a fly pattern straight down the left sideline. This time Dave lofts the ball over Dan's right shoulder and the long-legged boy runs under it for a touchdown.

But Patrick Spilling is equally good at finding his brother Dwayne with passes, and soon they score as well. In this manner, the game goes back and forth as shadows cast by the tall pines surrounding the field lengthen. Then Mrs. Spilling comes out and rings the dinner bell. "One more play and that's it," Patrick declares. At this point, his team is down by a touchdown, and they have half the length of the field to go. They huddle then, after setting up, Patrick receives the snap and hurls a Hail Mary for his brother. Dan leaps in front of Dwayne for the interception, and that ends the game.

On the way home, the Knight boys coast their bikes, "no hands," talking excitedly about their victory. When they get to the house, Dan opens a can of ravioli for dinner while Dave makes himself a peanut butter, cream cheese, and banana sandwich. It's so good, he has another.

After cleaning up, Dave goes into the living room to listen to the radio and read. A little later, his parents descend the stairs dressed for an evening out. Knight's in a gray flannel suit, white button-down shirt, and white, black, and red striped tie. Bobbie wears a pale green dress with a gold shawl. She has a gold locket around her neck and a bracelet on her wrist from Germany that's made from antique twenty-mark gold pieces.

"We'll be home early," Knight tells Dave. "Just have to make an appearance."

"OK, Dad, see you later."

After his parents leave, Dave turns the volume up on the stereo and sings along as "Cotton Fields" comes on the radio. "Hey, turn it down," Melissa hollers from upstairs. "I'm studying."

Dave waits until the song is over then reduces the volume while "Peppermint Twist" is played for what seems like the ten thousandth time. He picks up his book again and reads until midnight when the radio station signs off. Then it hits him that he has nothing to wear to school the next day.

Reluctantly, Dave puts the book aside and goes down to the laundry room. He finds one of his long-sleeve shirts and a pair of khaki pants in the washing machine. As they tumble in the dryer, he gets the ironing board and sets it up. A little later, he's ironing the pants when Melissa comes in and opens the washing machine. "I'm looking for my yellow blouse," she says. "You know the one with the white collar and cuffs."

"It's not in there," Dave replies. But Melissa must see for herself. She sorts through the damp laundry then angrily stalks out. Meanwhile, Dave finishes ironing and puts his clothes on a hanger. He goes upstairs and is walking toward his room when he hears a commotion down the hall.

"What's my blouse doing in your closet?" Melissa shrieks. Marie runs out of her room with Melissa close behind. The older girl grabs a handful of her sister's nightgown, but Marie desperately pulls away, and the flimsy material rips apart. Now completely naked Marie makes for the stairs. Dave lets her go by then blocks Melissa.

"Get out of my way," Melissa snarls.

"No."

"I'm going to kill her."

"You need to calm down."

"That bitch stole my blouse."

"You can tell Mom and Dad when they get home."

Melissa tries to bolt past Dave, and again he blocks her. She tries to hit him, but Dave easily deflects her blows. Melissa fixes her brother with a baleful glare. She starts after him again then hesitates. Spinning, she walks back down the hall and turns into the room Dave shares with Dan. She comes out moments later holding a book. As Melissa rips pages out, small squares flutter to the floor. With horror, Dave realizes it's his stamp collection. He sprints down the hall, shoves his sister flat, then holds her down while pulling his fist back for a punch. But Dan comes from behind, gets Dave in a headlock, and drags him off Melissa. After a brief struggle, Dan, by now a head taller than his brother, pins Dave to the floor and is in position to use either hand to hit him. But before Dan can swing, Dave relaxes and looks up at him with a grin. "You fight like a baby," he says. "Not like a man."

"What?"

"Yeah, here we are wrestling on the floor like little kids," Dave says. "Real men fight standing up, throwing punches."

"OK, let's go outside."

Dan and Dave go out the back door through the garage to the driveway. They clench their fists and warily circle each other. Both have cooled off now, and neither has his heart in fighting. Still, they don't know how to stop without one of them chickening out. That would be unthinkable, so they shuffle around each other, throwing an occasional punch. Finally, Dave grazes Dan's chin with a roundhouse, and the younger brother falls theatrically to the pavement. Dave helps him up, and the fight is over. Much later, lying in bed, they hear the distinctive rattle of the Opel's little four-cylinder motor coming up the driveway.

Overnight the wind shifts, and by morning what had been glorious autumn has turned to winter. It's chaos as the Knight children scramble to find coats and sweaters hidden in the backs of closets or buried in drawers. At school, a faint odor of mothballs hangs in the air.

Now the days get progressively shorter, and with darkness coming early, playground activities cease. It's a grim time of year, and since Knight will be on duty over the holidays, the family doesn't have a Florida getaway to anticipate. Instead, Elizabeth Hughes flies up from Coral Gables for a pre-Christmas visit. She makes an immediate hit with the Knight children by taking them to the PX to pick out presents. Melissa chooses Shalimar, her favorite perfume, while Perle and Marie get new bicycles. The boys select fishing rods.

Dave and Dan have seen anglers walking along the shore of Boardman Lake catching fish with spinners and plastic worms. Both want to try it, so they rush down to the water once they're home from the PX. But Dave's spinner immediately goes into a tree and won't come out. After that, he and Dan go over by the dam to fish where there are no obstructions. They don't get any bites, but they practice casting until it gets dark.

Later, Elizabeth, Bobbie, and Knight are having cocktails in front of the fireplace. Dave is upstairs reading when the phone in the hall rings. He goes and picks it up, but before he can speak, his father answers downstairs. "Colonel Knight's quarters," Dave hears him say.

"What have you done with my wife?" someone mumbles.

"Hello, Wilbur," Knight replies.

"Don't hello me."

"Ha-ha, well, how are you?"

"How in the hell do you think I am?" Wilbur slurs. "I'm all alone 'cept for my old pal Johnny Walker here." A slurping sound follows, then a belch.

"Well, you should have come along."

"On one of those puddle jumpers? No thanks."

"You want to talk to Elizabeth?"

"Sure as hell didn't call to talk to you."

There's a pause, and Dave knows he should hang up, but he holds one hand over the mouthpiece and continues listening. "Hi, sweetie," his aunt says.

"So sorry to interrupt," Wilbur replies nastily.

"Oh, we're just having drinks, honey, you aren't interrupting anything."

"Just having drinks, huh?" Wilbur says. "'Spect me to believe that? Ha. I know what you're doing. You're sucking your brother's dick."

Elizabeth giggles nervously. "Now, honey, that's ridiculous."

"Don't lie, just tell me," Wilbur demands. "You're in bed with him right now, aren't you? Naked with your legs spread open, just begging for it."

"Wilbur, for crying out loud," Elizabeth exclaims. But Dave has heard enough. He gently hangs up, hoping the click won't be too audible.

Elizabeth accompanies Bobbie and Knight to a holiday party at the Beauforts' the next evening, and more social events are on tap over the next several days. However, Wilbur keeps calling, so Elizabeth cuts her visit short. She changes her flight reservation and Knight takes her to the airport. Afterward, he swings by Sue Brandt's house. She has promised him a special Christmas gift, which turns out to be a brown, white, and gold bundle of fur. "What kind of dog is this?" Knight asks.

"Part collie among other things," Sue replies.

When Knight gets home, Perle is in the kitchen. "Oh, a puppy," she squeals. Marie comes running, and the other children follow. Knight puts the dog on the kitchen floor, and the animal wags its tail excitedly. Then it squats and produces a little yellow puddle. Melissa grabs a wad of paper towel to clean up. Then they take the new family member upstairs.

"Oh no," Bobbie exclaims.

"You guys have to take turns walking him and making sure the dog gets fed," Knight insists.

"We will," Dan promises.

"What's his name?" Perle asks.

"Let's call him Tex," Bobbie insists. No one objects.

Tex turns out to be a ravenous eater, and over the next several months he puts on weight and grows to be full collie size. Throughout the spring, the dog follows Dave and Dan when they go fishing, and the three of them are often seen prowling the lakeshore.

Fishing gives Dave yet another reason to avoid studying, so it's no wonder when, as the end of the school year approaches, he's called into the principal's office. "You failed algebra," she says. "It's a required course, so you'll have to come back to Langford and try again next year."

"But I want to go to ARC," Dave protests.

"Then you'll have to attend summer school and pass algebra."

"All right."

Dave only has one week of vacation before summer school, and he spends it sleeping, reading, and fishing. Then algebra class begins in an old elementary school located directly across a grassy field from ARC. A young man named Mr. Johnson is the teacher. "There's nothing mysterious about algebra," he tells the class. "It's simply a matter of following procedure. Now, who can tell me what seven times eight equals?"

"Fifty-six," Dave answers when the teacher calls on him.

"OK, good answer," Mr. Johnson says. "But there could be times when a problem presents itself differently. Who can tell me what number you would have to multiply by five to get forty?" No one else raises their hand, so Dave answers once more.

"Thanks, Dave," Mr. Johnson says. "Now tell us how you solved that problem."

"I just remembered the multiplication table."

"Very good, but imagine if we were dealing with bigger numbers, then that wouldn't work. Let me show you another way." Mr. Johnson goes to the blackboard and demonstrates the use of variables. Then he gives the class an assignment in the workbook and walks around the room helping where necessary. He stands next to Dave's desk for a moment, watching him work. "Looks like you've got it," the teacher says.

After an hour, Mr. Johnson removes his sports coat. The floor-to-ceiling windows are all open, but it's still warm inside the building because it's not air-conditioned. Still, the class continues the rest of the morning with just a couple of short breaks. Afterward, Dave walks downtown to catch the bus to Fort Gordon.

That evening Dave and Dan have baseball practice. "We may not be the best team in the league," Kinsey tells the Tigers, "but we'll be the fittest." So, the first half hour of practice is taken up with sprints, calisthenics, and a team run. Then Kinsey has the boys pair up and play catch. Dave takes the opportunity to work on his pitching technique. When practice is over, he approaches Kinsey.

"Coach, I've been working on my pitching."

"Not much hope for you there, Knight," Kinsey replies. "Phil and Mike are our regular starters; then there's Gary. You need to stick with the outfield."

"Yes, sir," Dave replies.

But on a Saturday morning midway through the season, the coach has a dilemma. Phil's family has taken him along on a vacation trip, and Mike is away as well. "You're pitching," Kinsey tells Dave after the fourth inning.

The Tigers are losing to the Cubs 6-0 as Dave takes the mound. He knows his fastball lacks velocity and his curve doesn't move. So Dave plans to keep the ball out of the strike zone. He does this and gets out of the inning by throwing nothing but junk. Then the Tigers get three runs in their half to narrow the score. Dave feels more confident going out in the sixth and again holds the Cubs scoreless by not giving them anything to hit. When it's their turn to bat, the Tigers get a rally going but only come away with one run. Nevertheless, Coach Kinsey is excited. "Three up and three down," he exhorts his team as they take the field for the top of the final inning.

The first Cubs batter hits an easy pop fly, and the second one grounds out, but Dave loses his concentration and throws a perfect strike to the third opposing hitter. It goes for a home run, and the Cubs end up winning 7-4. As the players are lining up to shake hands, Kinsey grabs Dave's arm and spins him around. "I told you, no meatballs," the coach growls, digging his thumb into the boy's wrist. Pain radiates up Dave's arm then Kinsey releases him as the Opel pulls into the parking lot.

It's the Fourth of July holiday, so the Knights' car is loaded with suitcases packed for a long weekend of water-skiing. Everyone in the family is going to Captain Kinsey's lake cottage except Bobbie, who is not well.

While Dave and Dan climb into the back of the station wagon, Kinsey comes over for a word with his boss. "Tough game," the coach sighs. "I was missing my two best pitchers."

"That happens this time of year," Knight commiserates. "People take vacations. There's nothing you can do about it."

"I guess."

"Hey lighten up, you can't win 'em all."

"No fear of that," Kinsey laughs. "Anyway, it's just a game. I'll see you at the lake."

"We'll be there."

Knight stops at the first filling station they come to after leaving Fort Gordon. He goes inside and gets popsicles for the children and a bottle of Coca-Cola for himself. After passing out the treats, he spikes the Coke then gets the car back on the road. A little later, the children are delighted when their father breaks into song. He delivers a rousing rendition of "Abdul Abulbul," then Perle pleads for "Paper Doll." Knight is happy to oblige. Afterward, he starts an Irish ditty the children all know, and they accompany him on it. The singalong continues until they reach the lake.

Tim comes up from the dock to help the Knights unload. Then the children change into bathing suits, and each has a turn water-skiing. Later everyone gathers in the kitchen where Phyllis has whipped up a spaghetti dinner. They eat, and then the grown-ups play cards while the young people go into the living room and set up Monopoly. This is a game that often leads to bloodshed in the Knight household, but on this occasion, they play peacefully until everyone except Melissa is bankrupt. Then she and Tim go for a walk by the lake while the others get ready for bed. Soon the house is quiet except for the kitchen where murmured conversation and the clink of ice cubes signify that the adults are still up.

Dave sleeps fitfully as algebraic equations go around in his head. Then he wakes to use the toilet. As he pads down the hall, Dave glances into the kitchen and sees Mrs. Kinsey seated on his father's lap. She has a drink in one hand, and her other arm draped across Knight's shoulder. Captain Kinsey is on the opposite side of the table. "Doc, I don't know what's wrong," he's saying. "Ever since the operation, I haven't wanted to eat anything except watermelon and fried chicken." Kinsey laughs, and the other two join in.

After two more days of water-skiing, the holiday is over, and it's time for the Knights to pack up and leave. They have a short but busy week ahead. Knight is scheduled to give the commencement address for the latest class to graduate from the signal school while Melissa goes back to work at the PX. Dave must return to algebra class.

As the summer heat settles in, Augusta bakes, and residents with vacation time use it to head for the mountains or shore. But Knight must work, so his family is stuck. Bobbie compensates by sending Marie and Perle to more weeks of camp. She signs Dave and Dan up for golf lessons then takes them to Fort Gordon's nine-hole course to play on afternoons when there's no baseball.

With all they have going on, school vacation seems to blow by for the Knights. Soon the newspaper is full of back-to-school ads, the baseball season is winding down, and summer school is coming to an end. Mr. Johnson spends the last week of algebra class prepping for the exam and Dave pays close attention. On the morning of the test, he breezes through it. "You're a great teacher," he tells Mr. Johnson as he turns in the answer sheet.

That evening Melissa comes home from the last day of her job. "What happened to the summer?" she moans. "All I did was work."

"Yeah, but look at all the money you made," Dan comments.

"It's all going for school clothes," Melissa replies. She'll be leaving to attend Florida State University after Labor Day.

"I learned some new water-skiing tricks at camp this year," Marie brags. "I can hold the rope with my foot."

"I'd like to see that," Knight exclaims.

"Maybe we can go to the Kinseys' this weekend?" Melissa says hopefully. "Marie could show us."

"I'll check and see," Knight promises. "But they might have something else going on."

The next morning when Knight gets to work, he invites Kinsey into his office. "The kids want to come up and water-ski this weekend," Knight says. "How does it look?"

"Well, the Pony League playoffs start Saturday morning," Kinsey replies. "Since we're in last place, we have to play the Yankees. If we lose, the Tigers are out of the tournament, and we could all go to the lake after the game. Otherwise, we play again on Sunday. Either way, I have leave coming and will be at the cottage all next week."

"What are the chances of beating the Yankees?" Knight asks.

"Slim to none," Kinsey laughs.

"That's what I thought," Knight chuckles. "We'll be ready to go right after the game Saturday."

"Sounds good."

On Friday the Knights pack for the weekend, and the next morning, they're ready to go to the lake. But first, they go to the ballpark where the Yankees are already warming up. When it's the Tigers' turn to use the field, they appear to be smaller than the Yankees and lack their razzle-dazzle. However, the Tigers get to bat first and score two runs. Then they take the field, and Phil goes to the mound knowing this could be the last game of his career.

Phil holds the Yankees scoreless until the fifth inning when he gets bombed for four runs. With the bases loaded, Kinsey calls on Mike to stop the bleeding, which he does. After neither team scores in the sixth, the Tigers come to bat in the top of the seventh and final inning, trailing 4-2. It looks like the game is going to end as predicted, but now the Yankees move their starting pitcher to first base and bring the first baseman to the mound to close. This looks to be a mistake when Dan leads off with a double. Then Mike helps his own cause by singling Dan home. Dave is up next and lashes the first pitch. He gets around on it late, resulting in a line drive into right field. The ball hits the ground just inside the foul line and rolls to the fence. As the Yankee right fielder runs after it, Dave chugs around the bases. Meanwhile, Kinsey windmills his arm. "Go, go, go," the coach hollers, "take home." Dave rounds third and heads for home plate just beating the throw. He runs the gauntlet of excited teammates then sits on the bench to catch his breath. The Tigers lead 5-4.

After Dave's home run, the Yankees' pitcher settles down and retires the next three batters in order. The Tigers pick up their gloves and return to the field with Mike still on the mound. This is the Yankees' last chance at the plate, and they collectively moan when their first batter strikes out. But the team's second hitter knocks the ball into a gap in the outfield for a stand-up double. As the next Yankee batter settles in at the plate, his teammates stand on their bench cheering. Mike checks the runner, nods at the sign from his catcher, and delivers a pitch. The crack of the bat seems to freeze time. Then Mike spears the line drive and calmly turns to double the runner off second. The game is over and the Yankees, who have led the league all season, are out of the playoffs.

Both teams line up to shake hands, and it's hard to say who's more stunned by the result. Several of the Yankees break down and cry while Tigers parents surround Kinsey and pound on his back. Melissa comes up to Dave. "You selfish brat," she says furiously. "All you care about is yourself." Melissa turns and stalks toward the parking lot where she accosts her father. Soon they're engaged in a fierce argument.

"Over here, Tigers," Kinsey calls. A reporter for the post newspaper wants a team picture. He has the taller players stand in the back and places the others in front. Once the newsman finishes, Knight approaches Kinsey. "Guess you won't be getting an early start on your leave after all," Knight smiles.

"I don't care," Kinsey says exultantly. "We're in the semifinal."

"The girls are pissed not to go water-skiing," Knight says.

"Are you kidding?" Kinsey exclaims. "We won. They should be happy."

"Melissa doesn't care about baseball; she wants to ski."

"Well, then, why don't I take Melissa and the others to the lake with me after we're done tomorrow, win or lose?" Kinsey suggests. "They can spend the week, and then you can come up Friday, stay over, and take them back with you Sunday."

"That's mighty generous of you," Knight replies. "I don't want to ruin your leave."

"Oh, they won't be any trouble," Kinsey assures his boss. "Phyllis will tend to them."

"OK, let's do that," Knight says. "Thanks."

The next afternoon, after another unexpected win in the morning, the Tigers return to reality in the final and lose to the Cubs. For most of the players, this is the end of the line. Only a few of them are good enough to play American Legion or high school ball.

Kinsey's chances of being named Pony League Coach of the Year have also ended. The disappointed officer helps Knight transfer the children's suitcases into his trunk. "Mike's arm was worn out," Kinsey explains. "Phil's too. I knew we were in trouble when I had to put Gary in."

"You had a good run," Knight replies. "Now go and enjoy your leave."

But Kinsey broods on the way to the lake as the late-afternoon sun glares at him through the windshield. Waist-high cotton plants in dusty red fields line both sides of the road. Occasionally they pass farmhouses where country people, out on their porches, wave as the car goes by. "Those people act as if they know us," Melissa exclaims.

Kinsey wakes from his funk. "They're hicks," he says contemptuously, "from the sticks. One car comes by every hour, and to them, it's a big deal." Now Marie and Perle stop waving back at the people.

It's near dark by the time Kinsey pulls up in front of the cottage. He and the Knight children unpack the car then everyone gathers around the kitchen table for dinner. "Let's make it an early night," Kinsey says. "Tim and I are going fishing in the morning."

"Oh, can I go?" Dave pleads.

"You don't want to," Kinsey replies curtly. "We're getting up at five."

"That's fine," Dave replies. "I can do that."

"I don't think so," Kinsey insists. "You won't like it."

"Honey, he wants to go," Phyllis interjects. "You need to take him."

"Oh, all right," Kinsey relents. "I'll wake you up, but if you aren't ready when it's time to leave, too bad."

The Kinseys go out on the patio to relax after dinner while some of the children watch TV. Tim goes down to the dock with his fishing rod, and Melissa accompanies him. It's very quiet at the lake, and there's nothing much to do, so the children are soon ready for bed. Marie and Perle will sleep in Tim's room as usual, but since Knight is back home, Melissa takes the guest bedroom. Once again, the three boys sleep in the living room.

It takes Dave a long time to drift off to sleep because he's excited about the fishing trip. Finally, he falls into a fitful slumber. It seems but a short while later that his rest is interrupted by a rough shake from Kinsey. Dave blinks his eyes and looks up. It's pitch dark, and he can barely make out his coach's face. "You don't have to get up if you don't want to," Kinsey whispers. However, Dave sits up and plants both feet on the floor. It's chilly in the house, thanks to the air conditioning, and he thinks how nice it would be to get back under the covers. Instead, Dave pulls on a pair of jeans and a T-shirt then slides his feet into well-worn tennis shoes. Someone's in the bathroom, so he gets his fishing gear together while waiting his turn.

Soon the three fishermen are on their way to the boat. They climb aboard, Tim casts off, and Kinsey steers the craft out onto the lake. It's a bright moonlit night, and there's a portent of fall in the cool air. Once they're well away from the shore, Kinsey gets the boat up on plane then pushes the throttle all the way forward. Now as a blast of air hits him, Dave wishes he had dressed warmer. Tim and his father are both wearing jackets.

Kinsey steers the boat several miles up the lake then backs off the throttle as they enter a cove. Rushes and reeds line the far bank, and lily pads dot the surface of the water. After stealthily anchoring the boat, Tim picks up his rod and releases the brake on the reel to free up some line. He has a 3/0 hook on the end with a red and white float suspended above it. Tim fishes around in the bait bucket, comes up with a big shiner minnow, and hooks it through the lips. Then he ducks the bait in the water and watches it swim frantically in circles. Satisfied, he casts toward a clump of lily pads. The big bobber dances as the shiner darts back and forth underneath. Meanwhile, Kinsey baits his hook and casts into another likely spot. He looks over at Dave who's holding his fishing rod expectantly. "That rig is too light for this," Kinsey says. "What have you got in your tackle box?"

"Just some spinners and plastic worms."

"Well, you can tie on a spinner and cast it out there," Kinsey says, pointing back the way they came.

"OK," Dave says excitedly. Soon he's busy casting his lure out and reeling it in while the other two fishermen wait for a bite. As the sky lightens, Kinsey's bobber suddenly disappears. "Fish," he whispers calmly while stripping line off his reel. He's giving the predator time to turn the bait in its mouth. Finally, Kinsey rears back on the heavy rod. It bends as he cranks on the reel. "Pull hard," Tim exclaims. "It's trying to get into the reeds."

Kinsey pulls the fish away from the shoreline, but then the tension goes out of his body, and his shoulders droop. He can tell from the lack of fight that he doesn't have a bass. "Bowfin," he says with a grimace.

"Shit," is Tim's comment.

After Kinsey reels the bowfin in, he puts a boot on it and removes the hook. Then he baits up again while the fish flaps in the bilge. Kinsey's not going to throw it back. He doesn't want the thing stealing more bait.

Dave looks at the worthless fish as it gasps for oxygen. It's a primitive creature and very ugly, especially compared to the beauty of a largemouth bass. He suppresses the urge to feel sorry for it. Bowfin eat baby bass as well as baitfish. They're a menace.

The sun is well up in the sky when Kinsey calls it quits for the day. On the way back, Dave's arm aches from hours of fruitless casting. The Kinseys aren't happy either. Several more bowfin have joined the first one in the scuppers. That's all they have to show for their morning.

The fishing Tuesday isn't any better, but on Wednesday things change. Word goes out on the bass grapevine: "Time to eat, guys. Bite anything." So, Tim catches a medium-size largemouth before the sun comes up, then he catches another. Meanwhile, Kinsey hauls in a five-pounder. After he places the big fish in the cooler, he becomes expansive. "Try throwing a plastic worm under those lily pads," he tells Dave. "I'll show you how to rig it so the hook doesn't snag."

After several casts, Dave sees his line turn and snake across the surface. A fish has picked up his lure. Emulating Kinsey, Dave waits to give it time then rears back to set the hook. His little rod bends double while the drag on the spinning reel screeches. Dave tightens it and manages to keep the fish from going into the reeds. It turns out to be a nice bass.

Back at the cottage, Dave curls up on his cot and has a nap. He doesn't wake for several hours and by then he's ravenous. After eating two sandwiches, Dave walks down to the dock to look at the water. It's crystal clear, and he sees that the shade underneath the walkway is home to a crowd of bream and bluegills. With the sun broiling down, the heat is miserable, but Dave doesn't mind. He runs back up to the porch and gets his fishing rod. When the panfish disdain his spinner, Dave finds a pack of trout-sized hooks in his tackle box and ties one on his line. Then he gets a piece of bread from the kitchen and forms a little ball of dough onto the hook. Kneeling on the pier, he dangles the bait in the water. A bluegill rushes out of the shade to grab it, and Dave happily reels it in. But after catching and releasing over a dozen little fish, he gets bored. So, Dave grabs his book and climbs into a hammock to read.

The heat dissipates late that afternoon, and it's time for water-skiing. Today Kinsey allows Tim to drive the boat. He and Phyllis are going to enjoy cocktails on the patio and watch.

Marie clamors to go first and has her wish. She gets up on one ski then Tim takes her around the cove before bringing her back past the dock. As she goes by, Marie holds the towrope with her foot. On the next circuit, she reveals a new trick. Kicking off her ski, Marie skims across the water barefoot. Then she releases the tow rope and sinks into the water.

Phyllis and Kinsey are on their feet applauding as Marie comes out of the water. Then it's Melissa's turn. She doesn't do any tricks but is so graceful she doesn't have to. After several loops around the cove, she lets go of the rope. "I'm done for today," Melissa says, climbing the ladder onto the dock. "Ready for a shower."

Dave puts on a lifebelt and jumps into the water. He's not much good at water-skiing but likes to catch as much air as possible jumping the wake. The wipeouts that result can be entertaining to watch, but now he manages several minutes behind the boat without mishap. So Tim pushes the throttle all the way forward, and Dave falls for it. He swings out wide then slingshots back, leaping off the wake into the air. Unfortunately, he gets discombobulated, catches his ski tip coming down, and then skitters, limbs akimbo, across the surface. Momentary concern among the spectators gives way to relieved laughter when Dave gaily waves to let everyone know he's all right.

On the patio, Kinsey rattles the ice cubes in his otherwise empty glass. "Got a dead soldier here," he tells Phyllis, getting up from his chair. "Need reinforcements, you?"

Phyllis holds her drink up to the light and swirls it around. Then she tosses back the remnants. "Sure," she says.

As Kinsey walks into the cottage, Melissa is coming out of the bathroom wrapped in a towel. Hastily, Kinsey puts the glasses down and follows Melissa into her room. She turns, and Kinsey shoves her down on the bed, then bends to kiss her. Melissa grits her teeth and tries to push him away, but Kinsey grabs her forearm, sinking his thumb into a pressure point. As pain radiates down to her fingers, Melissa's grip weakens, and Kinsey pulls the towel away. He runs his eyes over her body then tries to wedge his hand between Melissa's legs. "Relax, honey," Kinsey grins. Instead, Melissa screams. Kinsey moves his hand over Melissa's mouth, and she meets it with her teeth. The officer suppresses a cry when Melissa chomps down, then uses his free hand to hit her with a roundhouse slap. The retort seems to echo in the small room.

Leaping to his feet, Kinsey shakes his injured extremity in the air. "What the hell is wrong with you?" he scowls. "Tim said you liked it."

"Liar," Melissa shouts hysterically, "liar, liar, liar."

Kinsey lunges and takes Melissa by the throat, holding his other hand up threateningly. "Shut up," he hisses. Melissa's eyes bulge; she can't speak, can't breathe. Then Kinsey loosens his grip and roughly pushes her head back on the pillow. He sidles to the door then looks back. "If you think Tim and I keep secrets from each other, you're simple," Kinsey says. "He told me all about it. You're nothing but a slut." The officer goes out, shutting the door behind him.

By the time Kinsey returns to the patio, Perle is finished with her turn water-skiing, and Dan is having a go. He's no better than Dave at the sport, but unlike his brother, Dan avoids wipeouts. Once he's had his fun, skiing is over for the day, and Tim ties the boat up at the dock. Kinsey helps his son put the equipment away while the others go inside to shower and change.

Soon a group has gathered around the kitchen table to await dinner. Phyllis has some of the bass that were caught that morning in the oven. While the fish cook, Tim goes down the hall to see what's keeping Melissa. "Go away," she moans from behind her locked door.

Kinsey doesn't join them at the table either. Instead, he sits on the patio by himself. Later, as the others are eating, he comes in to freshen his drink. "Forget fishing in the morning," he tells Tim. "I need some rest."

It's late, and the sun has long been up when Dave rises the next morning. Perle, Marie, and Dan are clustered around the TV with the volume turned low so as not to disturb Tim, who's still snoozing on the couch. After eating a bowl of cereal, Dave goes outside. Other than an occasional puff of cloud, the sky is clear, so the sun's rays are unhindered in their assault on the landscape. Dave goes back into the air-conditioned cottage and picks up his book.

At Fort Gordon the next day, Knight has lunch at the officers' club. When he gets back to headquarters, he stops to talk with Sergeant Major Reynier. "I need to get an early start out of here now," he tells the NCO. "If anyone looks for me, say I'll be back first thing Monday."

"Yes, sir."

Bobbie declines to make the tedious trip to the lake, so Knight packs for the weekend and leaves by himself. When he gets to Kinsey's place, he finds the captain and his wife sitting on the patio watching Tim pull Dan around the cove. Perle and Marie are sitting on the dock waiting their turn. Dave is fishing.

Kinsey gets up to greet his boss. "Let me help you with that," he offers, taking Knight's suitcase. The two men go inside the cottage and down the hall to the guest bedroom. The door is locked, so Kinsey knocks.

"Leave me alone," Melissa says weakly.

"Your father's here. He needs this room," Kinsey replies.

Quickly the door is jerked open, and in a blur, Melissa rushes out and throws her arms around Knight. She presses her cheek against his chest and sobs, "Thank God, thank God."

"What in the world?" Knight exclaims.

"Take me home, please take me home," Melissa wails as Kinsey stands uneasily aside.

"But I just got here," Knight protests.

"I want to go home, please."

"Not till you explain what's going on," Knight replies. "This is crazy."

Melissa points an accusing finger at Kinsey. "He tried to rape me," she declares.

"I did nothing of the sort," Kinsey protests.

"He tried to kiss me, tried to put his hand between my legs, and when I screamed he clamped his hand over my mouth," Melissa insists. "So, I bit him. Look at his hand."

"I opened the door to see if she had any laundry that needed doing," Kinsey explains. "I didn't see Melissa's suitcase in the middle of the floor, tripped over it and fell on her. She started screaming in my ear, so I put my hand over her mouth to stop the noise."

"Liar," Melissa shrieks. "Dirty liar."

"No more of that," Knight says sternly. "Calm down."

"I want to go home," Melissa cries. "Right now."

"OK, I'll take you, just calm down."

Knight leaves Melissa to pack while he and Kinsey walk toward the front of the house. "It's better if I take her," Knight says. "God knows what's got into her."

"Yeah, that's probably best," Kinsey agrees.

Knight goes to the dock and calls the children together. "Something's come up," he tells them. "We've got to leave."

"Oh no," Marie wails. "I thought we were staying all weekend."

"Plans change," Knight replies. "I want to see all of you packed and ready to go in half an hour."

Phyllis gets up from her chair. "So sorry you can't stay," she says, taking Knight's arm. "I was so looking forward to the weekend."

"Melissa's not feeling well," Knight dissembles. "I have to take her back."

"Let me at least make you a drink."

"I need it."

"Me too," Kinsey says.

"You boys sit right there, and I'll be back in a jiff," Phyllis smiles.

"I just don't understand Melissa," Knight says after Phyllis goes. "I mean, the whole thing sounds perfectly innocent."

"She wouldn't listen, just got hysterical. It was incredible."

"Teenage girls," Knight says, shaking his head. "Be glad you don't have any."

"It's the hormones," Kinsey agrees.

CHAPTER SIX
GOING STEADY

Dave Knight loves everything about ARC except his classes. Every day they come at him inexorably like the cars of a slow-moving train. Sure, a couple of the courses aren't so bad: typing, which is something useful, and ROTC because it's simple, but as for the others, well, occasionally he tries to hop aboard, but mainly Dave sits in the rear of the classrooms and either reads or sleeps.

The best part of the school day is once it's over. That's when kids congregate at the Maglin Terrace playground, and lately, there are plenty of them. That's because the infantry has come to Fort Gordon bringing many new families. Now Dave has no problem organizing touch football games; especially on Fridays. That's when bookworms like Joe Bryan, and even guys who aren't any good like Gene Sexton, come out. Gene's father, an infantry major general, is the new commandant of Fort Gordon. They live in General Clifton's old house on a bluff overlooking Boardman Lake.

On this Friday afternoon at the playground, instead of choosing up sides, it's decided that the guys from Boardman Lake will take on Maglin Terrace. Soon the football game is underway, and while the older kids play, young children use the playground equipment. Meanwhile, a group of teenage girls strolls around talking, laughing, and taking everything in.

As usual, the game is a high-scoring affair featuring the increasingly bitter rivalry between the Spillings and the Knights. It goes on until all agree that it's too dark to see the ball. At that point, Maglin Terrace has the lead and so is declared the winner. As the Spillings celebrate, Dan gets on his bike and starts downhill. However, Dave can't find his jacket. He looks around then sees one of the girls wearing it. She's a cute junior high schooler named Diane Benson. Dave has noticed her on the bus, always joking and carrying on with the other girls. Now he accosts her. "What are you doing with my jacket?" he demands.

Diane gazes levelly at Dave, smiling mischievously. "It got cold when the sun went down," she explains.

"Well, I'm getting ready to go."

"So, you're gonna make me walk home in the cold without a wrap?" Diane pouts.

"Oh, all right, what if I walk you home?" Dave asks. "You can give me my jacket back when we get there."

"OK."

As they walk across the field toward the housing development, Diane takes Dave's hand. It's a portentous move, and Dave's heart is suddenly thudding. He's afraid his hand is sweating. They go up the walk to the front door of Diane's house, and she looks up expectantly. "Aren't you going to kiss me?" she asks.

"The deal was I get my jacket back," Dave stupidly replies.

"You have to kiss me first," Diane says with a mocking smile.

Dave looks at Diane's lips nervously. Losing patience, she goes up on her tiptoes and plants her mouth on his. Dave puts his arms around her, and Diane tugs him off the lighted doorstep, into a shadow. Then they are lying on the ground, and the kisses are getting longer. Neither wants to stop, but presently they hear the front door open. "Yoo-hoo, Diane," Mrs. Benson calls. The teenagers quickly scramble to their feet and brush their clothes off. Diane walks around to the front with Dave trailing.

"Oh, there you are," Mrs. Benson says. Then she spies Dave coming out of the bushes. "And who's this?" she calmly asks.

"Hi, Mrs. Benson, I'm Dave Knight."

"Oh, you're Colonel Knight's son."

"Yes, ma'am."

"Well, Diane has to come in now. Why don't you visit us another time?"

"I'll be happy to."

The next morning Dave sleeps late then, after getting something to eat, he climbs aboard his bicycle. He's a strong enough pedaller now to power up the hill, past Maglin Terrace, and across the post to the library. When he gets there, Dave returns several books, then finds some new ones. Afterward, he rides over to the indoor shooting range. Joe Bryan and Gene Sexton are already there. Back in September, all three boys took an NRA gun safety course, and they've been coming to the range on Saturdays ever since to work on their marksmanship qualifications.

The three boys spend an hour perforating targets, and then Dave rides home. He relies on fishing and reading to get through the rest of the weekend. On Monday morning, when the school bus pulls up in front of the house, Dave climbs aboard wearing the World War II-era army surplus uniform he was issued for Junior ROTC. Diane has saved a seat for him, and Dave casually takes it. This makes it official; they are going steady.

That afternoon Dave's ROTC platoon checks out vintage M1 Garand rifles from the armory. They go out to the drill field where the cadet officers conduct an inspection. "Why didn't you shine your shoes?" Cadet Lieutenant Johnny Samson asks the boy next to Dave.

"Sir, no excuse."

"Oh, come on, give me an excuse," Samson sneers. "Tell me your kiwi bird died."

"Yes, sir."

"Well, you better have your shit together tomorrow."

Samson is a tall, sturdy tight end for the ARC football team. After inspection, he drills the platoon, frequently halting the cadets for breaks. "Platoon at ease," he says. "Smoke if you got 'em."

The cadets only have drill on Mondays and Tuesdays. The rest of the week they wear civilian attire and attend ROTC classes inside. Master Sergeant William Tisdale is the NCO in charge. He teaches Army History and Tradition. "What's a salute?" he asks the class one afternoon.

"Sir, it is a gesture of respect," a boy answers.

"Don't call me sir," Tisdale snaps. "I'm not an officer. I work for a living."

"Then what should we call you?"

"Well, one of my men called me an SOB once," Tisdale replies. "He told me that stood for 'sweet old Bill.'" The cadets all laugh; they know what SOB really means.

"Seriously, you should just call me Sergeant, or Sarge for short," Tisdale says.

"Sarge, did you ever shoot anybody?" one of the students asks.

"I have no idea," Tisdale replies. "I shot at plenty of people, don't know if I hit 'em."

"How could that be?" the boy persists.

"Son, I was at the frozen Chosin in the freezin' season," Tisdale says. "The shambos came at us in waves, and we mowed 'em down in waves. The machine guns were firing so fast the barrels melted. Who knows who hit what; we just kept shooting till we were overrun. The only thing that saved us is the stupid gooks just kept going. They were so drunk none of 'em stayed to mop up. That's why a lot of us survived. Of course, many didn't." Sergeant Tisdale stares at his questioner placidly, but the student has no more questions. Then the bell rings, and the classroom quietly empties.

Meanwhile, out at Fort Gordon, Knight is whiling away the afternoon with nothing to do. That's because the infantry has taken over post headquarters, and he's lost his job as deputy commandant. A grunt brigadier from the pre-airborne training program is now ensconced in what used to be Knight's office. It's his turn to experience both the perks and humiliations that come with the deputy job.

At this time, Knight's office is in one of the decrepit buildings that line the parade ground. Down the hall is his new boss, Colonel Bryan. He was appointed commandant of the Southeastern Signal School when General Clifton left to take the helm of the Signal Corps. Bryan has just returned from Fort Monmouth and a meeting with Clifton. Now he summons Knight to his office. "How was your trip?" Knight asks once they're alone.

"Terrifying," Bryan replies. "I hate those puddle jumpers."

"They're better than helicopters," Knight comments. "Something about rotary I just don't trust."

"Oh, I agree," Bryan laughs. "You look at the contraption and have to wonder, is this pile of junk actually going to fly?"

"My thought exactly," Knight says.

"Next time I'll try to be thankful to at least be on something that has wings," Bryan says. "But in any case, this trip was well worth it."

"How so?"

"I learned that the defense authorization bill Kennedy recently signed includes funding for a new Southeastern Signal School."

"That's great news."

"Now we just need someone to build it."

"Yes, sir," Knight agrees.

"Well, General Clifton and I have our boy," Bryan says. "It's going to be you."

"That's a wonderful assignment," Knight enthuses.

"No one better to handle it," Bryan replies.

"Thank you, sir."

After the meeting, Knight excitedly calls Kinsey and Sergeant Major Reynier into his office. "We got money in the budget to build a new Southeastern Signal School," he tells them.

"About time," Kinsey comments.

"I've been handed the project."

"Congratulations, sir," Reynier exclaims.

"First thing I want you to do is to comb through the personnel files of every soldier in the Signal Corps," Knight orders. "We can reassign any who possess relevant experience or education to this office."

"Yes, sir."

"I want to have a team assembled by December 1. After that, we'll want to solicit proposals from architectural firms, so an RFP must be prepared. I want to see the first draft by the end of January, along with a list of DOD-approved architects."

"I'll get right on it," Kinsey says.

Sue Brandt opens the door. "Colonel, have you got a minute?"

"Sure, what do you need?"

"Some unsettling news has just come over the radio," Sue says. "President Kennedy has been shot."

At ARC, Dave is in typing class when Mr. Oldman comes on the intercom. "There's word that the president has been shot," Oldman announces. "It happened in Dallas. I'll keep you posted as more information comes in."

"I told you so," one of the boys in the class crows. "Didn't I tell you? My daddy said he wouldn't live out the year."

"Shut up," a girl hollers from across the room.

More arguments break out as Mrs. Fletcher, the typing instructor, tries to get things under control. "I'm sending you, you, and you to see Mr. Danforth," she says, pointing at the worst offenders. Danforth is the assistant principal for discipline, and no one wants to see him, so the students quiet down. Then Mr. Oldman comes back on the intercom. "It's with great sadness that I have to report: President Kennedy has died. The superintendent is canceling classes for the rest of the day."

Outside, students mill around aimlessly. Most are somber, and many are crying, but here and there knots of boys whoop and holler happily. A fight starts, but the combatants are quickly pulled apart by their classmates. Then a Pontiac burns rubber leaving the campus, and other cars rapidly follow. However, most of the students must wait for the buses to arrive.

The schools stay closed the following week, and Thanksgiving mournfully comes and goes. Then classes resume, and the students return to school hoping to pick up where they left off. Superficially, at least, they manage to do that.

On Friday, Bobbie is waiting for Dave when he gets home. "We need to go shopping," she says. "You need some clothes."

"What for?"

"We're going to Miami."

"For Christmas?"

"No, for Melissa," Bobbie replies. "She's coming out, and there will be lots of debutante parties between Christmas and New Year's. You're old enough to attend, but you'll need to dress up."

"Can I drive us to town?" Dave asks. He has his learner's permit, and Bobbie's been teaching him to drive.

"Sure," Bobbie replies.

At Cullum's Department Store, the tailor takes measurements while Dave stands on a pedestal in front of a three-way mirror. He takes this opportunity to assess his appearance and finds that his head is too big for his scrawny, long-limbed body. The frizzy hair on it is a disaster.

Bobbie picks out a blue blazer, gray dress slacks, some Oxford cloth shirts, two ties, and a new pair of penny loafers. They leave the sports coat and pants to be altered and take the other stuff home.

The next morning, in a further effort to get Dave ready for society, Knight takes him to the officers' club for a haircut. Jason Entlich has the barber concession. "Got a live one for you," Knight tells him. "Try to do something with that mop. I'll be at the bar."

Entlich drapes a striped cloth over Dave and tucks it under his chin. "My mother said to tell you not to use the clippers too high in the back," Dave says.

"All right."

After the haircut, Dave goes looking for his father and finds him sitting with a small cluster of officers at the bar. "You don't mess with Texas," one of the men is saying.

"His problem was more with Alabama," Knight comments. "What right does the federal government have to tell a sovereign state how to run its schools?"

"Hear, hear," the man says, taking a swig of his drink.

Knight turns to Dave. "Nice haircut," he says disinterestedly.

"Thanks."

"Kevin, get the boy a 7UP," Knight tells the bartender. "Put lots of cherries in it."

Kevin comes back with a tall glass filled with bubbling clear liquid and several maraschino cherries.

"Go watch some TV," Knight tells his son. "I'll be along presently."

Dave goes to the TV set in the corner of the barroom and finds that a football game is on. Michigan is leading Ohio State 10-7 with only a minute left on the clock. Then the OSU quarterback heaves a desperation pass into the end zone. The crowd erupts as the receiver makes a diving catch. Dave gets caught up in the excitement. "All right! Yeah!" he exclaims, pumping his fist.

Knight and one of the other barflies come over to the TV to see what's going on. The announcers are hollering madly, and time has run out. Ohio State players are carrying the receiver on their shoulders, and Dave is cheering. Knight takes in the scene then bends to hiss in his son's ear. "I can't believe you're rooting for a goddamn nigger," he says then turns to go back to the bar.

"What difference does his color make?" Dave calls after his father. "He made a great catch."

Knight ignores his son. "Bring us another round," he tells the bartender.

"What's wrong with that boy?" Kevin asks as he fixes the drinks.

"Oh, he's got that radio going morning, noon, and night listening to garbage and getting all sorts of crazy ideas," Knight says. "Hopefully he'll grow out of it."

On Monday morning Dave is back in his ROTC uniform with polished brass and shined shoes. That afternoon at drill, Cadet Lt. Samson calls him out in front of the platoon. "Now this is what a GI haircut should look like," Samson says. Dave flushes as the other cadets snicker. He silently vows never to get another haircut. For the rest of the week, he hides in the rear of his classes idly running his hand over his bristly scalp. A week later school lets out for the year, and it's almost time to head for Florida.

But first, the Knights spend Christmas at home. That morning, they unwrap presents then Knight takes the family outside. He points to a white 1962 Cadillac Sedan de Ville in the driveway. "That's ours," he declares as his children swarm the vehicle. "It's not a used car; it's pre-owned."

Early the next morning the Knights leave Fort Gordon in their new ride to go to the Rices' house. Dave gets to drive, and he spends his time behind the wheel surreptitiously increasing the speed until his father catches on, and then repeating the process. The Knights make record time on the trip and find Barbara still up when they get to Coral Gables.

The following evening, Dave is in the bathroom of the cottage he's sharing with his siblings, trying to knot his tie. He will soon be making his first foray into society thanks to Sid and Barbara, who are hosting a party in Melissa's honor. Try as he might, Dave can't get the tie right, so he finally gets his father to do it. Then music begins wafting across the lawn. "The dance is starting," Dave says.

"Right on time," Knight replies, glancing at his watch.

"Well, let's go."

"Relax," Knight tells his son. "It's gauche to get to a party early."

An hour later, the Knights stroll up the walk to the main house. Bobbie looks frail but radiant in a plum-colored short dress while Melissa is wearing a low-neck, floor-length blue gown. She has her hair up for the occasion and wears Bobbie's pearls. Inside, they find an orchestra playing a foxtrot. Gray-haired couples are dancing to the music. A few young people are on the fringes, mainly debutantes and their escorts. Melissa spots several friends from Florida State and walks their way. Meanwhile, Bobbie and her husband prepare to separate and work the room. "Make sure you dance at least one dance with Mrs. Rice," Knight admonishes his son. "It would be rude not to."

"And some of these unescorted older ladies would appreciate being asked as well," Bobbie adds. "So be gallant."

"Would it be all right if I have a beer?" Dave asks. He's seen several college-age boys walking around holding beer cans.

"Sure," Knight replies, "you're what now, sixteen?"

"Just make sure you only have one," Bobbie says sternly.

"Yes, ma'am," Dave agrees, and as his parents move off, he gets in line at one of the makeshift bars. Soon Dave's guzzling a beer, despite the bitter taste, and gradually an unaccustomed sense of well-being overtakes him. His senses tingle and a warm glow spreads within. He decides to have another.

Dave doesn't want Bobbie to see him in one of the bar lines again, so he goes to look for beer in the kitchen. There are none in the refrigerator, but several cases of liquor are stacked by the back door. Reaching into one, Dave pulls out a bottle of Scotch. Hurriedly he uses a paring knife to remove the seal. Then he fills his empty beer can. Presently Dave's back in the living room, sipping the drink.

As the orchestra breaks into a jitterbug, Dave taps his foot. He wants to dance, but Mrs. Rice is nowhere around. However, lots of old ladies are nearby, so Dave decides to be a gentleman. He asks an elderly woman in a red dress to dance, and she acquiesces delightedly. Dave rests his can of booze on a side table and goes out to cut a rug. He has no idea what he's doing, but that doesn't discourage his geriatric partner. She takes the lead and does her best to get Dave into some sort of rhythm. At the end of the number, he politely escorts her back to their starting point. "Thanks for the dance," Dave says with a little bow.

"You're perfectly welcome," the woman smiles.

Back on the sideline, Dave chugs Scotch as he takes in the scene. He's dazzled by the swirl of color as the dancers spin past. *What a lovely group of people*, he thinks. However, an older woman nearby seems sad, and Dave's heart fills with compassion. He takes another swig of his drink, puts the can down, and asks her to dance. The lady's expression takes on a youthful gaiety as he walks her onto the floor.

After dancing, Dave returns to his spot, and soon the beer can requires a refill. He makes his way back to the kitchen and tops up. When he gets back, the band has progressed to a hipper part of its repertoire. People are doing the twist, and Dave gets the urge to join in. He has no trouble finding a blue-haired companion.

Dave swivels himself into a frenzy, then escorts his partner back to the sideline. On the way, he receives several compliments on his twisting. Then Dave retrieves his drink and nurses it a while. Later he wends his way back to the kitchen again.

The crowd has noticeably thinned when Dave returns, but those who remain make up in enthusiasm what they lack in numbers. The band essays more rock 'n' roll and decorum is relaxed. Dave takes to excusing himself in the middle of dances to tend to his beer can, and no one takes it amiss. His partners wait happily in the middle of the dance floor until he returns.

As the hour grows late, Dave is slow dancing with a woman who must have been something in her prime. They are cheek to cheek, and she's gently caressing the back of his neck. That's all Dave remembers until he opens his eyes and sees the water. "Don't bite me, you son of a bitch," his father says.

Slowly Dave realizes that the object being pushed down his throat is his father's index finger. Knight's other hand is on the back of Dave's head forcing it into the toilet. Meanwhile, Dr. Wilbur Hughes stands swaying in the doorway. "He's got to throw up," the physician slurs. "Make him throw up."

Knight energetically reams Dave's oral cavity but fails to get the desired result. The tile floor is hard on his knees, so he stands and joins Wilbur in swaying. They look like two gentlemen aboard ship in a storm. "Son of a bitch won't vomit," Knight complains.

Dave laboriously pulls an arm up from the floor and rests it on the rim of the porcelain bowl. Then he lays his head on the sleeve. "Just want to sleep," he mumbles, "sleep."

"He can't sleep," Wilbur tells Knight. "That might be fatal. We have to walk him." The two men take hold of Dave's legs and drag him out of the bathroom and into the living room of the cottage. It's all they can do to hoist the boy to his feet. Then they force their shoulders under his armpits and haul him across the small room. After several turns back and forth, Wilbur and Knight agree to take a break. They plop Dave down on the sofa and fall into armchairs. Knight lights a cigarette.

A few minutes later, Elizabeth Hughes breezes into the cottage. "Well, that was a shock," she says. "Mrs. Ferndale couldn't believe it when he keeled over just like her late husband." Elizabeth finds a pillow and blanket in the hall closet, removes Dave's shoes, and covers him up. "Let's go," she tells Wilbur.

In the morning Dave is wretchedly ill. He has also worn out his welcome in South Florida society so will now spend the rest of the holiday with his younger siblings. They fight, watch TV, play Monopoly, and swim.

The following week, the Knights return home and find that an infantry officer named Colonel Gilder has moved into the house across the lake. The Gilders have a son, Mike, who's Dave's age and a daughter, Gillian, a couple of years younger. When school resumes, Mike Gilder eagerly joins in the after-school football games. He's a cute, fun-loving guy almost as tall as Dan but not as fast.

Mike also comes to the range on Saturdays. He's been shooting longer than the other boys and is rated "Expert."

On school days, Gene Sexton, Mike Gilder, and Joe Bryan sit together at the front of the bus while Dave happily rides with Diane a few rows back. A new song called "I'm Into Something Good" has been playing on the radio, and it perfectly describes Dave's happiness these days. He hums the tune incessantly and sings it in the shower or when he's out walking Tex.

The army is also into something good. War is in the air. At Fort Gordon, construction of the jump towers and other infrastructure for pre-airborne training has been completed, and the course is up and running. Every month airborne units from Fort Campbell and other bases come to perform demonstration jumps. Afterward, troopers throng the streets of downtown Augusta telling girls, "If you want it done, call the 101." Some drunkenly lean out of hotel room windows in varying stages of undress holding a liquor bottle in one hand and a hooker in the other. "Geronimo," they yell.

The Signal Corps is dull compared to the infantry, but they too have money to spend. Soon proposals from architects for the new signal school arrive at Knight's office. By the end of March, Kinsey and his team have narrowed it down to the five best submissions. They meet with Knight to present them. "These all look good to me," he says. "But I like Eckt's the best."

"His buildings have a nice open-air feel," Kinsey agrees. "The design is better suited to this climate."

"Well, Eckt is from Atlanta," Knight says. "Contrast his plans with what those New Yorkers sent."

"Yeah, their buildings look like bunkers," Kinsey laughs. "Blizzard-proof."

"Still, I want to present each of the finalists to General Clifton and Colonel Bryan," Knight insists. "I'm not going this alone."

"That's right, Dave," Kinsey says. "CYA all the way."

Two weeks later Knight and Bryan travel to Signal Corps HQ at Fort Monmouth to meet General Clifton. Bryan supports Knight in favoring Eckt's proposal, and Clifton concurs. After the meeting, Knight is ecstatic. The hardest part of the job is over, and all he has to do now is to have an RFP prepared and sent to qualified building contractors. The purchasing bureaucracy at the Pentagon will handle the rest. "Let's stop by the club before heading to the airstrip,"

Knight suggests as he and Bryan are leaving post headquarters. "I've got to have a drink before we get back on that goddamn puddle jumper."

"At least it's not a whirlybird," Bryan grins.

Diane and Dave are still going steady. She's now in the ninth grade while Dave has made it to the eleventh, thanks to summer school. Today they are tramping through the woods below Maglin Terrace taking advantage of the mild fall weather. The going is rough as they make their way downhill toward a pond, so the two teenagers take a rest. They sit on the trunk of a fallen tree, and Dave puts an arm around his girlfriend. As they kiss, he touches her breast, but Diane immediately moves his hand. Dave tries again, with the same result, so he gives up. Now they relax, breathe deep, and enjoy the view. Then Diane leaps to her feet. "Race you to the top," she says and begins scrambling up the steep slope. Dave quickly follows then grabs Diane from behind, pulls her down, and races ahead. "You're cheating," she laughs.

By the time Diane and Dave get to the top of the hill, they're both panting, not to mention dirty and sweaty. It's getting late, so after a brief dusty kiss, they part. But after walking a little way toward home, Dave turns and sees Diane up by the playground watching him. They wave then each goes a little farther until they both turn and wave again. Slowly the distance between them grows.

When Dave gets home, his mother and father are in the living room having cocktails. "Dinner's on the stove," Bobbie says. "You're late."

"Yes, where were you?" Knight asks.

"With Diane."

"Still robbing the cradle, huh?"

"She's fifteen years old, for crying out loud," Bobbie says.

"Yes, and Dave's seventeen. He should be dating girls his own age," Knight replies heatedly.

Dave gets his book and goes into the kitchen to escape the argument. After eating he has a shower and gets into bed. With Melissa away at college, Dave has her room, but he'll have to relinquish it when she comes back. For now, Dave's able to stay up reading into the small hours as the radio plays and the night envelopes him in its protective cocoon.

The next morning, Dave catches up on his sleep during class. It's inconvenient to have to get up and move every hour, but those disruptions don't keep him awake long. He's so far behind in his courses it doesn't matter what he does. Still, Dave's not worried; there's always summer school.

After lunch, Dave goes out the side door to the smoking area. Gambling is one of the main activities there, and he joins a group of smokers who are pitching nickels. Dave's good at this and is soon up by half a dollar. Then the bell rings, and it's time for ROTC.

Dave walks over to the drill field and lines up for inspection. Phillip Wilcox is now his cadet platoon leader. He's a short, powerfully built halfback for the Musketeers. "What have you got against Superman?" he asks Dave.

"Nothing," Dave replies.

"Then what's with all this kryptonite?" Wilcox points at Dave's belt buckle, which is turning green with tarnish.

"It happens."

"That will be one tour."

So, after school, Dave draws his M1 from the armory and marches back and forth in front of the tennis courts for an hour. As he walks, Dave sees his school bus come and go, but that's no problem, he'll walk downtown later and catch the Fort Gordon bus.

"Where were you after school yesterday?" Ethan Jackson asks when Dave gets on the bus the next morning. Ethan moved to Fort Gordon over the summer. He's living with his uncle who's a sergeant in the infantry.

"Had to march a tour for ROTC."

"I wanted to ask if you'd like to go to North Augusta with us tonight."

"Sounds like fun."

"OK, we'll pick you up around seven."

Dave goes directly upstairs after he gets home that afternoon and finds his mother in her room looking through a recent *LIFE*. "I'm going out with some friends tonight," Dave says. "Can you give me some money?"

"Of course," Bobbie replies. She wants Dave to have friends.

Dave eats a couple chicken pot pies for dinner, then showers and puts on fresh clothes for the evening. He sits on the front porch and reads until his ride pulls up an hour late. "Charley's dad didn't want to give him the car, but we finally talked him into it," Ethan explains.

Charley is Ethan's cousin and is driving the car. On the way into town, "I Get Around" comes on the radio, and they turn up the volume. The guys all sing along, and somehow the Beach Boys transport them from gritty Augusta, Georgia, to hip Southern California.

But reality is inescapable as they cross the Savannah River into North Augusta and pass several blocks of empty warehouses, abandoned textile mills, and boarded-up storefronts. It's a grim picture, but the one bright spot in South Carolina is the state-mandated drinking age of eighteen. When they come to a roadhouse with a neon Carling Black Label sign in the window, Charley parks. The three boys go in, and since Ethan is twenty, he goes to the bar. The others grab a table. Soon Ethan returns with a pitcher of suds and some frosted mugs.

The place is called the Heidelberg Inn. At the bar, several men clad in overalls sit hunched over their beverages. Posted on the wall in front of them is a handwritten notice proclaiming the management's right to refuse service to anyone for any reason. Another placard tells patrons what they can do with their personal checks. Next to the cash register are several display cards offering handy products like Gem fingernail clippers, Goody's Headache Powder, and Feen-A-Mint. A bottle filled with pickled pigs' feet is available for those in need of a tasty snack.

Dave quickly drains his beer and is hit with the same carefree feeling he experienced the previous year in Florida. He gets up, puts a quarter in the jukebox, and "You Really Got Me" comes blasting out of the speakers. Then he refills his mug.

Several rounds later, a pleasant humming fills the space between Dave's ears. It's as if a swarm of bees has moved in. He leans back, guzzles some brew, and studies Ethan and Charley who are deep in conversation on the other side of the table. Charley is a tall, muscular boy with light brown hair, a choirboy's face, and an even disposition. Dave knows him from the bus and has concluded that Charley is a simple soul who means no harm to anyone. His cousin is another story. While Ethan's an attractive kid, seemingly cool, he always has an agenda, and Dave doesn't trust him. Now, as if feeling Dave's gaze, Ethan looks his way. "Have you got your license?" he asks.

"Just got it," Dave replies.

"That's great," Ethan says. "Maybe you can drive next time?"

"I'll have to ask my dad."

"Ethan doesn't have to worry about that," Charley laughs. "His dad done threw him out."

"How come?" Dave asks.

"We didn't get along," Ethan explains uneasily. He gets up and goes to the bar.

Charley leans over the table conspiratorially. "Ethan got sent to reform school in Florida," he says. "When he got out, his father didn't want no more to do with him. That's how come he moved in with us."

Ethan comes back to the table with more beer, and they keep drinking until the place closes. On the way home, Dave vomits out of the window. When Charley stops at a filling station to clean the car door, Dave gets out and lies on the pavement. Ethan gets a cup of coffee from a vending machine, and he and Charley pour it down Dave's throat. It promptly comes back up and makes a steaming puddle on the driveway. Not knowing what else to do, Charley and Ethan take Dave to Boardman Lake and pour him out of the car onto the front lawn of his house. They speed off, and sometime later Dave gets to his feet, goes inside, then somehow makes it up the stairs. But just as he gets to the top, Dave falls over backward and tumbles back down. He's lying in the alcove mumbling curses when his father appears at the head of the stairs. "Shame you can't hold your liquor," Knight comments. "Now if you don't pipe down, I'm going to lock you out."

This time Dave crawls up the stairs on hands and knees and keeps the same low center of gravity going down the hall. He climbs into bed, but the room spins crazily, and he barely makes it to the trash bin in time. After a series of agonizing dry heaves, Dave gets into bed again. This time he puts his hand on the floor to keep it from moving.

The next day, Dave struggles through school with his tongue seemingly a foreign object. That, a throbbing headache, insatiable thirst, and profound queasiness lead him to swear off alcohol again.

For the next several weeks, Dave manages to stay out of trouble, but then he notices a flyer on a school bulletin board from the Young Republicans Club. They're chartering a bus to see William Miller who'll be making a campaign stop in Greenville, South Carolina. Miller is Barry Goldwater's vice-presidential running mate, and Dave likes Goldwater. Sure, the senator is crazy, but that's exciting. By contrast, President Johnson is boring. He looks and talks like a Baptist preacher. Dave can picture him and Lady Bird sitting on their porch waving at the occasional car that comes by. So, he signs up for the trip.

On the day of the Greenville excursion, all those going to South Carolina must first report to homeroom for attendance. After that, they go outside where banners with the slogan "AUH2O 64" are attached to the waiting bus. Dave climbs aboard and grabs a seat next to Alan Walters. He's a member of the Young Republicans and very active in school politics. Alan is also a hell-raiser who's often found smoking cigarettes and pitching nickels with the side door crowd.

As the bus heads east, sunlight pours cheerfully through the windows, and the party begins. Soon the vehicle is transformed into a gambling den. While the wealthier students play liar's poker, others match coins. In the rear of the bus, a fifth of Old Crow comes out, and the owner generously passes it around. Later a pint of Smirnoff gets the same treatment.

The fun continues until the bus arrives at the Greenville airport early that afternoon. "Hey, this is South Carolina," Alan says to Dave as they walk into the terminal.

"Then we're at the right place," Dave deadpans.

"What do you think of when you think South Carolina?" Alan persists.

"Well, there's your dogfighting, incest, and of course the trailer parks."

"How 'bout the eighteen-year-old drinking age?"

"Good thinking."

Alan and Dave find the small airport lounge deserted this time of day. A bored middle-aged woman sits idly behind the bar, and Alan approaches her. While short in stature, he's a good-looking boy with slicked-back black hair, intelligent eyes, and the serious expression of a physician. He's only seventeen, but the bartender does not ask for his ID when he orders two beers.

Dave and Alan perch on barstools then gaze out of the tinted plate glass window. It provides a view of the tarmac where a stage, covered in bunting, has been erected. Several photographers carrying bulky Speed Graphics cluster to one side, while members of a high school marching band wait nearby. Dave and Alan watch as the crowd gathers.

"You beat us to it," a boy from the bus exclaims as he and several more Young Republicans enter the bar.

"Can't help it if you're a bit slow on the uptake," Alan replies good-naturedly.

Soon the lounge is packed with ARC students. The air conditioning and cold brew provide a desirable alternative to being outside under the South Carolina sun. It's no joke even in October. On the tarmac, people in the crowd hold their hands up to shield their eyes. The Young Republicans in the lounge can practically see them sweat. Then Congressman Miller's plane arrives, and the band leader calls his ensemble to order. "Let's go," Alan says.

"Why?" Dave complains. "We can see everything from here."

"I want to get onto the stage."

"How?"

"I'll say I'm president of the Georgia Young Republicans," Alan replies. "You can be vice-president."

"No thanks, I'll wait here."

"You'll miss the speech."

"Too bad."

"Come on; you need to back me up."

Dave drains his beer and reluctantly follows Alan. Another ARC student immediately slides onto his barstool.

Outside Alan and Dave force their way through the crowd to the front of the stage. But when Alan tries to get on the ladder, he's blocked by a couple of serious-looking dark-suited men. "You can't go up there," one says.

"Sorry I'm late," Alan replies, smiling brightly. "I had a little car trouble, and now they're waiting for me up there. I'm president of the Georgia Young Republicans. Here's my card." Alan hands over his membership card, and one of the men takes it then consults his clipboard. "You aren't on the list," he says, handing the card back.

"Must be some mistake," Alan says. "You know, bureaucracy." He laughs jovially.

"Wait here."

Presently the man returns with a sharply dressed colleague. "I'm Gary Franklin," the newcomer says. "Can I help you?"

Alan extends his hand. "Hi, I'm Alan Walters, president of the Georgia Young Republicans. I'm supposed to be onstage with the other dignitaries." He gives Gary his membership card.

"Yes, well, I'm on the advance team for Congressman Miller," Gary says. "Responsible for credentials. You're not on the list of invitees. Further, this only says you're a member, not the president."

"You're making a big mistake," Alan blusters. "I'm friends with Senator Thurmond up there. He's not going to like this."

"I'll have to take that chance," Gary says. "If you were supposed to get an invitation and didn't, then I apologize."

"You haven't heard the last of this," Alan exclaims as Gary turns away. He's genuinely angry.

Onstage, a lady steps to the microphone and introduces the mayor of Greenville who launches into an impassioned speech of welcome. "Looks like it will be a while until Miller speaks," Alan says. "Let's get a beer."

"Hell yeah," Dave seconds the motion.

The little lounge is jam-packed when Dave and Alan get back, and they must fight their way to the bar. All the stools are now occupied, so they drink standing up. With everyone talking politics, the decibel level in the cramped space has gone way up. Soon Dave is deep in conversation with a boy from his history class. After a while, he glances out of the window and sees a distinguished dark-haired man on the stage speaking into the microphone. "Look, it's Miller," Dave says. He tries to get Alan to go back to the tarmac, but his friend is earnestly talking with an older man. "Be there in a minute," Alan says. "You go ahead."

Back outside, Dave stands in the rear of the crowd. "God bless all of you, God bless the state of South Carolina, and God bless these United States," Miller says. He lifts both arms and waves as the crowd applauds. Then the band breaks into a spirited rendition of "Dixie," and a chorus of rebel yells erupts from the spectators. But this burst of energy quickly fades. These people have been standing on the pavement under the southern sun for several hours. They are done.

Dave goes to the parking lot and finds his seat on the bus. After a while, someone roughly shakes him awake. It's the girl who organized the trip. "Where's Alan and the others?" she asks angrily. Dave is groggy, but he knows the answer to this question. "I'll get them," he promises.

The parking lot is empty now, and all the news vans, limousines, and taxis are gone. Inside, the terminal is equally deserted except for the lounge. Dave opens the glass door and his ears are assaulted by the din of inebriated conversation. "The bus is waiting," he hollers. "We've got to go." The ARC students reluctantly polish off their beers. Several line up at the bar to get one for the road as the place slowly empties.

Most of the students sleep the entire way back to Augusta. That night, when Dave gets home, his father is waiting. "How was the speech?" he asks.

"Brilliant," Dave replies. "Johnson doesn't have a chance. We're going to win."

"That's good," Knight smiles.

On Monday morning it seems like everyone at ARC is talking about the trip. So are Dave and several other Goldwater supporters who are waiting outside the door of their homeroom. "How much money did you lose?" a kid asks John Valeska, who was playing liar's poker all the way to Greenville.

"None of your fucking business," John replies.

"What did you say?" Mrs. Clover asks. The English teacher has come up behind them. She's a tall, broad-shouldered, sloe-eyed blonde, and Dave is enamored with her.

"I said, ah, how's the, uh . . . duck-hunting business?" John stammers. He's considered to be the cutest boy in the junior class and is in the school's best fraternity.

"Go inside," the teacher says disbelievingly, "all of you."

Dave loiters with a group of students in the back of the class. "Good thing the bus was equipped with puke bags," one of them says. "Henderson was barfing all the way back."

"I said sit down," Mrs. Clover orders, but when Dave turns to sit, one of his friends pulls the chair away, so he ends up sprawled on the floor. The room erupts in laughter, but the mirth quickly dies away as Mrs. Clover comes over to where Dave is lying. "That's it," she tells him. "Get out."

Dave stands in the hall while Mrs. Clover conducts class. Ten minutes later she allows him back in. "Have you learned your lesson?" the teacher asks.

"I give up," Dave replies, "have I?"

"Principal's office, now," Mrs. Clover snaps.

Mr. Raymond Danforth, assistant principal for discipline, is behind his desk smoking a cigarette when Dave is ushered in by the school secretary. Danforth is a former quarterback for the Musketeers, but his acne-scarred face and crew cut make him look more like a lineman than a quarterback. "Cutting up in class again, eh?" he smirks. "That'll be one hour of detention hall. Dismissed."

After sixth period, yellow buses line up outside the school, but Dave doesn't board his. Instead, he kills time out front until detention starts. As he waits, a white two-seat Ford Thunderbird pulls up in front of the school, and a pretty girl gets out. Then the driver floors it. A long patch of smoking rubber is all that's left as the T-Bird exits the campus.

Dave turns and goes inside the ground-floor entrance to the school. He has no problem finding detention hall, thanks to the raucous noise emanating from the classroom. He goes in, finds a seat, then pulls a paperback out of his bag and starts reading. A short while later he's rudely interrupted. "Pipe down," Coach Holloway hollers, coming into the room.

Holloway is a social studies teacher, but his primary job at ARC is defensive line coach. He's a tall, husky young guy who no doubt played on the line somewhere himself. The teacher has a blond crew cut, a twenty-inch neck, and a nose that appears to have been broken more than once. However, no one in the room pays any attention to Holloway. If anything, the noise level goes up.

The coach walks over to a group of girls who are laughing and joking among themselves. He sticks his face in and yells, "Sit down and shut up!" Sulkily the students comply. Then as Holloway turns to accost another group, a paper plane sails by his head. The coach quickly spins, hoping to catch the miscreant, but the kids in the back row are now wearing bored expressions. Suddenly a spitwad impacts on the wall above one of them. When Holloway turns to see who threw it, he's hit in the butt with a rubber-band-propelled paper clip.

Now the coach backpedals toward the front of the room where he can keep the entire class in view. "Whoever did that is going to pay," he yells, slowly swiveling his head from side to side. As his head rotates away, students shove wads of paper into their mouths and chew. They're making more spitwads.

"Today I have a stack of papers to grade," Holloway announces. "And I don't have time for this crap. Y'all need to get out a book and do some work." He glares at the students until he's satisfied that some at least are studying. Then he goes to the teacher's desk, pulls out the chair, and sits. He looks down at the sheaf of papers he brought, and instantly a massive spitwad flies by his head then splatters on the blackboard. "Who threw that?" the coach begs to know. He's once again energetically looking first at one side of the room and then the other.

As Holloway swivels his head, someone on the other side of the room lets out a wolf whistle. The coach's head snaps back, and at once a chorus of whistles erupts from the other side. "The next person I catch whistling will be sent to see Mr. Danforth," Holloway threatens. Then the coach head fakes one way and quickly looks the other, hoping to catch someone with pursed lips. Black circles of perspiration have appeared under the arms of his purple Musketeers polo shirt.

It's quiet in detention hall for a time as Holloway scans the room, then someone starts humming. It's hard to hear at first, just a low, monotonous drone, but other students pick it up, and presently the room sounds like an amplified beehive. "Who's making that noise?" Holloway shouts as the teenagers all sit, mouths shut, staring straight ahead expressionlessly, humming to beat the band. The coach leaves his desk and scuttles up and down the aisles bending his head in next to first one student and then another, hoping to pinpoint the source. But the sound is coming from everywhere and nowhere. As Holloway comes to the back row then turns toward the front, a fusillade of spitwads hurtles past. He whirls around, but the troublemakers are back in their innocent pose. The coach's eyes light on the wall clock. It's only four fifteen and detention hall is supposed to last until four thirty, but that doesn't matter. "Class over," Holloway bellows. "Get out, get out, get out!"

After detention Dave goes to the armory to draw his M1. "Where have you been?" Sergeant Tisdale asks.

"Detention hall."

"That figures," the NCO says, handing Dave his weapon. "And now you have a tour to march. What's got into you this year?"

"I don't know."

"Well, no need to come out for the rifle team again."

"OK."

It's dark by the time Dave arrives home, but there's a lasagna still warm in the oven, so he makes a plate. After eating he has a shower, then climbs into bed with his book. Hours later Dave wakes momentarily and turns off the radio.

At ARC, the next afternoon, Dave is outside the side door pitching nickels with some guys when Ethan comes over. "Ready for another trip to North Augusta?" he asks Dave.

"Why not?"

"Can you drive?"

"I'll see."

That night, after another drinking session at the Heidelberg Inn, Dave takes Ethan and Charley home. They live in a grim area of the post, filled with what the army admits is "substandard housing." The tan buildings aren't any different from the WWII-era wooden barracks that predominate on Fort Gordon, but these are divided into apartments for enlisted men with families.

After Dave drops his friends off, he goes to Maglin Terrace and parks the Opel near the playground. It's late, so he approaches the Bensons' house stealthily. Then he sits on the grass next to Diane's bedroom window. After five minutes of tapping, she opens it. "What are you doing here?" Diane whispers sleepily.

"Come to see you."

"Are you drunk?"

"Yes."

"What do you want?"

"A kiss."

"Impossible."

"Press your lips against the screen."

"OK."

They kiss with the screen in between, and it's not satisfactory. Then Dave gets an idea. "Can you go get a mouthful of liquor from your parents' bar?"

"What? I don't drink."

"You can pass it to me through the screen when we kiss."

"OK."

"Anything but Scotch," Dave insists.

After several liquor-infused kisses, Diane is giggling. "You're crazy," she says.

"Crazy like a fox."

"You should go."

"One more," Dave pleads.

"No, go home."

"I'm going to stay right here unless you give me one more bourbolicious kiss."

"If I give you one more, you promise to go?"

"I promise."

"You're not crossing your fingers, are you?"

"No," Dave says, showing Diane his hand.

"Let me see both hands," she insists.

Dave is true to his word, and after one more intoxicating kiss, he staggers off. Soon he's home and is surprised to find all the lights on and everyone in the living room. "Where in the hell have you been?" Knight asks his oldest son.

"What's going on?"

"There has been an accident," Bobbie explains. "Granddad and Vi. We're waiting for word."

"Oh." Dave is suddenly sober.

"You're never around when we need you," his father says bitterly.

"That's enough," Bobbie snaps.

The phone rings and Knight picks up. "Yes," he says and then pauses for a minute. "Well, I was expecting that." Knight bows his head. "What about you, sis?" he asks then listens for several moments. "Well, you've got to be strong," he says then puts the phone down. "They're gone," he says as tears stream down his face.

The children hardly knew their grandparents but are moved by their father's distress. Muffled sobs fill the room. After a while, Bobbie takes charge and gets the kids back in bed. "No use staying up now," she says. "There's nothing more to be done tonight."

In the kitchen, Dave makes a peanut butter and jelly sandwich and pours a glass of milk. As he's eating, his father comes in. "You don't care about anyone but yourself, do you?" Knight asks. "Out on the town, living it up while your grandfather's dying. Do you care? Hell no. You don't care."

Dave throws his paper plate into the trash. Then he rinses off the knife and puts it into the dishwasher. Upstairs, he quickly brushes his teeth and gets into bed. Then he reaches over, turns the radio on low, and douses the light.

Twenty-seven buildings are nearing completion on the campus of the new Southeastern Signal School, and Knight is out there along with his aide. "How is it that Kellogg, Brown & Root gets all the jobs?" Kinsey asks. He's looking at the construction company logo on a massive crane.

"Politics might have something to do with it," Knight replies. "Their headquarters is in Senator Tower's hometown. In any case, our hands are clean; we gave the ball to procurement and let them run with it."

"Absolutely," Kinsey agrees.

"Well, come on, let's go," Knight says. "These guys don't need us looking over their shoulder."

On the way back to the signal school headquarters, Knight's staff car is slowed by a platoon of airborne wannabees. The men are double-timing down the middle of the street chanting:

> *Hey Vietcong, Vietcong,*
> *Here we come, here we come.*
> *Hey Vietcong, Vietcong,*
> *Here we come, here we come.*

The driver takes a side road to get out from behind the troops then lets his passengers out at the office. Inside, Knight puts some coins on his secretary's desk. "Get us a couple Cokes, will you, Sue?" he asks.

"Yes, Colonel."

Soon the two officers are comfortably seated with drinks in hand. "Now I get a glimmer of how Eisenhower felt on D-day," Knight says.

"How's that?" Kinsey asks.

"Perfectly useless," Knight replies. "I mean, after Ike gave the go order he had nothing to do. His job was over. Sure, he went around and visited some of the units as they were gearing up. But all he did was get in the way."

"I see what you mean," Kinsey says. "All he could do was twiddle his thumbs."

"Same way here," Knight continues. "They don't want to see us out at the construction site. We only take up their time. My career is riding on this, and I'm helpless to affect it anymore."

"Then just relax," Kinsey exclaims. "It's going to be fine. Once the landscaping is in, it'll look great."

"I know," Knight says, "that's what I keep telling myself."

That evening Knight and Bobbie are listening to music in the living room when Dave comes in. "OK if I take the car tonight?" he asks. "There's a basketball game."

"All right," Bobbie says, "but it's a school night, so be back by twelve."

When Dave gets to the ARC gym, several boys he knows are by the door watching the game. It's midway through the first half, and the Musketeers are already leading the Grovetown High School Warriors 30-19. Grovetown is a small high school in the next county and in a lower division than ARC. "Why do we even play them?" Dave asks John Valeska.

"Who knows?" John answers. "I guess 'cause they're close."

By halftime, the Musketeers' lead has grown to twenty-five points. As the two teams head for their locker rooms, the ARC cheerleaders take the floor. "Come with us," John says conspiratorially.

Dave follows John and a couple of other boys out to the parking lot. They gather behind the school bus that brought the visitors, and John brings out a pint of vodka. He takes a swallow then passes it to Terry Ralston, a tall kid with bleached blond hair who looks like a surfer but isn't. Still, Terry's popular and belongs to the same fraternity as John. "Have you been to see Sexy Sally yet?" he asks Dave, passing him the bottle.

"Who's that?" Dave asks. He takes a swig of vodka and then passes it on.

"Her family moved here over Christmas," Terry explains, "into one of those apartments on Reynolds Street."

"All she wants to do is fuck," another boy says.

"Yeah, she's a nymphomaniac," Terry agrees. "But she loves John, now, doesn't she, boy?"

"That's because we only talk," John says. "That's all."

"Yeah, right," Terry laughs.

"Hey, give me that bottle," John insists. "I get to kill it; I brought it."

It's midway through the second half when the boys go back inside. The ARC coach has the second string in, but still, the game's a rout. "Anyone going to Timmerman's?" Dave asks once it's over.

"Nah, I got to get home," Terry replies.

"Ditto," says John. "If I'm not in by eleven, my ass is grass."

"OK, later then."

"Later."

At Timmerman's Drive-in, Dave has a cheeseburger for dinner. Afterward, he walks around the lot to see who's there. It's a slow weekday night, and Dave doesn't run into any friends. He pauses in front of a shiny black limousine, and as he's admiring it, the rear door swings open and a hood gets out. The kid's hair is greased back in a ducktail, and he wears a leather motorcycle jacket over a white T-shirt. "Like what you see?" he asks.

"She's a beauty," Dave replies.

"'Forty-eight Packard," the hood says. "Come have a look."

Dave approaches the vehicle and peers inside. The interior is cavernous, and a couple more hoods are sitting on the sofa-sized rear seat. "You wanna beer?" one of them asks, moving his lips around a lighted cigarette.

"Sure."

"Get in."

Dave climbs aboard and settles onto the facing seat. The gray herringbone upholstery is clean and very plush. One of the hoods reaches into a storage compartment, pulls out a Nehi bottle, and pries the generic bottle cap off. "We make it ourselves," the boy explains, and hands the beer to Dave. "My name's Vernon, this here's Zack, and that's Caleb."

"I'm Dave."

"Pleased to meetcha."

The bottle feels lukewarm in Dave's hand. Sediment lines the bottom. Nevertheless, he gulps down some homebrew. It's yeasty, but the alcohol comes through loud and clear. "Not bad," he says, smiling at his benefactors appreciatively. They smile back, showing off their dirty broken teeth.

Two more hoods walk up to the car and get in front. "Ain't no skirts here," one of them says, turning the ignition key. "Let's ride." The cabin of the limousine fills with a powerful rumbling sound, which grows into a muffled roar as the car slowly makes its way onto the street. They go toward town, past the high school to Kelly's, another hangout. The driver, a boy named Jimmy, backs into a parking space next to a red Mustang. A tall kid is leaning against it dressed preppie style. Vernon opens the door of the Packard and beckons him inside.

"Isn't it past your bedtime, Billy?" Caleb asks the newcomer once he's settled on the facing seat next to Dave.

"Had a basketball game," the kid says. "And don't call me Billy."

"Sorry, William."

"Eat me."

"I was at the game," Dave ventures.

"And who the fuck are you?"

"Relax, he's OK," Caleb says.

The basketball player glances at Dave. "Just call me Bill and we'll be good."

"I'm Dave."

"You wanna beer?" Caleb asks.

"Why not?" Bill says with a shrug.

"Might as well make it a round," Caleb suggests.

"Did you know Donny's back?" Bill asks while Vernon and Zack open bottles and pass them around.

"No shit," Caleb exclaims.

"Thought he joined the Marines," Vernon says.

"They unjoined him," Bill replies. "He's back at their trailer with a broken arm, broken ribs, and a messed-up face."

"What happened?" Zack asks.

"They told him to wash a stack of pots and pans that went from floor to ceiling," Bill says. "Donny told them to fuck off. Next thing he was in the hospital."

"Sounds just like Donny," Caleb laughs.

"His sergeant gave him two papers to sign then they dropped him at the bus station."

"What's he gonna do now?" Zack wonders.

"Too old to go back to school," Vernon says.

"What did them papers say?" Caleb asks. "Ones he signed."

"Ha-ha, he couldn't even read what all he signed," Bill says. "I read the papers to him. One said he swore up and down that nobody laid a hand on him. He fell down a flight of stairs. Ha-ha. His mark is on it and 'bout four or five other guys who signed where it said 'witness.'"

"And the other paper?"

"Oh, that had a whole lot of long words on it, but the main thing it says is 'Dishonorable Discharge.'"

"Shit."

"Yeah, he's fucked."

"You can't get no job with that paper hanging over you."

"Guess he should have thought of that before he opened his big mouth."

"Hey, we're out of beer," Vernon complains.

"Then let's go to Blacky's," Zack suggests.

"Want to go with us?" Caleb asks Bill.

"Nah, I got to get back to Grovetown," Bill says. He opens the door and gets out. "See ya," he says.

"Yeah."

Blacky's is a combination tavern and liquor store located about five miles up Walton Way. When they get there, Jimmy turns onto the rutted driveway that leads to the joint then parks underneath a tree in the dirt yard. "Let's get some money together," Caleb suggests.

"All I got is fifty cents," Zack replies, and Caleb holds out his hand. "I got a buck fifty," Jimmy offers. Dave keeps one dollar in his wallet and gives the other to Caleb, who adds to the kitty, then passes the cash to the driver.

Several elderly black men dressed in denim coveralls are standing around an oil drum near the back entrance to the ramshackle building. Flames flicker inside the drum, illuminating their tired faces. Now one of the men comes over to the car, and Jimmy rolls down his window. "Good evenin'," the man says. "Wasn't you gennelmens here before?"

"Yeah, that's right."

"Gin, warn't it?"

"You remember," Jimmy exclaims.

"Gilbey's," the old man smiles.

"That's it."

"Three dollah fifty."

The porter takes the money and shambles toward the service entrance. A few minutes later he returns and passes over a brown paper sack. Jimmy gives him a dollar tip. "That's might fine," the man says, beaming. "Look for me next time, you heah?"

Jimmy cracks the seal on the bottle, takes a swig of gin, and passes it to his copilot. Then the bottle makes its way around the back of the limo. Afterward, Caleb returns it to Jimmy, who looks at the level and shakes his head. "What a greedy bunch of bastards we got in the back of this vehicle," the driver says to his front seat partner. "We need to keep this baby up here for ourselves." Jimmy furiously works a crank, and a glass partition rises to separate the driver's compartment from the cabin.

"Jimmy, if you don't pass that bottle back here this instant, it's gonna be your ass," Caleb shouts. Jimmy turns sideways on the front seat and cups a hand to his ear while mouthing the words "can't hear you." Then he tilts the bottle back and takes a healthy gulp. Caleb jumps out of the car and runs up beside the driver's door. He pulls on the handle, but it's locked. Caleb cusses while Jimmy shows him the bird. Then Jimmy cranks the partition back down.

He hollers at Zack, "Quick, the door." Now Caleb is locked out of the car.

Jimmy passes the gin to the backseat crew and each takes a swallow. They make faces at Caleb, who's jumping up and down outside. But soon the hoods tire of the game and let their friend back in. "Guess the joke's on me," Caleb says sheepishly. Vernon hands him the bottle, and he chugs on it. "Who wants to finish this off?" Caleb asks.

"Not me," Jimmy says. "I got to drive." Vernon grabs the bottle, takes a swallow, then passes it to Zack who kills it. They leave Blacky's and return to Timmerman's. The Opel looks forlorn in the otherwise deserted drive-in.

"See you," Dave says, getting out.

"Not if we see you first," Caleb replies with a grin.

The next morning, Dave sits on the school bus by himself. He and Diane are not going steady anymore. They had a silly fight over the holidays and broke up. Dave ignored Diane's subsequent efforts to patch things up because he was tired of his father's jibes about her age. Now Diane sits with Ethan.

Later, during first-period English, Dave is paying attention for a change. They're studying Shakespeare, and he loves it. "'How sharper than a serpent's tooth it is to have a thankless child,'" Mrs. Clover reads. "What does King Lear mean by this?"

"Goneril bit him," Dave blurts out.

"Oh, come on, Dave," Mrs. Clover sighs.

"Oh, OK," Dave says. "What's happening is the old fool realizes that Regan and Goneril have taken him to the cleaners."

"That's correct," Mrs. Clover says. "If you would cut out the wisecracks and just answer the questions, we wouldn't have so many problems."

"Yeah, but think of how boring that would be."

The bell rings before Mrs. Clover can reply, and Dave makes a hasty getaway. He goes down the hall to chemistry class and spends an hour contemplating the periodic table in much the same way his ancestors pondered runes. After that, the day drags on until it's time for his least favorite class: Algebra II.

The students think that the algebra teacher, Mr. Beardsley, has been at ARC forever, and with his grizzled face, unkempt iron-gray hair, yellow teeth, and hobble, it's not hard to believe. The teacher wears an ancient brown corduroy sports coat to school every day along with a nondescript pair of rumpled dress pants. He also owns two shirts, which he alternates wearing under the sports coat. One of the shirts is orange with depictions of antique golf clubs; the other is lime green and features illustrations of colorful trout flies.

Mr. Beardsley follows the same routine for every class. First, he writes an equation on the board then solves it while explaining each step. Next, he assigns the students similar problems in the workbook. Then the teacher goes to the back of the classroom, sits at a desk, and smokes while the students work.

Today, however, Mr. Beardsley notices Dave once again sleeping. So, the teacher comes up with a little surprise for him. After finishing his exposition at the blackboard, Mr. Beardsley heads to the back of the classroom as usual, but instead of lighting a cigarette, he picks up the trash can.

Meanwhile, in his dream, Dave is looking into a beautiful lake. The water is so clear he can see a jumble of boulders and the distinct shapes of big fish far below. Suddenly they scatter, and a noxious odor replaces the fresh mountain air. Even asleep, Dave recognizes the mark of Mr. Beardsley. *Oh no*, he thinks, coming awake. Before he can move, the teacher hurls the metal trash can to the floor beside him, KA-BLAM. Instantly the class is in an uproar, as students stand and crane their necks to get a better view. Everyone is laughing, including Mr. Beardsley. "That's what you get for sleeping during my lesson," he chortles.

Dave looks up from his desk, and his eyes come to rest on the teacher's stomach where a picture of a yellow trout fly appears strikingly against his green shirt. The description written underneath is "Quill Gordon."

The class cheerfully settles back down, but Dave is depressed. *I'm nothing*, he thinks, *and I'll never be anything*. Immediately he brightens. There's a sense of freedom in knowing the worst. Idly Dave scribbles the line in his notebook. It looks like a bit of dialogue, so he writes more:

> *I'm nothing, and I'll never be anything, he says*
> *While knotting his tie, that is the secret to my success*
> *She casually rolls up a stocking*
> *And slips her foot into it*
> *Then languidly pulls the nylon up her calf and over her knee*
> *That's what I like about you, she says, fastening a garter*
> *Your complete and total lack of ambition*

Dave imagines Paul Newman as the man and Elizabeth Taylor as the woman and tries to write more, but nothing comes. So, he slowly removes the page from his notebook, inserts it into his mouth, and chews. After spitting the sodden pulp into his hand and rolling it into a ball, Dave looks for a target. Not finding any enemies nearby, he flings the spitwad straight up where it sticks to the ceiling, joining many other similar lumps plastered there. As Dave admires his work, he notices several sharpened pencils that students have similarly flung upward. Now they protrude from the ceiling tiles like arrows fired by wild savages.

The bell rings, and Dave goes downstairs and out the side door. There's a hint of spring in the smoky air, and a large crowd of bad boys is enjoying the sunshine while grabbing a cigarette between classes. Many have thrown out the Brylcreem and are letting their hair grow to emulate the Beatles. However, Dave cannot produce bangs. His frizzy hair only stands on end.

Dave goes back inside for his last class, and once that's over, he attends detention hall. Afterward, as he's walking downtown, Dave loiters along the way to read placards advertising music shows. Among them is a poster for an event starring Augusta's own James Brown. Dave resolves to ask his mother for money to go.

At ARC word spreads about the upcoming appearance of the region's only superstar. For the next several weeks, Brown is the main subject of conversation. Then the night of the show, Dave gets the keys to the Opel and some money from Bobbie. He drives to Timmerman's to meet up with Alan Walters, John Valeska, and Terry Ralston. Terry is driving his father's big Buick, so they all pile into it for the ride downtown. "We're going to stop by Reynolds Apartments on the way," Terry says.

"Not interested," John replies.

"Well, I am," Terry declares, and since he's the driver, the others have no choice.

Reynolds Apartments is a development of run-down, one-story, two-bedroom duplexes. The one Sally Riley lives in is on a corner. Several cars are parked there when Terry pulls in. A crowd of boys is outside the vehicles smoking and talking while a car radio plays. "Who's in there now?" Terry asks one of the guys.

"Bucky."

"Shit, he'll take forever," Terry exclaims. "Well, I'm getting in line."

"That means you're after me," a short red-faced kid says.

"OK."

During the next hour, several boys climb in and out of Sally's bedroom window. Meanwhile, the crowd in the parking lot gets rowdier, and eventually, a woman in a nightdress comes out of the building. "Go away," Mrs. Riley hollers. "For pity's sake, go and leave my little girl alone." She brings a wine bottle to her mouth and drains it. Then she throws the empty at the nearest group of boys. They scatter as it shatters on the pavement.

"Beat it, you old hag," one of them shouts.

"Not till you git," the woman screams. "You git or I'm callin' the police."

"Shit," Terry exclaims.

"That's why I didn't want to come," John says. "She's getting worse."

"A little nookie would've been nice," Terry sighs as he and his friends pile back into the Buick. They go downtown, park, then join the people streaming toward Bell Auditorium. Inside they find a preliminary act on stage, laying down a funky groove while dancers pack the floor. Groups of white students gyrate among the predominantly black crowd and segregation is forgotten for the night. It's the KKK's worst nightmare.

John goes to the men's room and comes back holding a pint of Jim Beam. He takes a swill then passes it to Alan. "They're selling everything you want in the bathroom," John says. "Terry, if you're still horny, they even have a hooker turning tricks."

"How much was the whiskey?"

"Five bucks."

"Ouch!"

"What the hell?" John says. "Who cares? It's James Brown."

The bottle gets passed around as another preliminary act takes the stage then, around midnight, Brown's band comes out. The horn section features an endless row of saxophones and they immediately settle into a one-two-three-four downbeat riff. On the first beat, the musicians all bend forward and lower their instruments; on the second, the entire line steps to the right; on the third, they raise the saxophones high; and on the fourth beat, they lower the instruments while stepping back to the left. Soon the trumpets and trombones kick in, and then the whole band is swinging as the percussionists thunder away in back.

After playing the same groove for half an hour, the Flames gradually lower the volume as the announcer introduces the "Hardest-Working Man in Show Business." James Brown enters from the wing and as the band launches into one of his hits, he dances from one side of the stage to the other on one foot. It was already a wild party, but now the afterburners have been lit. The crowd is jumping up and down as if on a trampoline. Brown's percussive voice is the dominant instrument onstage, and his dancing is just terrific. He pumps new energy into the musicians and the audience.

No one wants the show to end, but after a long, exhausting performance, Mr. Dynamite wraps up somewhere shy of 2:00 a.m. Dave and his friends are all tired, and the effects of the whiskey have long dissipated. Terry drops John, Dave, and Alan back at Timmerman's, and they all head to their homes to get some rest.

Augusta's mild winter never lasts long, and in the coming weeks, as the weather warms, the side door crowd at ARC grows. "Hey, look," a boy named Sandy Diehl says one morning before class. "There's Sexy Sally."

Sandy is a friendless boy who tries to be cool but fails. He's pointing at a short red-haired girl who has just gotten off a school bus. As Sally walks toward the front stairway, Sandy lets out a piercing whistle.

"Why be an asshole?" John snaps.

"Who are you calling an asshole?" Sandy asks. He takes a confrontational step toward John then hesitates. John has a lot of friends.

"Hey, did y'all see the paper?" Terry asks to change the subject. "We're getting integrated."

"What?" Sandy exclaims. "They're letting niggers in here?"

"Next fall," Terry replies.

"It's about time," Dave observes.

"Are you crazy?" Sandy asks.

"'The Times They Are a-Changin','" Dave replies. "Like the man says."

"You must be some kind of nigger lover," Sandy accuses.

"Must be," Dave agrees. "I recently paid good money to listen to a black man sing. He was pretty good."

"Black man?" Sandy raises his eyebrows. "Is that what you call them? Where I'm from, we call 'em niggers."

"Which trailer park is that?"

Sandy gives Dave a shove. "You sayin' I'm trash?" he asks menacingly.

"Not at all," Dave replies. "A cracker maybe, but certainly not trash."

"Meet me after school," Sandy scowls. "I'm gonna kick your ass."

"What a douche," John exclaims as Sandy stalks off. Then the bell rings, and it's time to go to homeroom.

Dave's too upset to pay much attention during the announcements, but he does hear Mr. Oldman say that there'll be a school assembly for a band recital after fourth period. Later, during English class, Dave quietly worries about the fight. He's too nervous to either read or sleep, and he remains that way the rest of the morning. After lunch, he goes to the drill field for ROTC and gets gigged for his long hair, grungy brass, scuffed shoes, and unironed uniform. That means he'll be marching another tour after detention hall, but he won't be the only one. More and more boys are rebelling against ROTC. They let their hair grow, don't shine their shoes, and allow tarnish to accumulate on their brass. Sergeant Tisdale has collected this group into what he calls "the goon platoon." They're kept separate during drill, and the goons often march their punishment tours together.

Today, after ROTC everyone is supposed to go to the band recital, but Sandy Diehl accosts Dave on his way there. "Let's go to the softball field," he says.

"Danforth said the assembly's mandatory," Dave replies.

"Cut the shit," Sandy exclaims, pointing to a carload of students that's quickly exiting the school. "They don't take attendance at assemblies."

Seeing no way out of it, Dave turns to follow Sandy to the softball field. They climb down the embankment and square off behind the backstop. "This is stupid," Dave protests. "I don't have anything against you. Hell, I don't even know you."

Sandy puts up his fists. "Can't chicken out now," he says. "I said I'm gonna kick your ass, and I'm a man of my word." Sandy takes a bold step forward and launches a roundhouse, but to Dave's heightened senses it appears that Sandy is moving in slow motion. Dave easily moves his head to avoid the punch then pops his opponent with a stiff jab.

"Fight, fight," someone hollers, and Dave risks a glance up the embankment. He sees that the Packard has pulled over and now Caleb, Vernon, Zack, and Jimmy are standing outside it. "Don't stop," Caleb orders. "We want to see a fight."

Sandy hunches his shoulders with renewed determination and wings another wild punch. Dave avoids it then counters with a jab, which Sandy clumsily ducks, offering his face as an easy target. Dave sets his feet and starts to uncork a straight right, but at that instant, the sight of Melissa's fist driving into Marie's nose flashes across his consciousness. As Dave hesitates, Sandy tackles him to the ground.

Now Dave is on his back with the bigger boy astride. Sandy comes down with a big overhand punch, and while Dave sees it coming, all he can do is lift his head at the last moment causing the blow to glance off his forehead. Desperately he squirms around and gets into a kneeling position using his arms and legs to push up. Dave hopes to throw off his antagonist, but Sandy's too strong. He pushes Dave facedown and administers a series of rabbit punches.

Dave feels himself going in and out of consciousness then suddenly the weight on his back is gone. "I said I want to see a fight," Caleb snarls, holding Sandy by the throat. "When I say fight, I mean stand on your two feet and throw punches. I ain't innerested in watching two guys roll around in the dirt."

Caleb releases Sandy as Dave regains his feet. Then the hood steps back and motions the two antagonists together like a prizefight referee. However, Sandy hangs back, and now the pugilists warily circle each other. "Let's go, let's go," Caleb exhorts. "This ain't no fight. Come on."

Sandy glances nervously at Caleb then up at the hoods by the car. He backs up a couple of steps and drops his hands. "I don't wanna fight no more," he says.

"What?" Caleb asks. "Didn't you hear me? I said fight." But Sandy stands idle with his hands by his side, anxiously darting glances right and left. Suddenly Caleb takes two quick steps and hits Sandy with a chopping overhand right. Immediately a gaping gash opens over Sandy's eye, and blood gushes down his face. He dazedly brings his hand up to the eye, lowers it, and looks at what the hand has carried away. Then Sandy turns and begins running across the softball field. Jimmy, Vernon, and Zack yell taunts at him as he goes.

Now Caleb rounds on Dave. "What the fuck's wrong with you?" he asks.

"I don't know."

"You have the motherfucker right where you want, and you choke."

"I know."

"Why?"

"Guess I felt sorry for him."

"Sorry? You felt sorry?" Caleb spits. "Goddamn, you never let up on a motherfucker like that. You do what needs doin' any and everything." Caleb drops his hand, and in a flash, he's holding an open switchblade under Dave's nose. "Any and everything," the hood repeats as he malevolently carves the air. With a flick of the wrist, Caleb disappears the blade back into his dungarees. Then he turns and climbs up the embankment toward the Packard.

"See you later," Zack hollers as he and his friends pile into the limousine. The big straight-eight comes to life, and the black car rumbles away.

"Not if I see you first," Dave murmurs once the car is out of sight. He goes into the school and washes up in a downstairs bathroom. Then with nothing better to do until detention, Dave goes to the assembly. He finds a seat in the rear of the auditorium balcony and, like the other miscreants there, puts his feet up on the chair back in front of him. Onstage, the band is murdering "I'm Gonna Wash That Man Right Outta My Hair." Mercifully it's the last number. Despite the paucity of applause, the bandleader has the musicians take several bows. Then Mr. Oldman takes the microphone. "We have a couple more things to do before we end today," the principal says, accompanied by the squelch of feedback. "If you recall, the juniors took the SAT back in January. Well, the results are in, and we have award certificates for our top performers. Let's bring up Mrs. Fielding to do the honors."

Mrs. Rebecca Fielding is the head guidance counselor. She's a slim, businesslike fifty-year-old woman. For twenty years Mrs. Fielding has been proudly ushering her top students off to the University of Georgia. She doesn't realize that Athens is the closest thing the state has to Sodom and Gomorrah.

Now Mrs. Fielding approaches the microphone holding a sheaf of papers. "Hello, Musketeers," she hollers then holds a hand to her ear. A desultory reply of "Hello, Mrs. Fielding," is her reward.

"My hat is off to our juniors for coming in on a rainy Saturday in January to take the SAT," the guidance counselor exclaims. "Today I'm going to present awards to the top performers. When I read your name, please come and receive your certificate. Now, the best score was Eddie Jason. He made 730 on the math section and 610 on the verbal for a score of 1340. Come on down, Eddie." A smattering of applause follows Eddie Jason to the stage. No one's surprised he did well on the SAT. Eddie's been the smartest kid in the class since Forest Hills.

The next three students called to the stage are also well-known brainiacs, but when Mrs. Fielding reads the last name on her list, it's a shock. "The final certificate goes to David Knight," she announces to stunned disbelief. "He made 450 on the math and 760 on the verbal, total of 1210."

"How do you cheat on the SAT?" the kid sitting next to Dave whispers. Disdaining to reply, Dave clambers over the legs of his neighbors and hustles down to the stage. He collects the certificate and has his photo taken with the others.

"This has been a great assembly," Mr. Oldman crows into the microphone. "So many wonderful things are happening here at ARC. And now before we go, I have it on good authority that Mr. Bones is not only ready but indeed willing to grace us with a performance."

The band breaks into an up-tempo ragtime number as Mr. Bones steps onto the stage and begins tap dancing. He's a seventy-year-old African American janitor who has worked at the school for fifty years. Nobody knows his real name, but the man is tall and gaunt, so he's known as Mr. Bones or just Bones. Over the years he has been called upon to dance at assemblies and during halftime of home basketball games. But now due to his advanced age, he tires easily. Soon Bones is done, and as he leaves the stage, the band plays the opening bars of "Dixie." The students leap to their feet and sing along. Then the assembly is over, and Dave goes to detention.

Lawrence Brown, the head football coach of the Musketeers, knows how to handle detention hall. He sits at the teacher's desk, puts his feet up, and pulls out a magazine. The coach reads while spitwads splatter, paper airplanes fly, and some rubber-band-propelled paper clips find their targets. However, half the detainees are soon asleep while the rest talk among themselves or read comics. The hour passes without incident then several boys migrate over to the armory, draw their weapons, and begin marching back and forth by the tennis courts. Sergeant Tisdale comes out to watch. "If any of you guys applied to work the tournament next week, you can forget about it," he tells them. "You look like shit."

"Fuck," Alan says under his breath, "I was counting on that money."

"Me too," Dave sighs. Last year he worked holding ropes at the Masters in his ROTC uniform and earned enough for a new fishing rod and some tackle.

"I want to watch Arnie," Terry complains. "Now I'll have to try and find a ticket."

Tickets to the Masters are hard to come by even in Augusta. Out at Fort Gordon, Knight has been working the phone trying to find one for General Clifton. The Signal Corps commandant is coming to inspect the new signal school and wants to see some of the tournament. So Knight decides to call Blake Beaufort. "No problem, Colonel," is Blake's response. "How many tickets do you need?"

General Clifton arrives the following week. He spends a morning at the Masters then goes to Fort Gordon for a meeting with Bryan and Knight. Afterward, the three officers go for a tour of the new Southeastern Signal School. Fortunately for Knight, the complex looks even better in brick and block then it did in pen and ink. The Eckt design and the Kellogg, Brown & Root construction have produced an understated but impressive campus. The buildings look solid but airy, durable but not stodgy. "This will stand here as a testament to your good taste long after we're all dead and gone," Clifton tells Knight.

"Sir, that sounds like a toast," Knight says hopefully.

"Hell yes, let's adjourn to the OC."

At the officers' club, General Clifton treats his subordinates to a round of drinks. "To the new Southeastern Signal School," he says, raising his glass.

"Hear, hear," Bryan seconds, and the officers drink to it.

"Dave, we owe you," Clifton says, settling onto his barstool. "You've done a lot of heavy lifting for the Signal Corps over the years, and now this. Problem is you took forever to make bird, so you're way down in seniority. Otherwise, I could get you a command."

"Sir, I understand," Knight replies.

"And we can't get you a star, 'cause you've been too busy doing this that and the other thing to go to Carlisle."

"That's a killer," Bryan agrees. He hasn't been to the Army War College either, so even with all his seniority, he'll never get promoted.

"So here's what I have in mind," Clifton continues. "I'm at Monmouth, got to be there."

"Absolutely," Knight agrees.

"Meanwhile we're getting the shaft at the Pentagon."

"Damn right."

"What say you go to Washington and take our part?" Clifton asks. "Most importantly appropriations, but also promotions, assignments, various boards, the gamut. You'll be deputy commandant of the Signal Corps."

"Sir, that would be great," Knight exclaims.

That evening Knight returns to the Fort Gordon officers' club with Bobbie, Dave, Dan, Marie, and Perle. While their parents drink rum and Cokes and eat New York strips, the Knight children gorge on 7UP, fries, and cheeseburgers. "I have something to tell you," Knight announces afterward. "We're moving to Washington."

"Oh no," Marie wails. "We can't move."

"Why the hell not?" Knight asks.

"What about my friends?"

"Honey, you can make new friends in Washington," Bobbie says soothingly.

"You make it sound so easy," Marie replies bitterly.

"When are we going?" Perle asks.

"Not until school is over," Bobbie answers. "You'll have plenty of time to say goodbye to everyone. Make sure to get addresses so you can write."

"No one ever writes back," Dan complains. "Everyone says they will, but no one ever does."

"That's not true," Bobbie argues.

"Enough of this nonsense," Knight interrupts. "I have my orders. We're moving. Make the best of it."

"Who wants ice cream?" Bobbie asks brightly. The children sullenly raise their hands.

Knight spends the rest of the weekend at the Masters with Blake Beaufort. They follow Arnie, of course, but Jack Nicklaus runs away with the tournament. Then the golfers leave town, and things in Augusta return to normal.

At ARC, two weeks later, Dave, Terry, and John are pulled out of Mrs. Clover's class and sent to see Mr. Danforth. Alan joins them as they wait in the reception area, then the four friends are called in. They stand in front of the vice principal's desk as he casually makes notes on some papers. After a while, the disciplinarian looks up and gives the boys a self-satisfied smirk. He pulls a pack of Lucky Strikes out of his shirt pocket and fires one up. "Yesterday morning I took the family outside to get in our car for the ride to church," he says then drags on the cigarette, tilts his head back, and lets the smoke float around inside his mouth. Abruptly Danforth vacuums the nicotine down, bends forward, and slams his hand on the desk. "That's when I found that my white Chevy II was purple," he exhales.

Dave tries to stifle the laughter, but it only makes it worse. Soon he's bent over with both hands on his knees laughing so hard his sides hurt. Terry, Alan, and John are in no better shape. As if expecting this reaction, Mr. Danforth leans back in his chair and calmly smokes as they laugh themselves out. "I know it was you," he says once it's quiet. "I have witnesses."

"I demand to talk to these so-called witnesses," Alan responds. "I know my rights."

"Are you denying it was you?"

"Absolutely," Terry says.

"Then who did it?" Danforth demands. "Tell me, and you're off the hook."

"I wouldn't tell you if I knew," John vouches.

"You haven't heard the end of this," Danforth threatens. "Now get out of here."

Later, out by the side door, the smokers talk excitedly about the unauthorized and unrequested paint job on the vice principal's car. Rumors abound, but no one's claiming credit. "I'm sure it was the seniors," Terry says.

"Then they're one up on us," Alan replies. "We have to think of a way to top them."

Several prank ideas are bandied about by the bad boys over the next few days. Most are old standbys involving toilet paper, cherry bombs, and the school's fire sprinkler system. None of the proposals are creative enough to suit Alan, however, and soon planning for the weekend takes precedence.

At Boardman Lake, Dave devotes the weekend to reading, listening to the radio, and sleeping, until Sunday afternoon when he awakens from his lethargy, gets his fishing rod, and strolls around the lake with Tex. He tries a few casts with a spinner at various spots along the bank, but mainly Dave wants to enjoy the sights and sounds of spring. At one point he has to hold the dog while a mother goose crosses the road followed by her offspring. Farther along, Dave spies the twisted shape of a water moccasin sunning itself in one of the lakeside bushes.

That night, Dave's in bed with the window open to let in the balmy air. Outside, frogs croak incessantly while crickets chirp in accompaniment. Then a bullfrog down by the water speaks, and Dave puts his book down to listen. Gradually an idea forms in his mind.

In the morning, Dave's up with the sun, quickly dresses, then goes down to the lake carrying a shoebox. Frogs are everywhere in the swampy area by the shore, and he has no problem catching one after another of the slimy creatures. Soon the box is jam-packed, so Dave takes it back to the house, cuts some air holes in the bulging cardboard, and tapes it closed. Then he showers and dresses for school.

When he gets to ARC, Dave puts the frogs in his locker and goes to class. He waits until midday, then retrieves the shoebox and takes it upstairs to the library. As usual, it's crowded at lunchtime. Dave sits at one of the tables, places the box on the chair next to him, and removes the lid. Then he nudges the container over so that the frogs fall onto the floor. Dave then leaves the library, goes downstairs, and out the side door. He finds John and Terry there with several other smokers. A few minutes later, Alan comes over. He has a pint of Old Crow tucked in his waistband, so his friends gather round to shield him from view while he drinks. Then the bottle makes the rounds.

"Thanks, I needed that," Dave says.

"Having a rough day?" Alan asks.

"Yeah."

The students pause to listen to a faint sound coming from the open windows on the third floor. It sounds like screaming. "I'm going up there," John says.

"Me too," another kid chimes in.

The side door gang rushes up the stairs to the top floor then down the hall to where a crowd has gathered outside the library. Inside, girls are standing on tables screaming like it's a Beatles concert. Several boys are chasing frogs. "There goes one," someone yells.

"Coming through! Move! Get out of my way!" Mr. Danforth calls, rudely elbowing his way past. As the vice principal rushes into the library, a kid corners a frog and brings his heel down. There's an explosion of blood and guts. "Stop that," Danforth shouts, grabbing the misguided youth by the elbow. The disciplinarian searches his mind for another approach but is distracted by higher-pitched screaming. It seems that an unmentionable part of the squashed frog landed on the leg of one of the girls. Now she, along with her friends, have redoubled their vocal efforts. They're jumping up and down.

Danforth gazes toward heaven for a solution and through the open library window sees nothing but clear blue sky. Inspiration strikes. He looks down just as one of the little fellows hops by. Danforth grabs it, then hurls the vertebrate out of the window and into the pitiless void of oblivion.

Now that he has the hang of it, Danforth scampers around the library chasing frogs down and throwing them out. He's like a man possessed, and soon the entrance stairs and pavement below bear gruesome testimony to his murderous efficiency. After the last vestiges of the amphibian menace have been ejected, the library begins to calm down, and the spectators disperse.

"Danforth still has quite an arm," John says as he and his friends go back downstairs.

"Yeah, you've got to hand it to him," Alan agrees. "He was throwing perfect spirals."

That afternoon, Dave's sitting at his desk in algebra class reading a paperback hidden in his textbook. Suddenly Mr. Beardsley is hovering over him. As usual, the teacher looks and smells like a compost heap. "What are you reading?" he asks.

"T. H. White," Dave replies, showing the cover.

"Great book," Mr. Beardsley comments. "But after a while, it seemed to just keep going on and on."

"Yeah, I'm at that point now," Dave agrees. He can't believe Mr. Beardsley is so friendly. Normally the teacher would grab the book and throw it in the waste bin.

Now Mr. Beardsley sits at a nearby desk and lights an unfiltered Kool. "Going to summer school?" he asks.

"Got to," Dave replies.

"Best thing for you," Mr. Beardsley says condescendingly. "Hey, it was you who let them frogs loose, wasn't it?"

"It was somebody at this school," Dave answers. "That's for sure."

"I'm just curious," the teacher says hopefully. "That's all. I wouldn't tell anyone."

Dave doesn't reply, and as the silence lengthens he looks at one of the illustrations on Mr. Beardsley's orange shirt. It depicts an iron-bladed golf club with a wooden shaft. The caption underneath is "Niblick."

"You won't be able to sleep your way through summer school," Mr. Beardsley declares, grinding out his cigarette on the linoleum floor. "Otherwise, you'll be right back here with me." Mr. Beardsley grins, relishing the thought, and Dave is reminded of corn on the cob.

Later, after detention hall is over and he has done his ROTC tour, Dave is dallying outside the school to put off the hike downtown. The day has cooled, and several members of the track and field team are out on the sports field. Dave watches a boy throw the javelin while nearby Johnny Samson and Phillip Wilcox are taking turns on the high jump. Then three African American teenagers wearing gym shorts and T-shirts walk up. When Samson notices the visitors, he goes over to talk. Then the black athletes join the practice.

One of the newcomers is quite good, and he competes with Samson as they keep pushing the bar higher. But after a while, no one is getting over anymore, and darkness looms. So, the athletes end their workout then shake hands all around. Soon everyone is gone, and Dave begins his trek to the bus station. When he gets home, Dave sees that his mother has started packing for their move to Washington. Several boxes hold carefully wrapped lamps, vases, and artwork. Bobbie is packing these herself before the movers come.

Dave stops cutting up in class now, and by the end of the last week of regular classes, he only has one hour of detention hall remaining. He's outside after school waiting to go in when he sees his ex by the bus stop. She's by herself, so he goes over to her. "Well, hello there," Diane says.

"We're moving," Dave announces.

"I know. I got the news from one of the girls, but I was wondering if you were going to tell me."

"I've been busy."

"I heard. How did you rack up so many hours of detention anyway?"

"Oh, sleeping in class, throwing spitwads, mouthing off at the teachers, stuff like that."

"Just being Dave Knight, I guess you could say," Diane says, flashing one of her old smiles.

"I guess."

"You'll never change."

"Probably not."

"Hey, you need to come by the house and say goodbye to my parents," Diane insists. "They ask about you all the time."

"I will," Dave lies.

A group of students comes out of the ground-floor entrance to the school, and Ethan is among them. His step quickens when he sees Diane talking with

Dave. "Come on," Ethan says, taking her arm possessively. She gives Dave a bleak smile and shrugs before turning away.

There are only six students in detention hall when Dave goes in. He gets out a paperback but finds that he's too depressed to read. So, Dave puts his head down and feigns sleep. Afterward, since he has no more ROTC tours to march, Dave is free to go home. When he gets there, Melissa is at the house. She has piled Dave's belongings out in the hall. Now he must move back in with Dan. Neither boy is happy, but it'll only be for a short while. Next week school is ending, and after that, they will leave Georgia for good.

The next morning, Dave follows his regular Saturday schedule and sleeps till noon. Then after getting something to eat, he grabs his fishing rod and walks around the lake to where a dirt road branches off. Tex eagerly follows as Dave hikes toward a remote pond where he's caught fish before. The dog likes to run ahead, make side trips off into the woods, then come back, tail wagging, to check on Dave.

After a couple of miles, Dave and Tex pass a gruesome scene where several acres of forest have been clear-cut. Two bulldozers and a tractor-trailer loaded with logs are parked nearby. Dave and the dog continue past the place another mile to an impoundment that's fed by the same stream that flows into Boardman Lake. In the clear water near the bank, Dave can see where bass created beds in the sand. But spawning season is over, and now the fish are in deeper water just beyond. They're hungry, and Dave catches and releases over a dozen eighteen-inch bass. The similarity in size means they were all stocked at the same time.

On the way back, Dave looks to see if the lumberjacks left keys in any of their equipment. He doesn't see any in the bulldozers, but when he climbs into the cab of the tractor-trailer, the keys are in the ignition. Dave gets behind the wheel, and Tex scrambles up to where Dave can haul him the rest of the way. Then Dave puts the clutch in and maneuvers the shift lever until he gets it into neutral. He turns the key and the motor fires right up. Dave finds the hand brake, releases it, and puts the transmission in gear. When he lets the clutch out, the truck lurches forward and keeps going as Dave feeds it more gas. He steers the eighteen-wheeler up the dirt road toward home then shifts gears. It's fun driving the behemoth, but then it occurs to Dave that there's no place to turn around before dead-ending at Boardman Lake. He suspects that driving a stolen log truck around the pond might not be a good idea, so he stops at the widest spot in the road he can find.

Dave cuts the steering wheel hard to the left, backs up, then pulls forward with the wheel twisted the other way. He does this several times then impatiently attempts to complete the U-turn by steering the vehicle off the road, hoping to loop back on. Unfortunately, there's a culvert partially hidden by roadside brush that Dave doesn't see. When the left front wheel goes into the drainage ditch, the tractor starts to tilt. Dave mashes on the gas and gets the front of the truck through, but when the dual rear wheels on the left side of the tractor go in, the whole rig teeters then flips over. Logs go rolling and crashing down the hillside.

When Dave comes to, Tex is squirming on top of him. The dog has lost control of his bladder, and the pungent odor of urine fills the air. "It's all right, boy," Dave mumbles as Tex desperately licks his face. Then Dave tries moving his arms and legs, and they are fine. He has a golf-ball-sized knot on the side of his head, but it's not bleeding. His priority now is to flee the scene.

Dave pushes Tex aside and stands on the driver's side door with the open passenger window directly above. He pulls himself up then climbs through the opening and sits on the outside of the truck with his legs dangling into the cab. Below Tex barks unhappily. "OK, boy," Dave says. "I'm not going to leave you." Dave lies on the door, reaches down, and lifts the mutt by the scruff of his neck. As soon as Tex is out of the cab, he scampers to the ground. Dave lowers himself back into the cab, takes off his T-shirt, and uses it to wipe the steering wheel and shift knob. After that, he grabs his fishing rod and pulls himself out again. He clambers along the windshield, leaps to the ground, and starts for home.

Once back at the house Dave goes into the bathroom, strips his clothes off, and has a shower. He's still feeling hyper afterward, so after changing into fresh clothes, Dave goes down the hall and knocks on Melissa's door. "Who is it?" she asks.

Dave opens the door and finds his sister sitting cross-legged on his ex-bed painting her fingernails. "I just stole a log truck and wrecked it," he says.

"You didn't," Melissa exclaims, staring at her brother wide-eyed.

"'Fraid so."

"Where's it at?"

"Just up the road."

"This I've got to see."

Melissa blows on the fingers of one hand while fanning the other in the air. "Get out," she says. "I've got to change."

Dave goes outside and takes a seat on the front porch. The sun is going down over the lake, and bats are emerging from wherever they spend the day. They wheel about in the air acrobatically, traveling almost too fast to see. Dave tries to track them until Melissa comes out wearing a T-shirt, jeans, and tennis shoes. They lock Tex in the house, then brother and sister start walking. Once they turn onto the dirt road, it doesn't take long until they round a bend and come upon the truck lying on its side. Oil and gas are draining out of the motor, and a hissing sound indicates that air is escaping from the hydraulic braking system. An ominous ticking is coming from somewhere in the engine compartment.

The two siblings walk around to the front and look at the smashed fender. The ground next to it is littered with shattered glass and the twisted remnants of the driver's side mirror. A swath of flattened pine saplings shows the path the logs took upon leaving the trailer. They've come to rest in a jumble against the trunks of some larger trees at the bottom of the hill.

"Those logs down there were on the truck?" Melissa asks.

"Yep."

"You're crazy," Melissa says, looking at her brother with newfound respect. "What if you get caught?"

"How?" Dave asks.

"I don't know, but it doesn't seem like someone should get away with this."

"I wiped my fingerprints off," Dave says. "But I doubt if they're going to send the FBI out here for a beat-up old logging truck."

"What a hoot," Melissa says giggling.

Dave lies low the rest of the weekend then on Monday morning he boards the school bus knowing that after three days of final exams he will be leaving ARC for good. When he gets to the school, Dave goes to the smoking area. The crowd there is unusually quiet, and no one is pitching nickels. Dave sees Terry and John standing off to the side and goes to join them. "Did you hear about Sexy Sally?" Terry asks him.

"What about her?"

"She fucking hung herself."

"Hey, how about showing some respect?" John snaps.

"Yeah, you're right, sorry."

"Sally's dead?" Dave asks in disbelief.

"Yeah, Saturday," John says. He grounds out his cigarette and walks away.

The ARC students are in shock, and they remain subdued that day and the next. But Wednesday, it hits home that this is the last day of school and spirits brighten. Dave goes to his English final in the morning and has no problem with the test. Afterward, the students are allowed out for a break, but ten minutes later they're called back for study hall, which will last until lunch. These long study halls between exams are tedious, so Dave, Terry, and John amuse themselves, when Mrs. Clover isn't looking, by throwing spitwads at the ceiling. Unfortunately, a particularly nasty blob fails to stick, falls, and lands on a girl's head. She leaps to her feet brushing madly at her hair, and the perpetrators crack up. John laughs so hard he slides out of his seat and lies on the floor cackling.

"Dave, John, Terry, get up here," Mrs. Clover exclaims.

The teacher scrawls a note and hands it to John. "Take this to Mr. Danforth, and make sure he signs it before you bring it back."

The three boys leave Mrs. Clover's class and head down the hall toward the principal's office. "Shit, we're going to have to sit there for two hours with the secretary and Danforth watching us the whole time," John complains.

"I've got a better idea," Terry pipes up. "North Augusta."

No one is supposed to leave the campus during the day, but now Terry, John, and Dave rapidly head for the parking lot. Once there they get into John's bright yellow Chevelle SS 396 and peel out.

The first roadhouse John drives to in South Carolina is locked tight, but the door to the next one swings open with a push. Inside, the bartender is washing pitchers in a sink behind the bar. "Hey, we're closed," he says.

"Oh, come on, Chris," John says, laying a five-dollar bill on the bar.

"Well, I already did the mugs, and I'm just finishing up the pitchers," Chris says, pocketing the cash. "I ain't gonna get them dirty again, so let me see if I can find something else to put beer in."

Chris rummages around in the clutter behind the bar and comes up with an empty two-gallon glass bottle. The label reads "Red's Pickled Pigs' Feet." After cursorily rinsing the container, the bartender fills it from the Black Label tap. Then the three boys carry their refreshments along with several Dixie cups to one of the tables. On the way, Dave stops at the jukebox, puts a quarter in, and makes some selections. Soon "Ticket to Ride" comes on and makes Dave feel secretly giddy about the changes taking place in his life. He hasn't told his friends that he's leaving.

"This beats the shit out of study hall," John says after draining a Dixie cup. His upper lip now features a white foam mustache.

"Show us the note Mrs. Clover gave you," Terry asks.

John unfolds the paper and lays it on the table. It reads: "Mr. Danforth, I don't know what to do with these boys."

"I know what I'd do with her," Terry smirks.

"Down boy," Dave says good-naturedly. He doesn't want to hear any garbage about Mrs. Clover.

"Did you see Mary Ellen jump when that mess landed on her pretty head?" John asks, changing the subject. The boys break into laughter and are again on the verge of losing it. They toss down one Dixie cup full of beer after another, and soon John is back at the bar with the nearly empty bottle.

As Chris is refilling the pigs' feet bottle, the front door opens, and another customer enters. He's an unshaven skinny old man dressed in dirty, ragged clothes. "Hey, Chris, gimme a beer, for Chrissake," the newcomer says. The bartender looks at him disdainfully but fills a couple of paper cups and puts them on the bar. With shaking hands, the man makes it to a corner table without spilling too much. He doesn't leave any money.

Herman's Hermits comes on the jukebox with "Mrs. Brown, You've Got A Lovely Daughter," and suddenly John is yelling. "Turn it off, turn it off." He rushes over, pulls the plug, and the record screeches to a halt. Then John covers his face with both hands, and his shoulders heave.

"Hey, man, what is it?" Terry says, putting an arm around his friend.

"Mrs. Riley, you've killed your lovely daughter," John moans through his hands.

"Come over here and sit down."

John finds his seat then sloshes more beer into a cup. "Sorry, that song just got to me," he says after a while. "It was Sally's favorite."

"What did you mean about Mrs. Riley?" Dave asks.

"Oh, she used to beat Sally and stuff," John says.

"Why?"

"Mrs. Riley went crazy when her husband left," John explains. "She always blamed Sally."

"Hey, it's getting late," Terry interjects. "We gotta get back." He takes Mrs. Clover's note over to the derelict at the corner table. "I need you to sign something for me," Terry says and hands him a dollar.

It's a short return trip to the high school and soon Terry, John, and Dave are strolling back into Mrs. Clover's classroom. "I smell beer," the teacher exclaims. "Where have you been?"

"Principal's office," Terry lies. He gives the note to Mrs. Clover, and she unfolds the damp paper. "That's not Mr. Danforth's signature," she exclaims. "You're coming with me, all three of you, now." Mrs. Clover shepherds the boys down to the administrative office, and the school secretary ushers them all in to see Danforth. "I sent these boys to you two hours ago," Mrs. Clover tells him, "with this note." She hands Danforth the paper. "They just now came back smelling like a brewery and, well, did you sign that?"

Danforth glances at the signature. "Hell no," he says. "I certainly did not." The vice principal smiles happily at the three students clutching the note like a winning lottery ticket. "You boys are in big trouble," he grins. "Forgery is a crime in this state, in case you haven't heard." Danforth pauses thoughtfully for a moment and then continues. "Tell you what, though," he says. "You've been a thorn in my side all year, so here's what we'll do. I'm not going to call the police; I'm just going to expel each of you."

"Sir, I have something to tell you," Dave interjects. "Terry and John had nothing to do with this. It was all my idea. I'm the one who signed that note. They didn't sign anything."

Danforth frowns. "Oh, come on," he says. "Do you take me for a fool? You're all in this together."

"I'm the one who did it," Dave insists. "Did it on my own. They knew nothing about it."

"Well, dammit then," Danforth concedes. "I guess you two can go." The vice principal flicks the back of his hand at Terry and John dismissively then turns his attention to Dave. "You're expelled," he says. "I'm putting it on your record."

After emptying his locker, Dave goes outside and idles away the afternoon. When the last exam period ends, hundreds of happy students come streaming out of the school. They mill about in the bright sunshine, laughing and talking excitedly. The Fort Gordon school bus pulls up, so Dave gets in line to climb aboard. He has a last look at ARC and sees clouds of confetti fluttering out of a third-floor window. Then a paper airplane takes flight. It spirals lazily down toward the throng of exuberant students below.

CHAPTER SEVEN
HOLIDAY BREAK

Cameron Stewart teaches world history at Fort Hunt High School in the affluent Washington, DC, suburb of Alexandria, Virginia. The school is in a generic one-story brick building. It's the kind of place you must circle twice to find the main entrance.

With his wavy dark hair and chiseled good looks, Mr. Stewart is considered "cute" by the Fort Hunt High School girls. He's from Massachusetts and recently got his bachelor's degree from Harvard. "Who can tell me what caused the decline of Greek civilization?" he asks his fourth-period class.

"They kept dropping the soap in the shower," Dave Knight responds.

Mr. Stewart grimaces. "You can do better than that," he says.

"Oh, OK," Dave sighs. "The city-states weakened each other with incessant warfare, leaving them vulnerable first to Macedon and later to Rome. They never unified."

"That's right," Stewart says as the bell rings. "Anyone care to elaborate? No? OK then, tomorrow we start Chapter 10, make sure you read pages 162 to 175 and be prepared to answer questions. Class dismissed."

Dave has physics next. He failed chemistry at ARC last year, so now he's trying another tack at getting the second science credit he needs to graduate. Currently, he's just keeping his head above water in the class.

One problem Dave has with physics is the math involved; the other is the teacher, Mr. Baxter. He's a frail, white-haired old man with piercing blue eyes and a deeply lined face. Baxter muddles through his lectures each day in a barely audible voice then sits while Patsy Whitaker, his teacher's assistant, helps the students with the practical portion of the class. Patsy's a Fort Hunt senior who belongs to the National Honor Society and has already completed all the graduation requirements. She's a pretty blonde with a mischievous smile and a buxom figure. Not what you'd expect from a brainiac.

Today, after Mr. Baxter finishes his lecture on the speed of sound, the students break into groups to conduct experiments. The idea is to use an oscilloscope to measure the difference between the time a noise is made and its echo comes back. While Baxter sits at his desk, Patsy moves around the lab helping students. Dave is completely baffled, but the other members of his group get it, and that's good enough.

Physics is Dave's last class of the day. Afterward, he goes out to the bus stop and sees Marie there talking with several friends. At age fifteen she's an attractive, vivacious girl who is very popular at Fort Hunt. Now she goes over to the parking lot and gets into a car with a boy.

On the bus ride home, Dave sits across the aisle from Vinny Rubio. His family lives down the street, and they've become friends. The pair listens to records together, watches TV, and gets into mischief around their neighborhood, which is a few miles south of Mount Vernon. It's a development of two-story faux-colonial homes, and Vinny's is near the first bus stop. "I'll come by your house after I change," Vinny says as he gets off.

A few minutes later the bus stops again, and Dave climbs down then walks the short distance to his house. It's eerily quiet inside with Melissa away at Florida State and Dan now attending a boarding school. Perle isn't home from middle school yet.

Dave goes upstairs and quietly opens his mother's door to see if he can get her anything, but Bobbie's asleep. So, he goes down the hall to his room and changes clothes. Vinny arrives a short time later.

The previous occupants of the house mounted a backboard on the garage, and now Vinny and Dave start a game of horse in the driveway. Neither is any good at basketball, and their athletic endeavor is short lived. "I need a smoke," Vinny says.

The two boys go around to the backyard, and Vinny gets out a pack of Marlboros. He offers it to Dave and then lights both cigarettes. "You hear of any parties tonight?" Vinny asks.

"Nah."

It's Friday, and there are no doubt several parties happening later among the teenagers who attend Fort Hunt, but neither boy was invited. "Guess we can always go to the beer garden," Dave says.

"All right," Vinny agrees. "Hey, what's this thing?" He's pointing to a rectangular-shaped wooden contraception lying in the yard. It's about twelve feet long and three feet wide.

"I don't know," Dave says. "It was here when we moved in, too small to be a sandbox."

"Looks like a homemade boat."

"Yeah, could be a skiff," Dave replies.

"We should try it out."

"Where?"

"The Potomac," Vinny says. "If you go all the way down to the end of the street then cut over, there's a road that leads to some private houses along the river. We used to play there when I was little."

"It's too late," Dave says, taking a final drag on his cigarette. "It would be dark by the time we got there."

"I was thinking maybe tomorrow?"

"Sure."

"OK, good," Vinny says. "Now I got to get home for dinner. Do you want to come by later, say around eight?"

"All right."

After Vinny leaves, Dave stays outside bouncing the basketball and putting up an occasional shot. Then a white car pulls up driven by a boy named Sid who Dave knows from Mr. Stewart's class. Marie's in the passenger seat, and when she opens the door to get out, a beer can clatters to the pavement. She bends to pick it up then tosses it back into the car.

It's grown dark, so Dave follows Marie inside the house. He finds Bobbie in the kitchen fixing herself a cup of chicken bouillon. "Hi, honey, when did you get home?" she asks Dave.

"A little over an hour ago. I've been playing outside."

"So that was you bouncing the ball?"

"Sorry."

"That's OK; I needed to get up and eat something."

"Is that all you're having?"

"No, I'll have toast with it."

"You should let me make you a peanut butter and banana sandwich."

"Maybe another time," Bobbie smiles.

"Do you have some money?" Dave asks. "Vinny and I have plans."

"Sure, just stop by and see me on your way out."

When Dave gets to Vinny's house later, he finds his friend waiting outside. They start walking toward Fort Belvoir, an army post located a couple of miles up the road. It's a crisp fall night, but the exercise soon warms them up. They come to Route 1 then go up the hill a short way and onto the base. It's a section of the post with the same sort of shabbily constructed wooden buildings that Dave is familiar with from Fort Gordon. He and Vinny go into one marked "Beer Garden." The bored PFC behind the counter fills a pitcher for them without asking for ID.

It's late in the month, and a long time since payday, so there are plenty of empty tables. Dave and Vinny choose one, sit down, and fill their mugs. "Why do they call this a beer garden?" Dave asks, looking around. "It's indoors, and there's not so much as a potted plant."

"What do you want them to call it?" Vinny asks, gazing at the bleak surroundings. "A beer sewer?"

"That sounds enticing," Dave laughs. "You've got a future in advertising. I can see you on Madison Avenue now, wearing your gray flannel suit."

"Don't worry, I'll stop by your shoeshine stand for a quick polish," Vinny promises.

"You're all heart," Dave says. "But seriously, what do you plan to do after high school?"

"Get as far away from my old man as possible."

"I need to get away from my entire family," Dave exclaims.

"My sister Kathy moved out two weeks after graduation," Vinny says. "Got a job working for the government and moved downtown."

"You never told me about her."

"Well, now I did."

"So, how long ago did she move?"

"It's been over a year. She hasn't been back since."

"Do you miss her?"

"Hell yes, but I don't blame her."

"I have an older sister too, at college."

"Do you miss her?"

"Nah, I got her room."

Dave and Vinny share another pitcher, then the place closes, and they begin the walk home. When they get to Vinny's house, his father, a Marine lieutenant colonel, is out in the yard with the family's dachshund. He quickly comes over to accost his son. "It's fuckin' cold, but you don't button your fuckin' coat," the officer snarls. "That's because it doesn't look cool buttoned up, right? Am I right?"

Lt. Col. Rubio is a short, stocky man with a swarthy square-jawed face and the sort of eyes that stare back at you from a mug shot. Cords stand out on his neck, and blood vessels throb at his temples as the officer wrenches Vinny's overcoat together then fastidiously buttons it, all the while jerking his son this way and that. "Well, I'm not paying good money for a fuckin' coat and have you waste it," he explains.

Vinny remains passive while trying to keep his feet. Meanwhile, Dave fights the urge to button his own coat. "See you later," he says weakly during a brief lull in Lt. Col. Rubio's tirade.

The next afternoon, Vinny comes over to Dave's house again. The two friends go into the backyard and look dubiously at the thing on the ground. Then Vinny takes hold of one end. "Let's see if it floats," he says. But the boys find that hauling the heavy contraption to the river is not easy. They can only carry it forty or fifty yards at a time before stopping to rest. Soon both are sweating even though it's a cold cloudy November day.

Eventually, Dave and Vinny make it out of the neighborhood and come to a private road that leads to a locked gate. Peering through the bars, they can see down a long white oyster-shell driveway until it bends. "There's a big house, farther down, that overlooks the river," Vinny says.

"How do we get past the fence?" Dave asks.

"We can go around it," Vinny replies. "It ends down there in the woods."

The two boys struggle along the fence line with their boat then turn toward the Potomac. Another half hour of hauling is required before they see the murky water through leafless trees. A few minutes later they're standing on the rocky shore. "It's beautiful," Dave says.

"Yeah, too bad the water's polluted," Vinny replies. "You go swimming out there and have an open sore, you'd be a goner—gangrene."

"What are we going to do for paddles?" Dave asks.

"Hadn't thought of that," Vinny replies. He walks along the bank, stopping here and there to pick up pieces of driftwood. "Here, look at this," he says, holding up part of a weathered board.

"That might work."

"Come help me find another."

After locating another suitable implement for pushing water, Dave and Vinny launch their craft. Soon they are a hundred yards offshore, and now they take a break from paddling to enjoy life on the water.

"See over there?" Vinny says, pointing to the Maryland shore.

"Looks like a Ferris wheel," Dave says.

"It's an amusement park, but it's closed for the winter."

"Too bad."

"Well, the pavilions are still open."

"What's in them?"

"Slot machines."

"You're kidding."

"No, really."

"Let's go," Dave says. "I have a dollar."

"That's a long way."

"You chicken?"

"OK, but we got to paddle hard."

Vinny and Dave paddle furiously and make steady progress. It's hard work but exciting. That's because the boat is slowly filling with water and they're not sure they'll make it. The craft wasn't blessed with much freeboard to begin with, and now it's sitting lower. Occasionally a rogue wave breaks over the side, adding to the water coming through the seams. Finally, a pier looms in front of them, and a few minutes later they ground the boat on the shore. It takes a massive effort to flip it over and empty the vessel. Afterward, they walk through the deserted park. The rides and pavilions appear to be from another century.

Inside one of the buildings are rows of slot machines, and a few people are scattered around the cavernous hall rhythmically pumping coins into the devices. Dave and Vinny get change and try their luck. However, the slots are ruthless, and both are soon busted. It's just as well since the day is waning, and the temperature is dropping. It's time for the voyage home.

Once back at the riverbank, Dave and Vinny flip their vessel right side up. It lands on a metal rod protruding from a chunk of concrete. The boys quickly lift it off the spike, but now there's a neat round puncture in the bottom of the boat.

"We need to plug that hole," Dave observes.

"What with?" Vinny asks.

"My socks maybe?" Dave sits in the sand and removes his sneakers. He takes his socks off and crams them into the hole. "We're going to have to paddle fast," he says. "That won't hold for long."

Vinny picks up a rusty can. "We can use this to bail with."

"Good idea."

Vinny and Dave drag the boat into the water and climb aboard. Then they paddle hard for the Virginia side. But it turns out Dave was right about the sock fix; it's worthless. Bailing helps, but when Vinny is bailing Dave is the only one paddling. Nevertheless, they make it to the middle of the broad river. Now there's no turning back.

As Dave and Vinny desperately work their highly inefficient driftwood paddles, the craft inexorably fills. Then Dave feels the stern sink beneath him. "Swim for it," he shouts.

It's difficult swimming in water-logged clothes, but fear of drowning is a powerful motivator. Even so, both boys eventually run out of gas. Vinny is the first to stop swimming and revert to treading water. His feet touch bottom. "Hey, I can stand up," he yells. Now they know they'll make it.

Both boys are violently shivering as they reach dry land. Their teeth click like Monopoly dice. "Let's run," Vinny says, and they take off for Dave's house.

"Goodness' sake," Bobbie exclaims when Dave bursts into her room, soaking wet.

"Vinny and I fell into the river," Dave says. "He's in the other shower. Can I use yours?"

"Yes, of course."

Later, after a hot bowl of soup, Vinny goes home wearing borrowed clothes. Then Dave gets into bed and burrows under the covers. He luxuriates in the warmth a few moments before plummeting into sleep.

On Monday morning Dave goes to his homeroom at Fort Hunt and takes his usual seat next to Madelyn Grimes. She's a cute girl who wears her thick dark hair parted down the middle. "How was your weekend?" Madelyn asks.

"Well, I'm still alive," Dave replies. "That's all I can say for it."

"Oh, come on."

Dave tells Madelyn about his boating adventure, and at first, she's aghast, then she can't help laughing. "You are truly crazy," she says.

"That seems to be the consensus," Dave agrees.

"Hey, we have playoff game today at four," Madelyn says. "You've been promising to come all season." Madelyn is on the Fort Hunt Federals field hockey team. Her petite size doesn't seem to count against her in the sport.

"OK, I'll be there," Dave agrees.

"You promise?"

"I promise."

Following homeroom, Dave goes to his American literature class and learns that Walt Whitman's poems don't rhyme. He thinks that's cool, but the teacher, Mr. Pritchard disagrees. "You may be unconventional if you're a genius like Whitman," Pritchard says, "but the rest of us need to follow the rules. Now let's talk about meter." The teacher launches into a lecture on the five basic meters and immediately loses Dave. He thinks Pritchard is taking all the fun out of poetry and tunes him out.

After lit, Dave has a ninety-minute study hall and then it's time for lunch. He eats what he can of the cafeteria food, then goes to Mr. Stewart's world history class. He arrives early and finds the teacher already there bantering with students as he waits for the bell to ring. "I can't believe you traded in your GTO for a Mini Cooper," Sid Warner is saying.

"Those three deuces were sucking down gas faster than I could pay for it," Mr. Stewart explains. "And it didn't handle. I took the Mini to a rally on Saturday, and that thing will turn on a dime."

"Well, we like Detroit iron around here," Sid insists.

"Guess I just don't fit in," Stewart replies. "Everything's so different in the South. For example, up north nobody ever refers to a Southerner as a rebel, but you Southerners are always calling us Yankees. Why?"

Dave cannot resist weighing in. "I've been living in Virginia for half a year," he says. "Before that, I lived in Georgia, and in all that time, I never heard anyone refer to a Northerner as a Yankee."

"Oh really?" Mr. Stewart says doubtfully.

"No, sir, it was always damn Yankee," Dave says. "Sometimes it was goddamn Yankee."

"OK, you got me this time," Stewart says good-naturedly. "I asked for it."

Dave intentionally misses the bus after school then sits on a bench to wait for the field hockey match. He gets out a book that he's reading for American lit and immerses himself in the troubles of Hester Prynne. Belatedly Dave remembers about Madelyn, so he goes to the athletic complex. He finds that the field hockey match is underway. To Dave's untutored eye, the game looks like croquet gone mad. There's something comical about the swarm of half-bent-over girls hacking away at the ball, but as he watches, Dave begins to appreciate the skill and physicality of the players. The stickwork is vicious, and Madelyn battles as hard as the rest. But in the end, the Federals lose and are out of the playoffs. Dave waits while the coach has a meeting with the team then runs to catch up with Madelyn as she walks toward the parking lot. She has an Ace bandage wrapped around her knee and is limping. "Thanks for coming," Madelyn says softly.

"Hey, you guys did great," Dave replies.

"Yeah, we gave them a good game," Madelyn sighs. "Springfield's number three in the state. We tried, but nobody thought we had much of a chance."

Dave spontaneously asks the dejected girl out. "Hey, you goin' to the football game Friday?"

"I was thinking about it."

"If you like, I'll meet you there. We can get something to eat afterward."

"I'd love to."

"OK then," Dave says, "see you."

On Friday night Dave is allowed use of the Cadillac. At Fort Hunt, he finds Madelyn inside the stadium by the concession stand. She smiles as Dave approaches, and her spirits have seemingly recovered. The area below her injured knee is still black and blue.

"How did you get here?" Dave asks.

"My parents dropped me off," Madelyn replies.

"I can take you home later," Dave offers.

"OK."

This night Fort Hunt is no match for Woodrow Wilson High School, and the Federals lose 31-7. After the game, Dave takes Madelyn to the Hot Shoppes in Alexandria. "I guess Marie Knight is your sister?" Madelyn asks between bites of her burger.

"That's right."

"She's very popular."

"Marie has a great personality."

"And she's so pretty."

"That too."

"Do you have any other sisters or brothers?"

"I have an older sister at college, another sister a year younger than Marie who's at middle school, and a younger brother away at boarding school."

"That makes five in all."

"Right."

"I'm an only child."

"Lucky you."

"It's boring."

"I'd like to try it," Dave says. "Tell you what, I'll trade with you for a week. You can move into my house, and I'll move into yours."

"That's silly."

"So, what are your plans after graduation?"

"My parents want me to go to college," Madelyn says. "But I want to be a stewardess."

"Can't you do both?" Dave asks. "You know, go to college and then get an airline job."

"Guess I'll have to," Madelyn sighs. "What about you?"

"I'm just concerned about graduating right now," Dave replies. "I'll see what comes along afterward."

Once they finish eating, Dave fights off Madelyn's attempts to go Dutch on the check. Then he takes her home. "This has been fun," he says after walking Madelyn to her door.

"Thanks so much," she replies. "I enjoyed myself."

It takes Dave a long time to find his way out of Madelyn's development. He keeps turning into cul-de-sacs but eventually stumbles onto the main road. As he drives home, Dave wonders what possessed him to ask Madelyn out. She's way too nice for him.

Two days later, Elizabeth and Wilbur Hughes arrive at the Knights' for a visit. It's Thanksgiving week, and they're taking a vacation from Wilbur's medical practice. That evening Bobbie bakes a Virginia ham for the occasion. The clove-tinged aroma coming from the oven whets everyone's appetite, and there's a rush for the dining room when Bobbie announces, "Dinner is served." Knight stands at the head of the table and carves.

"The ham smells great," Elizabeth exclaims, "and I'm starving."

"Pass your plate up here," Knight suggests. "I have the perfect slice for you."

"How has your trip been so far?" Bobbie asks.

"That interstate is the best thing Ike ever did," Wilbur exclaims.

"D-day was no slouch," Dave mutters. Then he shuts up under his father's wrathful glare.

"We stopped in Savannah," Elizabeth says brightly. "It's a beautiful town; our hotel was right on the river."

"When it comes to sight-seeing, Washington can't be beat," Knight brags. "We'll go to the mall tomorrow, visit the Capitol, and see all the monuments."

"Oh goody," Elizabeth says and beams at her husband. "Honey, this'll be like a second honeymoon."

"I hope not," Wilbur responds. "The first one was bad enough." Elizabeth's smile freezes on her face.

"Who wants dessert?" Bobbie asks to change the subject. "I made peach cobbler, and you can have vanilla ice cream on top." Dave, Marie, and Perle all wave their hands enthusiastically while their father glowers at them.

"I'd prefer a shot of something," Wilbur says.

"I can pour you a Cointreau, if you like," Bobbie offers. "We also have a decent brandy."

"Either will do," Wilbur shrugs.

"I'll have what he's having," Knight chimes in.

"Just don't give this kid anything," Wilbur says, jerking his thumb in Dave's direction.

The next morning, Knight takes Elizabeth and Wilbur into Washington. When they return that evening, Knight's toting a cardboard box full of lobsters. They blink their eyes and wave their claws.

"I always wanted to try lobster," Marie says.

"These are for the grown-ups," Knight replies. "I got flounder for you guys. You'll like it."

After the tourists have had time to freshen up, they gather in the living room for much-needed drinks. "Look what I got for Hailey," Elizabeth exclaims. She holds up a T-shirt that says: "I walked my ___ off in Washington, DC." A mule is pictured kicking up its heels.

"That's cute," Bobbie says.

"And it perfectly describes our day," Wilbur grumbles.

Once cocktail hour is over, Knight makes dinner for the kids and they eat in the kitchen. Afterward, he sends them upstairs. "I need you to find something quiet to do," he tells them. "Read, watch TV, whatever. I'm counting on you to let me entertain our guests without disturbances."

Knight returns to the kitchen to steam the lobsters while Bobbie sets the table and pours the wine. Then she calls the guests to the dining room, and in no time, everyone is busy dismembering the crustaceans. "This lobster is great," Elizabeth says between bites. "You know, the best part of today was that fish market."

"Very few tourists ever see it," Knight explains. "It's off the beaten path. The seafood all comes from the Eastern Shore."

"No wonder it's so fresh," Elizabeth enthuses. "It's too bad we have to leave. I'd go back tomorrow."

"Florida doesn't lack seafood," Bobbie observes.

"True, if you go to a restaurant," Wilbur replies, "or a seafood store, but I don't know any place where they sell it off the boat like that."

"Speaking of Florida, how does Melissa like FSU?" Elizabeth inquires.

"She loves Florida State, especially her sorority," Bobbie says. "She's going home with one of the sisters for Thanksgiving."

"What about grades?" Elizabeth asks. "Mindy joined a sorority when she went, and after that, all she did was go to parties."

"Melissa's getting straight A's so far," Knight says proudly.

"Hailey did the same when she was at FSU," Wilbur brags. "She learned from Mindy's mistake."

"Well, Mindy was never cut out for college," Elizabeth comments. "The main thing is she met Roger there. Now she's pregnant with number three, and he just opened another Burger King. Those things are gold mines. You should see the house they bought."

"As always, Phyliss is the problem child," Wilbur complains. "She married Larry Stallings even though we warned her about him. Sure enough, he was out in the bars again the week after they eloped. Then he got drafted because he wasn't in college. The army was going to send him to Vietnam, so he volunteered for airborne training. Larry thought he'd be safe because they don't parachute into the jungle, but now he has orders for Vietnam after all."

"It's nothing to worry about," Knight says. "He has as much chance of dying in a car wreck right here as he does to get shot in Vietnam."

"Phyliss is beside herself," Elizabeth says. "She wanted me to ask if you could do anything."

"Sure, I could get his orders changed," Knight replies. "But it wouldn't be right. I get these requests from people all the time. If I did it for Larry, I'd have to do it for all the others."

"But he's practically flesh and blood," Elizabeth persists.

"All the more reason why it would be wrong for me to intervene," Knight declares. "Tell Phyliss I said it's going to be all right. There are plenty of safe jobs Larry can get over there. For every soldier in combat we have nine in support; mail clerks, company clerks, drivers, cooks, just to name a few. Those guys are constantly completing their tours and must be replaced. When Larry gets in-country, he needs to ask his sergeant for one of those jobs."

"All right," Elizabeth agrees. "I'll tell Phyliss."

The next morning, Elizabeth and Wilbur leave for New York. After they're gone, Dave helps Bobbie gather the linens and towels from their room and put them in the wash. A little later, Dan calls. He's at the Greyhound station, so Dave is sent to get him. He finds his brother waiting outside the terminal looking princely in his gray military school dress uniform. "Get that bag and stow it in the vehicle, peasant," Dan orders.

"I'd rather be a peasant than a private," Dave grins, eyeing the lone chevron on his brother's sleeve.

"Hey, you've got to start somewhere," Dan laughs.

When the brothers get home, Bobbie meets them at the door. "Don't you look handsome," she exclaims, hugging her youngest son. Dan towers over her, his back as straight as the spike on a Prussian helmet.

Dan goes upstairs and quickly changes into jeans and a sweater. Then he settles in front of the TV. It's a good day for it, rainy and cold. Unfortunately, that's how the weather stays over the entire Thanksgiving holiday. Unable to go outside, the Knights rely on squabbling, gluttony, and televised football to get through the weekend. Then it's over, and Dave takes Dan back to the bus station.

That night Melissa finally calls. "How was Thanksgiving?" she asks her mother.

"Wonderful," Bobbie replies. "Aunt Elizabeth and Uncle Wilbur stopped by for a visit, and Dan came home."

"That's good," Melissa says. "I had a nice time too. Cynthia's family is great. They've asked me to come for Christmas as well."

"Absolutely not," Bobbie replies.

"Oh, come on, Mom," Melissa pleads. "I don't know anyone in Virginia. All my friends are here. I don't see why I can't stay."

"I'm not going to have you traipsing around Florida for the better part of a month sleeping on people's sofas," Bobbie replies. "You're coming home."

So, three weeks later, Melissa shows up in Alexandria driving the Opel. On Christmas Eve, she sits with the rest of the family as Knight recites *The Night Before Christmas*. It's a family tradition.

After Christmas, there's not much for the family to do out in the suburbs. Knight tries to organize a poker game one day but abandons the effort when both Melissa and Dan refuse. Monopoly is also a thing of the past. So, during their time off from school, the younger Knight children vegetate in front of the TV while Dave reads and Melissa talks on the phone. "How do you expect me to pay the long-distance bill?" her father demands.

"They call me just as often as I call them," Melissa retorts.

Finally, it's New Year's Eve. As the Knights prepare for a family celebration, Marie makes an announcement. "I have to go to a party," she says.

"What do you mean?" Knight replies. "We always stay home on New Year's."

"It's a sorority thing," Marie shrugs.

"Then go ahead," Bobbie agrees.

After Marie leaves, the rest of the Knights follow their usual New Year's routine. They gather in front of the fireplace and listen to music during the early part of the evening then Knight dons his tuxedo, Bobbie gets into an evening dress, and the children make themselves presentable. As the grandfather clock tolls midnight, the family sings a rousing "Auld Lang Syne," and Knight pops the cork on a bottle of champagne. Everyone's in festive spirits until a police officer knocks on the door. He's holding Marie up by the arm. She appears to be very drunk.

"I gave this one a summons for public intoxication," the cop says. "The kid who was driving is in jail."

"We weren't doin' nothin'," Marie mumbles.

"I'll take her," Bobbie says, pushing past her husband.

The patrolman seems relieved to have someone take Marie off his hands and quickly departs. Bobbie takes Marie upstairs while the rest of the family returns to the living room. But the fizz has gone out of the party.

Two days later Dan goes back to military school. The following morning Perle, Marie, and Dave must drag themselves out of bed in the darkness to resume their studies. However, Melissa is still on vacation and can sleep in. It's almost noon when she comes downstairs holding a folder.

"What have you got there?" Bobbie asks.

"Student loan papers Dad was supposed to sign. I forgot all about it," Melissa says.

"Let me see," Bobbie demands. She looks over the papers. "They wanted these back last month."

"Oh."

"You have to go to your father's office right away and take care of this."

"Can't it wait till he gets home?" Melissa asks. "How am I going to find him in that place?"

"No, it can't wait," Bobbie says. "We need to send these off today, or you won't have money for spring tuition. Go upstairs and get dressed. I'll write instructions for finding Dad's office and let him know you're coming."

Once she's ready, Melissa drives to the Pentagon and follows directions to Knight's office. Inside she finds the receptionist waiting for her. "The colonel was in a meeting," she says, "but he's hurrying back."

A few minutes later the office door is thrown open by Sergeant Major Reynier, who stands aside as Knight comes in. Melissa is shocked to see Captain Kinsey enter behind her father. "What's he doing here?" she gasps.

"Why, he works here of course," Knight replies.

Melissa backs away from her father as if he has suddenly sprouted horns and a tail. "You bastard," she cries then snatches a nameplate off a nearby desk and hurls it. Knight dodges the missile as Melissa rushes out of the office.

When she gets home, Melissa brushes past her mother and runs upstairs. Bobbie follows. "What's going on?" she asks.

"I'm getting out of here," Melissa says. "And I'm never coming back." She opens her suitcase on the bed and starts throwing clothes into it.

"What happened?"

"Dad brought Captain Kinsey up here with him."

"What's wrong with Captain Kinsey?"

"He tried to rape me."

"No!"

"Yes!"

"Why didn't you tell me?"

"I told Dad," Melissa replies. "Didn't want to worry you. I thought when we moved that'd be the end of it."

Outside, the high school bus pulls up with the middle school bus close behind it. As Dave, Marie, and Perle walk from the bus stop toward home, Knight speeds past them in the Cadillac. He parks then storms into the house as Melissa is coming down the stairs with her suitcase. Knight blocks her path. "What's got into you?" he hollers.

Melissa can't get past her father on the staircase. "Bastard," she hisses.

"You're not going anywhere unless you tell me what this is about," Knight exclaims.

"She tells me you know what it's about," Bobbie says from the top of the stairs.

"Oh, I know she has this cockamamie idea Captain Kinsey wanted to molest her," Knight replies. "It's all nonsense. The man tripped and fell on her. She went berserk, just like now."

"Tripped and just happened to jam his hand between my legs?" Melissa asks. "He tried to feel me up. That's what he did."

"You're lying."

"I don't think so," Marie says. She and Perle have come in the front door.

Knight turns. "What do you know about it?" he snaps.

"I know Captain Kinsey used to come to my bed at night," Marie answers. "He put his hand between my legs . . . and more."

Melissa looks at her sister aghast. "Why didn't you scream?"

"I don't know," Marie answers. "Maybe I was curious. He said I'd like it."

"Now you're lying," Knight says to Marie.

"No, she isn't," Perle murmurs. "I was there."

Bobbie leans against the wall and weeps as her husband descends the stairs and opens the door. "I'm not listening to any more of this garbage," he says. "I'll be at Belvoir."

"Better hurry," Marie suggests. "It's happy hour."

CHAPTER EIGHT
HOT WIRE

Kathy Rubio is Vinny's sister. She lives in a Catholic home for single women near Logan Circle in Washington, DC. Lately Dave and Vinny have been going to visit her nearly every weekend. Afterward, they stop off at a restaurant they found that sells Rolling Rock pony bottles for half a buck.

To get to Kathy's place, Dave and Vinny catch a bus to downtown Alexandria and then transfer to one that goes up 14th Street. It's tedious, but Dave doesn't mind. Kathy's a lovely dark-haired, dark-eyed girl and he has a secret crush on her.

Late one Saturday afternoon in April, Dave and Vinny are at Kathy's sparsely furnished efficiency. Vinny sprawls on a daybed while Dave sits in a small stuffed chair. It's coming to the end of visiting hours and residents in nearby apartments are cooking dinner. Many are from the Philippines, and the pungent odor of spicy food wafts down the hall. "How do you stand the smell?" Vinny asks his sister.

"It tastes better than it smells," Kathy says. "They often invite me to dinner, and I've come to like the food."

"What are they doing here?"

"They're hospital nurses," Kathy replies. "Not enough American women want to do it. I know I wouldn't."

"It probably pays more than you make as a secretary."

"Yes, but they send most of what they make home. None of them ever has any money."

"That reminds me, sis," Vinny says. "Would you be able to spare me a few bucks? You know, for bus fare."

"You mean beer fare," Kathy says, laughing. "I know you two aren't here just to visit me."

"You should come out with us sometime."

"Oh, I'm sure Father Martinez would enjoy hearing all about that at confession."

"Drinking isn't a sin."

"No, but gluttony is."

"I can't remember the last time I went to confession," Vinny sighs.

"Tell you what," Kathy says. "I can give you a five, but only if you promise to go to mass and make a confession."

"It's a deal."

"All right, then," Kathy says, getting her purse. "Will I see you next weekend?"

"Most likely."

Vinny and Dave make their way downstairs and out to 14th Street. Then they stroll up the block to the seedy little restaurant they've come to frequent. Inside, a few elderly men are eating dinner at tables scattered around the room. The two boys sit at the counter and order beers.

The only downside to Rolling Rock is that the little bottles don't last long. Soon Vinny and Dave have put away several. "Remember to save enough money for the bus," Vinny cautions.

"Yeah, we don't want to walk home," Dave agrees.

"Of course, we could always steal a car," Vinny fantasizes.

"What do you know about stealing cars?"

"You have to hot-wire it."

"Oh, I can do that," Dave brags. "Somebody showed me once. All you do is get a screwdriver and hold the metal end against the two contacts on the starter; that short-circuits it."

"We don't have a screwdriver."

"Guess we'd better save enough for the bus then."

"I hate riding the bus."

"I hate walking."

"We've got enough for one more round."

Dave and Vinny finish their beer, then go outside. They head down the street toward the bus stop. It's dark now, and a chill wind swirls around the squat buildings on either side. They approach a white Chevy Biscayne double-parked outside a liquor store. No one's inside. "Look, the motor's running," Vinny says, pointing to a cloud of vapor coming from the exhaust.

Dave walks around the vehicle and sees that the driver's door is unlocked. He opens it, slides behind the wheel then reaches over and pushes the passenger side door open for Vinny. "Get in," he says.

"This is crazy," Vinny protests, but he too gets inside.

Dave puts the car in gear, steps on the gas, and lets out the clutch. The car bucks and then stalls. *Must be some kind of trap*, Dave thinks. He panics for a moment then checks the hand brake and finds it pulled out. He releases it and tries again. Now they're rolling, and Vinny is giggling maniacally. "I can't believe this," he keeps saying. "I mean, I cannot believe this shit."

"We need to get out of DC and into Virginia," Dave declares. His heart pounds as they stop and wait for traffic lights. Finally, they're on their way across the 14th Street Bridge.

"Hey, you missed the turn for the parkway," Vinny exclaims as Dave merges onto I-95 toward Springfield.

"I thought better of it," Dave replies. "We don't want to drive this thing through Alexandria."

"Oh right," Vinny agrees. Alexandria is one traffic light after another all monitored by the local fuzz.

"We can take 95 to the Van Dorn Street exit," Dave explains. "Then go south until we hit Route 1."

"If you say so," Vinny replies. "I've never been that way."

"I did it every day going and coming last summer."

"How come?"

"Went to summer school at Edison."

"Oh."

"Yeah, we'll go right by the school," Dave says, "and believe me, Van Dorn will be deserted this time of night."

Sure enough, Van Dorn Street is mostly empty of traffic, and the rest of the trip home is uneventful. After dropping Vinny off, Dave drives to the next development, parks the Chevy in front of a darkened house, and wipes the steering wheel. Then he walks home, has a sandwich, and gets into bed.

On Monday morning Dave is back at Fort Hunt. He takes his usual seat in homeroom next to Madelyn. "How was your weekend?" she asks.

"Boring," Dave replies.

"Have you been to guidance about graduation?"

"Yeah, they wanted fifteen dollars to rent a cap and gown. I said no way."

"What do you mean? You have to be at graduation."

"Not according to guidance," Dave replies. "They said if I don't pay, I can't walk. They'll just mail the diploma."

"Oh, come on," Madelyn says, "what's fifteen dollars?"

"I'll think about it."

"Please, you've got to."

Madelyn is full of school spirit, but Dave has none. He only wants out, and that means he must pass physics. Dave grinds away at it over the next month, but he's still on the bubble as graduation approaches.

One day, after school, Dave is at the bus stop when a white car pulls up. "Hey, Knight," Sid Warner calls, "hop in." Marie's in front with Sid, so Dave gets in back with Patsy Whitaker, who's seated on the other side. "Hi, Dave," she says.

"Hey, Patsy."

"Your sister said not to, but I figured why not give you a lift?" Sid laughs.

"Thanks."

"You cracked me up in Mr. Stewart's class today."

"Mr. Stewart's cool, he can take a joke."

"Not like Mr. Baxter," Patsy says.

"He's awful," Dave agrees. "All he does is sit there. If it weren't for you, half the class would be failing."

Sid turns north on the parkway instead of south. "Hey, where are we going?" Dave asks.

"Drug Fair," Marie answers. "They have Schmidt's on sale for ninety-nine cents."

"It's always on sale for ninety-nine cents," Dave says.

A few minutes later, Sid pulls up in front of the drug store. "You go in," Marie says to her brother. "You look older." She hands Dave a five and Patsy gives him a dollar.

Dave goes into the store, gets an armload of six-packs from the cooler, and plunks them down next to the register. The woman behind the counter eyes him suspiciously. She appears to be close to seventy, with wrinkled skin that's just as gray as her hair. "How old are you?" she asks.

"I'm twenty-two but I know I look younger," Dave says, holding his driver's license out. He points at the birth date while the woman squints myopically. After giving her a long look, Dave pulls the card back. "I don't blame you for checking," he says in a friendly way. "You can't be too careful."

The woman uncertainly rings up the sale and gives Dave his change. He walks out carrying two paper sacks full of cheap beer.

"Hoowee," Sid hollers once Dave is back in the car. "I knew you could do it."

Sid drives them back to the parkway and heads south. Soon he pulls into an unoccupied overlook, and the high schoolers begin working on the beer. At first, Dave feels awkward drinking with his sister, but after a while, he doesn't care.

"Shit," Sid says, holding up a pull ring that has separated from the tab.

"I hate it when that happens," Dave comments.

"What I hate is breaking a nail," Patsy declares. "Open this one for me, will you?" Dave takes Patsy's can, pulls the ring, and starts to push it back into her beer. "That's dangerous," Patsy says. "What if I swallow it?"

"Don't be such a chicken," Dave laughs.

"I need to pee," Marie exclaims.

"There are some likely bushes," Sid says and points out his window.

"I'll go with you," Patsy offers.

"Where are you going to college?" Sid asks Dave once Patsy and Marie are gone.

"Nowhere," Dave replies. "I'm done with school for a while."

"I don't blame you," Sid agrees. "But my dad is sending me to Ohio State. That's where he went."

"Beats going to Vietnam, I guess."

"For sure."

The two girls come back to the car, and now it's Dave's and Sid's turn to take a nature walk. They find a spot then stand gazing across the river with the sun going down behind them. A nineteenth-century stone fort is partially visible among the trees on the far bank.

Back in the car, Marie and Sid start kissing while in the back Dave gingerly moves his feet trying to find room for them among the empty cans. He turns to grab another cold one, but Patsy is close by, and they too begin making out. Patsy's wearing a light fragrance; her lips are soft, and so is her hair. She's altogether delightful, but all too soon the car starts moving, and they must break their clinch. "Sorry, guys," Sid says, "but if I'm late for dinner, it's big trouble."

When Dave and Marie get home, they find a casserole warming in the oven. After making plates for themselves, they sit at the kitchen table to eat. A little later Bobbie comes in. "I'm glad you started on your dinner," she says. "I've been on the phone with Melissa."

"What about?" Marie asks.

"She got married," Bobbie replies. "To a boy from FSU. They eloped."

"Where are they going to live?" Marie asks.

"On the Eastern Shore of Maryland. That's where he's from."

"Oh, that's not far," Dave ventures. "Better than if she was going to stay in Florida or something."

"That's right," Bobbie says sadly, "not far. I'm sure we'll see her once in a while. Now you kids make sure you have dessert. Ice cream is in the freezer."

"Thanks, Mom."

The following week there's a flurry of senior activities at Fort Hunt, including prom and graduation practice, but Dave skips these. His only desire now is to graduate. That becomes a cinch the day before the physics final when Patsy comes up to him in the hallway and slips him some stapled-together papers. "It's the key to the exam," she whispers.

"Patsy, you're a lifesaver."

"Just don't do too well on it. Baxter would get suspicious."

"You don't have to worry about that."

Even though he has the answers, Dave doesn't score high enough on the physics exam to raise his D to a C. But he passes, and that means he'll graduate. Dave walks out of Fort Hunt for the last time without a backward glance.

CHAPTER NINE
ROCK CREEK

The want ads in the *Washington Post* have been full of openings the last few weeks, and Dave has been on several job interviews. However, he has yet to receive an offer. The problem isn't just his miserable high school GPA, the main impediment is Dave's 1-A draft classification. So after repeatedly striking out, he resolves to take what he can get. This turns out to be a minimum-wage gig as a desk clerk at Arlington Towers Apartments.

Mrs. Vanessa Richfield is the resident manager of Arlington Towers. She's a slightly overweight middle-aged lady with broad but attractive features. Mrs. Richfield has a charming smile, but Dave can tell that she's not the type to put up with any nonsense. In this regard, she reminds him of Mrs. Clover.

On his first morning of work, Mrs. Richfield is at the front desk waiting when Dave comes in. "You're early," she says approvingly. "How about a cup of coffee?"

"No, thanks."

"Don't you like coffee?"

"Not really."

"Well, I suggest you get used to it," Mrs. Richfield says. "It comes in handy on the graveyard shift."

"OK, I'll try some."

"Now you're talking."

Presently Mrs. Richfield and Dave are seated at the front desk sipping java. "Let me give you the lay of the land," the resident manager says. "This property has sixteen floors with twelve apartments on each floor, so we have as many people living here as some small towns. Your job is to answer the phone, greet the tenants as they come and go, be on the alert for anyone who doesn't belong, and operate the PBX switchboard."

"Sounds good," Dave replies.

"The PBX is mainly for switching internal calls, so it's not used much."

"Good."

"Most of the situations you will encounter at the front desk will be routine, but for anything out of the ordinary you are to call me."

"Yes, ma'am."

"Of course, in an emergency, I would want you to call the police or fire department first."

"That makes sense."

"You'll start on the day shift for three days, then have three swing shifts, and after that three midnights. Then you get three days off before starting on days again."

"All right."

For the next hour, Mrs. Richfield trains Dave on the PBX while pausing now and then to speak to residents who pass by on their way to work. Then she goes into her office nearby. "Call me if you need anything," she says.

"Will do."

The lobby stays busy for a while, and Dave tries to speak to each tenant, but gradually, traffic slows, and now he takes the opportunity to look around. Arlington Towers is a moderately priced apartment building with few pretensions. The spacious lobby is attractively but not opulently furnished. Light brown commercial carpeting gives the space warmth, and there are several seating arrangements. The sofas and chairs appear comfortable, but not enough to encourage people to linger. A series of unobtrusive overhead fixtures provide lighting.

Soon lobby traffic ceases entirely, and Dave gets a book out of his bag. He has discovered Barbara Tuchman, thanks to the Alexandria Public Library, and soon he's immersed in the run-up to the Great War. The phone only occasionally interrupts since most of the residents have direct lines. As Dave expected, this job will leave plenty of time for reading.

Over the next several months, Dave gets to know many of Arlington Towers' residents. He finds that the evening shift is best for this because people are in a much better mood coming home than they are leaving. Also, many of the residents seem lonely. They delay taking the elevator up to an empty apartment by loitering at the front desk.

Often, Connie Robinson stops to chat. She's a tall, sturdily built girl with a pleasant open face framed by long brownish blond hair. Connie owns a wig store in DC and often works late styling hairpieces. "It sucks having to work when everyone else is out on the town," she complains one Saturday night as she comes in.

"Oh, I don't care," Dave replies.

"Well, I do," Connie exclaims. "I hate it. Now it's too late for me to go out. By the time I'd be ready it would be after midnight."

"Nothing's to stop you from going upstairs and pouring yourself a drink after a long day."

"I don't drink when I'm alone."

"That's probably wise."

"Hey, I've got an idea," Connie says. "You get off at twelve, right?"

"Yes."

"You could come up and have a drink with me, couldn't you?"

"Of course," Dave answers. "I never turn down a drink."

"Sound policy," Connie laughs.

Dave's relief shows up an hour later, and after exchanging a few pleasantries with the elderly man, Dave leaves him at the desk then takes an elevator up to Connie's floor. She opens the door wearing a loosely fitting house dress. "I'm blow drying," she says. "There's liquor and beer in the kitchen."

Dave grabs a Budweiser from the refrigerator then returns to the living room. A little later Connie comes back. "Can I get you one of these?" Dave offers.

"Nah, I'm gonna make me a drink," Connie says as she saunters across the room, breasts swaying beneath the fabric of her dress. She dumps a good four fingers of Southern Comfort into a tumbler then plops down onto the sofa next to Dave.

"Imagine dropping off a wig at four o'clock on Saturday and expecting it to be ready to wear Monday morning," Connie says. "What's wrong with people?"

"It takes all kinds," Dave observes.

"The problem is I spoil my customers," Connie gripes. "But if I didn't, they'd go somewhere else."

"You're young to own your own business," Dave says.

"Oh, my parents set me up," Connie explains. "What happened is, well, you have to understand, I've always been crazy about wigs for some reason. So when it came time for me to go to college, I told my parents, 'Hey, just let me have the money for a wig store.' The rest is history," Connie laughs then downs the rest of her drink. "You done with that?" she asks.

"I am now," Dave says and polishes off his beer. He thinks that Connie's about to get them another round. But she has something else in mind.

"Good," she says, smiling broadly, "let's go to bed."

Dave doesn't get much rest that night. Connie is insatiable and seems determined to initiate him into every known sexual variation. But as morning light filters through the blinds, Dave remembers the advice boxing referees give fighters before every match: "Protect yourself at all times." He deploys a stout defense, which Connie playfully attempts to overcome. Eventually, she gives up, and the pair drifts off to sleep.

As time passes and Dave settles into his job, he discovers that the worst thing about it is the midnight shift. Reading won't keep him awake on the graveyard. Instead, Dave often goes out in the lobby and paces back and forth. It's usually dead quiet, but occasionally, determined revelers enliven the small hours with their comings and goings. One such is Connie, who brings assorted men into the building at odd times. She often winks at Dave as she passes the desk, and he isn't a bit jealous. Connie still invites him up occasionally, and he's always happy to oblige. There's nothing proprietary about their relationship.

During the spring, Dave gets to know Gary Brooks and Stephanie Podolski. They live in a one-bedroom on the tenth floor. Gary's most notable feature is shoulder-length silky black hair, which along with a scraggly goatee and a perpetually sympathetic expression gives him the look of an Old Testament prophet. He wears bell-bottom jeans, flowered shirts, and various ornamental accessories. Gary's always with Stephanie, a short, pleasantly plump redhead with a friendly freckled face. Her hair is usually in braids, Indian style, and when not in jeans she wears short "mother earth" smocks sans bra. Stephanie carries a fringed buckskin bag instead of a purse.

On a Saturday morning in April, Gary and Stephanie come off the elevator and stop by the front desk. "Too bad you're stuck in here all day," Gary says.

"Yeah, bummer," Stephanie agrees.

"Where are you two going?" Dave asks.

"To the beach," Gary replies.

"What beach?"

"The P Street beach."

Dave is baffled; the closest beach he knows is Ocean City. "Well, have fun," he says.

The following week, Dave sees Stephanie and Gary again on a Friday evening as they're coming in from work. "Must be nice having a job where all you do is read," Gary says jokingly.

"Hey, I have to answer the phone, water the plants, shoo the winos away, and a bunch of other stuff," Dave replies.

"Sounds tough."

"OK, so what do you do?"

"We work in the stacks."

"What's that?"

"Library of Congress," Stephanie says. "The books you see on display downstairs are just the tip of the iceberg. Most of the library's collection is on the top floors."

"In stacks?"

"They used to be stacked up back in the old days, and that's how it got the name," Gary says. "Nowadays they're shelved, but you wouldn't believe how many floors of shelves."

"Yeah, like acres and acres," Stephanie elaborates.

"So what do you do?"

"Well, say a reporter, author, congressional aide, whatever comes in and wants a book," Stephanie says. "They fill out a chit, give it to a librarian, she shoots it up to our floor, then one of us has to go find the book and send it down."

"Sounds easy enough."

"Problem is it's filthy up there."

"Yeah, some of those books haven't been read for a hundred years," Gary says.

"Imagine the dirt," Stephanie exclaims, "and it's always either too hot or too cold."

"So, they can't keep people," Gary elaborates, "and they hire anybody."

"Even longhairs," Stephanie says. "It's groovy."

"We all hang out at the beach when it's nice," Gary explains. "You ought to come sometime."

"OK, when?" Dave says. "I want to see this beach."

"How 'bout tomorrow?" Gary asks. "Are you off?"

"I start midnights tomorrow, so I have the whole day free."

"Good. Meet us here at noon."

"All right."

The next day, it turns out that the "beach" is a grassy field next to Rock Creek. To get there Stephanie, Gary, and Dave walk across Key Bridge through Georgetown. After crossing the P Street Bridge, they take a path down to the field where a good-sized crowd of young people has assembled. Some stand in groups talking while others throw Frisbees back and forth. Many lie on blankets to catch rays.

"What's with all these people?" Dave asks.

"It's a happening," Stephanie explains. She spreads an Amish quilt on the ground, and she and Gary sit.

"What's a happening?" Dave asks.

"People come, and we see what happens," Gary explains.

Stephanie reaches into her bag and pulls out a Sucrets tin. She opens it and removes a little square of blotter paper, which she offers to Dave. "This helps," she says.

"What is it?"

"LSD. Just put it in your mouth and swallow," Stephanie suggests. "We dropped ours already."

Dave hesitates a moment. He has read news stories about LSD and now here it is. *What the hell*, he thinks, then takes the paper, pops it into his mouth, and gulps.

"Hey, give him one more," Gary says. "For insurance."

"Yeah, it's a bummer when you don't get off," Stephanie says and gives Dave another hit.

"No worries here," Gary laughs.

"Me too," Stephanie giggles.

A black guy with a big Afro comes over. "What's happening?" he asks.

"You, man," is Gary's reply.

"Always."

"This is Dave."

"Hey, man, I'm Phil."

"Hello."

"This beats the hell out of the stacks, huh?" Stephanie says.

"Right on," Phil replies. "Fresh air, sunshine, what more could you want?"

"Oh, we're into sunshine, all right," Stephanie smirks.

"Big time," says Gary. They giggle.

"How can you do that shit?" Phil asks.

"How can you not?" Stephanie smiles.

"You bring your Frisbee?" Phil asks.

Stephanie gets the toy out of her bag and hands it over. "Get your lame ass up," Phil says to Gary. The two of them go off to play.

Dave takes Gary's place on the quilt, and since Stephanie's placidly taking in the scene and doesn't appear to be talkative, he stretches out. The sun feels good on his face, and soon he dozes off.

After a time, the hubbub from the happening becomes part of Dave's dream. He's in detention hall, and everyone's talking and laughing. Someone throws a paper airplane, and it floats out of the window, landing in a field of brightly colored quilts. It's shockingly vivid, and Dave comes awake, sits up, and opens his eyes. The light makes him squint, but he can make out the figures of Gary and Phil through the rippling air. Moving in slow motion, one of them elegantly pirouettes then releases the Frisbee. It sails through the air leaving a contrail like a high-altitude jet. "So, you finally woke up," Stephanie murmurs.

"This is wild," Dave declares.

"Like it?"

"Yes."

Dave gazes across the field at the trees along Rock Creek. Each is a mosaic of green colors, with every shade from light chartreuse to dark olive. *An artist could come here with only green paints and create a masterpiece*, Dave thinks. Then a gust of wind gets the entire leaf display shimmering and shaking. Dave wishes he had a movie camera to capture the effect. *People would pay good money to sit in a theatre and watch this*, he thinks, mesmerized. But as the afternoon wanes, the colors slowly lose their vibrancy. Then the sun goes behind one of the buildings that rim the park. Dave looks around and sees that many of the people have left.

"I'm gonna smoke a bowl," Stephanie says. "It makes coming down easier."

"OK," Dave replies.

"You want some?" Stephanie asks, holding up a corncob pipe.

"What is it?"

"Pot."

"Oh."

"So, you've never smoked."

"No."

"Well, come on, I'll show you."

"Where are we going?"

"Under the bridge," Stephanie says. "Can't smoke dope out here in the open." Dave gets stiffly to his feet and follows Stephanie. Her gingham smock billows around her as she walks.

Beneath the bridge, it's a different world, darker and much cooler. The low roof makes it like a cave. Stephanie climbs onto the broad wall that borders the creek and Dave follows. They sit and dangle their legs over the water that froths and foams as it rushes over and around boulders that give the stream its name. "Here, hold this," Stephanie says, handing Dave the pipe, which is lined with a square of perforated aluminum foil. She takes a film canister out of her bag and sprinkles some weed onto the foil. "It's not like smoking a cigarette," she tells Dave. "You don't take a puff and then inhale; you inhale straight down like this." Stephanie takes the pipe and holds it to her lips to demonstrate. Then she hands it back to Dave, strikes a match, and holds the flame over the bowl.

Dave draws the smoke straight down as directed, and it comes right back up in a paroxysm of coughing. He doesn't remove the pipe stem from his mouth, so the contents of the bowl are blown up into the air. For a moment the glowing embers hang suspended, then they flutter down and disappear into the turbulent water. "Never seen that before," Stephanie comments.

Stephanie reloads the pipe. "This time take it easy," she instructs. "You need to start with small tokes until you get used to it." Dave takes the pipe, and this time gets a little smoke down before passing it to Stephanie who takes a long slow pull. She holds her breath while Dave has another turn, then Stephanie sprinkles more pot into the bowl, and they repeat the process. "You good?" she asks afterward. Dave nods his head, so Stephanie puts her paraphernalia away. As she twists to put the bag beside her, the hem of the smock rides up her thigh. Dave can't resist touching Stephanie's bare leg, and at once they're passionately kissing. One thing leads to another, and the couple improvises a way to make love on the wall. Later, they go in search of Gary. "He's not my old man," Stephanie explains. "Gary's more like a roommate. My husband's in the Navy."

At midnight when Dave goes to work, he's still feeling high. But soon the bottom falls out. He paces all night trying to outrun a sense of foreboding. Frequently he goes outside to look at the sky, and eventually it lightens. A couple more hours pass and then his relief shows up. Dave endures the bus ride home then goes upstairs and throws himself fully clothed onto his bed. That afternoon when he wakes up, his brain feels like it's been wrung out.

Dave makes it through two more nights on the graveyard; then he's off for three days. During that time, Dave finds that he misses his friends from work. At this point, many residents of Arlington Towers won't pass the desk when Dave's on duty without stopping for a chat. He has become popular.

Over the summer Dave becomes friends with Suzanne Clark. She's a tall, stylish girl who works for a member of congress from her home state of Indiana. One evening, when Suzanne's loitering at the desk, Dave screws up the courage to ask her out. She accepts, and that weekend he wheedles use of the Cadillac for their date. Dave takes Suzanne to a movie, and then they go to a hole-in-the-wall Italian restaurant for beer and pizza. "I hate watching Paul Newman get beat up like that," Suzanne says while they wait for their food.

"It wasn't pretty," Dave agrees.

"At least they didn't break all his fingers in this flick."

"No, but they broke his spirit."

"Not really, he was just pretending."

"So, what's it like to work on Capitol Hill?" Dave asks.

"Low pay, endless hours, and lots of fat old married guys trying to get into my pants."

"At least your job has a future; I'm going nowhere."

"There isn't much of a future on the Hill either," Suzanne says. "Caseworkers like me are a dime a dozen. For everyone who makes it to chief of staff, hundreds get burned out and go home."

The pizza arrives, and Dave orders a couple more beers. After they finish eating, he takes Suzanne back to Arlington Towers. She politely invites him up to her apartment, which turns out to be an attractively furnished one-bedroom. "What would you like to drink?" she asks.

"A beer would be good."

Dave sits on the sofa with his beverage while Suzanne takes a stuffed chair across the room. Both are uneasy. "What do you miss the most about Terra Haute?" Dave asks to break the silence.

"My friends," Suzanne says without hesitation. "I'm used to having lots of friends."

"Haven't you made friends at work?"

"Not really. People on the Hill only care about themselves. They pretend to be your friend then stab you in the back."

"Sounds ugly."

"My folks are coming for a visit next month," Suzanne says, brightening.

"Bad timing," Dave observes. "There'll be hordes of tourists."

"Can't help it. Mom's a teacher."

"Oh, so she has to come when school's out."

"Yes."

Dave is running out of conversation, and optimism. He knows this girl is way out of his league. "It's getting late," he says. "I better get home."

"I understand," Suzanne replies. "Thanks for the evening. It was great."

Even though they don't go on any more dates, Suzanne and Dave remain friends, and she continues to spend time at the front desk. Stephanie and Gary are regulars there as well, and sometimes Dave accompanies the two hippies on forays into the city. Georgetown is an easy walk from Roslyn, so they often go across the bridge to hang out in the clubs and listen to live music.

Beyond Georgetown is Dupont Circle, another popular hangout. On weekends if he's off work, Dave goes there to take in the scene. Dupont is a mecca for Washington's misfits, including hippies, gays, street musicians, hookers, drug dealers, and aficionados of speed chess. The latter make good use of the concrete chess tables that ring the outer circle, while benches provide seating for those who congregate around the fountain in the center of the park. The grassy area in between is popular with picnickers, sun worshipers, and musicians. A drum circle forms under the trees there on weekends.

Toward the end of August, Stephanie's husband comes home from the Navy for a thirty-day leave. His name is Steve Podolski, but everyone calls him Ski. Gary isn't happy to see Ski show up. It means that he now must move back in with his parents. "They are so lame," Gary complains.

"Well, I'm off this weekend," Dave says. "Let's spend it downtown."

"I'll be there."

Dave makes it into the city around noon on Saturday, and within an hour has scored four hits of acid. When Gary shows up, they drop then go and get something to eat. Afterward, the two boys stroll around downtown Washington to trip, window shop, and people watch. Later they return to Dupont and sit on the low wall that circles the fountain.

As Dave and Gary rest, a girl catches their attention. She's moving around the inner circle, stopping for brief conversations with people on the benches. Eventually, she comes over to them. "Can you help me drive to New York?" she asks.

Dave looks the girl over. She's of medium height with short blond hair, a cute tomboyish face, sandals, cutoffs, and a Grateful Dead T-shirt that bulges promisingly. "Sure," he says. "I love to drive."

"Great," the girl exclaims. "I was about to give up. I'm Cindy."

Dave stands and makes a little bow. "My name's Dave, and this is Gary."

"Hi, Gary."

"You're kidding, right?" Gary says. "I mean about New York."

"Not me," Cindy replies.

"Come on, Gary," Dave says. "What else have we to do?"

Gary reluctantly gets up, and the two boys follow Cindy across the street to her car. She's driving a red Volkswagen with a roof rack that's piled high with trunks and suitcases. The passenger seat is empty, but the backseat has a stack of clothes on it. Cindy crams some of the garments into the already full trunk and folds the rest over to make room for Gary. Then Dave gets behind the wheel, and after Cindy gets in, he fires up the little motor and heads out of town.

"I left Virginia Beach late," Cindy says. "Had to work tearing down sets all day, so I'm exhausted."

Instead of responding to Cindy, Dave concentrates on driving. They're on Route 50 heading east. It's usually a drab stretch of road, but the acid improves it. Now the streetlights exude rainbow halos and pulsate like orbs. Neon signs on either side iridescently advertise the motels, fast food joints, and gas stations that line the road. They flash by bursting with color like the Stanley Kubrick film. Dave turns onto the Baltimore-Washington Parkway, and it's suddenly dark except for car lights. He notices a high-power line that snakes suspended alongside the road emitting a crackling purple aura. Dave wonders if he sees the electricity, or if it's another hallucination.

"What do you mean, 'tearing down sets'?" Gary belatedly asks from the backseat. It's been half an hour since Cindy spoke.

"I was working summer stock," Cindy explains. "You know, theater."

"Oh," Gary says.

"You want to get high?" Cindy offers.

"We're tripping," Dave replies.

"Oh, that explains it."

"Explains what?"

"Why you came with me," Cindy says. "It's karma." She pulls out the ashtray, where several joints are resting, takes one, and lights it. They pass it around happily burning their fingers at the end. Then "Ruby Tuesday" comes on the radio, and they all join in the chorus.

"I've never been to New York City," Gary says once the song is over.

"That's not where we're going," Cindy explains. "We're going to Bard."

"What's Bard?"

"My college. I'll be a senior this year. The fall semester starts on Monday."

"I thought you said New York?"

"That's right, northern New York State. We'll go by Manhattan and keep going."

"Too bad."

"By the time we get to the city, you'll be too tired to want to go in."

Cindy turns out to be right. No one's awake except Dave three hours later as the sun rises behind the skyscrapers of Gotham. He continues driving north until it's necessary to stop for gas again. Cindy and Gary wake up, and they all go into the station to pee. Afterward, Cindy provides directions to Bard, and they drive the remaining distance to her dorm. With all three of them working, the car is quickly unloaded. Then it's time to rest. "One of you can use the couch," Cindy says. "The other will have to share my bed."

Dave goes into the shower first, followed by Gary. Then it's Cindy's turn. While she's in the bathroom, the two boys talk. "Which one of us is going to sleep with her?" Gary asks.

"I drove," Dave replies.

"So what?" Gary asks. "I had to ride in the back of that thing."

"Guess we'll have to flip a coin."

"You call it," Gary says, reaching into his pocket for a quarter.

"Heads."

Gary tosses the coin up, catches it, and opens his hand. "Heads it is," he says disgustedly.

Dave goes into the bedroom and strips down to his underwear. A few minutes later Cindy comes in wearing a nightgown. She gets under the covers of the single bed as Dave lies beside her, on his back. That's the position he's in when he wakes up late that afternoon. The smell of bacon is what brings him around, so he hungrily wanders into the kitchen. Gary is already there drinking coffee while Cindy's at the stove frying eggs. "I went to the store while you were asleep," she explains.

Dave and Gary are going to hitchhike home, so after they've eaten, Cindy drives them to the outskirts of town. She pulls into a supermarket parking lot and lights a joint. "One for the road," she says, passing it to Gary. Then Cindy gets out a pen. "Give me your phone numbers," she says. "I'll call you next time I'm in DC." Dave and Gary provide the requested information between tokes, and soon not enough is left of the roach to hold. "Here, take these," Cindy says, handing Dave several joints and some matches. "I wrote my number on the matchbook cover."

After Cindy drives off, Dave and Gary go over to the highway and stick out their thumbs. It's a slow Sunday evening, but they finally get a ride to Poughkeepsie. They're stuck there for two hours until another car stops. The driver only takes them a short distance down the road. He drops Dave and Gary off in the middle of an agricultural area with no redeeming virtues other than a nearby roadhouse. When an hour passes without anyone stopping, they decide to go into the place for a beer. "Haven't seen you boys around here before," the bartender says as they belly up.

"No, sir," Dave replies. "We're from Virginia."

"Don't they have barbers down there?"

"We're working on it," Dave replies. "How 'bout a couple drafts?"

The bartender fills two mugs. "So what are you doing up here?" he asks.

"Hitchhiking."

"On this road? Good luck."

As the bartender moves away, his new customers take in their surroundings. It's a cozy place decorated with hundreds of black-and-white photos of men in WWII-era uniforms. A wooden prop dominates one wall with a painting of a Spitfire beneath it. Dave walks over for a closer look. "I was a pilot," the bartender says. "My name's Ricky; I own this place."

"You flew Spitfires?" Dave asks dubiously.

"Nah, B-17s, but we had Spits at the aerodrome as well. What beauties!"

"I've read about the air war; you were lucky to make it back."

"What did you read?"

"Oh, you know, *Twelve O'Clock High*, *Thirty Seconds Over Tokyo*, *God Is My Co-Pilot*."

"What about *Catch-22*?" Ricky interrupts.

"Can't believe I left that out," Dave exclaims. "Read it while I was in high school."

Ricky takes a picture off the wall and hands it to Dave. "That's me in the middle."

"You were a sergeant?"

"We were called 'flying sergeants.'"

"How did you come to be a pilot?"

"Aptitude test plus 20/10 vision," Ricky explains. "A bunch of us were selected out of basic and sent to Alabama for flight training. We all wanted to be in fighters, but after twelve weeks most of us were sent to Arizona for multi-engine training. Next thing I was in England."

"Guess it got pretty rough," Dave says.

Ricky refills the boys' mugs and pulls a draft for himself. Then he settles onto a stool and lights a cigarette. "It was hell above," he says thoughtfully. "My first mission was on a gray morning with drenching rain blurring the windshield. Low-to-no visibility, so just taking off and forming up was dangerous. There were hundreds of bombers circling among the clouds. It was like Piccadilly Circus on Saturday night. As we crossed the channel, the sun came out. Looking down you could see our shadows moving across the fields. Must have been a thousand planes. We headed toward Germany, and the flak was so thick you could have gotten out and walked on it. Swarms of FWs and Me 109s came at us from out of the sun. In training, they told us interlocking fields of fire would keep them at bay. What a crock! Bombers were being shot down right and left. Wings shot off, tails, bodies tumbling out of burning planes. When we got back, I tried to count the number of holes in our fort. Quit after a hundred, then went to see the flight surgeon and showed him my shaking hands. 'I'm not cut out for this,' I told him. 'Can you recommend me for a desk job?' He listened and was very nice, gave me a shot of brandy. 'Sure, no problem,' he said. 'We have plenty of administrative jobs here that need to be filled.' He handed me a red capsule with a glass of water to wash it down. Then I went back to my quarters and stretched out. Next thing I knew it was 4:00

a.m. and a flashlight was shining in my eyes. Two white-helmeted MPs were behind it. 'Let's go, Sergeant,' one of them said. 'Don't give us any trouble.' They marched me over to the briefing hut, and on the way, I saw several more pilots walking under guard. We got our mission, then the MPs put me in a jeep and took me to my plane."

"They put you on at gunpoint?" Dave exclaims.

"Oh, I wasn't the only one," Ricky says. "Not by a long shot. They said, 'Climb aboard or go to Leavenworth.' Bet you didn't read about that in any of those books."

"No."

"After that, I learned not to bother the flight surgeon," Ricky continues. "My hope was to complete twenty-five missions and go home. I made it to twenty; then the bastards raised it to thirty. Somehow, I survived, and I've been holed up in this joint ever since." Ricky refills the mugs without asking for money then turns to the sink and begins washing up. Meanwhile, Dave and Gary go and put some coins in the pinball machine. A while later Ricky comes over. "Sorry, but it's closing time," he says. "Take this with you." The bartender hands Dave a six-pack in a paper sack.

"Let me pay you for it," Dave offers, reaching for his wallet.

"No way," the owner replies. "We aren't licensed for off sales."

It's past ten when the two boys get back to hitchhiking. After several minutes, the headlights of a lone car approach. Dave and Gary wave their thumbs enthusiastically until they see the gumball machine on top. It starts flashing as the cruiser makes a U-turn and comes back.

"What are you doing out here?" the cop asks.

"Sir, we're waiting for a ride," Dave replies.

"There's no hitchhiking, county ordinance," the policeman says. "I saw you with your thumb out."

"Sir, I was just picking my nose," Dave explains.

"You some kind of smartass?"

"No, sir."

"Better not," the policeman says. "Tell you what, I'm making my rounds and will be back this way in an hour. You'd better be gone, or I'm running you in."

"Yes, sir."

After the officer leaves, Dave and Gary fire up a doobie and down some beer. During the next hour, a few cars come by, and they try to flag one down with no luck. Then an ominous-looking pair of headlights appear in the distance. Dave pops one of the remaining joints in his mouth and gives Gary the last one to chew. They kick the empty beer cans under a hedge, and then the patrol car pulls up. "Get in," the cop says.

The county jail is in back of the Poughkeepsie town hall. Dave and Gary get to share a cell. It isn't much, just a couple of military-style cots with wool blankets and no sheets. The striped pillows are egregiously stained, but no one comes with fresh pillowcases. So, the aggrieved duo takes to singing. First, they offer a rousing version of "We Shall Overcome." They only know the first verse, so that's repeated several times. Incongruously, the next song in their set is "Dixie." Then the vocalists segue into a rousing rendition of "Cotton Fields." They milk the song for all it's worth, but the deputy has heard enough. He comes into the cellblock holding a *Playboy* magazine. "See that," the peace officer says, pointing to a fire hose mounted on the cinder block wall. "We use it to rinse out all the blood and puke left over after payday weekends. We've also been known to turn it on the occasional rebel, or on people who sing off key. Do you catch my drift?"

"Yes, sir," Gary salutes.

"Hey, you just read that magazine for the interesting articles, right?" Dave asks.

"That's right," the deputy laughs. "I hope you don't think I look at the nasty pictures."

"No, sir."

"All right now, pipe down. I don't want to have to come back."

The deputy wakes Dave and Gary at five thirty Monday morning and sets them to sweeping and mopping the floor. Then they get to scrub the courthouse bathrooms. At ten o'clock the boys are taken before the magistrate. "Where's the arresting officer?" he asks impatiently.

"Here, Your Honor," the cop says as he strolls into the courtroom.

"Officer Wiggins, you're late as usual."

"I apologize."

"What's the beef?"

"Public intoxication, Your Honor."

"How do you plead?" the judge asks the two defendants.

"Not guilty," Dave declares.

"Present your case, Officer."

"Last night at approximately 10:00 p.m. I came upon these two outside Ricky's. They had obviously been drinking. I warned them that I would be back and gave them a chance to leave. When I returned, they were still there, so I brought them in."

"Is that all?"

"Yes, sir."

"What's your defense?"

"Sir, may I ask Officer Wiggins a couple of questions?" Dave inquires.

"Go ahead."

"Officer Wiggins, you had your first conversation with us a little after 10:00 p.m., is that your testimony?"

"That's what I said."

"Officer, if you had seen any sign of public drunkenness, I'm sure that being a staunch upholder of the law you would have arrested us, is that fair to say?"

"Absolutely."

"Just answer yes or no, please."

Officer Wiggins glares daggers at his antagonist. "Yes," he snaps.

"Now, what time does Ricky's close on Sunday?"

"Oh, everyone knows that," The policemen sighs. "At 10:00 p.m."

"Is Ricky's licensed for off sales?"

"No."

"So, where would the next closest place be to buy beer, wine, or spirits on Sunday night?"

"Nowhere."

"Then how could it be that we were not drunk at ten when you first spoke to us but were so messed up as to require incarceration an hour later?" Dave asks. "Where would we have gotten any alcohol during that time?"

Wiggins is mute. "I believe he's got you there," the magistrate chortles. "Case dismissed."

Out in the hall, Wiggins approaches his ex-prisoners. "If I see you hitchhiking, you're done." He scowls, then angrily stalks off.

Gary and Dave go outside to have a breath of free air. "There's no way around it," Dave says. "We're going to have to call our parents."

"Shit," is Gary's response.

An hour later, after making the dreaded calls, Dave and Gary pick up Western Union money orders at a nearby supermarket. Then they catch a commuter train into the city where they transfer to Amtrak. Gary's father is waiting that evening when they arrive at the New Carrollton station in Maryland. He eagerly takes custody of his son, sparing no more than a withering glare for Dave. Two hours later Knight shows up. Dave starts to say something as he gets into the car but is rudely interrupted. "I don't want to hear it," his father says.

CHAPTER TEN
SOUTHERN COMFORT

Knight is on a dais with five other officers. They're in a courtroom like the one his oldest son visited several months ago. It has rows of benches for spectators, tables for the contending attorneys, and a chair for witnesses. But there's no jury box, and instead of a podium designed to hold one judge, there's the long counter up front that Knight and the other officers sit behind. They will be both judge and jury for the court-martial.

General Novak, the president of the court-martial, reads a lengthy statement covering procedures. Then he addresses the defense attorney. "Major Wilkins, do you have any questions about the rules?" he asks.

"Sir, no questions," Wilkins replies.

After the officer who's handling the prosecution similarly agrees that he understands his job, Novak moves on to the next order of business. "Major Wilkins, name your peremptory challenge."

"Sir, I challenge Colonel Knight."

Knight gathers up his notes and begins shoving papers into his briefcase. "Colonel Knight," Novak says, "Thank you for your service on this board. You are dismissed."

"Yes, sir," Knight grins.

Captain Kinsey is at his desk when Knight returns to the office. "That was quick," he says.

"Pays to be known as a son of a bitch," Knight brags.

"Sir, you had several calls," Sergeant Major Reynier says, handing Knight a sheaf of messages. "Mrs. Hughes said it's an emergency."

Once he's at his desk, Knight calls Elizabeth. She picks up on the first ring. "Phyliss received a telegram from the Defense Department," she says breathlessly. "Larry's missing. Can you find out what's going on?"

"Sure, just hold tight, and I'll get back to you," Knight says reassuringly. Then he summons his aide. "This guy has turned up missing in 'Nam," he says, handing Kinsey a note. "Find out what we know."

"Got it."

An hour later Kinsey returns to the office with a document. Knight puts on his specs and begins to read:

CONFIDENTIAL

AFTER-ACTION REPORT

REPORTING UNIT: 101ST ABN PATHFINDER TEAM NO. 3

DATE OF REPORT: 12 DEC 68

DATE-TIME AND COORDINATES OF INSERTION:

161500 12 DEC 68 TT2251973 METHOD OF INSERTION: UH1D

DATE TIME AND COORDINATES OF EXTRACTION: 184245 12 DEC 68 XT5283534 METHOD OF EXTRACTION: UH1D

REASON FOR EXTRACTION: CONTACT KIA AND WIA

TEAM MEMBERS AND POSITIONS:

TEAM LEADER SSG LEMUS

ASST TL SGT FRANKLIN

TEAM MEMBERS

SGT RIDLEY PFC TRENCH

SP4 PRIOR PFC MCCORMICK

PFC WRIGHT KCS MYONG

PFC STALLINGS SSG PHILLIPS

MISSION: Mark LZ for air assault.

161500 Team 3 was inserted by UH1D in the vicinity of coordinates TT2251973. The team had moved approximately 50 meters into the wood-line on an azimuth of 290 degrees when they received five sniper rounds from an AK47 on an azimuth of 260 degrees, approximately 100 meters from the team. The team found a freshly dug bunker complex and took cover.

161920 Team 3 monitored seven single shots fired from an AK47 on an azimuth of 90 degrees, 200 meters from the team.

162825 Team 3 observed fifteen enemy soldiers moving on a trail 75 meters east of 3's position. The enemy were moving too quickly, and the distance was too great to effectively engage with small arms. The enemy were wearing NVA field gear, pith helmets, and were armed with AK47s.

163630 Team 3 observed twenty more enemy personnel moving south 75 meters west of their position. Again the enemy were wearing NVA ODs and were armed with AK47s.

164120 Team 3 began having .51-caliber rounds crack over their heads. The rounds were being fired on an azimuth of 160 degrees, 150 meters from the team.

164340 Team 3 called in a gunship, which was sent to 3's position. The team directed gun runs on enemy movement 50 to 150 meters north of their position.

165100 Team 3 monitored heavy movement heading toward the southwest, 100 to 200 meters east of their position. RPGs began impacting on team 3's position, fired on an azimuth of 180 degrees, 100 meters from the team.

165130 Gunship reported "hundreds" of NVA converging on Team 3's position.

165300 Team 3 moved on an azimuth of 220 degrees for 800 meters. While moving, the team was being followed by a large enemy force.

173140 SGT Lemus designated two-man elements and ordered E&E with rendezvous set for secondary extraction site at coordinates XT5283534.

184245 Team 3 reassembled at coordinates XT5283534 and was extracted by UH1D.

184510 Team 3 reported two KIA (WRIGHT, PHILLIPS), four WIA (LEMUS, TRENCH, MCCORMICK, RIDLEY), and two MIA (STALLINGS, PRIOR).

Knight puts the report down. "Check to see what's being done to locate the two MIAs," he tells Kinsey.

"I already inquired," the captain replies. "They conducted a battalion sweep."

"And?"

"Negative, the NVA are gone; *di di mao*. No sign of Stallings or Prior."

"What's next?"

"They'll insert a couple LRRP teams in the area to look around."

"OK."

Knight makes another call to Coral Gables, and Phyliss picks up the phone. "What have you heard?" she asks.

"Several thousand troops are out looking for Larry."

"Any news?"

"They'll find him," Knight replies evasively. "What was he doing in Pathfinders?"

"Oh, they lied," Phyliss says bitterly. "After airborne training, the army wanted Larry to go to Pathfinder school. They said he'd be trained to mark drop zones for parachute jumps in Germany. Instead, they had him setting up landing zones for helicopters in Vietnam."

"I'm sure he'll be all right."

"Let us know when you hear something, please."

"Right away," Knight replies. "I promise."

Knight hangs up then looks across his desk at Kinsey who's leafing through a magazine. "He's a goner," Knight says. "The NVA don't take prisoners."

"Neither do we."

"Anyway, she's better off without him."

"Why do you say that?"

"The guy was an alcoholic," Knight replies. "A bum. Always out in the bars chasing skirts."

"What's wrong with that?" Kinsey laughs. He gets to his feet and stretches. "'Bout time to call it a day," he says with a glance at his watch.

Meanwhile, Dave's workday is just beginning. At Arlington Towers he relieves Ryan Prince, another one of the desk clerks. Ryan is a former Marine, just a couple of years older than Dave, who supplements the income from his desk clerk job by working part-time as a bouncer. He's a nice-looking, clean-cut guy, so it's hard to picture Ryan throwing rowdy drunks out of a nightclub. "Are you going to the Hayloft later?" Dave asks him.

"No, I'm off tonight," Ryan replies. "Nothing's going on. But I'll be there tomorrow night. Phil Flowers is playing, so they expect a crowd."

"I don't know how you do it," Dave says. "Work here eight hours and then at that bar half the night."

"Neither job is much work."

"When I get done here all I want to do is vegetate."

"Yes, well you live with your parents," Ryan says, putting on his coat. "But I have rent to pay. See you tomorrow."

"See you."

Dave spends the next eight hours reading and talking with tenants. Afterward, he goes straight home and after getting something to eat climbs into bed with a book. The next morning he's in the kitchen having breakfast when Bobbie comes in. "A girl called for you last night," she says.

"Oh really? Who?"

"Cindy, from New York. She said you two are friends. We had a nice long chat."

"That's cool."

"She wanted to know if we'd be here this weekend, and I said yes."

"Why did she want to know that?"

"Cindy's going to visit some friends in Virginia Beach during Christmas and wants to stay over on the way down. Of course, I agreed."

"That's fine, Mom, Cindy's a nice girl."

Dave has several hours to waste before starting his commute to work. He goes to a window, pulls back the curtain, and sees the sun peeking out from behind a cloud. Quickly he gets into a sweatshirt and jogging pants then leaves the house. Soon he's striding purposefully toward the home of the country's first president.

On Friday evening, Dave is at home when Cindy arrives. He helps bring her things upstairs. "Why didn't you ever call me?" she complains.

"I used up all the matches and threw the book away," Dave mumbles. "Forgot your number was on it."

"Well, now that I'm here maybe we can do something."

"Sorry, but I have to work later."

"Too bad."

"I'll be off for three days starting tomorrow."

"I'll stay over another day, in that case," Cindy says.

"All right."

Cindy and Dave go into the kitchen and find Bobbie cooking dinner. "Hi, honey," she says, coming over to hug Cindy. "How were my directions?"

"Perfect, I only got lost once."

"I love those shoes. Where did you find them?"

"New York."

"Oh, of course. You know, I used to live in Manhattan."

"Really?"

"That's where I met my husband."

"How romantic."

Bobbie and Cindy talk animatedly all through dinner. Then Marie and Perle come in to fix plates for themselves. "When's Dad getting home?" Marie demands to know.

"He didn't say," Bobbie replies. "It's Friday, might be late."

"He promised us the car."

"Then I'm sure he'll be here."

"We'll eat in our room," Marie says. "Come get us when he shows up."

"At least say hello to Cindy."

Marie glances at the guest. "Hello," she says curtly.

"Hi," Cindy says brightly, but Marie and Perle are gone.

"I'm going upstairs to rest," Bobbie tells Cindy after the two of them have done the dishes. "I'll put a towel and washcloth in your room for you."

"Thanks, Mrs. Knight."

"You're welcome, honey, see you tomorrow."

Cindy and Dave go into the living room and put a record on the stereo. "We don't go in much for family meals," Dave confesses.

"So I see."

"What about you?"

"Punctually at six thirty whenever I'm home."

"Brothers and sisters?"

"An older sister and two younger brothers."

"Almost as big as my family."

"Where are the others?"

"Aside from the two you saw, I have a brother in military school and a sister who lives in Maryland."

The front door opens, and Knight comes in. "Turn that goddamn noise off," he orders. Then Knight sees Cindy and his expression changes. "Well, who's this?" he smiles.

"I'm Cindy."

"Is that your Volkswagen outside?"

"Yes, sir."

"I almost bought a VW bus when we were in Germany but got an Opel instead."

"Should have gotten the bus," Cindy smiles. "It's the hip thing to have nowadays."

"That's what I understand," Knight replies. "I'm going to have a rum and Coke. Can I get you anything?"

"Rum and Coke sounds good," Cindy agrees.

When Knight returns, he hands Cindy her drink then rejects the LP that's playing. He puts a Duke Ellington record on then settles into his chair. "Now that's music," he opines as the lush melody fills the room.

"It's lovely," Cindy agrees, and Knight beams at her.

Marie storms into the living room with Perle at her heels. Both are heavily made up and dressed to attract attention "Where are the keys?" Marie snaps.

"On the table," Knight says, pointing.

"You were late," Marie accuses, snatching up the car keys. Then the front door slams, tires squeal, and Marie and Perle are gone, leaving the cloying scent of Shalimar in their wake.

"So where do you live?" Knight asks Cindy.

"New Jersey, when I'm not at school."

"Where are you going?"

"Bard, I have one semester left."

"This guy barely made it through high school." Knight nods at Dave.

"I know a lot of kids who skipped college."

"To do what?"

"Go to acting school or work in shows."

"Oh, that Bard," Knight exclaims.

"Yes."

"Well, it's OK for a girl to go into the theater, I suppose, but a man should have a real job," Knight says, getting up from his chair. "Can I freshen your drink?"

"No, thanks."

"He's hopeless," Cindy whispers after Knight goes out.

"I know," Dave says. "Sorry, but I have to leave soon."

"Thought you didn't have to be at work till midnight?"

"It takes me over an hour by bus."

"I'll drive you."

"That's not necessary."

"I don't want to stay here."

"I see your point."

Cindy's low on gas, so they stop and fill up in Alexandria before driving the rest of the way to Arlington Towers. When they get there, Ryan's at the front desk. "You're early," he comments.

"I got a ride. Meet Cindy."

"Hey."

"Nice to meet you," Cindy smiles.

"If you can take over for me now, that would be great," Ryan tells Dave. "The Hayloft called, and they need me. It's the fifteenth and a Friday; you know what that means."

"Payday Friday," Dave answers.

"That's right, and the place is jammed; half doggies, half jarheads," Ryan elaborates. "Already been several fights and there are two hours left."

"You go ahead," Dave says. "The Marines need all the help they can get."

"Ha-ha."

"This is my least favorite shift," Dave says after Ryan goes out.

"Can't you get a better job?"

"I tried, but no one wants to hire a 1-A."

The lobby door swings open and Connie walks unsteadily toward the desk. "Hi, sweetheart," she says to Dave.

"Connie, this is Cindy."

"Oh, did you just move in?"

"No, I'm with Dave."

"Oh really." Connie winks elaborately at Dave.

"She drove down from New York this morning."

"You must be tired, honey."

"Getting there," Cindy admits, "but if I leave now, it wouldn't be long before I'd have to come back."

"I can take the bus home," Dave offers. "That's what I always do."

"Why don't you come up to my place?" Connie suggests. "You can rest on the sofa."

"No, I'm fine, really."

"Oh, come on, I need some company."

"Go ahead," Dave tells Cindy. "You can have a nap till it's time to leave."

After the two women go, a sepulchral silence settles over the lobby. Dave gets a paperback out of his bag and alternates reading and pacing as the remainder of the night drags slowly past.

That afternoon, Cindy and Dave drive out to Great Falls. It's a cold, dreary day and only a few other people are there. After parking, they head north on a trail that parallels the Potomac. The river is a jumble of rocky rapids this high up with ducks and geese sheltering in the pools. "Those birds look like they're freezing," Cindy says.

"Yeah, you'd think they would have migrated south," Dave replies. He expects Cindy to tire after a mile or so, but she keeps tramping along, stopping now and then to look out over the water. He's the one to finally suggest that they turn around.

By the time Cindy and Dave get back to the car, it's dark, and both are ravenous. So, they find a McDonald's and pig out. On the way home, the couple stops along the parkway to smoke a joint. Afterward, they get out to look at the river. It's much broader here, and the only whitewater is on the tips of the waves. In the darkness, they can't see far, and the wind is icy, so Cindy and Dave quickly get back in the bug. Once home they go in the living room, and Dave puts an album on the stereo with the volume turned low. "Where do you get your dope?" he asks.

"A guy at Bard," Cindy replies. "It's supposed to be Jamaican. Who's this?"

"Buffalo Springfield."

"Nice."

After listening to both sides of the record, they go upstairs. "See you tomorrow," Dave says.

"Good night," Cindy replies then turns to go down the hall.

But a little later Dave is tossing restlessly in bed when Cindy comes in wearing a nightgown. "I think we have some unfinished business," she whispers, shutting the door behind her. Then Cindy pulls the nightie over her head.

In the morning, Cindy and Dave are awakened by the hall phone. Knight answers it, and they can't help but hear his end of what becomes a heated conversation.

"Hello, sis."

"Still no word."

"I agree, it doesn't look good."

"No, please don't put her on."

"Hello, Phyliss."

"Now, wait a minute."

"Calm down."

"That's not right."

"Sure, they have other jobs there."

"He must have volunteered for it."

"That's not true; you have to volunteer for Pathfinders. Moreover, if you want out, you can quit."

"Then he lied. It's definitely an all-volunteer outfit."

"That's not fair."

"I did all I could."

"Don't talk to me like that!"

"Phyliss? Phyliss?"

Cindy sits up in bed. "Hey, look at the time," she says, "it's almost noon."

"No wonder I'm so hungry," Dave exclaims.

"Me too."

Dave makes a batch of French toast for brunch then he and Cindy take turns in the shower. Afterward, they go for a walk, and Dave shows Cindy the route he and Vinny took to the Potomac. When they come to the riverbank, she peers at the far shore. "You paddled all the way across?" Cindy asks in amazement.

"And almost all the way back," Dave laughs.

"You're lucky to be alive."

"God watches out for fools," Dave says. "I forget who said that."

"Where's Vinny now?"

"He joined the Marines."

"Too bad."

Cindy's supposed to meet her friends later, so when they get back to the house it's nearly time for her to leave. While she packs her suitcase, Dave makes them a snack. They're at the kitchen table eating when Marie comes in and grabs a beer out of the fridge. "See that sore on his lip?" she says to Cindy. "It's herpes."

"I know," Cindy replies. "He told me."

"Oh? Well, good luck, then," Marie says and goes out.

"She's awful," Cindy says quietly.

"You'd be awful too if you grew up in this family."

"Are you awful?"

"Yes," Dave admits.

"Well, at least you could call me once in a while."

"I will, I promise," Dave says. Then he cleans up what little mess they made and walks Cindy to her car.

It feels lonely after Cindy leaves, and Dave's almost happy two days later when it's time to go back to work. At Arlington Towers he finds a bleary-eyed Ryan waiting for him at the front desk. "I'm going to do nothing but sleep the next three days," Ryan says.

"You need to find a better job," Dave suggests. "In fact, two better jobs. That's dangerous what you're doing at the Hayloft."

"You want dangerous, try Marine Force Recon."

"Is that what you did?"

"Yeah, in Vietnam."

Suzanne comes off the elevator. "Hey," she says, flashing a bright smile. "Gotta run, I'm late."

"Nice girl," Dave says as Suzanne goes out.

"Truly," Ryan agrees as he gathers his things. "Anyway, I've been accepted at Georgetown starting in the fall. At that point, I'll be done here."

"Congratulations."

"Don't say anything."

"I won't."

"Don't know why I'm confiding in a fucking hippie."

"And the horse."

"See you on the flip side."

"Right on, Daddy-O."

Early that afternoon Stephanie and Ski emerge from the elevator. It's rare to see them anymore now that Ski is out of the Navy and Stephanie has quit the stacks. "Where have you been?" Dave asks.

"Norfolk," Ski replies. His hair is now down to his shoulders.

"But we're going to Constitution Hall tonight," Stephanie says, "to see the Who."

"Gary was going to come, but now his dad won't let him," Ski says.

"When's he gonna move out?" Dave asks.

"He can't stay with us," Ski says emphatically. "Two's company; three's a crowd."

"You can have his ticket if you want," Stephanie offers. "And we have acid."

"Any good?"

"Yeah, we did some last week. Very mellow."

"OK, thanks."

That night the concert crowd is a mix of stoned hippies and precocious teenyboppers, some with parents. They pack into Constitution Hall, and soon Pete Townshend's power chords are reverberating within the massive stone structure. Meanwhile, Keith Moon's drumming propels the band through its raucous repertoire. In between thrashing the skins and pinging the cymbals, Moon twirls his drumsticks like a majorette throwing first one then another up in the air and catching them behind his back. To the delight of the teenyboppers, the band plays their radio hit "My Generation" for the finale. As the song reaches its crescendo, the musicians preclude any possibility of an encore by thoroughly smashing their equipment. Moon drums all the way through the Armageddon then kicks his kit over. He dashes madly about, stabbing at the skins with a broken drumstick as the hall fills with electronic feedback and smoke.

On the walk home, Stephanie, Ski, and Dave stop at the Lincoln Memorial and go up the steps to spend some time with the great man. They stand at his feet and allow the stillness of the vast room to creep over them. To their LSD-addled minds, it's profoundly sad to think of Lincoln spending night after night alone like this. He seems comfortable in the chair but weary. They want to stay and keep him company but it's quite cold, so after a period of contemplation, the visitors leave. They cross the bridge to Virginia and walk the rest of the way to Arlington Towers.

Once they get upstairs, Stephanie puts Donovan quietly on the record player. Then she opens a piece of aluminum foil, revealing a big chunk of black hash. The three concertgoers pass the pipe around several times then sit back. "How does Keith Moon do it?" Dave wonders.

"Do what?" Stephanie replies.

"Catch those drumsticks behind his back."

Stephanie laughs, "He doesn't," she says. "I saw them at an outdoor festival last summer and wondered the same thing. So, I walked around to the side and saw that he keeps a coffee can full of drumsticks behind him. When he throws one up, Moon reaches back like he's catching it but actually just snatches another one out of the can and keeps drumming. I saw a roadie walk around after the show picking up sticks from all over the stage."

"Hey, this is good stuff," Dave marvels as the heavy weight of the hashish makes its presence felt.

"Glad you like it," Ski replies. "We got plenty more."

Stephanie shoots her husband a warning look. "Oh, relax, woman," Ski says. "Dave's OK." The ex-sailor goes into the bedroom and comes back with a metal attaché case. He opens it, and Dave sees that it's full of Hershey-bar-size packets. Ski takes one and carefully unwraps it. "This is Nepalese-government-inspected grade A," he says, showing Dave the stamp on a slab of hash.

"How does it get here?" Dave asks.

"Diplomatic pouch," Ski says. "It's foolproof."

"Damn, that's a lot of hash," Dave marvels.

"Only a month's supply for the Atlantic fleet," Ski smirks.

"Oh, so that's what you're doing."

"Got to make a living," Stephanie declares. "Beats working at the library."

The Donovan record comes to an end, and Stephanie gets up to flip it. "You can stay up if you want," Ski tells her, "but I'm done."

Stephanie looks at the clock. "No wonder," she says, "it's almost two."

"That's it then," Ski says. "Got to hit the hay."

"Me too," Stephanie agrees. "You can crash on the sofa," she tells Dave.

The hashish helps Dave quickly drift off to sleep, but he wakes up a few hours later when the sun shines through the window. After freshening up, he takes the elevator down to work. At the front desk, Dave again experiences the brain-dead feeling that comes after a trip. Any optimism or curiosity about the future is gone. Even drinking cup after cup of coffee doesn't help.

That afternoon a school bus pulls up in front of Arlington Towers as it does every weekday and Peggy Richfield, the resident manager's daughter, gets off. Mrs. Richfield is divorced, so it's only her and Peggy in their apartment. There's not much for a teenager to do at Arlington Towers, so Peggy often loiters at the front desk. She's a high school freshman with long reddish-brown hair and a round, nevertheless pleasant, face. Today, when she gets to the front desk, Peggy notices Dave's rough appearance. "Have you got a hangover?" she asks.

"Don't you have any homework?" Dave snaps. He told Peggy once that he was hungover, hoping to get rid of her. He has regretted it ever since.

"Yes, I have schoolwork, but I don't feel like doing it," Peggy retorts. "Anyway, you look awful. Isn't that the same shirt you had on yesterday?"

"None of your business," Dave protests. Thankfully, he spots his relief coming through the front door. "You're early," he says to Pat Hanrahan.

"Nothing else to do," the retired bus driver mutters.

"Well, if you don't mind taking over, that'd be great," Dave says. "I have a headache."

"I knew it!" Peggy exclaims triumphantly. "I'll get you some Tylenol."

Dave is at Arlington Towers on a rainy May morning waiting to be relieved after another midnight shift. Tenants dressed for the inclement weather are passing through the lobby on their way to work. Suzanne Clark comes off the elevator and approaches the front desk looking stylish in a Burberry raincoat. "Hey," she says.

Dave looks up from his newspaper. "Oh, hi, Suzanne, what's happening?"

"Not a whole lot."

"Would you like a cup of coffee?"

"No, I'm good, had two cups before I left the apartment."

"Well, I'm going to warm mine up," Dave says and splashes more of Mrs. Richfield's special blend into his mug.

"I've wanted to ask you," Suzanne says, "do you ever talk to Ryan? I try, but it's hard for me to get more than two words out of him."

"He was the same way with me when I first came to work here," Dave replies. "All business. But lately, he's been opening up more."

"You have to tell me your secret."

"Oh, I don't have any secret other than that people tend to be talkative late at night when it's quiet and no one else is around."

"I'm usually asleep then."

"Yeah, must be nice to work normal hours."

"Speaking of work," Suzanne says, glancing at her watch. "I better be going."

After Suzanne leaves, Dave goes back to the newspaper until Pat comes in to relieve him. The old man is carrying an umbrella and wears galoshes over his dress shoes. "Drivers in this town are the worst," he grumbles. "It's life-threatening to cross the street even when you have the light."

"Didn't you use to drive a bus?"

"Yes, and I always stopped for people in crosswalks."

"That's good," Dave says. "Well, I'll be off. See you tomorrow."

Once home, Dave eats breakfast then goes directly to bed. The rain and especially the overcast make for good sleeping, and he doesn't wake until late in the afternoon. By then, the precipitation has let up, so he goes for a long walk. Afterward, Dave zones out in front of the TV awhile before eating a late dinner. Then it's time for another graveyard shift.

Dave gets to Roslyn just before midnight and finds Ryan at the desk reading. "You can leave now if you want," Dave tells him.

"Oh, I got nothing to do," Ryan replies.

"Don't you have to go to the Hayloft?" Dave asks.

"No, there's no band tonight, so it'll be dead. But I'll be needed tomorrow; it's payday, and Phil Flowers will be back."

"Well, bust a few heads for me."

"Not if I can talk my way out of it," Ryan says. "Most situations I deal with can be handled verbally."

"Oh really? What do you say?"

"I tell them, 'Either cooperate, or you're gonna wake up in a full body cast.'"

"Short and to the point," Dave says admiringly.

"It's all in how you say it," Ryan laughs.

"Hey, mind if I ask you something?"

"What's that?"

"It's about Suzanne."

"What about her?"

"I think she's got a crush on you."

"Yeah, I can tell," Ryan says. "I like her too, but it's complicated."

"How so?"

"It has to do with my previous occupation."

"Force Recon?"

"Right. I've been thinking about Suzanne, and I would ask her out, but it wouldn't be fair. You see, I got shot over there . . . you know . . . in the wrong place."

"Oh," Dave says. "That's a motherfucker."

"Trust me."

"It's none of my business, but shouldn't you tell her?"

"You're right, it is none of your business," Ryan says and turns to leave.

"But, hey," Dave calls after him. "Suzanne's a sweet girl. She wouldn't care."

"Maybe not," Ryan says over his shoulder, "but I would." He goes out, letting the glass door close behind him.

Dave gets his book out, but soon he's too weary to read. As the long night drags on and the stillness penetrates every corner of the lobby, he cannot keep his eyes open. So, Dave resorts to a trick he discovered for staying alert. He takes an elevator up to the sixteenth floor, opens the exit door, goes into the stairwell, and climbs the short flight of stairs to the top. Dave has found that maintenance often leaves the entrance to the roof unlocked, and that's how it is now. He goes out onto the tar and gravel surface past several massive air-conditioning units then around the housing for the elevator mechanisms. A chill wind is blowing this high up, but Dave pays it no mind. He pauses on the east side of the building behind a low brick wall. Then he climbs over it, takes two steps, and now his toes are at the edge of the roof. The lights of Washington blanket the earth below and Dave forces himself to look down. His head spins, and he lurches back as a rush of adrenaline surges through him. "That should keep me awake for a while," he says with a laugh.

The visit to the roof does the trick, and Dave handily makes it through the remainder of the shift. On the way home, he changes buses in downtown Alexandria, and while there he treats himself to breakfast at the Waffle Shop. Afterward, he catches the bus home.

At the house, Dave is getting ready for bed when it occurs to him that Cindy hasn't called recently. He goes to the phone and dials the number for her dorm. After several rings, a girl answers and agrees to find Cindy. There's a long wait then, "Hello?" Cindy says sleepily.

"Hey, it's me."

"So, you're still alive."

"Last time I looked."

"I thought you'd forgotten about me."

"How could I forget?"

"Oh, I'm sure you have plenty of girlfriends."

"Actually, no; I'm saving myself for you."

"Well, lucky me."

"That's right; you are truly blessed."

"In more ways than one."

"I agree."

"What I mean is, I'm late."

"Late for class?"

"Don't be stupid," Cindy snaps. "I'm not that kind of late; I'm late, late."

"Oh," Dave says as it dawns on him that he's going to be a father. "Well, that's a surprise."

"Yes, isn't Mother Nature wonderful?"

"It's OK, we'll be all right," Dave says, thinking furiously.

"Glad to hear you say so."

"We'll get married," Dave blurts out.

"You mean it?"

"Yes."

"Do you love me?"

"Yes."

"Then OK."

"But you have to graduate," Dave insists. "There can't be more than a couple of weeks left in the semester."

"Sure, but I'm not going to walk," Cindy says.

"That doesn't matter."

"Are you excited?" Cindy asks.

"Yes."

"So am I."

After he gets off the phone, Dave goes to his room and tries to sleep. But his mind is full, and he doesn't get much rest over the day. That night on his way to Arlington Towers, Dave buys an extra-large container of rotgut 7-Eleven coffee. Mrs. Richfield's java tastes better but doesn't pack enough punch.

The next morning, after a long, tedious night, Dave starts on a three-day break. He's determined to get on a regular schedule and plans to stay awake all day then go to bed at a reasonable hour. So, instead of going home, Dave walks across Key Bridge, then stops at a coffee shop for a leisurely breakfast. Afterward, he wanders through Georgetown admiring the stately townhouses that prosperous merchants built during the port's heyday. When Dave comes to Rock Creek, he crosses the bridge then takes the path down to the beach.

The little park is an oasis of tranquility in the city's midst. Dave strolls along the stream bank, listening to the birds and the gurgling water. He goes under the bridge for old time's sake and finds a young couple using the secluded spot to get well. The girl has a needle in her arm and a belt clenched around her bicep. The boy holds the syringe. As he pulls the plunger back, the liquid in the chamber turns pink. "Bingo," he says. The girl's expression slackens, and her eyes melt as the boy slowly pushes the junk into her.

Dave has been morbidly staring at the addicts, but now he tears himself away and hastily leaves the park. He walks to Dupont Circle and goes into a movie theater where *The Endless Summer* is playing. It's an interminable film about surfing that kills off the better part of the afternoon. Afterward, Dave goes into the dive next door and orders a beer. As he's reading the paper, a man comes in and sits next to him at the bar. The newcomer wears dirty clothes and reeks of body odor. "I'll have a draft," he tells the bartender.

"Oh, it's you again," the barkeep says. "Have you got any money?"

The man puts several wrinkled dollars on the bar, then turns to Dave. "Do you know what you're reading?" he asks.

"The newspaper," Dave curtly replies.

"You mean the Jewspaper," the bum smirks.

"What?"

"The *Washington Post* is owned by Jews; it's a Zionist rag packed full of lies."

"Fuck off," Dave exclaims.

The bartender comes over with the man's beer. "Are you bothering customers again?" he asks.

"Nah, we're just having a friendly conversation."

"I'm tired of you running off my customers."

Dave drains his mug and gets up. "It's OK, I have to leave anyway," he lies.

Outside, the fresh air is most welcome. Dave breathes greedily, then walks to the corner to wait for a bus. When he gets home, Dave makes himself dinner then showers and goes to bed.

Much later, Dave's dream is infiltrated by music. He sleepily checks to see if his bedside radio's on, but the sound isn't coming from there. So, Dave goes to the window. He sees a car parked under the streetlight in front of the house and another one at the foot of the driveway. Several high-school-age boys are standing around listening to a car radio. Some are holding beers.

After getting into some clothes, Dave goes outside. Immediately, the kids scatter, so he gives chase. One of the teenagers is carrying a paper sack, and as Dave gains, the boy jettisons his load. Now beers are rolling and tumbling on the road. One is punctured and sprays foam as it madly spins. Dave hauls his quarry down from behind, pins him on his back, and cocks a fist. But the kid squirms and jerks his head so wildly Dave can't get a clean shot. Finally, though, the boy tires. "Go ahead, hit me," he cries. "Go ahead. But what good's it gonna do? Huh?"

Dave hears laughter behind him and turns to look. He sees Marie clambering down a tree that grows alongside the house with Perle right behind her. They reach the ground, scamper across the lawn, and get into a car. Tires squeal, and they're gone. Dave turns his attention back to the terrified boy beneath him. His friends are gone and so's his beer, but the pimples remain. Dave gets up. "Beat it," he says.

Two weeks later, Dave's at home killing time before going to work when the phone rings. "I just had my last exam," Cindy says excitedly.

"How did it go?"

"Piece of cake."

"So, when are you coming?"

"Tomorrow, I still have to pack."

"Sounds good."

"You sure everything's set for the wedding?"

"Yep, all taken care of. The only thing missing is you."

"I'm happy."

"Me too."

"See you tomorrow."

Dave takes the bus to Roslyn and gets there right at 4:00 p.m. Ryan is happy to see him and quickly departs to get ready for his second job. After settling in at the desk, Dave greets residents who are coming in from work. Then as traffic through the lobby slows, he gets out his book. Around ten o'clock, Connie comes in, all alone. "What are you doing after work?" she asks.

"Nothing," Dave replies.

"Want to come up?"

"Sure."

At midnight, Connie comes to the door wearing a sheer negligee. "Is that a banana in your pocket or are you just happy to see me," she purrs in her best Mae West impression.

"I'm getting married, my little chickadee," Dave drawls, W. C. Fields style.

"Why in hell would you do that?"

"For the obvious reason."

"That little girl I had up here?"

"Yeah."

"She's cute."

"Yes, she is."

"Then I need to give you a proper send-off," Connie says, picking up a bottle of Southern Comfort.

"Not for me," Dave exclaims. "That stuff's too sweet."

"Just like me," Connie simpers. "But go ahead and open that bottle of Jack if you prefer."

"That's more like it."

This night Dave manages to outlast Connie. She passes out around 4:00 a.m., leaving him to his own devices. So, Dave sits on the living room floor and takes a swig of whiskey. But with Connie out of the picture, it's lonely, and he wishes he had someone to talk with. Dave thinks of Gary. He finds his wallet, takes out a scrap of paper with Gary's home number, and carefully dials it. After six or seven rings, an irate voice answers. "Who's this?"

"Oh, hi, Mr. Brooks, it's Dave Knight. Is Gary home?"

"Do you have any idea what time it is?"

"No."

"Well, it's four fucking o'clock."

Dave belatedly jerks the receiver away from his ear as the phone on the other end crashes down. He tilts the whiskey bottle back, but it's empty. What's left of Connie's Southern Comfort is nearby, so Dave has a taste. It's not that bad. Still, he's lonely, so Dave decides to call his sister. She seemed downright friendly the last time they spoke. Dave finds a scrap of paper on the floor with a phone number, so he dials it. "What the hell?" a man bellows.

"Hi, it's Dave. May I speak to Melissa?"

"Are you out of your mind? There is no Melissa here. Don't call this number again. I mean it."

This time Dave anticipates what's going to happen and gets the phone away from his ear before the crash. Then he notices that the record has stopped, so he re-sleeves Neil Young and puts on another LP. As Dylan sings about his lost love from the north country, tears course down Dave's cheeks and splash onto his bare chest. It feels cold, so he gets dressed. "Now if only there were someone to talk to," Dave says to himself. "What about Ryan?" He finds the number and dials.

Sometime after dawn, the Southern Comfort runs out, and when he can't find anything else to drink, Dave departs. He takes the bus to Alexandria then goes into the Waffle Shop for breakfast. After ordering, Dave lays his head on the counter. Soon a policeman shakes him awake. "Hey, you can't sleep here," he says.

"'Pon my oath," Dave slurs. He's back in W. C. Fields mode.

"Whew, you smell like a distillery."

"And you, sir, you smell like a horse's hind end."

"That's it," the cop growls, jerking Dave off the stool.

"I say, unhand me, my good man."

The Alexandria City Jail dispenses with any refinements such as pillows or mattresses, stained or otherwise. In his cell, Dave finds that a perforated metal slab attached to the cinder block wall is the only bed. It will do. He lies on it and soon is in never-never land. Later he's awakened by the cries of the other inmates. They stand at the front of their cells and beg for deliverance. "Let me out," the man next to Dave keeps hollering. He grasps the bars of his cell and tries to shake them.

From time to time a deputy comes into the cell block and leads one of the inmates out as the clamor from the others rises. Finally, Dave's turn comes. Outside he finds Dan waiting. "What are you doing here?" Dave asks.

"Got home from school this morning," Dan replies. "Dad told me to come get you." He hands Dave a manila envelope with his belt, shoelaces, and wallet inside.

When they get home, Bobbie has a meatloaf ready for lunch, but just the smell of food makes Dave want to hurl. He sits at the table and dizzily guzzles water. Then Cindy pulls up in her VW and Dave goes to help her unload. "I'm going to have a nap," he says when they finish. "I'm not feeling well."

Several hours of sleep later, Dave wakes feeling marginally human. He has to begin work at four, so Cindy takes him to Arlington Towers. For the next eight hours, Dave manages to stay out of trouble. At midnight his fiancée comes to pick him up. They stop at a Little Tavern on the way home for a bag of burgers and fries, which they consume at the kitchen table. Dave will be off work until midnight the next day.

In the morning, Cindy and Dave sleep late, have a leisurely breakfast, then go for a walk. When they return, it's time to dress for the wedding. Dave puts on his blazer and ties his tie while Cindy gets into a simple yellow frock. When they come downstairs, Dan's in the living room. "What are y'all dressed up for?" he asks.

"We're getting married."

"No shit."

"Why don't you come?" Dave asks. "We need witnesses."

"Nah."

"Oh, come on, I'll buy you a beer afterward."

"Now you're talking."

Stephanie, Ski, and Connie are waiting outside the Alexandria courthouse when the bride and groom arrive with Dan. A few minutes later, Ryan walks over from the bus stop. It's a perfect early summer afternoon, so the wedding party remains outdoors until it's time for the ceremony. Then they go in, and Dave spends a few minutes with the clerk of court going over the paperwork. Afterward, they're shown into a nondescript room with a few uncomfortable-looking chairs. Before they can sit, the magistrate appears. He's a portly fellow with a jovial manner. "Are you folks ready?" he asks. "'Cause this ship's about to sail."

"Ready as we'll ever be," Dave answers carelessly. Then the judge shows the couple where to stand and guides them through the proceedings. Afterward, Cindy and Dave kiss, exchange cheap wedding bands, sign several papers, and soon they're all back outside. "So, what's the plan?" Dan asks. "I believe someone said something about a beer."

"Let's go to Mac's," Dave suggests, naming a Georgetown bar known for its cheap brew and fabulous jukebox.

"I've got to go to work," Ryan says.

"I'll relieve you at midnight," Dave promises.

"If you're late, I'll understand."

After Ryan leaves, the others split up with plans to reconvene in Washington. It's rush hour but they are going into town, not out, so the traffic's a breeze. The hard part is finding a parking spot in Georgetown. Dave gets lucky when a car just ahead pulls out of a legal place. He gets to the prized real estate first and slides the little car in. Then Dave pumps several quarters into the meter, and he, Cindy, and Dan make the short walk down M Street to the bar. Inside they take chairs at the end of one of the long tables and Dave orders a pitcher of draft. When the suds arrive, he fills the mugs. Then the door opens, and Connie comes in. She plops down on a chair next to Dan. "I feel sorry for all the poor bastards leaving the city," she exclaims. "They were parking on the other side."

Dave sloshes some refreshments into a mug for Connie and does likewise for Stephanie and Ski who come in a few minutes later. The pitcher's now empty, so he motions to the waitress for more. Then Dave gets up and puts some quarters into the jukebox. When he returns, Connie and Dan are deep in conversation. "The townies hate us," Dan is saying. "So, if we want to go into Waynesboro, it's best to go with friends."

"Why do they hate you?" Connie asks.

"Oh, we come to town in our dress uniforms and get all the girls. Those hillbillies can't stand it."

"I'll bet you look handsome in your cadet uniform."

"Here's a photo," Dan says, removing a snapshot from his wallet. In it, he's holding a sword and wearing a long gray coat with a maroon cape. Snow covers the lawn in front of the turreted barracks in the background.

"How romantic," Connie sighs.

The door to the bar opens, and Gary enters. "Sorry I couldn't make it this afternoon," he says. "My boss is a prick." The long-haired librarian leans in and kisses Cindy on the cheek. "Good luck with this idiot," he says then grabs a chair and pours himself some beer. "My father says if he ever sees you again, he's going to kill you," Gary informs Dave.

"What?"

"Yeah, he hated you before, but now it's out of control."

"Why?"

"You know," Gary says, "the other night, you wouldn't stop calling."

"Really?" Dave says. "I don't remember."

"Cut the shit," Gary replies. "Hey, next pitcher's on me."

"So, when do you go back to school?" Connie asks Dan.

"Just graduated," he replies. "I'm done with that hellhole."

"So, what are you going to do?"

"Air Force," Dan says. "One thing I learned at military school—steer clear of the army."

"What about the Navy?" Ski asks. "I spent four years, safe and sound."

"Problem is he was never home," Stephanie says plaintively.

Gary turns to Cindy. "You know, with a little luck, I might be sitting where Dave's sitting right now," he says. Quickly, Dave kicks his friend under the table.

"Yeah, you know that night we met," Gary persists, and Dave kicks him again, harder. Gary moves his chair out of reach. Then he looks at Dave and laughs. "As I was saying, Cindy, that night we met. Well, we couldn't decide which of us would share your bed, so we flipped a coin. Dave won, and now here we are at your wedding." Gary has a big smirk plastered on his face, but now the fireworks erupt. "You flipped a coin for me?" Cindy cries, leaping to her feet. "You're joking, right?"

"Uh, it's . . . it's . . . not what you think . . ." Dave stammers.

"Asshole," Cindy shrieks. She empties her beer mug over her husband's head then storms out. Dave rushes after his wife and has no trouble catching up. She's five months gone.

"Are we having our first fight?" Dave asks Cindy while walking beside her.

"You smell like beer," Cindy laughs. She's already cooling off.

"Listen, I didn't know you then and, anyway, I wouldn't have let Gary near you that night."

"Why not?"

"I already knew I liked you."

"And now?"

Dave pulls out the heavy artillery. "Now I love you."

The newlyweds stop in the middle of the sidewalk and exchange a long slow kiss. "Let's go home," Cindy says.

"OK, I'll get Dan."

"And my purse."

The jukebox is blasting when Dave goes back inside, and the wedding reception is in full swing. "We're leaving," Dave yells to make himself heard. "Come on, Dan."

As Dan tries to rise, Connie seizes his arm and drags him back down. "You can't leave," she pleads.

"Then how's he gonna get home?" Dave demands.

"I'll bring him," Connie promises.

"That's right, little brother," Dan says, placing a familiar hand on Connie's leg. "You can run along. I'm in good hands."

So, the newlyweds drive home by themselves to tell Dave's parents. The Cadillac is in the driveway when they get to the house, and they find Knight in the living room. "Cindy and I got married today," Dave tells him.

Knight looks up from his *U.S. News & World Report*. "You what?"

"We got married," Dave repeats.

Knight looks at Cindy. "Is he serious?"

Cindy holds her hand up, showing off the wedding band. "It's true," she smiles. "We're married."

"Honest to God," Knight exclaims. "I thought you had more sense; him not, but you."

"Where's Mom?" Dave asks.

"Upstairs," Knight says. "But it'll be better if I break the news. For one thing, you stink of stale beer."

Dave showers and gets into fresh clothes while Knight talks to his wife. A little later the newlyweds and the parents of the groom gather in the living room. Everyone is determined to put the best face on things, and Knight pops the cork on a bottle of champagne. He fills four glasses then offers a toast: "Here's to young love, may it triumph over all."

"Hear, hear," Bobbie seconds and they each have a sip of wine.

"This champagne's delicious," Cindy exclaims. "It's so light."

"What did your parents say?" Bobbie asks her new daughter-in-law.

"We haven't told them yet," Cindy replies. "We're going to see them Thursday."

"Well, we want to meet them, so we have to arrange something," Knight insists.

"I'll tell them," Cindy agrees.

"You two can stay with us as long as you wish," Bobbie declares.

"Thanks," Cindy replies. "This already feels like home."

Knight goes around the room refilling glasses, but Bobbie declines. "One glass is enough for me," she says. "In fact, I'm a little under the weather, so if you don't mind, I'll excuse myself."

Knight helps his wife upstairs and then comes back down bringing Marie and Perle. The younger girl's hair is wet. "Dad says you have some news?" Marie says impatiently.

"Cindy and I got married."

"Really?"

Knight comes in with a couple more champagne flutes for his daughters. After filling them he offers another toast. "Here's to Cindy. Welcome to the Knight family."

"Yes, welcome," Perle echoes, taking a delicate sip.

Marie gulps some bubbly then looks at Cindy. "Do you have any idea what you're getting into?" she asks.

"Oh, I doubt it," Knight interjects. "I'm sure Dave hasn't told her. Cindy, you've married into one of the most ancient and honorable of the Highland clans. Why, in 1328 when Robert the Bruce was scrambling for his kingdom . . ."

"Hey, we've heard all that stuff before," Marie interrupts. "Besides, we're busy dyeing Perle's hair. Can we leave?"

"Oh sure," Knight replies, "go right ahead. Now, where was I?" He has lost his train of thought.

"Dave tells me that you and Mrs. Knight have been married for over twenty years," Cindy says to fill the gap.

"Yes, it's true, twenty-six great years. I was fortunate to find a wonderful woman, and for whatever reason, she's been willing to put up with me," Knight says modestly. "So, tell me, what do you see in Dave?"

"It's karma," Cindy explains. "Like we knew each other in a previous life."

"Don't you think one life with Dave is enough?" Knight asks.

"Hey, I've got to go to work," Dave says.

"What about your honeymoon?"

"I have a three-day break coming. We'll go then."

Dave drives himself to work in the VW, and Ryan is impressed to see him come in exactly on time. "Thought you might be a little late today," he says.

"And leave the Hayloft without their favorite bouncer? No way. You go ahead now, I got this."

After Ryan leaves, Dave starts a pot of coffee then gets out his book. Around 2:00 a.m., he's at the front desk when his brother gets off the elevator and strolls over to the cigarette machine. Dan puts some change in, pulls a knob, and picks up a pack of Marlboros. Turning, he sees Dave. "Doesn't she ever quit?" he asks.

"No," Dave replies.

"Oh well," Dan sighs.

Two days later Dave's off work, and he and Cindy are on their way to break the news to Cindy's parents. They live in Princeton, New Jersey, where her father works at the college. When the newlyweds get to the white-painted brick colonial Cindy grew up in, they find Mrs. Brewster at the kitchen sink. "Hi, Mom," Cindy says.

Mrs. Brewster whirls around. She's a slim, middle-aged woman with a careworn face. "Where have you been?" she asks her daughter.

"Virginia," Cindy says. "I told you I was going to Virginia."

"That was a week ago."

"This is Dave Knight," Cindy introduces. "The boy I've been telling you about."

Mrs. Brewster gives Dave a curt nod then goes back on the attack. "You don't call for a week? When have you ever gone that long without calling me?"

"I'm sorry, Mom."

Mrs. Brewster turns and fishes around in the soapy water. She pulls out a plate, runs a sponge over it, then puts it into the rinse. "We got married," Cindy blurts out.

"Oh great," Mrs. Brewster replies. "I imagined all sorts of horrible things, but you have exceeded my worst fears."

"Mom, you should be happy for me."

Mrs. Brewster turns to face her daughter. "OK, fine, I'm happy, just look at me, see how happy I am? Now get your stuff and get out. I don't ever want to see you again." Mrs. Brewster abruptly drops onto one of the kitchen chairs and puts her hands over her face. Cindy sits next to her at the table and puts an arm around her mother's shoulder.

"Now, Mom, don't take on so. We're in love."

"Love? What do you know about love?" Mrs. Brewster moans between sobs. "I had such hopes for you."

"It'll be all right, Mom, you'll see."

Slowly Mrs. Brewster cries herself out. It takes a long time, but finally, she wipes her eyes with a tissue then looks at Dave. "I'm sorry," the woman says, fussing with her hair. "What must you think? Let me get my husband." Mrs. Brewster gets up from the table and disappears down the hall. Several minutes later she returns leading Professor Brewster. "This is Cindy's father," she says. "Honey, I want you to meet . . ."

"Dave," Cindy supplies.

"Of course, Dave," Mrs. Brewster says. "How stupid of me."

Professor Brewster is wearing jeans and a T-shirt. He's a tall man with a full head of sandy hair and an intelligent, friendly face. "Your mother says you have some news," he says.

"We're married," Cindy exclaims.

"Eloped, huh?" Professor Brewster says, looking first at his daughter then at Dave.

"Yes."

"That's how they used to do it in the old days."

"We're very happy," Cindy says desperately.

"I'm sure you are," the professor agrees. "Where are you going to live?"

"Virginia."

"That's not so far away."

"No."

There's an awkward silence. No one has anything to say. Then Cindy's father gets to what's on his mind. "I was watching the Yankees," he says to Dave. "They're playing Boston."

"No love lost there," Dave comments. He doesn't follow baseball, but he knows that much.

"Not hardly," the professor grins. "Want to watch the game?"

"Sure," Dave says. He follows his father-in-law downstairs to the finished basement. It's outfitted with a bar, bumper pool table, and comfortable seating around the TV. "Care for a beer?" Professor Brewster asks.

"Yes, please," Dave says gratefully. Then he sits on the sofa with his drink while Cindy's father turns his attention back to the game.

Two hours later the Yankees are sitting on a three-run lead going to bat in the bottom of the eighth. "I wonder who Houk will bring on to close," Professor Brewster says. "Hamilton came in for two innings Saturday and one on Sunday, but only threw sixty-three pitches, so he should be good to go."

"Then he'd be a good bet," Dave musters. He longs to pick up a *Field & Stream* lying nearby but doesn't want to be rude. So, he watches the Yankees explode for four more runs, draining what suspense there was out of the contest. A few minutes later Cindy comes down. "It's time to go," she says.

At the door, Cindy hugs her mother. "You have to stay longer next time," Mrs. Brewster says.

"We will, Mom, I promise," Cindy replies.

It's a tedious drive back to DC, and well past midnight by the time Cindy and Dave get home, but Knight is still up. "Are you off work again tomorrow?" he asks Dave.

"Yes, sir."

"Can you pick your mother up at the hospital in the afternoon?"

"Fort Belvoir?"

"No, Walter Reed."

"What's she doing there?"

"They have a machine that cleans the blood when the kidneys aren't working," Knight explains. "I'm taking Mama there first thing, and she'll be done by two o'clock. But I have an all-day conference and wouldn't be able to pick her up again until late."

"What's wrong with her kidneys?"

"They shut down when her blood pressure gets too high."

"I thought she was taking blood pressure medicine."

"It's not working."

There's a pause in the conversation while Dave mulls what Knight just said. Then Cindy speaks up. "It's no problem, Colonel," she says. "We'll be happy to go get her."

The next day, after lunch, Cindy and Dave leave the house. It's smooth sailing getting into Washington, but then the traffic is stop-and-go all the way up 14th Street because of the lights. Finally, they get to Walter Reed Army Medical Center and find Bobbie inside waiting. "Honey, you're beginning to show," she tells Cindy.

"I know," Cindy replies. She's wearing one of Dave's shirts with the tails out, but there's no hiding the thickness around her middle.

"How do you get into those shorts?"

Cindy briefly pulls the bottom of the shirt up to show Bobbie that her cutoffs aren't buttoned and are only partway zipped.

"We need to stop by Hecht's on the way home and get you a few things."

"Oh, that's not necessary."

"Come on; I want to."

"OK, thanks."

At the department store, Bobbie and Cindy have fun shopping while Dave sits on a bench perusing the paper. Then the three of them have coffee in the store's cafe. When they get home, Cindy puts on a fashion show. Dave thinks the maternity outfits look ridiculous but keeps that thought to himself. He's feeling glum because his break is ending, and tomorrow will be a workday.

To make the most of Dave's last night off, he and Cindy decide to go out. They see a movie then stop at Hot Shoppes on the way home. Cindy gets the double-decker burger and an Orange Freeze. "Shouldn't you be drinking milk?" Dave asks.

"This is just as good," Cindy declares. "It's loaded with vitamin C."

"That was the best movie ever," Dave proclaims.

"And how."

"They say Steve McQueen did his own driving in that chase scene."

"Of course, he did," Cindy replies. "He's a race car driver in real life."

"Oh, come on, he's not a real race car driver. Racing's just a hobby he can afford because he's rich from acting."

"You're just jealous."

"No, I'm telling it like it is. You want dessert?"

"Of course."

The house is dark when Cindy and Dave arrive home, so they get ready for bed quietly then go to sleep. But in the middle of the night, Cindy gets up. Eventually, Dave hears her faint cries coming from the bathroom. "Don't come in here," Cindy whimpers when Dave tries to open the door.

"OK, but what do you want me to do?" Dave asks.

"Get your mother."

Bobbie is quick to react after Dave wakes her. She goes into the bathroom then a moment later sticks her head back out the door. "She's lost the baby, call for an ambulance."

Dave rides with Cindy on the way to the hospital and holds her hand. "I'm sorry," she says. "I'm so sorry."

"It's not your fault," Dave replies. "It just happened."

But that's not the way they see it in the emergency room. Cindy's lying on a gurney when an Alexandria police detective arrives. "Who helped you with this?" he asks.

"What are you talking about?" Cindy moans.

"You're telling me that you didn't see anyone or do anything to induce this?" he asks.

"No."

"What are you suggesting?" Dave asks angrily.

"Who are you?"

"Her husband."

"Oh, you're married?"

"That's right."

The policeman snaps his notebook shut and turns to leave. "You better not be lying to me," he threatens. Then Cindy is wheeled into a room for treatment. Afterward, she's released.

When Cindy and Dave get home, Bobbie immediately takes charge of her daughter-in-law. She props Cindy up in bed with a collection of pillows and spoon-feeds her milk toast. "Come now, Mrs. Knight," Cindy protests. "I can feed myself." But Bobbie will hear none of it, and soon the hot buttered milk has the desired effect. "I know you're sad now," Bobbie whispers as Cindy's eyelids droop. "But you'll soon realize that this was for the best."

CHAPTER ELEVEN
THUMPER

Cindy and Dave are renting a one-bedroom apartment just off Route 1 in Alexandria. Now that they both have jobs, they can afford it. The problem is that Cindy's working at the Colony 7 dinner theater in Maryland and needs the Volkswagen to commute. This means Dave is back riding the bus to work. But now he has other plans. It's Sunday and Dave's calling people with motorcycles listed for sale in the newspaper. "Any luck?" Cindy asks, coming out of the bathroom. She's towel drying her short blond hair.

"Not yet," Dave answers. "You'd think it would be a buyer's market now that fall is here, but no."

Dave is seated on the floor next to the phone. Aside from a mattress and a portable stereo, the apartment is unfurnished. But the shag carpet is comfortable to sit on. Dave looks at an ad in the paper and dials the number. "I'm calling about the motorcycle for sale," he says, then listens with a frown. "Oh, I see. Well, thanks anyway."

"What's the story?" Cindy asks.

"He said his ad's been running since Friday, and he sold it last night."

"Too bad."

Dave tries another number. "Is the motorcycle still for sale?" As he listens to the reply, Dave gives Cindy a thumbs-up. "But no one's put a deposit down, right?" he asks. After a pause, Dave says, "Great, what's the address?" then scribbles on the margin of the newspaper. "Thanks, we'll be there in an hour."

After hurriedly dressing, Cindy and Dave drive to Laurel, Maryland, and find the address. It's a garden apartment building, like theirs, with a red Triumph Trophy 250 parked out front. Dave's immediately in lust with it. He buzzes the apartment number, and soon a young couple comes down to meet them. "Hi, I'm Stan," the man says. "This is Sharon."

Cindy and Dave introduce themselves then Cindy walks over to peek at the bundle in Sharon's arms. "And who's this?" she asks.

"Stanley Jr.," Sharon answers proudly, looking down at her baby.

"How old?"

"Just two months."

"Now you see why I'm selling the bike," Stan explains. "But I'm going to miss her. She's only a year old, just twenty-seven hundred miles, never been raced, never been down." He climbs aboard and uses the kick starter to get the little motor thumping. To Dave's ear, the exhaust note is as alluring as a siren song.

Stan puts the Triumph in gear and makes a loop around the parking lot. Then he pulls to a stop. "Want a test drive?" he asks.

"No need," Dave replies. "I'm sold."

Dave gives Stan a deposit and agrees to be back with the rest of the cash the next day. Then he and Cindy return to Virginia, stopping for fast food along the way. When they get home, it's almost Cindy's bedtime, but Dave's on midnights and must soon go to work. He kills some time with a book, then leaves to catch the bus.

After his shift is over in the morning, Dave goes back to the apartment, has breakfast, then crashes for a while. But he's ready and waiting when Cindy comes home that evening. "How was your day?" he asks.

"Not so good."

"What happened?"

"I had a lousy crew in to hang the lights," Cindy seethes. "They gave me nothing but trouble. I told them how I wanted it done, but they wouldn't listen. The guy kept saying, 'I'm the electrician here, little lady.'"

"Couldn't have been easy for those good ole boys to be taking orders from a little slip of a gal like you."

"Not funny," Cindy scowls. "I finally had to get the director. It was embarrassing."

Cindy changes out of her work clothes then the couple drives to Laurel. When they get there, Stan invites them upstairs. He counts out the cash Dave gives him then signs over the title. Afterward, they go outside where the bike is waiting. "There's a little trick to starting her up," Stan says. "I'll show you."

"Yeah, that would be good," Dave says. "I've never ridden a motorcycle."

"And now you're driving back to Virginia?"

"Sure, I just need you to show me the basics."

"Whatever you say," Stan agrees.

Ten minutes later Dave has learned how to start the Triumph, change gears, and brake. "It's no different than the Volkswagen," he reassures Cindy after Stan's gone. "Just follow me."

Soon they're on the Beltway, and Dave has the motorcycle up to its maximum speed. All's well until a dragonfly mistakes his face for a windshield. It's like getting shot between the eyes with a BB. Then an eighteen-wheeler rumbles past and tries to suck the Triumph into its slipstream. Dave manfully resists. He battles insects and trucks the rest of the trip, but his biggest scare comes on the Woodrow Wilson Bridge when the bike nearly wobbles out of control on the grating. Dave's happy to get off at the next exit.

"How was it?" Cindy asks when they get home.

"Great," Dave enthuses.

"Well, I want a ride."

"Let me get used to it first."

Dave has several close calls during the next few weeks while riding the motorcycle to and from work. Despite what he told Cindy, it's a lot trickier than driving a car. But gradually the near-death experiences become fewer, and eventually he feels confident enough to take his wife riding. Cindy is smitten. "Let's ride it to the concert next week," she suggests.

"It'll be chilly at night," Dave replies.

"We can bundle up," Cindy insists. "If we take the car, we'll have to park a mile away."

On the night of the concert, Dave easily finds a parking spot for the motorcycle only a block from the venue. It's a roller rink in downtown Alexandria, and when he and Cindy get inside, the crowd is sitting on the skating surface listening to Jeff Beck. He's playing an instrumental, and while many in the audience are focused on the guitar god's licks, others are passing joints and rapping. But conversation fades as the band segues into a vocal number and Rod Stewart steps to the microphone. His distinctive voice has people looking at each other quizzically and asking, "Who's that?"

After Beck's set, Big Brother takes the stage, and there are no more questions about who's singing. As the roar of feedback guitar and thrashing drums fills the hall, Joplin's voice cuts through the din like a chainsaw. Simultaneously everyone in the arena leaps to their feet. No one sits the rest of the night.

Once the concert is over, Cindy and Dave make a quick getaway on the motorcycle. Soon they're back at the apartment and have the Triumph on its stand for the night. "What a beauty," Cindy says, gazing at their chrome and crimson steed. "If we'd taken the car, we'd still be stuck in the traffic back on King Street."

The next morning, Cindy leaves for work at the Colony 7, and Dave heads for Arlington Towers. He's on his third cup of coffee when his father calls. "I may have a solution to your furniture deficiency," Knight says.

"That sounds good."

"Yes, well, we finally sold Grandad's house, and your Aunt Elizabeth has taken all the stuff out she wants. Several pieces of furniture remain, including a sofa. She says you're welcome to everything that's left, but it has to be out by closing."

"How do you suggest I haul the stuff up here?"

"You can rent a trailer."

"I can't pull a trailer with the Volkswagen; besides, Cindy needs it for work."

"Then you can take the Cadillac. Dan will go along to help."

So, during his next three-day break, Dave makes a whirlwind trip to Florida with Dan. Inside their grandparents' former home, they find an old but nicely upholstered sofa, end tables, lamps, and a cocktail table. A glass-fronted bookcase is in the den, full of musty tomes. Upstairs the brothers find an antique marble-top dresser. There's an oak table with chairs in the kitchen. After loading everything into the trailer, Dave and Dan take turns driving back to Virginia. It's late when they get there, but Cindy wakes and wants to see what they got. Dave opens the trailer, and she shines a flashlight inside. "You drove all that way for this junk?" Cindy exclaims.

It's cold, and a steady rain is falling the next morning, so Dave takes the bus to Arlington Towers instead of riding the Triumph. A white-haired gentleman named Jack Rawlings is waiting at the front desk. He's a retired mail clerk who has replaced Ryan. The bouncer is now a full-time student at Georgetown.

After Jack leaves, Mrs. Richfield stops by. "Just made a fresh pot," she says. "Help yourself."

"Thanks," Dave smiles. He fills his mug then sips coffee and watches people stream through the lobby. Some speak, others wave, but no one stops to chat. The people Dave got to be friends with when he first started are all gone now. Stephanie and Ski invested some of their ill-gotten gains in a suburban house, Suzanne has returned to Terra Haute, and Connie moved into an apartment closer to her store. The new tenants are mainly military types. It seems like every escalation in Vietnam brings more of them to Washington.

When Dave gets home that evening, a W. C. Fields poster welcomes him from the wall above his grandfather's sofa. Other furnishings from Coral Gables add to the cozy atmosphere in the apartment while rock concert posters lend a modern touch. The bookcase looks inviting, so Dave picks one of the volumes at random and starts reading.

"How 'bout unloading the car?" Cindy exclaims, coming in the door with her arms full of groceries. Dave complies and then helps put everything away. Afterward, he works alongside his wife in the kitchen. She makes a sauce for spaghetti while he chops up stuff for a salad. The kitchen is warm, and the air is full of good smells from the oven where a loaf of garlic bread is browning. Soon everything's ready.

As the Thanksgiving holiday approaches, the weather deteriorates, and Dave can no longer ride the motorcycle to work. Cindy takes him when she can. Otherwise, Dave rides the bus while the Triumph sits forlornly in the parking lot. After the first snow, they buy a cover for it.

For Christmas, Cindy and Dave go to Princeton. They attend a midnight church service with her parents and open presents with them the next morning. Afterward, they return to Virginia since both must work the next day.

The following week, the young marrieds go to spend New Year's Eve with Dave's family, but when they get to the house, nobody's home except Knight and Bobbie. "Where is everybody?" Dave asks.

"Some girl came by and picked Dan up about an hour ago," Bobbie replies. "Big girl."

"And of course, your sisters had to go out," Knight grumbles. "I've told all of you; only fools go out New Year's Eve."

Knight puts a Glenn Miller LP on the stereo, starts a fire blazing, then makes drinks for everyone. They listen to records until almost midnight when the phone rings. Knight picks it up and identifies himself. He listens for a moment, then says, "I'll be right there."

"Dave, you need to take me," Knight says. "Marie and Perle have been in a wreck."

"I'm coming too," Bobbie exclaims.

"No, better you stay here with Cindy," Knight insists. "To answer the phone."

Knight and Dave go out and get into the Volkswagen. Soon they're speeding south on Route 1 through a darkened Fort Belvoir. Coming over a rise just south of the base, the night gives way to a sea of flashing lights. Patrol cars are drawn up across the highway while more vehicles line the shoulders on both sides. Dave pulls over and parks. He and his father hurry past several fire engines and an ambulance to find what's left of the Cadillac plastered against an overpass wall. Two men kneel next to the driver's door. They wear white overalls, heavy gloves, and helmets with face shields. One holds an acetylene torch. Sparks fly around them like fireflies.

Off to one side of the wreck, a group of firemen in full regalia wait along with several state troopers. One of the policemen spots Knight and walks toward him. The flashing lights of the emergency vehicles create a strobe effect, and the officer appears to move jerkily. "I'm Sergeant Bellamy," he says. "Are you Colonel Knight?"

"That's right."

"We traced the registration to you."

"Yes, officer," Knight says impatiently.

"Well, the vehicle appears to have been traveling south at a high rate of speed then veered across two lanes into the overpass wall," Bellamy says. "Alcohol may have been a factor." The policeman shows Knight an empty bottle of vodka. "We found this under the passenger seat."

"What about injuries?"

"The passenger was thrown clear," Bellamy says. "She's been taken to Fort Belvoir Army Hospital."

"And the driver?"

"Still trapped in the vehicle."

"What's her condition?"

"Faint pulse and light breathing last time we checked."

The technicians start a compressor thumping then use a power tool on the door. After several minutes it comes off, and Marie can be seen pinned to the back of her seat by the steering column. The transmission and drive train have buckled through the floor beside her.

Now a member of the ambulance crew kneels beside Marie and holds a stethoscope to her chest. Next, he tries the carotid artery. He looks up and shakes his head. Dave's in shock. His father remains stone-faced. Then the medic gets to his feet. "She's gone," he says.

Dave numbly drives them to the Fort Belvoir Hospital where Perle is in intensive care. They're not allowed back, so father and son wordlessly settle down to wait. An hour later a young doctor comes out. He's a dark-haired serious-looking man with a five-o'clock shadow. The physician is dressed in light green scrubs and wears the talisman of his profession around his neck. "She's lucky to be alive," he tells them. "Skull fracture, broken collarbone, busted ribs, a punctured lung, and internal injuries. We performed emergency surgery to repair the spleen and managed to salvage it."

"When can we see her?"

"Check back this afternoon, that's all I can tell you."

Bobbie and Cindy are seated in the kitchen drinking coffee when Knight and Dave get home. They look up expectantly. "It looks like Perle will eventually recover," Knight says. "But Marie didn't make it."

Bobbie's anxious expression collapses and her eyes well with tears. "That poor girl," she moans. "It's all my fault."

"It was an accident," Knight says. "No one's at fault."

"I was weak, too weak," Bobbie sobs.

"They ran off the road. It was nothing to do with you."

"I should have taken the kids and left you a long time ago, back when it might have done some good," Bobbie cries. She glares at her husband through her tears.

"Bobbie, this isn't the time," Knight says gently.

"That's what you always said," Bobbie cries. "This is not the time. And I listened to you. Why? Because I'm weak, that's why. And now look at us. This family is doomed." Bobbie picks up a table napkin and wipes her eyes. "Where have they taken Marie?" she asks.

"The hospital," Knight says. "I have to call a funeral home."

"And what about Perle? When can we see her?"

"Maybe this afternoon."

Bobbie looks down for a long moment then slowly gets to her feet. "I'm going upstairs," she says.

"I'll go with you," Cindy says, taking Bobbie's arm.

Over the next several days, word gets around about the crash, and a small contingent of Fort Hunt students turns out for Marie's funeral. Dave recognizes some of the kids but doesn't know any of them. He and Cindy endure the proceedings along with Dan, Bobbie, and Knight. Melissa is a no-show.

The next day Cindy goes back to work at the Colony 7 while Dave returns to Arlington Towers. Over time, as both settle back into their work routine, they talk less about what happened New Year's Eve. Soon the weather improves, and Dave again commutes to work on two wheels. That's easily the best part of his day. Otherwise being at Arlington Towers is a drag. The new tenants are not nearly as much fun as the ones who moved out, and the only person who regularly lingers at the front desk anymore is Peggy Richfield. She has just turned fifteen and is a bundle of curiosity. "Why don't you wear a helmet?" she asks Dave one day.

"Don't have one."

"But it's not safe," she says.

"Not true," Dave replies. "I have better peripheral vision without a helmet."

"What's peripheral?"

Dave looks up from his newspaper. "Don't you have anything to do for school?"

"Nah, did all my homework between classes."

Mrs. Richfield comes out of the office. "Honey, maybe you could help me with a couple of things," she says to her daughter. The resident manager smiles at Dave and shrugs her shoulders.

On a Friday morning early in May, Dave finishes a stint of midnights. That means he and Cindy will have a rare weekend together. So, the next day they pack a few things and ride the Triumph out to the mountains. Near Front Royal, they turn south on a twisty two-lane highway. After a nice ride on the scenic stretch, they turn again and follow a farm road down to the Shenandoah. When they get to the river, Dave parks, and he and Cindy get off to stretch. "My butt aches," Dave complains.

"And I have a massive wedgie," Cindy laughs.

"This is beautiful, though," Dave says. They're at a spot where the river makes a sweeping turn then descends through a boulder field over a ledge and into a deep pool. Whitewater breaks over the rocks and standing waves form at the base of the rapid.

Cindy spreads a blanket over the grass, sits, and lights a joint. They share it, then Dave puts on an old pair of tennis shoes and wades in to fish. Immediately he's catching smallmouths in the fast-moving water. They put up a tremendous fight on the ultralight spinning rod he uses. After releasing several fish, Dave sloshes out of the water and joins Cindy for a picnic. She's packed sandwiches, chips, and beer.

Once they're done eating, Dave goes back into the river. The fish like the feathered spinner he uses, and he throws more back. Meanwhile, Cindy reads as shadows cast by the trees on the far bank lengthen. All too soon it's time to go.

The return trip is uneventful until Cindy and Dave are on the Beltway nearing their turnoff. That's when Dave checks his rearview mirror and finds it full of flashing lights. He pulls over, then he and Cindy wait as a young state trooper gets out of his cruiser and walks up.

"Your tail light is out," he says. "Have you got your license and registration?"

Dave hands over the documents. "Wait one," the patrolman says as he turns to go back to his vehicle.

"Hope he doesn't want to search the bag," Cindy says.

"I doubt it," Dave replies.

After several minutes the officer comes back and hands Dave his papers. "Nice bike," he says.

"Thanks. We rode out to the mountains today. It was beautiful."

"I bet, but you kids need to be careful. Be sure to get that taillight replaced."

"I'll take care of it tomorrow."

The policeman has another look at the shiny little motorcycle then darts a final glance at Cindy and Dave. They appear impossibly young, foolish, and happy. He's only a few years older but has a wife and two young children waiting at home. The trooper shakes his head and returns to the patrol car while Cindy and Dave get back on their ride to head home. "All I want is a nice hot bath," Cindy says when they get there.

"I'll join you," Dave suggests.

"OK."

The young marrieds take it easy the next day. They sleep in then watch the Redskins beat the Cardinals. Afterward, they go to have dinner with Dave's parents. Dan is reporting to the Air Force in the morning, and they want to say goodbye.

When Cindy and Dave get to the house, they find Bobbie in the kitchen. She has a hen roasting in the oven and is cutting up potatoes on the kitchen counter. Bobbie's wearing a cute housedress and is carefully made up but can't help looking frail. "What can I do?" Cindy asks her.

"You can help with the cornbread."

"Great. I want to learn your Texas recipe."

"It's simple," Bobbie says, holding up a box of Jiffy cornbread mix. They laugh. "Actually, I have a few extra ingredients we'll put in there."

"Good, then I'll have the secret!"

"That's right."

Dave kisses his mother then wanders into the living room. Dan's sitting on the floor shining shoes. "Hey, bro," he says.

"You're not spit shining them, are you?" Dave asks.

"Nah."

"Then I'll help." Dave sits on the floor next to his brother. He picks up a shoe brush and lightly buffs one of the dress shoes. "Are you excited?" he asks.

"Oh yeah," Dan replies. "Excited to be getting out of here."

"That bad?"

"He's drunk every night," Dan whispers, "and Perle's not much better."

Once they finish polishing, Dan takes the shoes upstairs. He comes back down holding a chess board. "Might as well have a game," he says.

"Why not?" Dave agrees. "What have we got for music?" Dave sorts through the rack of LPs and finds one of his old Kingston Trio records to put on. Then the brothers settle into their game, and as usual, Dan is wildly aggressive. Dave spends the first half hour defending himself while gradually building up his position. Then he begins to take advantage of all the openings his brother left.

"I'll take the winner," Knight says, coming into the room. Ice cubes clink, and a piece of lime floats in his drink. He sits in his chair and lights a cigarette.

"Check to your queen," Dave says.

"Oh fuck," Dan replies.

"Hey, it's that Everglades song," Knight exclaims. He goes to the stereo console and turns up the volume. "You used to sing this in the car, remember?"

"Sure," Dave replies.

The song ends, but Knight picks up the needle and starts it over again. He sings along with the opening lyrics snapping his fingers. Then he settles back into his armchair tapping his foot along with the music.

"What's that crap you're listening to?" Perle asks, sauntering into the room. She's wearing a tank top and frayed bell-bottom jeans and holds a beer. Her wavy chestnut hair is unkempt but somehow looks glamorous that way. She kills the beer, throws the empty into the trash, then settles onto her father's lap. He tries to bring his cigarette up, but Perle takes it from his fingers and has a drag. "Ugh," she exhales distastefully. "How can you smoke those things?"

"Nobody's asking you to smoke my cigarettes," Knight replies.

"Well, I'm going to High's for some Marlboros," Perle declares. "Give me some money." She kisses her father on the cheek.

"I gave you a twenty yesterday," Knight says.

"Well, it's gone."

"Get off me then, and I'll find my wallet."

After getting the money, Perle departs, and Dave returns his attention to the chess board. The match is nearing its predictable end, but Dan won't give up. Finally, Dave succeeds in checkmating him, so now he and his father can go to war. They have had many chess battles, but Dave's never won. This time is no different. He loses his queen to his father's knight early on, and it's all downhill from there. Afterward, Dave goes into the kitchen for a beer. He finds Perle has returned from the store and is sitting at the table talking with Cindy. "Then I told her, don't do the crime if you can't do the time," Perle is saying.

Cindy laughs, "That's telling her."

Bobbie takes the potatoes off the stove. "Can you help?" she asks handing a potato masher to her husband. Knight quickly passes it to Dave. "Here, make yourself useful," he says.

So, Dave puts his beer down and goes to work on the spuds. Meanwhile, Bobbie goes into the dining room to set the table. When she returns, the others have disappeared, and Dave's the only one left in the kitchen. "Where did everyone go?" Bobbie wonders. "We're ready."

"I'll get them," Dave offers. He goes into the living room and finds Dan and his father. "Dinner is served," he proclaims. Then Dave goes upstairs and follows the pungent odor of marijuana down the hall. Cindy is in Perle's room, and they are sharing a joint. "Want a toke?" Perle offers. Dave takes the short end and gets a good drag off it before dropping the last tiny bit in an ashtray. "Time to eat," he exhales.

After supper, the family sits around the table, talking. "I grew up in the Everglades," Knight tells Cindy, "while my father was building the Overseas Railway. One time a friend and I were out fishing in this little rowboat. It was hot, so I decided to go for a swim. I stripped and stood on one of the seats. The boat rocked as I began to dive then, at the last moment, I saw two beady eyes pop up. I was halfway into the water at that moment but somehow got back in the boat without getting wet. A man can do miraculous things when sufficiently motivated."

Dave turns to his brother. "Where's basic training?" he asks.

"Lackland," Dan says quietly. He has become subdued over the course of the evening.

"They call it basic," Knight sneers, "but in the Air Force it's nothing. You want basic training, go to Fort Benning."

"And I'm sure the Marines would say army training is nothing," Dave retorts. He knows how to push his father's buttons, and sure enough Knight gets angry. "The Marines are a bunch of glory hounds," he snaps.

"No one's covering themselves in glory nowadays," Dave quickly replies.

"You're wrong about that," Knight exclaims. "Every day American soldiers are out there fighting and dying so that you and your hippie friends can have all the freedoms you so take for granted."

"You mean every day American boys are being used as cannon fodder in an endless meaningless war that only benefits the military-industrial complex," Dave rants.

Bobbie energetically rubs her temples. She's heard Dave and her husband litigate this issue many times. "I'm going to bed," she proclaims.

"Me too," Dan says.

Cindy helps Knight clean up. Afterward, he puts ice cubes into a glass. "Care for a nightcap?" he asks.

"I'd love one, Colonel, but we have to go," Cindy smiles.

"Another time, then," Knight replies.

It's a little before one in the morning on a soft midsummer night when Dave pulls into the parking lot of the apartment building where he and Cindy live. He has just finished a swing shift and will have the next day off before going on the graveyard. After resting the Triumph on its stand, he turns the key to lock the handlebars. Approaching the building entrance, Dave spots Perle's white Corvair parked out front. Knight bought it for her used.

Dave lets himself into the apartment then pushes through a bead curtain into the living room. In the semi-darkness he sees Cindy and Perle sitting on the floor behind the coffee table. A Simon & Garfunkel LP is playing quietly on the stereo while candles flicker and shadows dance to the music. Two cans of cheap beer rest alongside an overflowing ashtray.

"You're just in time," Cindy says, holding up a doobie. So, Dave joins them on the floor and takes his turn with the joint. Afterward, Cindy gets up to flip the record over. "Perle is bummed out," she says.

"It's nothing," Perle exclaims.

"So, tell me anyway," Dave suggests.

"It's just some of the girls at school," Perle shrugs.

"What about them?"

"They've been talking about me, that's all."

"And they've been bad-mouthing Marie," Cindy says.

"That's sick," Dave declares.

"Sickening is more like it," Perle says, draining her beer. "That's why I hardly go out anymore. When I do, all I hear is nasty shit." She gets up to go into the kitchen. "Anyone else want one?"

"I'm sure Dave could use a beer," Cindy says.

Perle comes back with the beverages, and the conversation resumes. "They're just jealous," she says bitterly. "Just a bunch of jealous bitches. They didn't dare speak when Marie was still around. She'd beat their ass, and they knew it. But now they're brave enough to pick on me."

"I hated high school," Cindy says. "Me and the other kids in the theater group were the geeks. They laughed at us."

"I'm dreading going back in September," Perle sighs.

"You just need to hang in there one more year," Cindy replies. "Afterward you'll be off to college. Going from high school to college is like if you grew up in some little hick town then moved to New York City. It's a different world."

"That sounds good."

"I've got the munchies," Dave says. "Anyone else want some PB&J?"

Both girls raise their hands, so Dave goes into the kitchen and makes enough sandwiches to go around. Then they sit around the coffee table and eat. "You need to stay here tonight," Dave tells Perle afterward. "You can sleep on the sofa."

"Oh, that's all right, I can make it home."

"No, Dave's right," Cindy insists. "It's late, and we've been drinking. You don't want to get into another accident."

Cindy gets some bedding and makes up the sofa. It's after 2:00 a.m. now and everyone's tired. They take turns in the bathroom and get ready for bed. Before turning in, Cindy goes back into the living room to check on Perle. She's lying on the sofa staring at the ceiling.

"Everything OK?" Cindy asks.

"Just perfect," Perle replies. "But that was no accident, you know."

"I suspected as much," Cindy says. "You're lucky to be alive."

"Marie's the lucky one," Perle says bitterly.

"You'll see it differently one day, I promise you."

The next morning, Cindy tiptoes around the apartment as she gets ready for work. Then she quietly leaves without waking anyone. Several hours later Dave gets up. He goes into the kitchen and finds Perle reading the newspaper. "I see you're having your Wheaties," Dave says.

Perle holds up her beer. "'Breakfast of champions,'" she smiles. "Want one?"

"Might as well," Dave allows.

Perle gets her brother a cold one from the fridge. "I brought in the mail when I got the paper," she says. "There's an official-looking letter for you."

Dave picks up the envelope and sees that it's from the county draft board. Inside is the notice he's been dreading: "Greetings, you are ordered to report for induction into the Armed Forces of the United States." Quickly he rereads it, but there's no mistake.

That night Cindy freaks when Dave shows her the letter. "I'm going with you," she declares.

"That's impossible," Dave replies. "Read it again. I'm the only one invited. If Nixon wanted you along, he'd have mentioned it."

"There's no law says I can't move to Richmond if I want."

"Richmond is just where they take us for induction," Dave replies. "After that, who knows? Might be Georgia, or South Carolina, maybe even Missouri."

"Wherever it is, I'm going."

"There wouldn't be any point."

"You don't want me?" Cindy cries. "Is that it?"

"Of course I want you," Dave says, putting an arm around his wife. "But soldiers are not given any free time during basic training. We'd never see each other."

"How do you know that?"

"Honey, I grew up on those bases, and I know how draftees are treated. You see them on Saturdays and Sundays walking along the roadside picking up cigarette butts or in the officers' yards pushing lawn mowers, raking leaves, whatever shit jobs need to be done. Basic trainees are the lowest form of life on an army post. They never get passes."

Cindy wipes her eyes then goes to the bathroom. She comes out blowing her nose. "Well, what about after basic?" she asks. "What then?"

"Advanced individual training," Dave replies. "It's not much better."

"But it's better?"

"Yeah, a little."

"Well, I'll stay here until you get out of basic, if that's what you want, but that's it."

Cindy glares at Dave with fierce determination, and he gives in. "All right, you can come along wherever they send me after basic training," Dave says. Cindy jumps into her husband's lap and smothers his face with kisses. After a while, he comes up for air and says, "I don't know how we're going to afford it, though."

"We'll make do," Cindy declares. "One way or another, we'll make do."

Two weeks later Dave stops by Arlington Tower to pick up his final paycheck. "Thanks again for giving me notice," Mrs. Richfield says. "It was a big help."

"And thank you for all the donuts and free coffee," Dave replies. He sticks out his hand, but Mrs. Richfield sidesteps it and wraps Dave up in a hug. He briefly returns the gesture then makes his escape. Out in the parking lot he's getting ready to start the Triumph when the school bus pulls up. Peggy gets off then hurries over with her book bag dangling from one arm. It bangs against her leg as she runs.

"You weren't going to leave without saying goodbye?" she pants.

"No way," Dave lies.

"I'm so sorry you're going."

"Me too."

"We had such fun."

"Yes."

"I'll miss you so much."

"I'll miss you too."

The wind blows a wisp of Peggy's hair across her eyes, and she reaches to brush it away as traffic whizzes around Roslyn Circle. Overhead, tall buildings blot out the sun. "You'll be going off to college in a couple of years," Dave says. "That's going to be so much fun you won't believe it." He puts the gearshift in neutral, opens the choke, and rests his foot on the kickstarter. Then he offers his hand, and they shake. "Take care of yourself," Dave says.

"You too," Peggy replies with a wan smile.

Now Dave's life of freedom is growing short. He places a weekend newspaper ad to sell the Triumph, and first thing Friday the phone begins to ring. Dave rolls out of bed to get the first call. "No, I don't want to negotiate, take it or leave it," he growls. The other party hangs up, and immediately the phone rings again. "That's right," Dave says. "Only six thousand one hundred miles. She's never been raced, never been down."

Just before noon a guy comes over and agrees to pay the advertised price for the Triumph, which is what Dave spent a year ago. The man leaves a deposit and promises to be back at five with the rest of the money. Once he's gone, Dave calls the *Washington Post* and cancels the ad for Saturday and Sunday. Then he gets his sunglasses and jumps on the bike.

Dave steers the Triumph north on Route 1 then goes south on the George Washington Parkway to ride along the river. Sunlight sparkles off the waves as he twists the throttle as far as it will go. She's up close to seventy, and he has to lean the motorcycle into the curves. It's fun, but too soon Dave runs out of Parkway and must slow down. He's out of park police territory, and into the realm of the dreaded Alexandria fuzz.

Shortly after passing his old neighborhood, Dave reaches the junction with Route 1 and heads back toward the apartment. On a whim, he stops at a particularly horrendous-looking roadhouse and goes inside. It's early afternoon and the joint's regular clientele are still on duty at Fort Belvoir. Nevertheless, a worn-out dancer is bumping and grinding on the stage while three fiftyish-looking gents sit at the bar ignoring her. They are nursing mugs of draft beer, so that's what Dave orders from the over-endowed woman behind the counter.

Riding is thirsty work, and Dave quickly drains his first brew. While tending to the next, he surreptitiously sizes up his drinking companions. All three are crew cut and tattooed. Dave guesses that they are retired NCOs and have now dedicated themselves to a new mission—drinking up their pensions.

The old soldiers are not gregarious, so after tossing back another draft, Dave decides to break the ice. "I'm going into the army next week," he blurts out. The men turn in unison and look him over like farmers eyeing a dubious specimen at a livestock auction. Dave is an emaciated string bean, but the lifers can imagine what several months of PT and good army chow might do for him. "This calls for a beer," one of them proclaims.

Dave's money is no longer any good in the place, so it's with great reluctance that he bids farewell to his new pals several hours later then dizzily speeds home. There he finds the Triumph's soon-to-be new owner impatiently waiting. After money changes hands, Dave signs over the title, then sadly watches the motorcycle exit his life. He's disappointed that she leaves so readily and without a backward glance. *"There's a lesson to be learned here,"* Dave drunkenly muses. *"Something to do with unrequited love."*

The following week, on Sunday morning, Cindy gets Dave up early to enjoy his last day of being a civilian for a while. She packs a picnic lunch and they drive to Great Falls. Once inside the gate, they head to their favorite parking space at the north end. After a long hike, up the river and back, Cindy and Dave sit at a picnic table and pop the tops on beers they are not supposed to have in the park. Still, the suds go well with the cold fried chicken and cornbread Cindy packed. After eating they pass a joint back and forth while gazing out over the rocky gorge and down to the cataract below.

An intrepid fisherman has climbed down to the base of the falls, crossing over half a mile of jumbled boulders. Cindy and Dave watch the angler cast a shiny lure. The sun is out, so it's far from ideal conditions for fishing. Nevertheless, the man's rod suddenly bows over and for half an hour he battles a mighty fish. Eventually, he gets the thing close, and the sun's rays flash off the startlingly bronze sides of a huge smallmouth. The fisherman kneels and tries to haul his catch out of the water, but every time he gets it near, the fish struggles away. Finally, his line breaks and the bass regains its freedom.

That night Cindy and Dave go to visit the Knights. When they get there the colonel's new Buick is parked in the driveway. He's in the living room listening to Benny Goodman tootle his clarinet. "To what do we owe the honor of your presence?" Knight slurs.

"I'm going into the army tomorrow," Dave says.

"Oh, that's right," Knight replies. "I knew it was coming up. Don't tell me it's tomorrow already."

"'Fraid so," Dave says.

"We need to give you a proper send-off," Knight exclaims. "I'll open some champagne."

"We'll have a toast when I get out," Dave replies. "I don't feel like celebrating right now."

"Then at least let me make you one of these," Knight says, holding up his drink.

"Beer is fine for me," Dave insists.

"Well, I'm sure Cindy will have a drink with me," Knight pleads. "Won't you, honey?"

"Sure, I will, Colonel, I love rum and Coke," Cindy says brightly. "Let me help you."

Dave gets a beer out of the refrigerator and takes a few sips. Then he puts the can down and goes upstairs. After gently opening the door to his parents' bedroom, Dave tiptoes inside and sees Bobbie lying on the bed with a damp washcloth over her eyes. It's humid even with the air conditioning, so she has kicked the covers off. Dave notices that his mother's once glamorous legs are now mottled with bruises. "Who is it?" she asks softly.

"Dave," he says.

"Oh, hi, honey."

"Hi, Mom."

"Where's that sweet little girl of yours?"

"Downstairs with Dad."

"I see."

"How are you, Mom?"

"Oh, about as good as can be."

"Are you in pain?"

"Just my head."

"I'm so sorry."

"That's OK, sweetie, nothing you can do."

"I'm going into the army tomorrow."

"So soon?"

"It's been a month."

"Oh."

"I'll write."

"Yes, do that."

"Can I get you anything?"

"No, but stay for a minute," Bobbie says. "I wanted to tell you something."

"What's that?"

"I just wanted to say that you'll be all right."

"Thanks, Mom."

"I mean it. You know I've never worried about you."

"I'm glad."

"I've fretted endlessly over the others but never about you."

"That's good."

"It's because you always land on your feet somehow," Bobbie says. "Always have."

"That's right, Mom. Someone up there likes me."

"Must be," Bobbie says faintly. "Now I need to rest. Take care of that girl, you hear?"

"Yes, Mother," Dave says quietly, but Bobbie's breathing deeply now. She has faded out.

By the time Cindy and Dave get to Fairfax the next morning, a crowd has gathered outside the draft board. On one side, a group of protestors wave signs and chant tired antiwar slogans from behind a barrier. The draftees are opposite them. Most have one or more loved ones in tow, but no one is talking. So, it's a relief when a Greyhound appears. Now people hasten to say their final goodbyes. "Here's looking at you, kid," Dave says.

"Not funny," Cindy sniffles.

"Sorry, but I hate goodbyes. Why don't you leave and go to work? I'll see you in a couple of months."

Cindy gazes at the depressing scene around them, then faces Dave again and they kiss. "Oh, all right," she says, "I'll go."

As Dave watches the VW drive off, a Red Cross volunteer approaches and hands him a paper sack containing toothpaste, mouthwash, deodorant, and a pack of peanut butter crackers. Then he boards the bus and finds a window seat. When the doors close, the voices of the demonstrators can no longer be heard. In the silence, their animated gestures and contorted faces appear comical. Dave laughs as the bus rolls past them. Later, at the Armed Forces Induction Center, he takes one step forward. It's like going back.

CHAPTER TWELVE
BENNING SCHOOL FOR BOYS

After completing eleven weeks of basic training at Fort Benning, Georgia, Dave Knight is now at Fort McClellan, Alabama, undergoing Advanced Individual Training (AIT) for his Military Occupational Specialty (MOS), which is Light Weapons Infantry (11B). Over the last several months, the army has packed thirty pounds of lean muscle on him. He's sunburned, and his hair is cropped short. The boy has never looked healthier.

Dave's company has just returned from a long night of practicing small-unit tactics. They had several simulated firefights during the evening, and now the men are back in the barracks cleaning weapons. Because the blanks used in training emit more carbon than real bullets, most of the soldiers' rifles are filthy. But not Dave's. He never fires his M16 when they are out at night. In the dark, the cadre can't see who's shooting and who isn't.

Even though Dave's M16 is spotless, he tries to look busy by idly running a cleaning rod up and down the barrel. He's biding his time until the armorers start accepting weapons. Meanwhile, Wade Bayliss is sitting on a footlocker nearby earnestly working on his rifle. Wade and Dave have been bunkmates since AIT began seven weeks ago.

Wade is from a hollow in the hills of Eastern Kentucky and doesn't talk much. So, after several previous attempts at conversation with the taciturn mountaineer, Dave has given up. He is therefore surprised when Wade suddenly spouts out a comment on the evening: "That there lying on the cold ground hurts. I still feel it."

"Oh, really?" Dave says disinterestedly.

"It's 'cause of all them plates, rods, and screws they put in me when I was a young'un."

"What?!" Now Dave tunes in. He hopes Wade is going to tell him that spacemen installed a miniature radio receiver in one of his teeth and that he's getting messages from Martians.

"It was after I got run over ridin' my bike," Wade elaborates.

"Oh, so you got hit by a car and they had to use a metal rod to reset a broken bone?" Dave's disappointed that this has nothing to do with Mars.

"It was a bus, not a car, and it dint hit me, it ran over me," Wade replies. "They used them metal things on just about all my bones and my head at that there hospital in Lexinton."

"You have a metal plate in your head?"

"Yeah, right heah." Wade points to the side of his skull. "It hurts bad when it gets cold."

Dave stares intently at Wade and for the first time notices that his head is somewhat asymmetrical. It looks like a partially deflated volleyball. "OK, so where are these rods?" Dave asks.

Wade points to an ankle, his wrist, and several other places. "They used screws and pins to fix this part heah," he says, indicating his groin.

"You fractured your pelvis?"

"Yeah, my pelvis, that's what they called it."

"What about the physical exam when you got drafted?" Dave asks. "Didn't you tell the doctor about this?"

"Tried to, but he was in a hurry," Wade replies. "He told me once I got to Fort Benning I could go on sick call, and they would take care of it."

"OK, so you went on sick call. What did they say?"

"Guv me a cold pack and said come back if it keeps bothering me."

Dave knows that a cold pack is a paper bag containing analgesics, throat lozenges, cough syrup, and other drugstore remedies. Just about everyone that goes on sick call receives one, no matter what ails them. But clearly, Wade needs more. In the harsh light of the barracks, his face is tightly drawn with pain. He certainly has no business running up and down mountain trails all day and then lying on the cold hard ground half the night waiting to spring an ambush. And after AIT, it gets worse. Most of the company will be going to Vietnam, though Dave will not be joining them. He has been selected to attend Officer Candidate School (OCS).

Now Dave notices the bustle around them. Guys are coming back into the barracks without their M16s. They are heading toward the latrine to shower and get ready for bed. It looks like the armorers are accepting weapons now.

"Bayliss, here's what you need to do," Dave says as he stows his cleaning gear away. "Go on sick call tomorrow, and when you get to the hospital tell them you want full body X-rays. Do not let them give you a cold pack and send you back here. You must stay and not leave until they take X-rays."

"You reckon I oughta?"

"For sure."

"OK."

Dave takes his rifle to the armory where it quickly passes inspection. Then he comes back, gets his shaving kit, and goes to the latrine.

Early the next morning, after too little rest, the platoon assembles for a PT session followed by breakfast. Then they fall into company formation. Those who are going on sick call, including Wade, fall out and climb into the back of a three-quarter-ton truck for the ride to the post hospital. Everyone else gets their field gear, draws their weapons, and waits for transportation. Soon a line of deuce-and-a-halfs appear. The soldiers mount up for the ride out to the ranges.

As the trucks leave the company area, the trainees fall asleep. Dave jostles along with the rest, his mouth open, swaying to and fro, head bobbing, and with saliva drooling out of the corner of his mouth. He holds his M16 between his legs and like the others manages not to drop it even though deep in never-never land. Sometimes he falls over to one side and rests his head on a neighbor's shoulder; at other times it is his shoulder that's used as a pillow. In this manner, the soldiers ride out to the hinterlands of Fort McClellan for a day of marksmanship training.

That afternoon, after a long, fitfully sleepy ride back to the base, Dave dismounts from the big truck and carries his rifle into the barracks. He has a real cleaning job to do on his M16, and he wants to be done by five o'clock. That's because it's Friday and he has a weekend pass.

Approaching his bunk, Dave glances at the one below. Wade's sheets, blankets, and pillow are gone. His mattress is rolled up, and the lock is missing from the Kentuckian's footlocker. Dave idly lifts the lid expecting to see what he sees, which is nothing. *"How did that guy get through eleven weeks of basic and almost seven weeks of AIT?"* Dave muses as he gets out his cleaning kit. Then he disassembles his weapon and gets to work.

An hour later an armorer accepts Dave's rifle after a thorough inspection. Dave returns to the barracks, packs his overnight bag, and goes to the parking lot to wait for Cindy. When the VW pulls up, he gets into the passenger seat and bends over for a kiss. Then Cindy puts the car in gear, and they head off post. "You wouldn't believe what Bayliss told me yesterday," Dave says.

"I thought you said that he's practically mute," Cindy replies.

"Well, he finally spoke up, and it turns out he's a one-man hardware store," Dave laughs. "Bayliss said he was in a wreck as a child and now all that's holding him together is some nuts and bolts."

"Poor guy."

"I insisted he go on sick call today, and we'll never see him again. All his stuff was gone when we got back."

"You need to try that."

"The only metal in me is some fillings," Dave replies. "That ain't gonna get me out."

"Guess not," Cindy sighs.

That night Cindy and Dave simply enjoy being home together and don't go out. They're both tired at the end of the week, Dave for the obvious reason and Cindy because of her job selling magazines door to door. So they dine on Chinese carryout and spend the evening in front of the TV. But early the next morning they pack some sandwiches and drinks then drive to a nearby state park. They leave the VW at a trailhead and spend the day hiking in the mountains. "The guys in my platoon would think I'm crazy if they could see what we're doing," Dave says while he and Cindy are taking a break. "This is similar to what we do during the week."

"See, the army's not so bad," Cindy smiles.

"A lot of what we do in the infantry is fun," Dave replies. "The problem is the people I'm doing it with."

On the way back to Anniston, Cindy and Dave stop at a Winn-Dixie to pick up a few things. It's a mild autumn day, so they plan to grill hamburgers on the patio. When they get home, Dave gets the charcoal going while Cindy opens a couple beers. As they're waiting for the fire to die down, a tall, ruggedly handsome man walks up. "Hey, Cindy," he says, "is this your husband?"

"Yes, this is Dave," Cindy replies.

"Hi, I'm Sergeant Garrison," the man announces and offers his hand. Dave takes it then suppresses a scream while Garrison grinds his knuckles together.

"Can I get you a cold one?" Cindy offers.

"Sounds good," Garrison says. He releases Dave's hand and sits on one of the patio chairs.

"Jim is my neighbor," Cindy tells Dave when she returns with the beer.

"I've been looking out for her during the week," Garrison explains. "Hope you don't mind."

"Not at all," Dave replies. "This seems like a safe area, but you never can tell."

"Cindy tells me you're in AIT," Garrison says.

"Yeah, we just finished the seventh week."

"You'll be done soon; then it's Benning for OCS, I hear."

"That's right."

"I was a black hat at the jump school there for a while."

"Oh?"

"It's one of the few places in the army where an NCO can smoke an officer," Garrison says. "Man, did we light into those butter bars."

"What are you doing now?"

"Oh, I'm not supposed to say, but what the hell, everybody knows we have Special Forces here. We train up in the mountains between deployments, and of course we get some R&R."

"Got it," Dave says. He drains his beer and gets up. "Can I get you another?"

"Nah, I've got to run," Garrison says. "But we got to party sometime. Cindy tells me you two like to drop a little acid now and then. I can get us some hits, and we can trip together. What do you say?"

"That would be cool," Dave lies. He doesn't offer to shake hands as Garrison takes his leave.

Cindy takes Dave back to Fort McClellan the next evening, and on Monday at 0530 hours, a PT session kicks off another week of AIT. The trainees spend the next several days at various firing ranges working on marksmanship and weapons familiarization. Then Thursday evening, the cooks bring Murmansk cans full of hot food out to the field. The soldiers eat while waiting for it to get dark. They are going to run the night infiltration course.

In the twilight after chow, the company is assembled in bleachers by the drill instructors. It's still too light out to begin the night's activities so Sergeant Forester, the DI for Dave's platoon, will lead the men in song. He often does this, and everyone loves it.

Forester is a handsome black man who carries himself with all the swagger expected of a DI. He has a fabulous baritone and a penchant for old-time spirituals. "Steal Away" is the song he has selected for tonight.

"Now, listen up," Forester bellows. "I'm going to sing the chorus then you will repeat it."

> *Steal away, steal away, steal away home,*
> *Steal away, steal away,*
> *I ain't got time to stay here.*

The trainees in the bleachers practice this part several times until Sergeant Forester is satisfied. Then he delivers the first verse solo:

> *My lord, my lord, he calls me,*
> *he calls me by the thunder*
> *the trumpet sounds within the pit of my soul*
> *I ain't got time to stay here.*

Now the massed voices of the over one hundred soldiers come back with the chorus, and then Forester performs the next verse. The troops carry on singing this way for many more stanzas while darkness descends. As the last note hangs in the air, an owl hoots, and then a burst of machine-gun fire sends a stream of tracers downrange. It's time to go to work.

The night infiltration course involves low crawling through mud bogs, concertina wire, and various obstacles while cadre toss smoke grenades and artillery simulators alongside the trainees to add realism. The last fifty yards requires that the soldiers stay low enough to avoid getting snagged on strands of barbed wire suspended overhead. Meanwhile, M60 machine guns fire live rounds above the men's heads.

Dave nervously waits in line for his time to go. He hates low crawling and has no talent for it. Nevertheless, when his turn comes, Dave applies himself to the ground, cradles his M16 in his arms, and moves out using his elbows and knees for locomotion. It's rough going first over sand then into a muddy bog. After he emerges from the pit, Dave crawls through a concrete drainage pipe. When he comes out, he's under the barbed wire and tracers begin to fly overhead. The air snaps, crackles, and pops as it's ripped apart by flying lead. Dave keeps his chest to the ground as he slithers along like a copperhead. He's on the final stretch and can hear the DIs. "Get down, get your ass down," they yell. "Go, go, go! Why are you stopping, maggot? Keep moving."

After the soldiers have all finished the course, they gather by the trucks waiting for the order to mount up. Spirits are high as they have been dreading this night and are happy to have it over. The DIs are also glad to have this part of the curriculum behind them. They don't like night exercises any more than the trainees.

It's past midnight when the company gets back to the barracks. First, the men go into the showers wearing full combat gear and carrying their M16s. The soldiers wash themselves and their equipment to get some of the worst gunk off. Then they change into skivvies and get to work on their weapons. The sun is coming up by the time the last one is turned in.

After that, the troops change into fresh fatigues and go to chow. They spend the rest of the morning washing out ponchos, canteens, canteen covers, web belts, ammo pouches, and all the rest of their gear. They are done with this by noon but then have to GI the barracks. That takes the rest of the day.

Cindy picks Dave up that evening after he receives another pass. Neither of them is up for any outdoor adventures this weekend, so they stay in Friday night, then after lazing around the apartment most of the following day they go downtown for a burger and a flick. *Easy Rider* is playing, and the theater is almost empty for the 7:00 p.m. showing until several police officers file in. They stand in the back of the theater armed and ready. "Guess this is part of their drug education program," Cindy whispers.

"Probably as close to seeing a hippie as any of them will get," Dave replies.

For brunch the next day, Dave whips up a batch of French toast using his father's recipe, which substitutes cream for milk and calls for thoroughly soaking each slice of bread before dropping it into the sizzling bacon fat. Once their bellies are full, Cindy and Dave curl up on the sofa and watch televised football until it's time for Dave to report back to the base.

Dave's company goes to the firing range Monday for one last practice session. The following day it's the real thing, and each soldier must qualify with the assault rifle. Dave considers intentionally failing the test, but that would mean repeating AIT. Instead, he focuses on his shooting and ends up earning the coveted expert badge.

Now AIT is coming to an end, but before graduating each trainee will have to spend a night alone in the woods practicing escape and evasion. To prepare, they spend all day Wednesday at the land navigation course following azimuths from one checkpoint to the next. That evening, the company cooks bring out a hot dinner. After eating, the men climb onto the trucks again.

As soon as they are underway, the soldiers nod off. They sleep restlessly for nearly an hour as the deuce-and-a-halfs carry them deep into the Talladega National Forest. Then the vehicles turn onto a fire road, and the lurching wakes the troops. After a short distance, the column halts at a numbered stake and Forester comes to the rear of the first truck. He calls a name, and the soldier leaps down. The DI gives him a card with the azimuth to the rally point. "It's twelve miles thataway," he says, pointing. "There will be a big bonfire you'll be able to see a mile away. Try to get in before sunup."

The column proceeds a quarter mile to another numbered stake, and the next man is called out. After several more stops it's Dave's turn. He gets down, receives his marching orders from Forester, then watches the trucks drive off.

It's a clear night and a half moon provides illumination. The forest smells of clay, loam, pine, and decay. Stars are spilled across the sky like salt.

Dave opens his compass and has no problem reading the luminous dial. Now his only worry is being captured. The DIs informed the men that cadre from the training brigade will play the part of an enemy force called the Blue Army tonight. They will be out and about trying to capture trainees in the woods. The blues will roughly interrogate their captives, but the trainees cannot give out any more than their name, rank, and service number.

After an hour of walking, Dave comes upon a rocky stream that flows in roughly the same direction as the azimuth to the rally point. He figures that the sound of rushing water will cover any noise he makes, so Dave walks along the streambed. He's in defilade so it would be hard for the "blue meanies" to spot him.

The stream water is cold and delicious, so Dave takes frequent breaks during the night to drink, cherish the feeling of freedom, and listen to the sounds of the forest. But all too soon he sees a distant light flickering through the trees. The blazing bonfire makes it easy to hone in on the rally point. As he gets closer, Dave becomes cautious with his movements, guessing that the last mile would be the best place for the blues to set up an ambush. But he's unmolested and has no problem getting in.

As Dave approaches the bonfire, Sergeant Forester hurries over. "How did you get here so fast?" he asks.

"I followed a stream, Drill Sergeant."

"That's good. The captain has been waiting for you."

Dave has never seen the company commander, but now Sergeant Forester takes him over to the fire and introduces him to the officer. "Sir, this is Private Knight."

Dave salutes, and the captain touches his cap in return. "Very good, Sergeant," he says. Forester snaps a salute then makes his escape.

"You made excellent time," the officer says to Dave.

"Thank you, sir."

"I'm Captain Morris; I was ordered to come get you."

"Sir, I don't understand."

"It's your mother," Morris says. "She's gravely ill. You're needed back in Washington."

"Yes, sir."

"I have my car and can take you where you need to go."

"Thank you, sir."

Dave follows Morris over to a white Chevy parked behind the trucks. He takes his helmet and web gear off, stores the equipment in the backseat, and climbs in front. After several minutes of driving, the incongruity of an army captain chauffeuring a private strikes home. "Sir, did the Red Cross contact you?" Dave asks.

"Negative, it was someone at the Pentagon who called and talked to Colonel Geddings at Battalion. He reached me at home several hours ago and asked me to find you."

"Yes, sir."

"Where are you from?" Morris asks. There's no resentment in his voice about having to get out of bed in the wee hours of the morning to pick up a private.

"Sir, I was born at Fort Leavenworth but don't consider that home," Dave replies. "What about you?"

"Plano, Texas," Morris declares proudly, "just outside Dallas. I was born there, grew up there, played high school football there, and then went on to the University of Texas."

"Did you take ROTC?"

"That's right."

"Are you married?"

"Yes, to my high school sweetheart."

"Was she a cheerleader?"

Morris laughs, "Why, of course."

The sky ahead glows from the lights of Anniston. "Shall I take you to the bus station, or do you need to pick up your stuff at the barracks first?" Morris asks.

"Sir, my wife lives in town. If you could drop me off at our apartment, that would be fine."

When they get to the apartment complex, Dave gets his gear out of the back. "Sir, I appreciate this," he says. The officer sticks his hand out, and they shake. "I'm sorry about your mother," Morris says.

Dave walks past the VW and up to the apartment door. There's no response when he knocks, so he goes around back and lets himself in through the sliding glass door. No one's home.

After changing out of his fatigues and into blue jeans and a sweatshirt, Dave gets down a suitcase. He throws in a few pairs of underwear, socks, some T-shirts, a sweater, and a spare pair of jeans. His shaving kit is at the barracks, but he can pick up a razor and toothbrush anywhere.

As Dave finishes packing, he tries to think of where Cindy might be at this hour of the morning. She only has one friend in Alabama that he knows, so Dave goes outside, puts his bag in the VW, then goes to Sergeant Garrison's apartment. He knocks on the door then steps back. That's good because Garrison quickly appears, thrusts the storm door wide, and steps onto the stoop. He's wearing Vietcong black pajamas and Ho Chi Minh sandals. He scowls at the intruder, beetling his eyebrows.

"Hey, man, what's happening?" Dave asks.

"Nothing much," Garrison replies to buy time. He's trying to decide between a sidekick and a roundhouse. The commando makes up his mind and settles into a horse stance. But at the last moment, a glimmer of recognition crosses his mind. "Why aren't you out at the base with your AIT company?" he exclaims.

Dave ignores the question. "Is Cindy here by any chance?" he asks.

Garrison pauses then replies, "Yeah, she's in the living room."

Dave follows Garrison into his place. It's furnished with souvenirs from the Far East and junk from Pier 1. Cindy is sitting on the carpet in front of the fireplace wearing raggedy cutoffs and one of Dave's white undershirts. Her nipples raise bumps in the thin material. "Mom is near the end," Dave says. "I have to go home."

Cindy looks up, cheeks flushed in the firelight. She seems bewildered, so Dave tries again. "I'm going to drive to Washington in the Volkswagen," he explains.

"Do you want to come with me?" The implication that her husband might drive off without her has the desired effect. Cindy looks around for someplace to rest the half-full wine goblet she's holding. Dave takes it from her and puts it out of harm's way.

"Ah, that's an awfully long drive," Garrison stammers. "You could stay here." His face wears the stunned expression of a poker player who sees his flush bested by a full house.

"No, I have to go," Cindy declares, getting to her feet.

The sun is up by the time Cindy has packed, and she and Dave hit the road. They stop for coffee when they get to the interstate then head east. Twelve hours later they pull into the driveway of the Knights' house in Alexandria. No one's home but the door isn't locked, so Cindy and Dave unload the car and carry their things upstairs. They're sitting at the kitchen table eating sandwiches when Knight comes in an hour later. "She's in a coma," he says. "But the doctor told me that people who are comatose sometimes wake up and can remember what was said to them. So, we're taking turns sitting with Mom and talking to her. Perle just took over from me. Dave, you can relieve your sister after you've had some rest."

"All right," Dave replies.

In the morning Dave slips out of bed quietly so Cindy can sleep. At Walter Reed he finds Perle sitting with Bobbie. "I've been talking to Mom all night," Perle says. "She squeezed my hand once. I know she hears me."

Dave looks at his mother. Bobbie's mouth is agape, and her lips are pulled back into a grimace. Both hands are frozen into claws. Dave is shocked, but he quickly gets hold of himself. "Hi, Mom," he says, smiling. "What are you doing? Sleeping in? Well, that's good. You need the rest." Perle gets up to leave, and Dave slides into the chair. He takes Bobbie's clenched fingers in his hand and continues the patter.

Late that afternoon Knight arrives with Dan. The airman takes one look at Bobbie and starts bawling. Knight hustles him out of the room, but they return five minutes later. "Hi, beautiful," Dan says and kisses Bobbie's cheek. He takes Dave's place in the chair and holds his mother's hand. "You wouldn't believe what the women wear in Saudi," Dan says. "In that heat! I'm going to tell you all about it."

Knight and Dave go out in the hall. "Perle is all in," Knight says. "She and I have been taking turns here all week, and I'm done in myself. So, you're going to have to come back for the midnight shift. Best go home now and sleep. I'll be along shortly."

Dave goes down the hall and is waiting for the elevator when the doors open, and Melissa gets off. "Oh, it's you," she says.

"Mom's down the hall, Room 212."

"Where's Dad?"

"In there, along with Dan."

"I don't know if I can stomach the bastard."

"That's harsh."

"If you only knew."

"Tell me."

"What good would that do?"

"Get it off your chest."

Melissa laughs bitterly. "You are so naïve," she says. "I hope you stay that way. Now I'm going to see Mom, and if that SOB says anything to me, he'll be sorry."

Back at the house, Dave sleeps for several hours then heats some chicken pot pies for a late dinner. He and Cindy eat while watching the ten o'clock news. Then Dave returns to Walter Reed and sends Dan home. He begins telling Bobbie about basic training, but her stentorian breathing is his only reply. After a while, Dave props his feet on the bed, tilts the chair back, and dozes off. Later a change in Bobbie's breathing wakes him. She's rasping. It's a hoarse, desperate sound. Dave pushes the button for the duty nurse, and she's quickly there. "It won't be long now," she says.

Dave runs down the hall and pumps coins into a pay phone. First, he calls the house, then the Hilton where Melissa is staying. He hustles back to Bobbie's room and finds a doctor by her bedside. They wait as the rasping becomes more guttural. A few minutes later it stops, and Bobbie is still. The physician holds his stethoscope to her chest. He knits his brows in concentration for a time then looks up. "She's gone," he says. Bobbie recently turned fifty-seven. Now her short, unhappy life is over.

The sound of rushing footsteps echoes down the hall then Knight comes into the room with Perle and Dan. The doctor whispers something, and Perle silently bows her head. Dan begins wailing like a banshee. Knight tries to hush him, but Dan roughly pushes his father away. Then Melissa comes into the room and immediately takes Dan into her arms. He struggles distractedly for a moment then buries his face in Melissa's shoulder, weeping inconsolably.

Dave envies Dan. He wishes he could cry, but there's something wrong with him; with all of them, except Dan. Dave looks at Melissa's face, at Perle's, and his father's. Each wears the same stoic expression, and they are all thinking the same thing: "*This too shall pass.*"

Two days later Cindy and Dave are at the kitchen table having coffee when Knight comes in. "Gram's laid up and won't be able to attend the funeral," he says. "So Aunt Penny is coming instead. Can you pick her up at the airport?"

"Sure," Dave replies.

Penelope Colby is Ethel's sister. She and her husband Lee still have a home in Oakwood, but they have long lived in Michigan where Lee is a big shot in the car business. When Dave picks his great aunt up at the airport, he's apologetic about the VW. "Guess you're not used to riding in one of these," he says.

"No, but honey, these little cars are the coming thing," Penny says graciously. "Detroit's all in a dither about it."

It's a short drive from National Airport to the funeral home in Alexandria. When they get there, Penny signs the guestbook then she and Dave go into the viewing room. Bobbie's coffin is on a bier. Penny strides over to it while Dave hangs back. "She seems so peaceful," Penny says after a while. "Don't you think?"

Dave feels obliged to look and wishes he hadn't. Bobbie's heavily made-up face is that of a wax figure. It looks nothing like her. He struggles for something to say. "It's as if she's only sleeping," is all he can muster.

Penny joins the rest of the family at Arlington Cemetery the next morning for a memorial service followed by the interment. Afterward, Knight offers to treat everyone to brunch, but there are no takers. Cindy and Dave bring Penny back to National Airport then swing by the house to get their bags. Upstairs

Dan is in his room packing. "Dad's taking me to Andrews," he explains. "I'm going to try for a military hop."

"Hope you don't get stuck out there," Dave says.

"Oh, I'll get a ride eventually." There's an awkward pause, then they hug.

The men of OCS Company 54 file into a classroom at the US Army Infantry School at Fort Benning and Dave Knight is among them. As the officer candidates stand at attention, an instructor walks to the lectern. "At ease," he commands, and the OCs immediately shift position. "Take seats," the officer shouts.

The OCs let out a roar then holler: "Sir, OCS 54, sir, mobile, agile, and hostile, sir." They simultaneously drop onto their chairs.

Now the instructor presents a mortar problem to the class, and most of the soldiers get busy with their plotting boards. But Dave sits motionless. He doesn't know how to triangulate targets even though this is his second attempt at this phase of officer training. He failed the mortar exam on his first try and was put back from OCS Company 39 to this one. At this point, Dave has been at Officer Candidate School for over five months and is getting burned out. However, he sees no viable alternative. If he quits OCS, he will surely go to the land of the little people. "Little people" in army vernacular are the Vietcong.

As his fellow OCs work on the mortar problem, Dave idly spins the azimuth wheel on his plotting board. The company was out on a tactical exercise the night before and up early again this morning for PT. Dave's head bobs, and he drifts off to sleep.

That evening after chow, Dave is called in for a meeting with Lt. Ronald Takitas, the tactical officer for his platoon. When Dave gets to the TAC's office, a line of OCs is outside. As he waits, several more join the queue.

"You were sleeping in class again today," Takitas says once Dave gets into his office. "I'm assessing you five demerits, which gives you a total of fifty-eight. You are getting dangerously close to a dismissal panel."

"Yes, sir."

Lt. Takitas glances at the file of OCs outside his door and sighs. He hands Dave a quarter. "Go get me a Lemon RC," he orders.

"Yes, sir."

Dave leaves the barracks and double-times up the street. It's spring, and the dogwoods along the way are in full bloom. He jogs past a row of two-story cinder block barracks then stops at a kiosk containing several vending machines. Nearby, a TAC stands over his platoon. The OCs are all down in the push-up position, waiting for their comrades to come out of the barracks and join them. "Take note of those slackers," the TAC shouts, pointing at laggards still coming out of the barracks. "They don't care about the rest of you."

Dave puts a coin into the soda machine then scoops up the drink. Meanwhile, another OCS platoon double-times up to an adjacent barracks. "Platoon, left face," hollers the OC platoon leader. "At ease." The newcomers spot their neighbors on the ground struggling to hold the push-up position, so they begin singing:

> *Far across the Chattahoochee*
> *To the Upatoi,*
> *Stands our loyal alma mater,*
> *Benning School for Boys.*

It's mandatory for everyone to stand when the OCS alma mater is performed so now the OCs on the ground happily leap to their feet and sing along:

> *Forward ever, backward never,*
> *Faithfully we strive*
> *Till we reach our destination.*
> *Follow me with pride.*

Dave smiles as he jogs back to the company. When he gets there, Takitas has Steve Draper in his office. The TAC sees Dave outside and motions him in. "I never wanted to be an officer in the first place," Draper is saying. "It was all my father's idea." Dave slides the cold RC and the change onto Takitas's desk and backs away, snapping a salute.

Later, after mandatory study hour, the OCs get ready to turn in. It's Friday, so they don't have night training, nor will any classes be held during the next two days. But that doesn't mean Saturday won't be another miserable day. That's because the TACs will be in charge.

So, at 0530 hours the next morning, Company 54 lines up for inspection in spit-shined boots and starched fatigues. The TACs walk up and down the lines nitpicking the men's appearance. "Totally unacceptable," they agree. "Once around the barracks, low crawl."

After circuiting the building on their bellies, the OCs are allowed back inside to break starch on fresh uniforms and go to breakfast. They eat then draw their weapons from the armory and fall out for a twelve-mile forced march. The OCs are inured to this kind of thing and grind out the miles in good style all the while muttering wisecracks among themselves. In Dave's platoon, many of the comments are at the expense of their TAC, who is out of shape. By now Takitas's uniform is soaked with sweat. The officer audibly huffs and puffs as he jogs up and down the line of marching OCs, calling out corrections: "Knight, straighten up that weapon. Colombero, put out road guards at the intersection. Draper, get in step."

The OCs would love to have a change of pace and be able to alternate walking, jogging, and backpedaling like the TACs. It's constricting to have to march at the same pace hour after hour, so they have no sympathy for Takitas. He graduated OCS a year ago and lives off base with his wife. The lean physique he must have had as an OC is all behind him now.

Company 54 gets back to the barracks in time for lunch then spends the afternoon cleaning weapons and equipment. Afterward, Takitas has an announcement. "Now, listen up," he says. "I will inspect the barracks after church tomorrow. If you pass you will receive post privileges." Post privileges means having the freedom of leaving the company area to go anywhere on base, including the PX, movie theaters, bowling alley, or beer garden. The best post privilege is renting a room at the guest quarters. OCs with wives or girlfriends can have conjugal visits there.

So, after breakfast the next morning, the OCs in Takitas's platoon get to work on their bay. They know what the TAC looks for, and by noon the men are confidently standing at attention waiting for him. However, Takitas comes in, takes a cursory look at three or four quads, and renders an unsettling verdict. "Totally unsat," he shouts. "I'll be back in two hours. Get this barracks squared away."

The OCs of Takitas's platoon are baffled. They have become very good at inspections and usually pass with no problem. Uncertainly, they get out the buffers, brooms, and mops again. While two OCs polish the floors, the rest use dusters and cleaning supplies to perfect the latrine, common areas, and living quarters. By the time Takitas returns, the platoon bay is gleaming, but the TAC doesn't see it that way. "This place is filthy," Takitas hollers. "I will be back in another two hours to give you one last chance."

"Guys, there is no point in slaving away any longer," Gary Colombero, the OC platoon leader, says. "Takitas is just fucking with us. He's not going to cut us loose today." Colombero is a decorated veteran of two tours in Vietnam and wears jump wings and the combat infantryman badge (CIB) on his uniform. So, the other candidates listen to him. They accept that they're stuck in the company area and might as well make the best of it. Some of the guys sit on their footlockers and write letters while others read. A few brave souls nap on their bunks, destroying the trampoline-like tautness of the covers.

Dave looks out the window and sees the VW in the rear of the parking area. He slips outside and finds Cindy in the car, reading. "I thought you were supposed to be done by one," she complains.

"No such luck," Dave replies. "Ronnie's wife must be away. He appears to have nothing better to do than mess with us today."

"Shit, I planned a nice dinner," Cindy sighs. Lately, she's been smuggling Dave off base on the Sundays when he has post privileges.

"Sorry, but I'll be eating in the mess hall," Dave says. "You might as well go home."

Back inside the barracks, there's a flurry of activity as the OCs get ready for the next visit from Takitas. But he bursts in early and finds the platoon bay in disarray. "Fall out with full field gear and weapons," Takitas snaps. "Formation at 1600 hours."

Now there's a mad scramble to put on web gear and get to the armory to draw bayonets and M14s. As the OCs run out of the barracks, Takitas drops them into the push-up position to await the slowpokes. Once the last man is in place, the TAC brings the platoon to attention. Then he takes the OCs to a track at the Airborne School and orders them to double-time around it.

As the OCs monotonously run laps around the oval, the Airborne School's 250-foot jump towers loom overhead. Nearby the streets are empty, while in the distance billowing clouds sail along like tall ships. It's a quiet Sunday afternoon on a sleepy army post, except for the officer candidates of Takitas's platoon.

Dave struggles to keep his M14 at port arms. The bayonet scabbard slaps his thigh with every step. He concentrates on the back of the OC in front of him, taking care not to clip his heels. After a while, the guy staggers and then falls out of formation. On the next lap, Dave sees him kneeling in the grass. As the punishment continues, more men straggle. Eventually, the platoon is strung out around the track.

"Close up ranks," Takitas calls. "One more lap with everyone together and that will be it."

"WETSU," Colombero hollers, and the platoon closes up, dresses ranks, and runs a full lap in perfect formation. WETSU is an airborne jump cry. It stands for: "We eat this shit up."

"Do one more lap," Takitas yells as the platoon comes around.

The OCs groan and curse in response to the TAC's double cross. "Come on, we got this," Colombero hollers, but the formation quickly falls apart. Guys are lying down or kneeling next to the track. Stragglers cannot keep up. Still, Colombero leads Dave and a few others as they continue to circle the track in formation. The diehards are like automatons; united in their determination to outlast Takitas. They focus on taking one more step, then one more. Finally, the TAC calls a halt. "Take 'em back to the barracks," he tells Colombero.

At 0530 hours the next morning, Company 54 holds morning inspection then the OCs do some push-ups and low crawling at the behest of the TACs. Afterward, they break starch on clean uniforms then go to breakfast. Meanwhile, Draper and two other guys line up outside Takitas's office. Each holds a letter of resignation. The company started OCS with 160 members ten weeks ago and is now down to ninety-three. Takitas's platoon has been hit hardest; only nineteen OCs remain out of the forty who started with him. Perhaps that's why the following Sunday the TAC grants post privileges after his first inspection of the barracks.

Whatever Takitas's reason, Cindy is happy on Sunday when Dave comes out of the barracks, throws his helmet liner into the back of the VW, and climbs into the passenger seat. After a lingering kiss, she murmurs, "Let's get you home."

On the way off post, Cindy pulls into an empty parking lot so Dave can climb into the back of the car. He hides as they pass the MPs at the gate. A few minutes later, Cindy turns onto a dirt road that leads to the trailer park where she has found a home. The floor of the single-wide crunches as they enter. "I sweep it out five times a day," Cindy says. "I don't know how the sand keeps getting in here."

"It gets into everything," Dave replies on his way to the refrigerator. "Want a beer?" he asks.

"Sure," Cindy replies. She sorts through some LPs then puts one on the turntable.

Dave changes into a pair of running shorts and a T-shirt. It's great to get the heavy jump boots off his feet and to hang up his uniform for a while. They sit on the vinyl sofa that came with the trailer, sip beer, and listen to the Byrds. Presently Cindy lights a joint and they pass it back and forth until it's gone. Then Dave flips the record over and gets a couple fresh brews from the fridge. "Draper, Samuels, and Wright all quit this week," he says.

"No surprise about Draper," Cindy replies. "But I thought Samuels and Wright were gung ho."

"They let their hatred of Takitas get the better of them."

"So now they go to Vietnam, not much of an improvement."

"No."

"I'd rather have you right here, even if we only see each other once a week."

"Thanks, honey," Dave says. He kisses Cindy, then kisses her again. After a little more of this, she pulls away and takes Dave's hand. "Let's go down the hall," Cindy suggests.

Later Dave hears a faint noise that doesn't belong in his dream. It sounds like a phone ringing somewhere far off. Slowly the sound gets louder, more insistent, and Dave realizes that it's coming from right next to him. He sits bolt upright as the phone on the nightstand continues to ring. The clock next to it reads 7:00 p.m. He was supposed to be back at the company for evening formation an hour ago. A feeling of dread overcomes him as he picks up the receiver.

"Hello?" Dave says.

"You are in some deep shit now, Knight," Takitas yells.

"Yes, sir."

"Get your ass back here."

"Yes, sir."

Cindy sits up and rubs her eyes. "What was that?" she asks.

"We overslept."

On the way back to the base, Dave ponders his predicament. Missing a formation is called "failure to repair" in army legalese and is a court-martial offense. "What's going to happen?" Cindy asks.

"I don't know," Dave replies as they pull up in front of the company. "I'll call you when I can."

Dave goes inside where Captain Foster, the company commander, is waiting along with First Sergeant Thompkins and all four of the company's TACs. Foster is furious. This won't look good on his record. It's as if he's a prison warden and one of the inmates escaped. So the officer's face keeps getting redder as he yells at Dave. Soon it's purple, and veins are throbbing on his forehead. Abruptly, Foster turns and stalks out.

After Foster leaves, the TACs relax, and Sergeant Thompkins takes over. "You are fortunate to be in a unique legal status as an officer candidate," the NCO tells Dave. "Otherwise you'd be on your way to the stockade. As it is, you will be paneled in the morning, and with the demerits you have accumulated already plus the ones you get for this violation, you can expect to be dismissed."

"Yes, Sergeant."

"Report back here at 0700 hours," Thompkins orders.

"With all your shit," Takitas snarls.

"That's right," the first sergeant says calmly. "You will be transferred to the transient barracks after the panel, so pack your duffel bag."

Dave goes upstairs to the platoon bay. Guys on either side are in their quads polishing brass, spit shining boots, or studying for the upcoming mortar exam. Some look up, see him, and scowl. But as he moves around getting ready for bed, Dave detects a hint of admiration on one or two faces. This is no doubt due to the sheer enormity of his crime.

In the latrine, as Dave is brushing his teeth, Colombero comes to the sink beside him. "Gotta give it to you, though, Knight," he mutters. "When you fuck up, you don't half-step."

"Thanks," Dave whispers. "Good luck."

"You too, buddy, you're gonna need it where you're goin'."

An army transient company is a place where soldiers who are in between duty stations spend their time. Dave is on the roster of one operated by the First Training Brigade at Fort Benning. Thanks to the time he spent at OCS, his rank is now specialist fourth class. Being a spec 4 doesn't get Dave out of performing details like guard duty and KP, but it does mean that he gets more pay than a private. Also, he can live off post.

One morning Dave's checking the transient company bulletin board and finds a request for a typist to work in the company office. He volunteers for the job, and after a brief demonstration of the keyboarding skills he learned in high school Dave gets the gig. That night he's waiting at their trailer when Cindy comes home from a day selling magazines. "Guess what?" he says. "Our company clerk left, and I got the job."

"For how long?" Cindy asks.

"Just until my orders come through."

"Oh."

"Hey, it means no more details. I'll have nights and weekends off."

"Well, that's something," Cindy says, brightening. "Let's celebrate." She gets out the rolling papers and a bag of dope.

Cindy rolls a fat joint then takes a long slow toke. As she passes the doobie, her cheeks bulge like a chipmunk's and Dave has to laugh. "Hey, if you aren't going to smoke it, give it back," Cindy exclaims, coughing out a vast cloud. Now

Dave remembers the burning reefer between his fingers and begins inhaling while Cindy looks on approvingly.

The Knights have their stereo cranked up, but through the wall of sound created by Crosby, Stills, and Nash they hear pounding on the door. "Are you guys burning rags in there?" yells Sergeant Ray Gillis, a neighbor three trailers down. He opens the door without being invited, comes in, and plops down on an aluminum kitchen chair. "You shouldn't smoke that shit," Ray declares.

"Try it, you'll like it," Cindy says and offers Ray the joint.

"Nah, I have a big enough problem with this," Ray says holding up a can of Pabst Blue Ribbon.

The trailer park is home to many draftees like Ray who have already done their twelve months in Vietnam but still have time left to serve in the army. Cindy has introduced Dave to Ray and several of his buddies, including Tom Ferguson and Gary Fiddler. They all served in the same mechanized infantry unit in 'Nam. Tom and Gary are friendly, uncomplicated country boys but Ray is a maniac. With his sandy hair, freckles, and Tom Sawyer face, he looks like a choirboy but is anything but. Now Ray has a question for the Knights. "Have you got five bucks?" he asks.

"What for?" Cindy inquires.

"Beer bust," Ray replies. "Tomorrow's Friday, and we're going to have a bonfire."

"Sounds like fun," Cindy says and digs the money out of her purse.

Early the next morning Dave drives to work at the transient company and begins typing reports. The work is tedious, and Dave's restless mind struggles to focus. He keeps making mistakes and having to start over. It's frustrating, so by the end of the day he's ready to cut loose. So is Cindy; she's had a good day selling magazines and is happy that the weekend is here.

Ray lights the fire just before dark, and soon most of the trailer park residents are gathered around it holding beers. However, many of them have young children, so after a couple of hours the crowd thins. That leaves a small group of hardcore partiers with Cindy and Dave among them. By midnight even they have had enough. "Great party," Dave says to Ray. "See you later."

"Oh, have another beer," Ray insists. "You paid for it."

"Why not?" Cindy agrees. The Knights grab a couple of cold ones out of a cooler, then join Ray, Tom, and Gary by the fire. Ray's wife, Maureen, is sitting on a camp chair nearby. She's a willowy blonde along the lines of Tammy Wynette.

"So how does a Yankee boy like you come to be livin' in a redneck trailer park?" Ray asks Dave.

"I'm for sure a Yankee," Cindy interrupts. "But Dave's not; he's from Virginia."

"He don't sound like it."

"I've moved around," Dave says. "Guess I never picked up an accent."

"His dad's in the army," Cindy elaborates. "That's why they moved."

"A lifer, huh?" Ray snorts.

"He's an officer," Cindy says defensively. "Works in the Pentagon."

"If I knew someone at the Pentagon, I sure as shit wouldn't be sitting here waiting for no orders to Vietnam," Tom says heatedly.

"My father and I don't get along," Dave declares, then he changes the subject. "Anyone want another beer?"

"I do," Ray says, shaking his nearly empty can.

Dave walks over to the coolers, but Gary and Tom follow him. "You have no idea what it is like over there," Tom says.

"No fucking idea," Gary agrees.

"We'll tell you a little war story," Gary offers. "Maybe you'll get the picture." He turns to Tom. "Remember Hoc Noi, in the highlands?"

"Oh fuck," Tom says.

"Our Third Platoon got pinned down by an NVA unit," Gary begins. "They were raining fire on 'em from a little village on top of a hill. Third Platoon was in deep shit. We heard it on the radio. KIAs, WIAs, awful. So we were ordered to take our APCs up there and engage the enemy with our fifties. Meanwhile, jets were pounding the gook positions. There was only one way up or down the mountain, and that was a narrow road. As we were hauling ass up it, crowds of refugees from the village came streaming down."

"We couldn't wait for them to pass since every minute meant more KIAs in Third Platoon," Tom interjects. "Besides, there wasn't hardly any space for them to get around us."

"The only choice was to run right over 'em," Gary says sickly.

"We just ground them under the tracks like hamburger and drove on," Tom elaborates. "Old men, women, babies, they were screaming." He looks down at the ground and shakes his head. "Ray still ain't got over it," he concludes.

"So do you get the picture?" Gary demands. "Or you want to hear more?"

"Believe me, we got more," Tom threatens.

"So you best do every motherfucking thing you can to keep from going," Gary tells Dave.

"Up to and including calling your big-shot father," Tom agrees. "Or we're gonna kick your ass."

"Hey, where's my beer?" Ray hollers.

Dave takes Ray's beer to him then stands by the fire next to Cindy who is deep in conversation with Maureen. "You can choose any seven magazines you want and get 50 percent off the newsstand price," Cindy is saying. "Then you get three for free; it's a package deal."

"Do you have *Photoplay*?" Maureen asks.

"Sure," Cindy says, "we have any magazine there is."

"What about *Playboy*?" Ray leers.

"*Playboy* too," Cindy smiles.

Dave yawns. "It's late," he says. "I'm going to bed."

"Why don't you go to bed with Maureen?" Ray suggests. "I ain't innerested, so she might as well get some from you."

"Now, Ray, I'm sure Cindy would have something to say about that," Maureen says nervously.

"Oh, come on," Ray insists. "This is your chance to do it with a college boy."

"I didn't go to college," Dave protests.

"Bullshit. You use all them fancy words. If you dint go to college, then what?"

"Oh, knock it off," Tom says.

"Well, I went to the school of Charlie," Ray persists, then he points at Dave, "while you and your hippie friends were burning your draft cards."

"They were smart to burn 'em," Tom says. "Anything's better than the 'Nam."

"What do you know about it, you fuckin' REMF?" Ray asks.

"Eat me," Tom replies.

"Fuck you," Ray exclaims, turning to face his friend. Meanwhile, Dave takes Cindy's hand and pulls her away from the firelight. Cloaked in darkness, they make their getaway.

But late the next morning while Cindy and Dave are still sleeping, bam, bam, bam; Ray pounds on their door. "Wake up in there," he hollers. "You can't sleep all day." After giving Cindy and Dave a decent interval to put on some clothes, Ray comes in with a big grin on his face. "How did you like the party?" he asks.

"Just great," Cindy mumbles.

"Well, it gets better," Ray exclaims. "Today we're going to the lake. Be ready in an hour." Ray is gone as suddenly as he arrived.

"How 'bout a glass of cold orange juice and some Tylenol?" Cindy inquires of her husband.

"Hell yeah."

Cold showers, OJ, and acetaminophen combine to improve the Knights' outlook on life. Cindy makes sandwiches and packs a cooler while Dave gets towels and bathing suits together. Then they join the convoy going out to a swimming hole Ray discovered some time back. Many of the people who were at the party the night before are along.

Soon the line of cars following Ray's pickup turns onto a two-lane country road. After several miles, they pull over and park on the shoulder near a spot where a trestle bridge crosses the finger of a reservoir. There's a sandy beach along the lakeshore, and the crowd gathers there with coolers, blankets, and towels. Then Ray leads the way out to the middle of the bridge and jumps off. The others follow, and then they all swim to the bank, climb out of the water, and do it again. Later, after more bridge jumping and lots of whooping and hollering, it's time for the hair of the dog. There's plenty of beer left in the coolers, and soon hangovers are a distant memory.

Across the way, cows munch grass in a pasture. Then the animals move down to the water, and the leaders slowly wade in. "Just what we need," Ray complains. "Soon we'll be swimming in cow shit."

"Let's go in again before it gets too bad," Maureen suggests.

Cindy and Dave swim out to the middle along with everyone else. "This is wild," Dave says. "I can feel several temperature gradations down my body. It's warm around my shoulders, cooler by my stomach, and downright freezing at my feet."

"That's normal," Cindy laughs.

Dave flips over and dives deep. He wants to get his entire body into the cold layer, and soon he's touching the muddy bottom of the reservoir. It's blissful down there, so he comes up for air then dives again. Meanwhile, the others start swimming back to the picnic area. After one more deep dive, Dave follows. As he wades through the shallow water near the shore, Dave hears others splashing behind him. Then a mud ball hits him in the back. "Got you," Ray hollers. Dave dodges Ray's next throw then goes back into the deeper water to rinse his back.

Cindy has a sandwich and a beer waiting when Dave returns to the picnic area. They sit with the others and eat. "What are you going to do when you get out of the army?" Ray asks Dave in his fake friendly way.

"I have no idea," Dave answers.

"Oh, you probably have some cushy job waiting for you."

"Knock it off," Gary says. He's been buddies with Ray for a long time but has little influence on him.

"College boys always get over," Ray says. "Me? I'll have to work for a living."

"Maybe you should go to college, if it's all that great," Tom says.

"Oh, I don't have some rich army officer father to pay my way," Ray says bitterly. He crushes his beer can and goes to get another.

With Ray gone, Dave sits on his towel and takes in the scene. It's a great spot, even better than the P Street beach. Although the cattle have now taken over the swimming hole, Dave doesn't begrudge them their turn. He stretches out and closes his eyes.

Early the next morning, Dave is back at work. Sergeant Calhoun, the first sergeant for the transient company, is his boss. He's a nice portly man with a fatherly air about him. The two of them work on the morning report then Dave takes it to headquarters. On the way back he stops at a phone booth. Inside, it smells like urine, as they always do. It's because soldiers get drunk on 3.2 beer then want to call someone, and while they're talking, nature calls. Dave has been guilty of this himself. Now he gets a card out of his wallet, lines up some change on the shelf, and dials his father's work number.

"Colonel Knight's office, Sergeant Major Reynier speaking," comes a voice Dave has known since childhood.

"Hi, Sergeant Major, this is Dave Knight, Colonel Knight's son."

"It's nice to hear from you," Reynier says. "I'm sure the colonel will be pleased. Just hold for a moment." Dave waits a few minutes then his father comes on the line.

"How are you able to get away this time of day?" Knight demands.

"It's easy," Dave says. "I'm done with OCS."

"What happened?"

"I got kicked out."

"OK, so you recycle, I'll take care of it."

"There's no point; I'm never going to pass mortars."

"You're not trying," Knight complains.

"It's just a jumble of numbers to me."

"But I've arranged to make the commencement address for OCS 54."

"Better let someone else do that."

Knight sighs, "So what now?"

"Cindy and I are heading for Canada."

"What?!"

"I'm going AWOL."

"You can't be serious."

"Dad, I went along with the draft out of consideration for your career, but I'm not going to Vietnam."

"If you desert, you'll pay the rest of your life."

"And if I go and kill someone or get myself killed, then what? It's all for nothing."

"It's not for nothing. You're just too stupid to understand. Eighty percent of the world's oil supply goes through the Strait of Malacca, and whoever sits in Cam Ranh Bay controls it. The Russians want that port. That's it, that's what the war is about."

"Well, I'm not willing to kill anybody or get killed over the Strait of Malacca," Dave exclaims. "So you better start thinking about how you're going to explain to your buddies at the Pentagon that you have a son AWOL in Canada. I'm just calling to give you notice. Now I have to go. My coins are running out."

"Son, don't do anything irrevocable," Knight pleads. "Let me see what I can do. Can you call me back this afternoon?"

"Sure."

"Stay put till we talk again."

"You got it."

After hanging up, Dave is mildly ashamed that he lied to his father about going to Canada. At least he didn't pee in the booth.

Back at the transient company, Dave only has two reports remaining, and he knocks the work out before lunch. That afternoon there's nothing for him to type except the next day's duty roster. Once he's finished, Dave posts it on the bulletin board. Then he goes to the parking lot and checks under and between the seats of the VW, finding several coins among the marijuana seeds. He takes the money to the phone booth and makes another call to the Pentagon. This time his father picks up. "Hi, Dad," Dave says.

"Do you want to go to Germany or Korea?" Knight asks abruptly.

"Germany," Dave replies.

"OK, but you should know that troops are often levied from Germany to Vietnam. Not so with Korea. It's a hardship post, so you cannot be transferred from Korea to Vietnam."

"Then make it Korea."

"All right," Knight says. "Now you sit tight until your orders are ready."

"Thanks, Dad," Dave starts to say, but his father has hung up.

Over the next month, Dave and Sergeant Calhoun become a team. They work from seven to four Monday through Friday and are off the rest of the time. There are only a couple of hours of work for them to do each day, so they strive to make it last. The first thing they handle is the Morning Report. Once that's done Dave gets an *Atlanta Constitution*, and the two men divvy it up and proceed to read it line by line, swapping sections as they go. The greatest time waster in the paper is the comics section where they find the *Jumble*. It's a clever puzzle that often takes them an hour or more to solve.

After that, Calhoun makes some phone calls to his buddies around the brigade to see how many bodies they each need the next day to pull details. Meanwhile, Dave types the Personnel Status Report.

In the afternoons Calhoun gives Dave the duty roster for the next day. After typing it, Dave posts the form on the company bulletin board so the transients can see which details they are assigned to pull. After that, Dave's free to goof off unless the phone rings or he has to process someone into or out of the company. Sergeant Calhoun doesn't mind if Dave leaves the office to run personal errands in the afternoons as long as he doesn't stay away too long. They rarely see the company commander or the two lieutenants who are nominally in charge.

For now, time passes uneventfully for Cindy and Dave. They go to and from their jobs every day like civilians then explore the countryside on weekends, often ending up at the swimming hole Ray showed them. At night they sometimes take advantage of the low ticket prices at the movie theaters on base or go bowling. It's idyllic compared to what they've been through in the army thus far.

But the good life comes to an abrupt end one afternoon when a full-blooded sergeant major throws the transient company office door open and stomps in. "Where is Specialist Knight," the NCO demands. "Is he out on detail?"

"No, this is Specialist Knight," Sergeant Calhoun says, pointing to his clerk.

Dave nods at the impressive figure of the sergeant major. He's a large black man with a neatly trimmed mustache bristling martially on his lip. The name tag on his starched fatigue shirt reads McKenzie. "You are wanted at personnel ASAP," he tells Dave.

McKenzie strides out of the building with Dave following. As they parade down the street, Dave recalls how the Knight children used to fall in behind their father and follow him into the commissary or other places on base. Now he gets that same feeling of insignificance.

When they get to the sprawling World War II-era wooden building that houses First Training Brigade personnel, McKenzie leads Dave inside. They go up an aisle past rows of government-issued metal desks each occupied by a busy clerk. The sound of typewriter keys thudding against paper and bells ringing fills the air. At the rear of the building, McKenzie stops before a mahogany door with a brightly polished brass sign that reads, "Major Gleason, Commanding Officer."

After opening the door, McKenzie ushers Dave into an anteroom where a white-haired woman sits at a desk typing. An empty desk opposite her has McKenzie's nameplate on it. There's a water cooler next to another mahogany door. The sergeant major strides over to it and raps twice.

"Enter."

McKenzie throws the door open for Dave who marches over to the major's desk, stands at attention, and salutes.

"Sir, Specialist Knight is reporting as ordered."

Gleason doesn't return the salute, nor does he put Dave at ease. Instead, he shuffles papers on his desk while looking down at them intently. Meanwhile, Dave examines the major's shiny dome. There's a fringe of close-cropped hair encircling it, and the back of Gleason's neck is wrinkled like a walrus's.

Finally, Gleason looks up and distastefully holds out a piece of paper like it's a stool specimen. "What's this?" he asks.

Dave peers at the paper. "Sir, it looks like orders," he says.

"Goddamn it, of course it's orders," Gleason explodes. "Orders to Korea. Well, nobody goes to Korea from here. Someone has gone over my head, and I demand to be told what you know."

"Sir, I don't know anything," Dave lies.

"You don't know anything?" the major drawls sarcastically. "Look at this." He points to a block on the form labeled "Authorization Code." Normally an alphanumeric sequence goes in that space, but this set of orders only has the word FONECON there. The major angrily stabs at the paper with his finger as if FONECON is a personal insult. "I'm in charge here," he thunders. "I will brook no interference with my command. You will tell me what you know or wish you had."

While the major continues to vent, Dave scans the rest of his orders. He will have a month's leave then must report to a transient company at Fort Lewis to await transport to the Republic of Korea. Upon arrival in the ROK, he will join the Second Infantry Division as a rifleman.

Slowly, Major Gleason runs out of steam. "Here are three copies of your orders, your medical records, and personnel file," the officer mutters, thrusting the folders at Dave. "Included are travel vouchers good for your airfare to Fort Lewis and meals in transit. Keep one set of orders on your person at all times until you reach your next duty station. Now get out of here."

Dave walks straight back to the transient company office. As he comes in carrying his records, Sergeant Calhoun looks up anxiously. "Vietnam?" he asks.

"No, Korea."

"What?"

"Yep, I'm going to the 'Land of the Morning Calm.'"

"Cut the shit."

"No lie."

"Knight, I've been here going on three years, and no one, I repeat, no one has ever gone to Korea from here."

"Well, I am."

"That's wonderful!"

"You're going to have to find yourself a company clerk."

"Don't worry about me," Calhoun exclaims.

Dave processes himself out then says farewell to Sergeant Calhoun. When he gets to the trailer, Cindy is out selling magazines, so Dave opens a beer and starts packing. He has the VW loaded by the time Cindy's boss brings her back in his big white Oldsmobile. "Your wife sold eighteen deals today," the sales manager tells Dave through a rolled-down window.

"Too bad we're leaving," Dave replies.

"Oh no."

Cindy settles up with her boss and gets out of his car holding a nice commission check. After changing into travel clothes, she helps Dave tie two full trunks onto the luggage rack. The bug is stuffed now, but several items remain. Cindy finds Maureen and gives her the ironing board and several other things that didn't make the cut. "Thanks," Maureen says. "If you ever come to Little Rock, call me."

"OK," Cindy replies, "give me your number."

As Cindy and Maureen are exchanging addresses and phone numbers, Ray comes over. "You did the right thing," he tells Dave. "Never thought I'd admit it, but you did."

"Thanks, man," Dave says. "Now you take care, you hear?"

"Oh, go fuck yourself," Ray suggests.

On that note, it's time to leave. Cindy squeezes into the passenger compartment of the VW while Dave gets behind the wheel. As they drive away, he glances into the rearview mirror and through a haze of red dust watches the trailer park recede from view. They are on their way to Princeton to spend his leave.

CHAPTER THIRTEEN
LOCK AND LOAD

The Boeing 707 left Anchorage half a day ago with Dave in a center seat wedged between two beefy sergeants. They are monopolizing the armrests, so Dave tucks his elbows in and reads *Billion-Dollar Brain*. It's a wacky spy thriller by one of his favorite authors.

The plane has been descending for some time, and now it breaks through the clouds just south of Seoul's Kimpo Airport. "There it is, gentlemen," a sergeant says, "your home for the next year." He's pointing out of his porthole at a sea of treeless mountains.

A few minutes later the plane jolts down on the runway then taxis past a row of F-4 Phantoms parked in sandbagged revetments. Unmanned .50-caliber machine guns are on the terminal roof overlooking the fighters. These warlike scenes have a forlorn aspect since the Korean War ended in a truce almost two decades ago. The only fighting on the peninsula nowadays is an occasional clash in the DMZ.

After deplaning, Dave and the other newcomers wait on the tarmac. It's early morning, but heat is already radiating from the runway. A conveyor is wheeled up to the aircraft, and duffel bags begin rumbling down it. The soldiers claim their belongings then board a bus for the short ride to the Replacement Processing Center. Once there they go into a hangar furnished with long rows of tables and chairs. A broad aisle runs down the middle, and a stage is up front. "Welcome to the Republic of Korea," a middle-aged master sergeant says into the microphone. "Please pass your records toward the center aisle."

It takes a while to get all the soldiers' personnel records piled onto the table ends. Then the master sergeant announces, "Smoke break. Return in half an hour."

Billion-Dollar Brain is coming to a dramatic conclusion, so Dave doesn't leave the hangar with the others. He continues reading but gradually becomes aware of the master sergeant repetitively coming down from the stage, picking up stacks of records, then carrying them back. Dave lays the book down. "Hey, Sarge, could you use some help?" he asks.

"That would be great, we're shorthanded today."

With both men working, it doesn't take long to get the rest of the files. Then Dave helps organize them on work tables at the rear of the stage. "Where are you headed?" the sergeant asks after they finish.

"Second Infantry."

"Oh," the sergeant frowns. "Well, you've been a big help."

"No problem," Dave replies.

After the break, the soldiers return to their places, and a captain mounts the stage to deliver a lecture on the Status of Forces Agreement. "You men need to know that if you commit a crime away from a United States military reservation, your ass belongs to the ROK," he tells them. "You will be subject to whatever kind of kangaroo court they might or might not accord you. In other words, you better get to like kimchi because that's all you will be eating for the next long time. Now if you commit a crime on one of our bases, you'll be arrested by the MPs and will be prosecuted under the US Military Code of Justice and whatever kind of kangaroo court they may or may not . . ." The officer trails off while the men laugh at his joke.

After the captain gets done, the soldiers at each table are taken to a nearby Quonset hut to exchange their greenbacks for Military Payment Certificates (MPC). Then an officer sternly advises the troops that they have one last chance to turn in any contraband without fear of prosecution. He orders the soldiers to walk through another Quonset to ditch any illegal items into a barrel. The army defines contraband as pornography, drugs, illegal weapons, and just about anything else a red-blooded American soldier might want to own. Few would be foolish enough to throw any of these goodies away, and sure enough, as Dave walks by the barrel, he sees it's empty except for a couple of well-thumbed horrible porno mags.

All this takes an interminable amount of time, and perhaps that's the idea because, meanwhile, the staff has been busy sorting out the soldiers' files and many are now ready for out-processing. The replacements are ordered to go back to their tables in the hangar and wait to be called.

As they wait the men talk among themselves and the rumble of conversation and laughter reverberates inside the metal hangar. Dave is reading but glances up from time to time to see if anything's happening on the stage. Then he notices the master sergeant walking down the center aisle peering intently at the rows of faces on either side. The sergeant stops when he gets to Dave's row and stares at him. "Knight," he calls, "I'm gonna make an MP out of you."

It suddenly gets very quiet around Dave, and several men turn to glare at him. "No, Sergeant, you got the wrong guy," Dave protests. "I can't be an MP."

"You'll thank me this winter when you're in a nice warm guard tower instead of freezing your ass off in a foxhole on the DMZ," the master sergeant declares. He turns and walks back up the aisle while Dave fumes.

Soon the master sergeant is back onstage. "At ease," he hollers, and the noise level in the hangar dissipates then tails off completely. "When you hear your name called, come forward, pick up your records, then go get your duffel bag. Transportation is waiting."

Over the next several hours, most of the replacements are called up and given their marching orders. In the end, only a few remain, including Dave. "You men head over to supply and draw bedding," the master sergeant tells the holdovers. "You will be here at least one more day. Pay attention to the PA system tomorrow. When your name is called, come to the office and get your new orders."

Once again Dave is a transient. He expects to be assigned to a detail, but the next morning when he checks the bulletin board, there's no duty roster. So, after breakfast, he sits on the front steps of the barracks to wait. Later a staff sergeant joins him. "This sucks," the soldier says. "They got my orders all fucked up."

"That's the army for you," Dave blandly replies.

"Same thing happened last time I came through."

"You've been here before?"

"Second tour," the NCO says. "You?"

"First time."

"It's good duty."

"I was expecting to see my name on the duty roster."

"Ha-ha, there is none."

"Who does KP?"

"The Koreans do that; they do everything."

"Sounds good."

A burst of static comes over the PA as one of the holdovers is called up for out-processing. Then the two men go back to talking. "You have houseboys in the barracks that make the beds, shine your boots, and keep your equipment in order," the staff sergeant says. "Off base, you can rent girls by the month, cheap."

The PA crackles again, and the staff sergeant hears his name. He leaps to his feet and rushes away. A few minutes later, the NCO is back holding his records. "Camp Humphries," he beams. "Don't know why I had to stay over; I mean, that's just what it says on my fucking orders." The staff sergeant disappears into the barracks, gets his bedding, then goes to the supply hut.

Two days later Dave finally hears his name called and goes to get his new orders. "What took so long?" he asks the master sergeant.

"Had to get you a security clearance."

"But I'm not MP material, trust me."

"This isn't going to be line duty," the master sergeant explains. "You're going to be a tower guard, that's all."

"Oh."

"Believe me, you don't want to go to the Second Infantry. It's the Wild West up there. Nothing but race riots, liquor, drugs, and everyone walking around with a loaded M16."

"All right, Sarge," Dave says, "guess I owe you one."

"Damn straight," the master sergeant smiles. "Now go turn in your bedding."

Soon Dave is on an army bus heading for Seoul. Ramshackle buildings line the road on either side and locals wearing loose white jackets over baggy pants walk along the rubble-strewn shoulders. Most have plastic sandals on their feet, while others wear primitive clogs. The older men have long wispy beards.

As they near the city, all sorts of fantastic conveyances jam the roads. Water buffalo pull two-wheeled wooden carts while bicycles are used to carry unbelievable loads. Dave sees one with a live hog on the back. The pig's head lolls drunkenly.

The traffic gets heavier with more cars and buses as they near downtown. Modern multistory buildings line the streets and crowds of pedestrians, many dressed in western attire, jam the broad sidewalks. Japanese cameras and consumer electronics fill the store windows.

Eventually, the bus turns onto a quiet treelined block with a cinder block wall bordering one side. It's the perimeter of Yongsan Army Garrison. At the entrance, an MP takes a cursory look at the bus driver's ID then waves him through. Inside they are back on US territory, and Yongsan Garrison looks like any stateside army post. The bus stops at a terminal across from the PX. "Everyone off," the driver says. "If you're a cherry and don't know which bus to take from here, you can look it up on the bulletin board."

As he waits for the next bus, Dave takes in the scene. Shoppers, including American women and children, are coming out of the PX carrying packages. It looks much like a weekend shopping day at Fort Benning, only it's a half a world away. Then Dave's bus pulls in, and soon he's on the final leg of his trip.

The highway south is a broad expanse pockmarked with holes and lined with ruts. It's crowded with bicycles, taxis, buses, and vehicles powered by a variety of animals. After an hour of jolting along this thoroughfare, Dave's bus turns onto a worse road that runs through the sort of town that springs up outside military bases all over the world. Shacks and ugly little buildings crowd each other on either side. Signs for pawn shops, tailors, massage parlors, and nightclubs hang everywhere. Then the bus stops. "This is as far as I go," the driver says.

Dave is left standing with all his worldly possessions in front of a fifteen-foot-high concertina-topped gate. A sign over it reads "83rd Ordnance Battalion." The gate is open, so he picks up his bags and carries them over to a guard shack just inside. An attractive Korean woman dressed in a miniskirt is there talking to the MP. The guard picks up a field phone and cranks the handle. "I need to speak with Sergeant Wilson," he says.

As Dave waits for the guard to get off the phone, he gazes down the gravel road that leads into the compound. It goes straight for about half a mile. On the left, there's an assortment of buildings set back from the road. The biggest looks like a movie theater. On the right is a sea of Quonset huts laid out with the sides of the buildings parallel to the road.

"Hey, Sergeant, your yobo is up here, she wants to see you," the gate guard says into the phone. He hangs up then turns to Dave. "Replacement?" he asks.

"Yeah."

"Which company?"

"The 260th MP."

"Same as me," The guard smiles. "I'm Johansson."

Spec 4 Johansson is a massively built blond-haired, blue-eyed guy who looks like he should be out terrorizing medieval monasteries, not manning a guard shack in Korea. He picks up the field phone and cranks the handle again. "Hey, I've got a cherry up here with all his shit. Can someone come get him?"

Presently a cloud of dust appears at the far end of the gravel road. A jeep is racing up it toward the guard shack. The vehicle stops along the way to pick up a soldier then comes barreling up to the gate. The driver cuts the wheel and slams on the brake, so the jeep slides to a halt. Then a black sergeant jumps out and strides over to the woman. They walk away from the gate to talk in private.

The driver comes over, picks up Dave's duffel bag, and throws it onto the backseat of the jeep. "Where are you from?" he asks.

"Washington, DC."

"Oh fuck, a Yankee," the soldier exclaims. He's bareheaded, and his long dark bangs hang almost into his eyes. The last name, O'Reilly, is stenciled onto the unbuttoned fatigue shirt he wears over his bare chest.

"Actually, DC is below the Mason-Dixon line," Dave says, climbing onto the passenger seat.

O'Reilly gives Dave a baffled look as he floors the accelerator and pops the clutch. This produces a minor amount of wheel spin and flying gravel, but not much. Jeeps have about as much horsepower as a go-kart.

There's nothing but block after block of Quonsets on Dave's side, so as they head down the gravel road he looks past the driver at what's on the left. There's a mess hall across from the movie theater, and a Special Services recreation building next door. The battalion headquarters is on the next block, and then they pass the motor pool, which is surrounded by a chain-link fence. The short ride ends at the rear of the compound, and they park next to a big wooden sign with "260th MP CO" emblazoned on it. O'Reilly slides out of the jeep and opens the screen door of the company office. Dave catches it before it slams and follows him in. "He's a Yankee," the driver says to a scrawny spec 4 seated with his feet up on one of the desks.

"Shit," the spec 4 says. He has the sort of pinched face and sallow complexion often seen in Appalachia. A sparse little mustache is trying to grow on his upper lip. The name tag on his fatigues reads "Gibson."

Dave glances at the clock. It's going on 7:00 p.m. and other than O'Reilly and Gibson no one else is on duty. "We're really shorthanded," Gibson mutters. He looks Dave up and down then comes to a decision. "You're going to be in our squad," he says. "I'll show you where to bunk."

Outside, Gibson grabs Dave's carry-on bag out of the jeep, leaving the new guy to shoulder the duffel bag. They walk down the company street to one of the Quonsets. Inside, ten cots face each other across a center aisle. In between the cots are wall lockers, and on one of them, a reel-to-reel tape is turning as speakers blast out the dulcet tones of Grand Funk Railroad. The tops of many of the other lockers also hold high-end Japanese electronic gear.

Slumbering GIs occupy several of the bunks in the barracks. On one, a man is writing a letter while in the middle of the hut four guys sit at a table playing cards. A pedestal fan near the back door strives to keep the air moving. Open windows mounted head high along the walls help with ventilation.

Gibson walks a short way down the center aisle then throws Dave's travel bag onto the bare springs of a cot. The mattress is rolled up at the end. Dave opens the door to one of the nearby wall lockers and finds that it's empty except for a few hangers. The other locker is just as barren. There's an empty footlocker under the cot.

The front door of the hut opens, and O'Reilly comes in carrying a stack of bedding. He dumps the load onto the bare cot. "Sign here," the driver says, handing Dave a clipboard. Then O'Reilly and Gibson go back to the office.

As Dave unrolls the mattress and starts to make his bed, one of the card players looks over and starts laughing. The others are soon cracking up as well. "Hey, cherry," one of them says. "We don't do that shit here." He puts his hand down and motions Dave to follow him. "My name's Smitty," the soldier says as they walk toward the rear of the Quonset. "I'm an acting jack. The lifers appoint some of us to be acting sergeants so they can chill in the vill with their yobos."

"What's a yobo?"

"A whore who gets paid by the month to shack up."

Outside the back door, there's a concrete stoop and a grassy area where two Korean men are squatting on their heels shining boots. "Hey, Kim, we got a new guy," Smitty says. Immediately one of the Koreans jumps up and comes over.

"*Yeoboseyo*," Kim says, bowing his head.

"He needs to get his shit squared away," Smitty demands.

"I come mos rikki-tik," Kim says, "finishee Lee boots." He squats and goes back to furiously buffing the boots.

"Kim's our houseboy," Smitty explains. "Every payday we each give him ten bucks." Smitty is a tall, broad-shouldered guy with a cruel Teutonic face.

"That's a lot," Dave says. "What if I want to take care of my own stuff?"

"Are you fucking joking?" Smitty asks. He turns and goes back into the hut.

Kim gets up holding several pairs of footgear. "You come," he says, prying the screen door open with an elbow. Inside, the houseboy stops at several bunks to deposit boots. When they get to Dave's area, Kim pulls the footlocker out and motions for Dave to sit on it. Then the Korean neatly and efficiently makes up the bunk. Next Kim begins hanging Dave's uniforms in one of the wall lockers. Smitty looks up from the card game and sees Dave relaxing while the houseboy works. "That's right, cherry," the acting jack hollers. "Now you got it."

Kim hangs Dave's civilian clothes in the other locker. Then he motions for Dave to get up and stores his shaving kit, books, underwear, and other incidentals in the footlocker. When the houseboy gets to the bottom of the duffle bag, he finds the Corcoran boots Dave got for OCS. "Jump boots numba fuckin' one," Kim exclaims as Dave winces. The Korean's breath smells like something a buzzard wouldn't eat.

Suddenly the hut grows quiet. The tape has run out and now one of the card players goes to the stereo receiver and shuts it off. Then the other three get up, and they all go out the front door. "They go movie," Kim says. "Maybe you?"

"No, I go shower," Dave replies. He can't help copying Kim's speech pattern. "Where's the latrine?"

"You come," Kim says and leads Dave out the back door. He points to a cinder block building a short walk away.

"Thanks," Dave says.

"*Aniya*," Kim replies with a friendly smile. Dave's been trying to think of who the houseboy resembles, and now it hits him—Mickey Rooney. Kim has the same cherubic face complete with dimples, but he's not young. Dave wouldn't want to guess how old, but for sure the houseboy is not young.

After showering, Dave gets into bed to read. Soon his attention wavers and the book drops to the floor. He sleeps soundly for several hours but is awakened in the middle of the night by a commotion. "Get up and fight, you white motherfuckers," someone hollers. Dave makes out the shape of a large soldier staggering up and down the center aisle. He freezes, hoping the intruder won't see him lying there in the dark. "I'll fight any one of you, any two of you. Oh fuck, I'll fight all of you white bastards right now," the soldier offers. But no one takes him up on it. "You're nothing but a bunch of fucking pussies," the frustrated fighter complains. Then he goes out, slamming the screen door behind him. Immediately several whispered conversations break out around the hooch. Some of the men are quietly giggling in the darkness. "Who was that?" Dave asks his neighbor.

"Chief Thunder. He hates white people."

"I gathered that."

The other guys are still sleeping when Dave gets up in the morning. He goes to the latrine to brush his teeth, shower, and shave. Then he changes into fatigues. Dave is curious to see what the day will bring but decides to fortify himself at the mess hall first.

There are only a couple of other men at chow when Dave arrives, so he expects to get plenty of everything. However, as he goes down the buffet line, nothing looks edible. The scorched bread is nothing like the Knight family's conception of French toast, the powdered eggs are excessively watery, and the sausage does not bear thinking about. Dave missed dinner the night before and is starving. So with a look of distaste on his face he fills his tray and takes it over to one of the tables.

After eating what he can of the food, Dave remains at the table reading. He's engrossed in the book and doesn't see his squadmates come in. Suddenly Smitty is looming over him.

"Whatcha reading?" the acting jack demands.

Dave holds up his paperback so Smitty can see the cover. It's *The Spy Who Came in from the Cold.*

"Any good?" Smitty asks.

"It's great," Dave enthuses. "This is the second time I've read it."

"Didn't get it the first time, huh?" Smitty says smugly. "You must be fucking stupid." He smiles down at Dave condescendingly while O'Reilly and Gibson stand on either side of their leader laughing inanely.

"Yeah, I'm not that bright," Dave agrees. "That's why I'm sitting here at the ass end of the world, wearing a silly green suit, and eating this shit food. So tell me, what brings you here?"

Now O'Reilly and Gibson round on Smitty. "Yeah, genius, what brings you here?" O'Reilly cackles.

"You had to be real smart to get your ass sent to this fucking place," Gibson piles on.

"Eat one, Gibson," Smitty exclaims. He turns in a huff and walks off.

"Ha-ha, that was good," O'Reilly laughs. Then he and Gibson turn and follow Smitty.

A short while later, Dave returns to the hut, gets his records, then goes to the company office. Several soldiers are standing at the rail waiting for the company clerk to get off the phone. Two other clerks are at the desks up front. One is sorting mail; the other is typing. Meanwhile, all the desks in the back are empty. There's no sign of the first sergeant or any officers.

The company clerk's name tag reads Harris. He's tall and thin and has thick army glasses perched on the bridge of his long prominent nose. He seems exasperated. "Well, what am I supposed to do with them?" he whines into the phone. "So, when is he expected back? OK, sheesh, guess I'll have to handle it." He hangs up and sees Dave standing there.

"Knight?"

"That's me."

"When did you come in?"

"Last night."

"Shit, which hooch did Gibson and O'Reilly put you in?"

"Theirs."

"Ha, that figures," Harris laughs. He opens a three-ring binder and thumbs through it until he finds what he wants. "Well, I guess that's all right," he says. "You'll be in First Platoon, Second Squad. Are those your files?"

Dave gives the clerk his personnel file, medical records, and a set of orders. "When's the last time you got paid?" Harris asks.

"August."

"OK, we'll get you caught up next week."

"Sounds good."

Now Harris addresses the other men who have been waiting: "Guys," he says, "welcome to the 260th MP. I'm sure that the captain would like to greet you personally, but he's in Seoul. So, I want you all to come back after lunch, say 1300 hours, and we will get you processed in."

Dave follows the other replacements out the door. They stand uncertainly in the company street. No one says anything, so Dave breaks the ice. "When did you guys get in?" he asks.

"I been here mos a week," a muscular African American PFC named McGriff complains. "Every day the man say we gonna process, but nothin' ever get done."

"Same ole lame-ass army," another black soldier says. His name is Jeffrie; he's a tall skinny private with a mustache and as much of an Afro as he can get away with.

The other two guys in the group are white. Spec 4 Castle is almost as big as McGriff. He has a homespun face and looks like he should be pushing either a plow or a blocking sled. Next to him is PFC Montgomery, an overweight, acne-riddled soldier who does not appear very happy about life. "Me and Montgomery got in Saturday," Castle says. "We were supposed to meet the captain and the first shirt Monday, but neither of them showed up. Been waiting ever since."

"This shit be all fucked up," Jeffrie exclaims.

That afternoon Harris gains the cooperation of the supply sergeant and the armorer and manages to get all five replacements assigned weapons and issued field equipment. Afterward, Dave brings his gear to the hut and Kim puts it away. Then he goes to the company office to complete processing. "We got one more thing," Harris says, holding up a Polaroid. "Stand over there." Harris snaps a picture and affixes it to a card. "Sign at the bottom," the clerk says.

"What this for?"

"It's your gate pass; you need it for work, so make sure you keep it in your wallet."

"OK, is that it?"

"Yep, you are done," Harris says. "First Platoon goes on days tomorrow, and you'll go with them."

"OK," Dave replies. "But I got a question. What's the address here? I've got to let my old lady know where to write me."

"It's simple," Harris says. "She can send letters to you at 260th MP CO, APO SF 96301."

"Got it."

Dave goes to the canteen and buys some stationery and stamps. Then he returns to the hooch and drafts a short letter to Cindy. After mailing it, he goes to the mess hall for dinner then kills a couple of hours at the movie theater watching *Five Easy Pieces*. It's a depressing flick.

All is quiet in Second Squad when Dave gets back from the movie. He's glum, and so is everyone else. The platoon is at the end of a three-day break, and in the morning the MPs begin a nine-day stretch of tower guard doing rotating shifts. Dave is familiar with shiftwork, thanks to his time at Arlington Towers. He's not thrilled to be back at it, but it beats being in Vietnam all to pieces.

As the soldiers sullenly get ready for bed, conversation is subdued. Most are asleep by 11:00 p.m., but Dave can't seem to doze off. He keeps thinking of Cindy so far away. She's the source of the optimism that has buoyed him over the last year. Without her, he feels anxious and depressed.

Smitty cuts the lights on at 0530 hours. Grumbling, the soldiers climb out of their cots, grab their shaving kits, and go to the latrine. They wash up then return to the hooch and get into uniform. After stomaching what they can of breakfast, the men fall out in the company street for roll call. Standing in the ranks, Dave gets his first look at the platoon NCOs. They are not an impressive bunch. None look like they could pass a PT test.

Once roll call is over, the MPs draw their weapons from the armory and board the waiting bus. Soon they have exited the compound and are wending their way through the village of Seoksu-dong. The signs on the shacks promising unlimited vice appear particularly tawdry in the faint dawn light. When the bus gets to the highway, it turns south toward Anyang. Before reaching the city, it turns again, this time onto a one-lane dirt road that leads into an agricultural area. Here rice paddies jam every bit of arable land on either side. They extend off into the distance then become terraces going up into the mountains. Picturesque thatched roofed villages perch precariously in the hollows.

The bus ride continues for another ten minutes passing only one building of note. It's a grim two-story edifice constructed of mud and thatch. About two miles past this place, the vehicle stops at a fenced-in military installation. After dismounting, the MPs pass through the entrance under the gaze of two tired guards. Then they fall into ranks for the duty formation. As they're waiting for the platoon sergeant to appear, Dave turns to Gibson, who's standing next to him. "What exactly are we guarding?" he asks.

"Nukes," Gibson replies, "along with some other stuff."

"What other stuff?"

"No one knows for sure," Gibson says. "This is a Special Ammunition Depot."

"You've got your liquid and your nonliquid," Smitty explains. "It's all stored in there." He points to a sandbagged gate ahead of them. The sign on it reads "SAD."

Dual chain-link fences surround the SAD, and mercury vapor lamps illuminate the perimeter. These lights are still on in the early morning gloom, and it's as though a giant incandescent necklace has been dropped onto the horseshoe-shaped ridge that encompasses the site. The elevation of the ridge increases as it curves until reaching a peak in the center; then it gradually tapers off as it curls back around. A conical hill rises in the middle of the horseshoe, and a gravel road runs between it and the base of the facing ridge. Bunkers line the road on either side in this area. They tunnel underground, providing storage for the special ammunition. The bunkers are called Stradley magazines and look like something out of a sci-fi movie.

Finally, the platoon sergeant comes out of the guard office with the duty roster. He's a heavyset staff sergeant named Erik Anthony. "At ease," the NCO calls, and conversation in the ranks tapers off. "It's First Squad's turn for QRF," Anthony announces, and there's a cheer from the front rank. Then the platoon sergeant reads off a series of names and assignments for the gates and towers. Anthony concludes by issuing the password for the day. It's "lemon lullaby," the assumption being that this would be a mouthful for the average North Korean.

"Platoon, atten-hut," Anthony hollers. The MPs adjust their posture slightly, and Anthony quickly cries, "Dismissed." The men line up to draw their C rations then begin passing through the SAD gate. Now each tower guard must hand over his pass and insert a full magazine into his M16. The NCOs and gate guards carry sidearms, so they slide clips into their .45s.

"You'll need a ride," Smitty tells Dave once they are both cleared into the secure area. "O'Reilly will take you."

A jeep is parked just inside the SAD gate with O'Reilly behind the wheel. The driver grins as Dave climbs onto the passenger seat. Then two more guys jump into the back. One is McGriff, who Dave knows from in-processing, the other is Peterson, who was writing a letter the night Dave arrived. He's a tall humorless Midwesterner who's always writing letters and ignoring his squadmates.

O'Reilly starts the motor and turns onto a partially washed-out road that follows the curve of the ridge just inside the fence line. Wooden guard towers stand at prominences along the ridge, each about half a mile from the next. The lower ones are within walking distance, but Dave is in tower 6, which is near the top of the mountain.

As the grade steepens, and the ruts in the road become gullies, O'Reilly keeps the little four-wheeler in low. The soldiers in back hold on tight as the vehicle bucks and bounces. At one point it sways so far over, Dave's afraid it's going to flip. O'Reilly stops about a hundred yards shy of tower 5. "You're up there," he tells McGriff, and the PFC wordlessly starts walking. Meanwhile, a figure begins climbing down the ladder of McGriff's tower; it's the guard who was up there the previous night.

The road ahead is impassable. "How do I get to tower 6?" Dave asks.

"Take the Choji Trail," O'Reilly replies.

"Where's that?"

"Come on, I'll show you," Peterson offers.

O'Reilly leans against the jeep and lights a cigarette. He will have to wait until the guards who were in the higher towers come down. "Later," he says.

Peterson sets off up the ridge with Dave following. They climb until they come to where the Choji Trail forks off from the old roadbed then pause for breath. Below them, the site is open to view. It's heavily forested, and birds fly among the treetops. Across the way, on the peak, Peterson's tower stands outlined against the sky. "Tower 7 is the best and the worst," he says.

"How so?"

"It's the worst because it's the hardest one to get to and it's the best 'cause it's the hardest one to get to," Peterson laughs. "No one messes with you up there."

The two soldiers start up the Choji Trail. It's a narrow path through immature forest that traverses the ridge. As they go up, a tower guard from Fourth

Platoon brushes past going the other way. He barely acknowledges them in his haste to get down the hill to where the jeep is waiting.

After ten minutes on the Choji Trail, the two MPs emerge from the woods into a clearing below the base of tower 6. "I'll be back this way at the end of the shift," Peterson says. Then he starts the trek across the long saddle that separates tower 6 from tower 7.

Dave is tired and ready to sit down somewhere, but first, he must get to his place of business. There's a wooden ladder on the tower, so he begins climbing. In a short while, he steps onto the catwalk, and the view is spectacular. One mountain ridge follows another in every direction. In the valleys, rice paddies surround thatch-roofed villages. Most of the mountains are bare, but tall trees grow among the rocks on some of the highest peaks.

Once he has admired the view from all sides, Dave unslings his rifle and ducks inside the enclosure. He does a quick inventory of the items inside: binoculars, field telephone, footlocker, folding metal chair, and heavy-duty wire cutters. Then he unstraps his web belt and shrugs out of the shoulder harness. His gear drops to the floor. Dave sits on the footlocker and in the stillness feels very much alone. "This is going to be all right," he says.

Somehow it doesn't feel at all strange for Dave to be talking to himself in the tower. Who's going to know? Likewise, who's going to see that he's reading? Dave unzips his gas-mask pouch and pulls out a paperback. It's *The Quiet American*, one that he's read before. Loath as he is to admit it, Smitty is right. Dave rarely "gets" a book on the first read-through.

Reading while on guard duty is forbidden, so the next day when Dave draws tower 12, he must be careful. It's the closest tower to the guard office, and the one the NCOs check most often. He spends most of the day out on the catwalk and only goes inside to sneak glances at his book when he knows it's safe.

The following day, Second Squad lucks out and is assigned to be the Quick Reaction Force (QRF). This means that their only job is to be available to rush to the scene of an emergency. Since there haven't been any Commies spotted in the vicinity since 1953 the men are not worried about being called out. Instead, they rush to claim one of the bunks in the ready room. Dave is slow getting there and has to settle for an upper. He has a long nap then spends the rest of the day either reading or just hanging around the guard office building.

After dinner that evening, the Second Squad hooch empties. Some of the guys go to the NCO club for a beer while others attend a movie. No one is worried about morning formation because there won't be one. First Platoon is going onto the swing shift, so the next formation won't be until 3:00 p.m. the following afternoon. In the empty hooch, Dave sits on his footlocker and writes a long letter to Cindy. Then he reads until it's time to turn out the light.

Only a few guys go to breakfast in the morning but by 10:00 a.m. the MPs of Second Squad are all up. Soon the card game regenerates itself, and Dave goes over to watch. "What are you playing?" he asks.

"Spades, of course," Smitty replies, but this provides little illumination. The only card game Dave knows is poker. He watches a few minutes longer then leaves the hooch. He wants to visit Special Services and see what they have to offer.

It's a short walk up the gravel road to Special Services. Inside, Dave nods to the spec 4 at the front desk then goes to check the place out. There's a library, a room for arts and crafts, and a game room. Dave enters the game room, gets a cue off the rack, and pulls several balls out of the pockets of one of the pool tables. He practices basic shots while the rock opera *Tommy* booms from a pair of speakers on the wall. An hour goes by then the tape runs out, and the room grows quiet. It's time for lunch.

On his way out, Dave spots a poster for the Armed Forces Institute promoting college correspondence courses. There's a display with brochures, and he takes one. Then he goes to the mess hall and gets a tray of food. Once again, it's deplorable: stringy baked chicken, powdered mashed potatoes, watery mixed vegetables, and a hard brownie for dessert. The bones of the chicken are black.

Dave reads the AFI brochure and decides to sign up for a college course. So, after returning his tray, he goes back to Special Services. "Glad to see you again," the spec 4 says when Dave comes in. "You gonna work on some bank shots now?"

"Not until I can consistently make those simple straight-in shots," Dave replies.

"Yeah, those are not as easy as they look."

"Oh, and I want to take a correspondence course."

"College?"

"Yes."

"That's good," the spec 4 says, handing Dave a registration form. "You know, some guys complete several courses during their tour. They leave with a buttload of credits."

"That would be good."

"Of course, that's rare. Most of these idiots completely waste their time in-country. You know, drink, smoke pot, whore around in the vill, all that shit."

"I couldn't afford all that even if I wanted to," Dave says. "I'm sending most of my pay home." He hands the Special Services guy the completed registration form.

"OK, this looks all right," the spec 4 says. "*US History to 1865* is a good one. You'll get the course materials in the mail." Dave starts to leave but is drawn back into the game room. Two of the pool tables are busy, but the other one is free. He goes back to practicing.

Later, Dave is returning to Second Squad when he's startled to see a tall, attractive blonde coming out of the company office. She's wearing hot pants, platform shoes, and a blouse with the shirt tails tied together, so it comes up shy of her bare midriff. He stops, mouth agape, but is brought up short when a captain comes out behind her carrying a bag. "Pop your eyes back into your head, troop," the officer snaps.

"Yes, sir." Dave salutes, but now the captain ignores him.

"You'll never guess what I just saw out in the company street," Dave exclaims, bursting into the Second Squad hooch.

"Oh, we saw her too," O'Reilly says. "That's Captain Pfeiffer's fiancée."

"She loves to parade around the company area like that while we drool over her," Gibson explains.

"That's what keeps him in Seoul," Smitty declares. "She's a donut dolly, works for the Red Cross."

"Hey, formation is in half an hour," O'Reilly says. "We got to get our shit together."

That evening in tower 14, Dave begins to understand what he's up against. For the first several hours he can read, but then the sun goes down, and there's no light in the tower. He spends the next four hours either sitting in the dark or walking around the catwalk looking at the stars.

Dave is having lunch at the mess hall the next day when Smitty comes over. "Hey, you got any money?" he asks.

"A few bucks. What for?"

"We need beer. Tomorrow is our last night on swings, and we're having a party."

"Sure," Dave says, reaching for his wallet.

When First Platoon comes off the swing shift the next night, they have twenty-four hours of free time coming before going on midnights. In the Second Squad hooch a waist-high stack of beer is waiting when the MPs come in shortly after 1:00 a.m. Smitty starts a Rolling Stones tape playing on his reel-to-reel then, like the others, he changes into civilian attire. Soon most of the men are in a circle drinking suds and jiving to the music. But Peterson is having none of it. He sits on his bunk at the rear of the hooch writing a letter to his wife. Jeffrie is also missing. He has gone to the Fourth Squad hooch to party. There are brothers there, and soul music is more to his liking.

The remaining Second Squad guys all participate, and several men come from other hooches to join the festivities. Not all are in for the duration, however. Most of the guys are tired after a long day and just drink a beer or two before ambling away to get some rest. After a couple of hours, it's only the hardcore who remain.

Now Smitty invents a drinking game. He opens a beer, takes a slug out of it, then passes it to Gibson. "It's called the circle game," Smitty declares. "If you want to play, you have to be in the circle and take a drink of every beer then pass it on." Gibson does as instructed while Smitty quickly opens another can, swallows some, and then this beer too starts making the rounds. There are ten guys in the circle to start with, including Dave, who intentionally misquotes Ken Kesey. "You're either in the circle or out of the circle," he shouts. This sounds profound, so he repeats the mantra—over and over again.

The partiers find themselves drinking with one hand while holding out the other to receive reinforcements. Some hold a beer in each hand and keep another in the crook of the arm. Meanwhile, Smitty is maniacally opening cans one after the other, and presently guys begin staggering away to find their cots. But Gibson doesn't make it to his. Instead, he kneels with his face in the trash can, throwing up. Then the beer runs out, so Dave, Smitty, and a couple of other stalwarts stagger out back for a last pee before they too take to their bunks.

It requires all morning for the swing partiers to recuperate, but by noon most of the guys are at least able to eat lunch. When Dave gets back from the mess hall, a letter from Cindy is on his cot. He opens the envelope and learns that she got her old job back at the Colony 7 and has found a nearby apartment. It's nice to know that Cindy received his first note and now has his address. Dave scribbles her back a letter describing the insanity from the night before.

After dinner that evening, the MPs mope around the barracks waiting to go on midnights. They're so bummed not even the card players feel like playing. It's almost a relief when the time comes to get ready for formation.

When they get to the site, Dave draws tower 7. O'Reilly takes him as far up the ridge as he can, then Dave hikes the rest of the way. He plans to kill off the night by exercising so he puts his gear away then begins walking around the catwalk, pausing now and then to do calisthenics. Slowly his motivation ebbs, and after a while, he goes inside to rest. Dave knows that sleeping on guard is court-martial offense, often punished with a dishonorable discharge. But the NCOs rarely if ever check tower 7, so he lies on the footlocker using his gas mask for a pillow and the folding metal chair as a footrest.

In the darkness, Dave brings pleasant memories to mind, and soon he and Cindy are riding the Triumph down a twisty road in the Shenandoah Valley. She sits behind him with her hands on his hips as the pulsating exhaust of the single cylinder motor echoes under an overpass. All is well, and slowly Dave drifts off to sleep.

In his dream, Dave is working at the front desk of Arlington Towers. He talks to a pretty girl, and she invites him to come up and see her when he gets off work. Later, Dave takes an elevator to the girl's floor and knocks on her door. He's surprised when Dan opens it. "What are you doing here?" Dave asks.

"None of your business," Dan replies.

Dave punches Dan in the face, and his brother falls to the floor with his nose grotesquely bent to one side. Then Marie appears and grabs Dave's arm. "Don't hit him anymore," she begs. Dan is gasping, and blood bubbles from his nose. Then someone pounds on the door: "Military Police, open up."

With a determined effort, Dave wakes himself from the nightmare. He thinks of Marie and is overcome with remorse. As the night drags on, he wallows in melancholy. Eventually, the sky lightens, and Dave goes onto the catwalk again. He can make out the geometric shapes of rice paddies far below. Lights flicker in the mud-walled houses of the peasants then a rooster crows and is joined by many others. Nearby mountains appear stark and treeless in the dim light.

An hour later the bus pulls up in front of the main gate, and Third Platoon gets off. Dave waits to leave his tower until they hold formation and he sees the jeep start up the perimeter road. As he climbs down the ladder, the full canteen bobbles awkwardly on his hip. The water tastes awful, and Dave didn't drink any. He stumbles along the Choji Trail then down the hill to where the jeep is parked. "Hey, what's happening?" O'Reilly asks.

"Miserable fucking night," Dave replies.

A stream of MPs begins filing out of the SAD. The gate guards return their passes then the men clear their weapons. They walk past the infantry barracks and the guard office building then line up to go out the main gate. The soldiers come through single file and shamble over to the bus. There is no banter, the men's faces are expressionless, and their eyes are glazed over.

Over the past couple of months, Second Squad's swing parties have caught on. Last night's edition attracted participants from all over the compound. Now, even though it's afternoon, Dave is lying on his cot recuperating. A shadow falls across his face, and he looks up to find Smitty hovering over him. "What's that thing on your lip?" he asks.

"It's just a cold sore," Dave replies.

"Looks like a pussy-eating sore to me," Smitty says. "Sure you ain't got the clap?"

"I'm sure."

"Well, never mind, we need you for spades."

"Never played."

"Nothin' to it," Smitty replies. "I'll learn you."

Dave gets off his bunk and goes to the card table where O'Reilly and Gibson are seated across from each other ready to partner. While Smitty tells Dave the rules, O'Reilly deals, and soon they are playing. Dave's strongest card is the ace of clubs, and he happily wins a trick with it. Next, he leads the queen of diamonds and Gibson takes that trick with the king. Gibson adds insult to injury by winning the next one with the jack. Then he leads the deuce of diamonds having determined, based on Smitty's look of disgust, that his partner, O'Reilly, has the ace. Smitty seems to be doing everything he can to hold himself back from throttling Dave. "Did you count the queen as one of your three?" he seethes.

"Yes," Dave admits as he catches on to the enormity of his crime.

"But you threw her out there without a dress," Smitty snaps.

"Hey, relax," O'Reilly says. "What do you expect from a cherry?"

Dave realizes that if he wants to avoid getting killed by his partner, he better bring his scant powers of concentration to bear. There are only thirteen cards in each suit and just four suits. How hard can it be? Over the next couple of hours, he focuses but still makes mistakes. However, Dave gradually learns the game and begins to appreciate the potential it offers for surprises. Better yet, Smitty stops yelling at him and is even gracious at the end when O'Reilly and Gibson are first to five hundred. "'Bout time you losers win one," he says while putting the cards away.

Smitty and his sidekicks leave the hooch, allowing Dave to return to his bunk. He dozes off, and when he wakes, it's time for dinner. Dave goes to the latrine, splashes some cold, chemically treated water on his face, then walks to the mess hall. After eating overcooked spaghetti with anemic tomato sauce, Dave goes to Special Services and spends an hour completing the latest assignment for his correspondence course. Then he gets in line to play pool. It takes a while, but then it's his turn to rack the balls. Dave handily wins the first game but scratches on the eight ball to lose the next. That means he must go to the end of the line. Instead, he returns to the hooch and starts getting ready for work. First Platoon is going on midnights.

Out at the site, Dave is assigned to tower 10, which is unlike the other towers. It sits on top of the conical hill in the middle of the SAD, and its round shape and white paint job make the guard post look like a UFO. Because of its spaciousness, tower 10 is a popular roost, but the guard office is not far away, so the round tower is frequently checked by the NCOs.

Once through the SAD gate, Dave trudges up the hill. He's breathing heavily when he gets to the base of tower 10 and pauses to catch his breath. Looking up he sees a hole in the Milky Way created by the bottom of the tower. Stairs lead from the ground to a landing then one more flight of steps goes up to a trapdoor built into the tower floor. Dave climbs the stairs then pushes the trapdoor open and pokes his head inside. He removes the M16 from his shoulder, slides it into the tower, and climbs in after it. Once Dave's inside he flips the trapdoor closed.

Dave has had tower 10 before, but the circular guard post is still a novelty. He quickly sheds his web gear and goes out on the catwalk. It's dark, and there isn't much to see other than lights twinkling mysteriously in the mountains. The crisp air is a foretaste of the bitter Manchurian cold that's on the way.

It doesn't take long for Dave to get bored pacing around the catwalk in the dark. He goes back inside and sits on the metal folding chair as random thoughts bounce around in his head. After several months of solitude in the towers, he has exhausted the capacity to sustain a coherent daydream. Now it's more a matter of fighting off unpleasant memories. In the towers, troublesome thoughts have a way of springing forth jack-in-the-box-like to cause Dave's heart to race, his skin to dampen, and his dread to deepen. It often takes a major effort to harness these goblins and tamp them back down into their holes.

At present, however, Dave's main enemy is drowsiness. So he goes back out on the catwalk and spends another hour walking laps. It's a clear night, and the sky is ablaze. He picks out some well-known constellations and wishes he knew more.

The temperature has been dropping all night, and even though Dave has his field jacket liner zipped in, he eventually gets cold. The guard office building below appears moribund in the wee hours, so Dave goes back inside and lies on the footlocker, covering himself with his poncho. The electric heater provides some warmth.

It's almost 3:00 a.m., and Dave feels a peaceful drowsiness as he stretches out. It doesn't occur to him that he's lying on top of enough "special ammunition" to kill every man, woman, and child within a thousand miles. He closes his eyes but can still visualize the night sky. Planets, stars, and distant galaxies drift slowly past. It's delightful, but after a while, Dave feels a faint vibration, like someone may have stepped onto the tower stairs.

Still, Dave doesn't panic; he continues to drift along in a semiconscious state as another minute passes. But then he feels the vibration again. "Motherfucker," he mutters, coming fully awake, "sneaky motherfucking bastard."

Dave reaches for his M16 and drops to the floor. He assumes the prone position in front of the trapdoor, then snicks the bolt of the rifle back. A click signifies that the catch has engaged. Dave checks to make sure the safety is on then he looks over the sights and waits.

As time passes, the interval between steps grows shorter as whoever is on the stairs loses patience. Finally, the intruder reaches the top, and the trapdoor silently begins to rise. A hairy hand wearing a cheap Timex is pushing it up. Next, a green army field cap comes into view then slowly the face of Sergeant Anthony appears under the brim. He looks to the right then swivels his head until his eyes are staring down the barrel of Dave's M16. They widen, and at that moment Dave releases the bolt catch. The clash of an assault rifle being locked and loaded reverberates through the tower as the trapdoor slams shut and Anthony tumbles back down the stairs. Dave gets to his knees and flips the trapdoor up again. He looks down to see the disheveled NCO crumpled on the landing below. "Oh, Sergeant Anthony, it's you," Dave exclaims innocently. "I thought it was a North Korean infiltrator."

"You dirty motherfucker," Anthony moans, looking up at Dave with murderous intent. The NCO gingerly moves his limbs. Finding his arms and legs still in working order, he now pats himself down as if checking to make sure he's still all there. Satisfied, Anthony looks at Dave again. "You tell anybody about this, and it's going to be your ass," he says. "You hear me?"

"Yes, Sergeant," Dave says nodding his head affirmatively.

But of course, Dave can't wait to tell what happened. His chance comes several hours later after Third Platoon comes to take over security at the site. He tells his story as the guys are waiting to board the bus. "Bullshit," Smitty declares. "You wouldn't have the balls."

But O'Reilly is more positive. "Oh shit, I wish I coulda seen that motherfucker rolling down them stairs," he says. This comment meets with great acclamation, and some of the other guys in the platoon come over to see what Second

Squad is carrying on about. Tom Hanson is among them. He's a member of First Squad, which is known as a haven for drug addicts, alcoholics, and hippies. "What's happening?" he asks.

"Knight locked and loaded on Anthony," Gibson says excitedly. "The motherfucker tried to sneak up on him in tower 10."

"No shit," Hanson says, giving Dave a thumbs-up. "Very cool."

"Hey, mount up," Smitty hollers. "Let's go."

Back at the compound the tired tower guards shower then go to breakfast. Normally, they would return to the hooch and sleep once they've eaten, but this is payday. So, after chow, First Platoon holds formation and then one by one the MPs go into the company office to see the paymaster. Each man must wait while his allotment of MPC is counted out, then visit various stations to contribute money for the orphanage, company fund, and houseboys. The lower-ranked enlisted men normally end up with a little over two hundred dollars in MPC, but Dave only has eighty bucks when he emerges from the office. That's because he has money deducted for Cindy every month to add to the spousal allowance she gets from the army.

After putting his money away, Dave goes to sleep. But that afternoon he's awakened by Carlos Santana's "Black Magic Woman" blasting out of one of the stereos. A raucous payday poker game is going on in the middle of the Quonset with Smitty in the midst of it, grinning and talking trash. "Whores, fours, and one-eyed jacks," he calls, then allows a lit cigarette to dangle from his lip as he deals.

Dave tries to pick up where he left off in the book he's reading, but the noise proves too much. He gets up to see how the poker game is going and finds Smitty with a big stack of MPC in front of him. Gibson and O'Reilly are also at the table and appear to be hurting, while a shifty-looking sergeant from ordnance named Gullickson has almost as much cash as Smitty. Next to him, Sergeant Wilson from Fourth Squad is limping along with a modest pile of currency on display.

Now Smitty rakes in the pot, having assembled enough wild cards to beat O'Reilly's full house with four of a kind. "I can't win for losing," O'Reilly moans and gets up. One of the bystanders immediately takes his seat.

"Tough luck," Dave says as O'Reilly comes over to join the spectators.

"Oh, I never win," the driver says. "Don't know why I even play. Let's go to the NCO club and have a beer."

"Sure."

The NCO club is at the rear of the compound just a short walk away. It's crowded on payday, and the tables are full, so O'Reilly and Dave sit at the bar. Presently they each have a frosty can of Olympia in front of them and are taking in the scene. Many of the soldiers have brought their yobos, who are dressed to kill in heels, minis, and slinky, low-cut blouses. While the men focus their attention on the cheap booze, their dates devour plates of fried chicken. "Payday is about the only time you'll see all these lifers on base," O'Reilly explains. "Most of the month they're out in the vill eating ramen with their yobos."

The lights in the club are turned low. Onstage, a Korean band covers the Beatles. "All you need is rub," the singer croons as amorous couples stagger around the dance floor. Meanwhile, O'Reilly succumbs to the southern fried aroma coming out of the kitchen and orders dinner. Dave follows suit and they eat, leaving nothing but a pile of chicken bones on their plates. "Colonel Sanders would give his left nut to cook like that," O'Reilly intones.

"Beats the hell out of mess hall food," Dave agrees. "Hey, we better leave. Don't want to get caught drinking before going on duty."

Two days later, First Platoon starts a three-day break. With money to spend, the village rats quickly shower, change into civvies, and head for Seoksu-dong. They are objects of scorn for the southern boys in Second Squad who seldom mingle with the natives.

First Squad is not fond of the vill either. They head for the bright lights of Seoul when they have money. The story is that most of First Squad were once on line duty with the 728th MP Battalion at Yongsan Garrison. That is, until the commander of the seven-deuce-eight decided to get rid of all his disciplinary problems by shipping them to the 260th.

Happy to be done with midnights, Dave has a long nap. Then he gets into some warm clothes and goes for a walk. He takes a trail out of Seoksu-dong that follows a rocky stream up into the mountains. It's a broad well-traveled dirt path that leads to a Buddhist monastery. There's a resort halfway there where the stream has been dammed to form a pond. Several small hotels dot the area along with some ramshackle bars and restaurants. It can get crowded on summer weekends, but now, at the beginning of October, the resort area is quiet. As Dave continues climbing, he passes small groups of Koreans also making the trek to the monastery. They carry bundles of food and other gifts for the monks.

By the time Dave reaches the mountaintop, the fortress-like monastery is closed to visitors. However, Dave can see inside where a bronze statue of the Buddha is centrally located. Hundreds of lit candles surround the serene figure while saffron-robed monks scurry past, tending to their evening chores.

Dave heads back down the trail and gets to the compound in time for chow. After eating he stops by the canteen and picks up a six-pack of beer. When he gets to the hooch, several new faces are seated around the poker table along with Smitty, Gullickson, and Wilson. A Led Zepplin tape is playing on one of the stereos. Dave opens a beer and puts the rest in his window to stay cold. Then he gets out his writing materials and dashes off a letter to Cindy. Afterward, he reads until he can't keep his eyes open any longer.

When Dave returns from breakfast the next morning, he finds that the mail clerk has been around. A letter from Cindy is on his bunk along with an oversize manila envelope from the Armed Forces Institute. Dave quickly opens Cindy's missive and finds it full of the cheery goings-on at Colony 7. They are doing *Bye Bye Birdie*, and thanks to excellent reviews and good crowds, the run of the play has been extended.

Inside the large envelope is the final exam for the correspondence course Dave has been taking. He brings it to Special Services and the spec 4 at the desk watches while he sits the test. It's all multiple choice, true/false, matching, and fill-in-the-blank. Once he's done, Dave turns in the answer sheet, but it was too easy. There's no sense of accomplishment. "Let's pick out another course now," the desk clerk says.

"Not today," Dave replies. "I need a break." He goes back to the hooch, grabs his field jacket, then goes to the canteen to buy beer. After exiting the compound, Dave stops at a pawn shop in Seoksu-dong to exchange MPC for Korean currency. He walks to the highway and gets on the first bus that stops. It's a rickety beat-up conveyance that's been down a lot of bad roads. Dave goes all the way to the back where he can stretch his legs. The capacious pockets of his field jacket are full of beer. He gets one out and pulls the ring. Then he drops the tab back into the can and takes a swallow. As the bus bumps along, Dave looks out the window and tries to grasp the incredible foreignness of everything he sees. They pass a Korean man pushing a bicycle with eight cages stacked high on the rear fender. Each holds a live rooster. Another man rides a moped with an impossibly tall stack of wicker baskets full of radishes lashed to the back.

The bus stops at random places along the rutted highway to let some passengers off and others on. It's getting full, but people shy away from sitting next to Dave. They prefer to stand. Finally, the vehicle enters Seoul and comes to a terminal in a shopping district. It's the end of the line, and everyone must disembark.

Dave goes in search of somewhere to pee, but it doesn't look promising. Crowds of people are everywhere, wandering among stalls that sell toys, cheap colorful clothes, plastic shoes, electronics, liquor, cigarettes, and food. Then he passes a construction site where several men are hard at work. One is casually pissing on a freshly cemented cinder block wall. Dave happily irrigates a spot a little farther down. Afterward, he goes back into the market and gets a bowl of soup. It's a clear broth containing seaweed mixed with white cubes of tofu.

Thus fortified, Dave goes back to the terminal. Several buses are waiting while the drivers stand outside talking and huffing on foul-smelling Korean cigarettes. Dave goes over to the men. "*Anyang?*" he asks, holding both hands out palm up while shrugging his shoulders. The drivers turn to look at the American. One holds out his hand.

"Cigarette me," he demands. "Winston numba one."

Dave takes a half-empty package of Marlboros out of his pocket, keeps several for himself, and offers the rest of the pack to the driver. The man snatches it. "*Anyang,*" he says, pointing to a bus that's slowly pulling into the lot. A couple of hours later, Dave gets off the rattletrap at the stop for Seoksu-dong.

The next day is the last day of break, and Dave is depressed. In the afternoon he tries to sleep, but the poker game is still going on. Music blares as the cards make the rounds and the windows are full of cold beer. The guys still playing this long after payday are all winners and they're a boisterous bunch. Several have come to Smitty's table from other units. There's even an officer present, a lieutenant from the artillery company.

Since sleep is impossible, Dave gets his wallet and takes a seat at the table. When Smitty looks up from shuffling the cards and sees Dave sitting across from him, his eyes light up. "Fresh meat," he crows. But over the next several hours, Smitty's luck goes south while Dave wins. The acting jack vents his frustration by downing beer after beer.

It's getting late when the game ends in dramatic fashion. Smitty has the deal and calls his favorite game: seven-card stud with queens, fours, and one-eyed jacks wild. "Ante," he says and tosses a buck onto the table. After the others pony up, Smitty doles out two down cards and one showing to each player. Dave receives the four of hearts and seven of diamonds facedown with the nine of diamonds up. Smitty has the high hand with an ace, and he throws out a small bet, which the other players all call. On the next round, Smitty gets the queen of spades to go with his ace and ups the bet to five dollars. The other players all fold except Dave, who has also received a wild card.

The price of poker goes up the next round when Smitty deals himself another ace and quickly throws in a ten spot. Dave hesitates a moment, then matches it. After neither player gets any help on the next round, Smitty deals the final cards facedown. Dave peeks at his last card and is happy to view the five of diamonds. When Smitty tosses in another ten-dollar MPC note, Dave tops it with a twenty. "Ten more," he says.

Smitty leans forward, peering across the table at Dave's unimpressive up cards. Irritation is written all over his face that a cherry would try to bluff him. So the acting jack snatches up his last twenty and throws it into the pot. "Back at you," he snaps. After Dave calls the raise, Smitty flips his hole cards over. "Four aces," he declares. "Read 'em and weep." As Smitty begins to rake in the pot, Dave reveals his down cards. "Straight flush," he says. "I've got you beat."

"Bullshit," Smitty declares with an impatient glance at Dave's jumble of cards. He reaches for more of the money, but Dave pushes his hand away. "Motherfucker," Smitty growls then rises out of his chair and rushes around the table. Dave is slow getting up, so he catches a punch on the side of his face. He comes to on the floor, lurches to his feet, and belatedly gets his hands up to fight. But there is no need. Smitty is holding his right arm up and cursing a steady, monotonous stream. His wrist is bent at a peculiar angle, and he winces with pain. O'Reilly and Gibson come over to help.

"We got to go to the infirmary," O'Reilly says.

"Fuck no," Smitty snaps. "I'll be OK."

"Let's just have Doc look at it," Gibson persists.

"Swelling up like a balloon," O'Reilly observes.

"Oh, OK," Smitty says. "But get my money off the table."

"The pot belongs to Knight," the lieutenant insists. "He won the hand."

"Who gives a fuck?" Smitty says as O'Reilly picks up the acting jack's few remaining bills. The others pocket their cash as well since the poker game is obviously over.

After putting his wallet away, Dave gingerly runs his tongue along the inside of his cheek. It's all cut up, and he detects the coppery taste of blood. So he guzzles some beer then goes out back for a quick pee before returning to lie on his bunk. Suddenly he's exhausted.

Someone turns out the light, and it grows quiet in the hooch. A few minutes later, Peterson comes staggering in the front door. The spec 4 is known for his pious ways, but now he drunkenly sits on his bunk and buries his face in his hands. "Why, why, why?" he moans.

"Hey, quiet," a voice calls in the darkness. "We got to get up in five hours."

But Peterson has no intention of quieting. "Why?" he asks. "How could I?" The hooch shakes as Peterson slams his fist into the wall next to his cot.

"Why what?" someone asks.

"Why did I do it?" Bam. Peterson punches the wall again.

"Do what?"

"Give her all that money. I gave her sixty dollars."

"Sixty? Are you nuts? The going rate is ten."

"She promised to yobo me."

"Who?"

"Lisa."

"At the Flamingo? Lisa at the Flamingo?"

"Yes."

"You stupid shit, she butterflies like crazy."

"I know, I know," Peterson sobs. "My wife and kids, they need that money."

"You should have thought of that while you were balling her," another voice calls out. "Now shut the fuck up. We got to sleep."

It's Gibson, not Smitty, who cuts the lights on in the morning. "Hands off your cocks and grab your socks," the redneck hollers in imitation of a Fort Benning drill instructor.

The men grumble as they come awake and contemplate going back to the towers. One by one they get their shaving kits and head for the latrine. Once his head clears, Dave joins them. On the way, O'Reilly falls into step beside him. "Smitty's at the Yongsan hospital," he says. "I rode there with him last night."

"What did they say?"

"Torn ligament."

"Too bad," Dave shrugs. He goes into the latrine and takes care of his morning business then looks in the mirror. His left cheek is swollen, but not so anyone would notice. Still, he has no stomach for the mess hall's idea of breakfast, so Dave goes back to the hooch and lies on his bunk until time for roll call. Then he goes out to the company street where the men of First Platoon are waiting. They're talking animatedly, but the conversation tails off as Dave approaches. In the sudden silence, Tom Hanson calls out, "Hey, what happened between you and Smitty last night?"

"He pissed me off, so I punched him in the fist with my face."

The guys are still laughing when Anthony comes out of the company office with his perpetual scowl on his face. "Fall in," he hollers. The men oblige haphazardly then, having got the best response obtainable, Sergeant Anthony bellows, "Attention. Stand ready for inspection by the captain." This adds some starch to the men's lackadaisical posture.

After a short wait, the door of the company office opens, and Captain Pfeiffer appears. He marches to the front of the formation and exchanges salutes with Sergeant Anthony. Then the pair proceeds to stride up and down the lines of troops. "You need a haircut," Pfeiffer tells a miscreant, and Anthony makes note of the man's name. Pfeiffer finds fault with several other soldiers, then he resumes his position in front of the formation and gives a motivational speech. "Men, we have the CMMI coming up next week. All is in readiness for the inspection. It simply remains for each of you to have all your equipment prepared, know your duties, and respond appropriately to the inspectors. I know that I can expect your very best at this important time." Pfeiffer then turns the platoon back over to Sergeant Anthony.

"Platoon dismissed," Anthony hollers, and the men go to draw their weapons.

Dave prefers the day shift to any of the others. He can read, gaze at the magnificent scenery, and have fun with the farm children who climb the steep ridge to beg. "Cafe, cafe," they shout, or, "Cigarette me now, GI, you numba fuckin' one."

The kids know the contents of each C ration and what's most in demand on the black market. The coffee packet is the hottest item, followed by the four-pack of stale cigarettes included in each box. But the children will take anything, including cans of ham and lima beans, the least popular C ration entrée. Dave feels munificent as he tosses the requested items over the fence to the children below.

As the day wears on, Dave alternates time outside in the cold with periods of reading inside where the little heater rattles while kicking out very few BTUs. Heeding Captain Pfeiffer's wishes, Dave puts his book aside for a while and studies the guard orders for the tower. He is thus prepared that afternoon when First Sergeant Williams makes the rounds quizzing each MP on his duties. "What are your general orders?" he asks Dave.

"I will guard everything within the limits of my post and quit my post only when properly relieved," Dave recites. "I will obey my special orders and perform all my duties in a military manner. I will report violations of my special orders, emergencies, and anything not covered in my instructions to the commander of the relief."

"What is the muzzle velocity of your M16?"

"It's 3,110 feet per second."

"And what special equipment are you responsible for?"

"Wire cutters, smoke grenades, field telephone, binoculars, and a flare gun."

"What is the purpose of the wire cutters?"

"In the event of an emergency, wire cutters are to be used to cut through the fence in order to exit the site and rapidly evacuate the area."

"Very good, Knight, now keep studying; no one knows what the inspectors might ask."

Smitty is sitting on his cot when the rest of the squad returns to the hooch that evening. His lower right arm is in a cast. "Sorry about last night," he tells Dave. "I was drunk."

"That's OK," Dave says grinning. "You got the worst of it."

"You got that right," Smitty laughs. Then he and several other guys go to chow. A few minutes later Tom Hanson strolls into the hooch. "You gonna eat?" he asks Dave.

"Yeah," Dave replies and grabs his field jacket. On the way to the mess hall, he and Tom come upon Chief Thunder, who is out in the middle of the road. The Indian has gotten hold of a meat cleaver from the mess hall and is waving it over his head. "I'll kill you," he shouts. "Gonna scalp all you white motherfuckers."

A crowd of soldiers including Sergeant Williams and Captain Pfeiffer is watching the Native American from a respectful distance. Tom and Dave skirt the throng and keep going. "Appears Chief got into the firewater again," Tom observes.

"Might be a good time to see if he wants to sell his tribal lands," Dave jokes.

"You go ask," Tom laughs. "I'll wait here."

"What's up with him anyway?"

"Tower fever," Tom replies. "Chief used to be the strong silent type, but one night he was in tower 10 and thought he saw the entire Korean People's Army coming over the mountain. He started firing his M16 and kept the QRF pinned down for over an hour. Chief hasn't been allowed back in the towers since."

After they've eaten, Tom and Dave go their separate ways. But the following day, when First Platoon gets back to the compound after a stint in the towers, Tom takes Dave aside. "You want to get high?" he asks.

"Sure," Dave replies and follows Tom into his hooch.

Inside First Squad, the usual array of Japanese stereo equipment is on top of wall lockers. In the rear of the Quonset, a bead curtain sections off the space where Tom and his friends live. Inside, four bunks are arranged in a square with a couple of footlockers in the center. Moments after Tom and Dave push through the curtain, they are joined by another MP. He's a scraggly haired, mustachioed spec 4 with a bead necklace. "Do you know Kris?" Tom asks.

"That would be me," the soldier says with a friendly grin.

"Oh yeah," Dave replies. "I've seen you around."

"Me and Tom came here from the seven-deuce-eight."

"This is a far cry from Seoul."

"Too true," Kris says. "But we make do." He puts a Neil Young LP on the turntable then he and Tom sit on bunks across from each other and use the footlockers in the center as a table. A bag of dope comes out, and they begin rolling joints. Dave pitches in to help.

Before they get the first joint lit, another soldier comes in. "Those motherfuckin' lifers in supply," he complains. "Try to get another canteen, and they act like it's their fuckin' money. I mean, who's paying for this shit? Joe Taxpayer, right? I mean, am I right?"

"You shouldn't have thrown your canteen at those kids," Tom says mildly.

"What? Are you kiddin' me? I'm up in my tower tryin' to sleep and them little bastards keep tormentin' me. 'Cafe, cafe,' they holler. So I give them the coffee, but now they want the fuckin' smokes. Well, guess what? I need them cigarettes 'cause I'm all out. Next thing you know it's 'motherfuckin' GI numba fuckin' ten,' and they're droppin' trou and shinin' me. I threw everything I could at the little fuckers. They're lucky I didn't lock and load on their sorry asses."

"Here, smoke this," Tom says. "You need to mellow."

The newcomer sits on the bunk next to Kris and takes a toke. Then in a practiced way, he stacks another deep drag on top. With veins bulging all over his forehead, he looks for someone to pass the joint to. His eyes light on Dave, and he suddenly expels a vast cloud. "What are you doing here?" he exclaims.

"Relax, I invited him," Tom replies.

"Shit," the man says. His name tag reads "Bryant." Like Tom and Kris, he wears a bushy mustache, and his sideburns and hair are as long as he can get away with. "This weed is worthless," Bryant complains. "I need something stronger to settle my nerves."

Bryant opens one of the wall lockers and comes out with a bowl of pills. Some are green and others red. He grabs a handful indiscriminately and washes them down with a Coke from the window. Kris selects some reds, and he too opens a can of Coke. Meanwhile, Dave looks at the pills curiously. He figures that they're cheap Korean knock-offs of real drugs. The red ones look like Seconal, and the greens appear to be Dexedrine. But Dave can't believe they are the real thing. *Why would Bryant take uppers and downers at the same time?* He wonders. *How could anyone eat that many and still function?* Dave looks in the windows for a beer, but all he sees are soft drinks and fruit juice. Then Tom glances at his watch. "Uh-oh," he says, "chow's over in twenty minutes, let's go."

As the soldiers walk up the company street, none wear the despised army field caps. They pay no attention to Sergeant Williams, who is coming toward them. "Where's your cover, men?" the NCO barks.

"Don't fuckin' worry about it, Sergeant," Tom shoots back. The men laugh and push past the open-mouthed first sergeant without breaking stride. Dave expects Williams to come after them, but nothing happens.

After eating, Tom and his friends go to a movie, but Dave has seen it. He goes back to Second Squad and joins in a spades game. It doesn't break up until late then the soldiers get ready for bed. They must be up early again for their last day shift of the cycle.

As they're going to chow the next morning, the MPs see several staff cars come through the front gate. "Must be someone important," Gibson says.

"Only if you think a CMMI is important," Smitty laughs. "Don't you remember? We have the inspection this week."

The CMMI team sniffs around the compound for several days, paying close attention to the company armories, the motor pool, and the filing cabinets at battalion headquarters. Then they go out to the site and spend a full day there. First Platoon is on midnights by then and the inspectors are gone by the time they get there.

Two days later First Platoon goes on break, and as usual Tom Hanson and his friends in first squad head for the big city. This time Dave is invited along. They take the shuttle to Yongsan then go out the gate and walk into town. As the MPs stroll down the busy boulevard, they pause to look into store windows filled with Japanese cameras and electronics. "Don't ever buy anything at one of these places," Tom tells Dave. "The prices are much better at the PX."

A little farther on, the MPs come to a Chinese herbal medicine store and stop to peer into the window. It's crammed with fluid-filled bottles containing snakes, frogs, mushrooms, bats, birds, fetuses of various animals, and lots of ghostly ginseng roots. The men are both awed and disgusted, but finally, they tear themselves away. On the next block, they come to a pharmacy and go inside. The owner is at the counter, and he immediately recognizes Bryant. "*Anyoung hashimnikka,*" the man exclaims. "No see long time."

"Too much workee," Bryant replies.

"But you OK, samo, samo?" the man asks.

"No, me sick."

"What you need?"

Bryant puts a stack of MPC on the counter and jerks his thumb up. After counting the money, the owner goes in back and gets a vial of green capsules. He pours a large quantity of these into a container. Now Bryant places more MPC on the counter and gives the thumbs-down. This time the owner returns with a vial of reds.

Soon the soldiers are back on the street. They gather outside the store to make plans. "Let's go to Itaewon," Tom suggests.

"What for?" Dicky Bowman asks. He's a slightly built, acne-faced junkie that no one likes.

"To see the acid queen," Tom says.

"Count me out," Bowman says. "I'm goin' to the USO."

"See ya later," Tom replies unconcerned.

"I'll keep you company," another junkie pipes up, and as the two needle freaks take their leave, a couple more hastily follow. The remaining men flag down taxis.

Like Seoksu-dong, the Itaewon district of Seoul thrives on the wallets of American GIs. However, the streets are paved, and the clubs are nicer. When the MPs arrive, Tom leads the way up a hill to a souvenir store. Inside they pass a display of black silk jackets embroidered on the back with a color map of Korea and the phrase "When I die I know I'll go to heaven because I've served my time in hell." Smitty has a jacket like that with his name embroidered on the front.

Down the next aisle, they find a mama-san standing behind a glass display case. It holds a collection of commando knives, switchblades, brass knuckles, nunchucks, and other items that would come in handy should your neighbor allow his dog to shit on your lawn. The woman seems thrilled to see Tom. Beaming, she exclaims, "Whatsamatta, you? Where you been? No see long time."

"Oh, come on," Tom replies, laughing. "I was here just a month ago."

"You not like me no more?"

"I like you too much," Tom says, smiling boyishly. "But I stay in Anyang now."

"No seven-deuce-eight?"

"No."

"Too bad," the proprietress exclaims. "So what you want?"

"Happy pills."

"Good, I got numba-one stateside," the mama-san says. She reaches under the counter and pulls out a jar filled with tiny round purple tabs. After removing the lid, the shopkeeper lets the men peek inside. Each tablet has a black dot in the middle. "Three dollah," she proclaims.

Bryant hastily pulls a ten out of his wallet. "I'll take three," he says. The other MPs opt for two hits each.

After the transaction is complete, Tom leads the way to a nightclub on the corner. It has a sign over the door emblazoned with a pair of intertwined horseshoes. Below are the words: "Lucky Club." Inside, rock music blares from speakers located on either side of a stage.

It's still afternoon, and the dim interior of the nightclub is sparsely populated, so the MPs have their choice of seats. They pick a comfortable booth located along the back wall and Tom distributes the acid. Then a cute waitress comes around, and the men all get Cokes. The drinks are useful in washing down the little pills but hardly necessary.

"So why did those guys want to go to the USO?" Dave asks.

Tom quickly replies, "Must be the donuts."

Then Kris adds, "And the free coffee."

"Don't forget the ping-pong," Bucky Walker throws in with a laugh. He's a blond-haired, blue-eyed Virginia boy who lives in the curtained-off section of the First Squad hooch with Tom and his friends.

"They don't actually go to the USO, numbnuts," Bryant snaps. "It's the neighborhood around the USO."

"That's right," Tom explains patiently. "They go there to get smack."

"The USO is kind of like a Greyhound bus station," Kris says airily. "In any stateside town, if you need something, that's the neighborhood you go to."

"Yeah, and in this town that area around the USO is where you go for junk, skivvy shows, blow jobs, and every disease known to man," Bucky declares.

"Hey, how 'bout that fucking Wilson?" Bryant asks, changing the subject.

"Yeah, I heard he paid Connie two hundred bucks for yoboing him," Bucky exclaims.

"Well, she don't normally yobo black guys," Bryant replies. "Says they're too big."

"Plenty of chicks don't care if you're black, white, green, or yellow," Bucky says. "Long as you got MPC."

"Wilson's OK," Tom insists. "NCOs and officers have to pay more, that's just the way it works."

Dave's not interested in platoon gossip, so he relaxes and listens to the music pouring out of the club's PA system. Over the next hour, the place slowly fills as GIs get off work at Yongsan Garrison. The soldiers occupy tables near the dance floor or booths along the wall. Meanwhile, business girls dressed in colorful miniskirts and blouses congregate at the bar. Occasionally two or more get up and dance, swinging their long black tresses to and fro. Dave is reminded of the way strands of kelp move in the ocean current. He's getting off on the acid now as Van Morrison belts out a rousing "Domino." The pounding rhythms set every cell in his body vibrating while a slight but delicious current courses through him.

A Korean lady stops by the table dressed in a green knee-length dress that shows off her slim figure. The woman is quite beautiful, and Tom goes off with her. Meanwhile, Kris and Bucky get on the dance floor with a couple of girls they seem to know. At a nearby table, Bryant is deep in conversation with a tough-looking Korean man who wears a leather jacket.

As the hour grows late, Dave finds himself sitting alone. He's lost track of his friends and doesn't care. Mick Jagger is singing "Ruby Tuesday," and Dave quietly joins in; it's a heartrending song. Then a cold Coca-Cola mysteriously appears on the table in front of him, and Dave drinks thirstily. "Want to get high?" Tom whispers.

"Why not?"

"Come on."

Dave follows Tom out the front door of the club. They go down an alley that leads into a warren of houses and small apartment buildings. Tom goes up to a cottage and ushers Dave inside. Bryant, Kris, and Bucky are there seated around a low table with several girls. Then the woman in the green dress enters carrying a brown paper sack. "Michelle, this is my friend Dave," Tom says.

"Welcome," the hostess smiles.

Tom opens the paper bag, which contains pot. No one has any papers, so the soldiers get busy emptying tobacco from cigarettes and replacing it with marijuana. Soon several filter-tipped joints are circulating. The women smile benevolently as the soldiers smoke but don't touch it themselves.

Michelle puts an LP on the console and lights some joss sticks. Meanwhile, Dave gazes intently at his palm peering through the translucent skin at the blue and green blood vessels that weave through the tendons and bones deep within. After a while, he looks up and sees that Kris, Bucky, and Bryant have departed with their girlfriends. Tom is sitting on the sofa talking with the lady of the house. He looks up and meets Dave's gaze. "You doin' all right?" Tom asks.

"Yeah."

"I'll show you where you're going to crash."

"OK."

Tom leads Dave into a den with a colorful Chinese rug, a sofa, and a tropical fish tank. An inlaid black lacquer desk is at one end of the room. "This is Michelle's office," Tom says. "She owns the Lucky."

"I see."

"We're going to turn in."

"Cool."

"Will you be OK on the couch?"

"Sure."

Dave spends the next few hours watching the fish. There's something electric about the finny little creatures. Bright blue jolts almost meet pink sparks then somehow avoid colliding with neon-green flashes. On the aquarium's sandy floor, a ruined castle attracts schools of the tiny fish. They wander past the battlements and in and out of the gate. It occurs to Dave that the inhabitants of the tank behave just like he and his friends. They school up for mutual reinforcement then mindlessly dart this way and that. *Only we're in a bigger bowl,* he thinks.

Tom wakes Dave late the next morning. Once the other MPs are ready, they take cabs to Yongsan then catch the shuttle back to the compound. In Second Squad, the inevitable spades game is going on when Dave comes in. His hoochmates glance up from their cards then resume what they're doing. The cherry has spent his first night out, but no one comments. Dave gets his shaving kit and goes for a shower. Afterward, he comes in the back door of the Quonset with a towel wrapped around his waist and stops to watch the card game. "Who's winning?" he asks.

Smitty looks up from his hand, stares intently at Dave's bare chest, then points. "Is that a crab?" he asks.

"Where?" Dave demands. He drives his chin into his sternum to peer down.

"There's another one," Gibson exclaims. He too is pointing at Dave's chest hair.

"Oh my God," Dave cries. He grabs his toilet kit, shoves his feet back into his shower clogs, and rushes to the latrine again. There he turns the water up as hot as it will go then lathers and re-lathers his chest. "Fucking whorehouse," Dave keeps muttering. "What do you expect?"

After a while, Dave can't take any more of the steamy shower, so he dries off and goes back to the hooch. "Let's see," Smitty says when Dave returns.

"Not nearly as many as before," O'Reilly reports.

"There goes one," Gibson says, pointing.

Dave grabs his shave kit to go for another shower. He rushes to the door then on a whim turns and looks back at the card players. They are silently cracking up. Gibson is hugging himself and rocking back and forth to contain the outburst that is building. O'Reilly is holding both hands to his mouth and stamping his foot to suppress his glee. Now they see that Dave has finally caught on and a torrent of mirth breaks out around the hooch. "You got me this time," Dave says, sheepishly. He puts his shower gear away and gets into bed.

The next night is the end of the long break, and after chow Dave joins Tom and his friends in the rear of the First Squad hooch. As the evening wears on, visitors come and go while the men commiserate with each other about having to go back to work in the morning. Joints are continuously making the rounds and it's standing room only.

Josh Roberts is one of the guys who push through the bead curtain to hang out in the back of First Squad this night. He's a good-natured alcoholic who is once again sloppy drunk. The guys enjoy bantering with him when he's polluted, but now a tall, redheaded E-5 named Simpson goes too far. "How did a fat slob like you make it through basic?" he asks Josh.

"Same way you did," Josh smirks. "I kissed the drill sergeant's ass."

"Sucked his dick, you mean," Simpson replies.

"Oh, is that what you did?" Josh giggles.

Simpson rushes Josh and pushes the drunk up against a wall locker. "I'm gonna fire you up," he snarls, pulling back a fist. But Bryant, who has been sitting on the edge of his bunk, rises and hits Simpson with both forearms like a linebacker hitting a tackling dummy. The bully staggers back but somehow keeps his feet. "You touch him again, and you'll answer to me," Bryant says.

"Motherfucker can't talk to me like that," Simpson protests.

"Oh yes, he can," Bryant declares.

Simpson is a full head taller than Bryant and much heavier, but he doesn't like the madness he sees in the smaller man's eyes, so he turns away. Slowly calm returns to the room as Bryant reclaims his seat and casually reaches into the pill bowl for a handful of capsules. He tosses them back nonchalantly and takes a swill of his Coke. Then Bucky follows suit. Dave is sitting across from them and decides that a few reds might help him sleep. He washes them down with Coca-Cola.

It's still tense in the hooch because Simpson hasn't left, but a half hour later the big man sidles out. "God, how I hate the army," Tom exclaims once the E-5 is gone.

"It's assholes like Simpson that give it a bad name," Kris smiles.

"What's not to like?" Bryant asks. "The army gives you the opportunity to travel the world, learn about different cultures, meet interesting people, and kill them."

"That was funny back in first grade," Bucky laughs.

"Oh, come on," Bryant complains. "You must mean junior high?"

"Are you going to light that?" Tom asks.

"Coming right up," Bryant says. He holds a lighter to the joint he's been rolling, takes a long drag, and passes it to Kris.

"Has anyone heard how we did on the CMMI?" Bucky asks.

"The official report won't be out until next month," Bryant says.

"I'll be gone by then," Bucky exclaims. "I'm so short I came in under the door."

"Me too," Tom smiles. "Just twenty-seven and a wake-up."

"Right behind you, man," Bryant exclaims.

"Come see me in Philly," Tom says. "A good time is guaranteed."

"I'll be there."

Dave can't relate to being a short-timer, so he tunes out the conversation. The grass they're smoking seems unusually strong, and he enjoys the sensation of floating. Gradually his body grows numb, and a warm, vaguely sexual glow spreads within. "This is what drinking is supposed to be like but never is," he murmurs.

"What?" Tom asks.

"Nothing," Dave slurs, "nothing."

"Hey, you better hit the sack," Tom suggests. "And that goes for all of us. It's late, and tomorrow's going to come early."

At 0530 hours when Smitty cuts on the lights in Second Squad, Dave doesn't budge. He sleeps while his squadmates shit, shower, and shave, then snores as they make their way back and forth to chow. Finally, Smitty spots Dave still under the covers and roughly shakes him. "Formation in ten minutes," he says. "What's the matter with you?"

Dave rises like an automaton, shifts his legs around, and plants his feet on the floor. He reaches into his wall locker and gets a pair of fatigue pants. Then he pulls them over his uncooperative legs and, after zipping them up, gets his boots on. Next Dave stands and leans on the wall locker. Supported thus, he buttons his shirt and tucks it into his trousers. Pulling his web gear off the rack, Dave puts one arm through and then another. He snatches up his field cap, takes several steps toward the front of the hooch, then finds himself sitting on his butt. Slightly baffled, Dave rises and again strides toward the door. This time he almost makes it.

Formation is going to start any minute, and this is becoming serious. With a determined effort, Dave gets to his feet and lumbers to the door. He steps outside and walks toward his comrades. They and he are equally chagrined when Dave's knees buckle, and he makes a three-point landing on the company street.

"What's wrong, Knight?" Sergeant Anthony inquires. "Are you unable to report for duty?"

"Just tripped over my own two feet," Dave mumbles. "I'm fine." He gathers himself and staggers into the formation, coming to a stop between a couple of guys in Fourth Squad. They take hold of his elbows and keep him vertical long enough to get through the morning roll call.

Out at the site, Dave draws tower 6. This is one of the least visited guard posts, so once he manages to get across the Choji Trail and climb the ladder to his perch, he's able to go back to sleep. At the end of the shift, as the men wait to board the bus, Dave is accosted by some of the guys from Fourth Squad. "Man, you had the staggers bad this mornin'," McGriff says.

"Thanks for helping," Dave replies.

"Hell, half the platoon be staggering out there, but the man, he don't know nuttin'," McGriff says. "Till you go and fall on your puny ass. Could've got us all busted."

"Guess it was the reds," Dave allows.

This provokes much laughter from the group, and PFC Jeffrie joins in. "Man, you just too deep in that shit," he says sarcastically.

"Yeah, I didn't know how strong they were," Dave replies. "So I took three."

"Three? That's all? Sheeet, you let three of them dolls put you on yo candy ass?"

"Hey, what the hell?" Sergeant Anthony hollers from the front of the bus. "You men mount up now."

"Damn lifer," McGriff glowers as he boards the bus. "He just want to go fuck that ugly yobo he got."

"What did you say?" Anthony asks.

"You heard me," McGriff snaps as he brushes past the platoon sergeant and makes his way to the back of the bus.

"You got sumpin to say, say it to my face," Anthony bellows.

"Oh, fuck this shit," Jeffrie interjects. "Let's go now fo we all late to chow."

CHAPTER FOURTEEN
VILLAGE RAT

It's shortly after 2:00 a.m. on New Year's Day. Snow is falling, and Dave's feet squelch as they sink into the fresh powder. He wanders the deserted streets of Seoksu-dong, passing walled courtyards, small apartment buildings, and seedy nightclubs. Everything is shut tight. "*Yeoboseyo*," Dave cries, "*yeoboseyo*." He has nowhere to go since the gate to the compound is locked and will not reopen until morning.

Dave's friends in First Squad all went home before Thanksgiving and, left to his own devices, he has become a village rat. Now Dave frequents the clubs of Seoksu-dong to drink and play pool, especially the Flamingo. As a regular, he's allowed to run a tab there.

The Flamingo has a separate pool room with two tables. At night they are always in use and guys who are waiting a turn line the walls. They slug down whiskey Cokes, smoke, and try to talk above the din of music coming from the main room. It's much livelier than Special Services, and the business girls at the bar are enticing. They are always friendly, but not in a vulgar way. Most are looking for a steady relationship but will take a soldier home for the night if adequately compensated. Dave, however, refuses to pay. He has the reputation of a deadbeat, and so far none of the girls has been willing to give him a freebie.

At this time, all is quiet in the village, except for Dave's plaintive cries which echo off the cinder block walls. He's lonely and cold. "*Yeoboseyo*," he wails as puffs of white smoke from charcoal heaters rise above the houses. Impossibly long icicles hang from the eves.

As Dave passes the Flamingo, a side door opens and an apparition appears which turns out to be the club owner, Mr. Park, dressed in a long white nightshirt. "Knight-san," he exclaims. "Why you no sleepee?"

Dave raises a bottle of clear Korean liquor to his lips and pours some of the fiery beverage down his throat. Shaking his head, Mr. Park steps onto the snow and gently removes the container from the soldier's hand. "You come," he says, taking Dave's arm. Mr. Park leads Dave into the building and down a hall. Opening the door to a small room, he ushers Dave in and points to a rumpled bed. "Sleep," he commands.

A girl stirs in the bed. It's Sue, one of the Flamingo bar girls. She peers up at Dave, then at Mr. Park. He says something to her in rapid-fire Korean, and she snaps back at him. They have an argument, but it doesn't last long since he's the papa-san. In a huff, Sue scoots over to make room for Dave. He strips then gets under the warm covers. As Mr. Park closes the door, Sue squinches as close to the bedroom wall as she can. Dave takes the hint. He closes his eyes and is out. But a few hours later Sue wakes him with an elbow to the ribs. "You pay," she demands, eyes flashing.

The normally alluring business girl looks less than stellar with no makeup and a severe case of bedhead. Insistently she holds her hand out for money. Dave groggily fishes around on the floor for his jeans. He extracts the wallet and shows Sue the emptiness within. "You numba ten," she says, pointing to the door. "Go."

Dave stumbles back to the compound and stretches out on his cot, but rest proves elusive. The alcohol is wearing off, and a massive hangover is crowding in behind it. Then the alarm begins to wail. Some sadist has decided to have an alert on New Year's Day.

Now every man in the battalion not currently on duty is expected to go to the SAD and help prepare it for demolition. So while a few guys hide in their wall lockers, and others dash for the latrine, Dave along with most of his squadmates, begin getting into fatigues. They'd rather go to the site and be busy than hide in the compound. As the men are getting ready, Sergeant Anthony bursts into the hut and glares at the inhabitants. "I better see you outside in five minutes," the NCO hollers.

"Or else what?" Jeffrie says flippantly. The PFC seems to be dancing a two-step as he buttons his fatigue shirt. He has the staggers.

The bus is waiting outside, but as the MPs wait to board, O'Reilly pulls up in his three-quarter-ton truck. "Room in the back," he calls, so Dave and Jeffrie climb in. Then tires crunch on frozen snow and the little convoy starts off. Once they're clear of the compound, Jeffrie pulls a doobie out of his shirt pocket and fires it up. Then he passes the joint to Dave. The weed does not help Dave's head, nor does the jouncing of the little truck. His stomach lurches, but somehow he manages not to puke.

At the site, Dave joins a group of MPs who are stringing detonation cord from one Stradley to the next. Afterward, they stand guard outside the open magazines while ordnance technicians place charges inside. Meanwhile, the tower guards carry their wire cutters down to the ground and prepare to cut their way out of the site. In the guard office, the clerks gather sensitive documents to burn. After everything is ready, several officers conduct an inspection. Once they are satisfied that the facility is prepared to blow, they issue the all-clear. It takes the soldiers over an hour to remove the charges and put everything away.

The paymaster comes the next morning, and First Platoon goes to the head of the line since they are on the day shift. After collecting their meager wages, the men draw their weapons and get on the bus. They spend the day at the site with a month's pay burning a hole in their pockets. That evening after chow, there's a rush to get out to the vill.

Dave is among those hurrying off the compound in search of recreation. First, he goes to the Flamingo to pay his bar tab. The place is rocking when he gets there. Soldiers and business girls jam the dance floor as music blasts from the speakers. Dave looks for Mr. Park and finds him is in his customary spot on a stool behind the bar. The papa-san is a bulky middle-aged man unusually tall for a Korean. He's a former ROK Marine, so when Mr. Park asks you to leave the Flamingo, you go. But now, as Dave approaches, the bar owner smiles at him benevolently. "Knight-san, you finishee workee?" he asks.

"Yes, for today, tomorrow more."

"You take it easy now. You too much workee."

"That's right, Mr. Park."

The two men quickly run out of small talk, but the papa-san is too well mannered to mention Dave's bill. He waits until Dave brings it up, then Mr.

Park gets out his little black book and they settle up. It's not much since Dave only uses the tab when he's broke at the end of the month.

After a few more pleasantries with Mr. Park, Dave goes to the bar for a whiskey Coke. He only has enough money in his wallet for pool and a couple more beverages, but not enough for the more basic entertainment available. This way, even if tempted, Dave cannot break his cardinal rule against paying for companionship.

In the pool room there's a long queue to get on a table, but finally, Dave gets up and racks the balls. His opponent is a tall ordnance NCO. The sergeant shatters the rack complacently then follows up by running several more balls off the table. But Dave is able to make a nice run of his own when his turn comes. He long ago mastered straight-in shots, and now through practice and much play Dave has discovered a talent for cutting balls. He's not good at bank shots, however, so if he can't find a straight-in shot or a ball to cut, Dave looks for a leave. That's what this game comes down to. With only the eight ball remaining, the players compete to see who can give the other the worst shot. Finally, Dave's opponent leaves the cue ball at one end of the table and the eight ball just off the rail at the other end. He expects Dave to try a difficult bank shot. Instead, Dave calls for the far corner then shaves a millimeter off the eight ball, sending it slowly along the rail into the pocket. Now he doesn't have to get back in line again.

For the next half hour Dave manages to hold the table against mediocre opposition, but then he's dethroned by a hustler from the motor pool. As he waits in line for another turn, Spec 4 Johansson strolls in holding a drink. "Why ain't you playing?" the gate guard asks Dave.

"Lassiter beat me," Dave explains, pointing to the wiry PFC from Chicago who's busy running the table on another victim.

"He's good," Johansson replies. "I better try my luck on the other table."

"Guess I'm a glutton for punishment," Dave says. "I'm four back to play Lassiter again."

"Whatever you do, don't bet."

"You don't have to tell me."

"You know, it's a good thing most of the guys around here can't really play," Johansson says.

"That's right," Dave replies. "You actually just got Lassiter, Bridger, and that cat from battalion HQ, what's-his-name."

"Yeah, I know the one you're talking about."

"I feel pretty good playing anyone but them," Dave says, "and of course you."

"Ha-ha."

"I'm goin' to the bar. You want one?" Dave offers.

Johansson looks at his half-full whiskey Coke. "No, I'm OK."

At the bar, Dave places his order then looks around the main room of the club. Most of the patrons are on the dance floor, but at one table Peterson is deep in conversation with Lisa. She's a cute business girl with a buxom figure, short hair, and bangs. Dave often flirts with her.

Now Lisa drains the remnants of her drink, and after Peterson follows suit, she comes to the bar with the empty glasses. Lisa presses her hip against Dave as she waits for refills. "So you got that idiot buying watered-down drinks for you," Dave comments.

"Whatsamatta you?" Lisa scowls as the barmaid returns and puts her drinks on the bar.

"I bet there ain't no whiskey in your whiskey Coke," Dave says.

"You mo betta samo samo," Lisa replies seriously. "You drinkee too much whiskey."

"At least I get what I pay for."

"You no get nothin'." Lisa giggles and rotates her hip a little as she leans into Dave. She picks the drinks up and sashays back over to Peterson who's been glaring at them.

In the pool room, Lassiter has made short work of two opponents and is now destroying the third. So Dave is soon racking the balls. His strategy this time is to focus on his leaves from the get-go. Therefore, Dave delays his fate without altering it, and presently he's back at the bar. As he waits for another drink, Dave notices that the crowd has thinned. Many of the couples have left, and now the dance floor is deserted except for several bored business girls who are dancing together. Dave is surprised to see Lisa among them. She spots him at the bar and comes over.

"Where's Peterson?" Dave asks.

"He go compound," Lisa says. "He angry."

"Oh."

"You come my hoochee?" Lisa asks. "Yes?"

"Yes!" Dave agrees.

Lisa leads the way to a nearby apartment building, and Dave follows her up the icy staircase. Once they're in her room, she goes behind a screen. Moments later Lisa comes out naked. Dave only has a moment to admire her lush body before she pushes him down on the bed, plasters her lips against his, and commences flopping about like a freshly caught fish.

At first, Dave finds Lisa's gyrations comic, but soon her efforts obtain the desired result. Recognizing this, Lisa slows her passionate ministrations then whispers enticingly in Dave's ear, "You souvenir me ten dollah."

Dave's heart sinks. At this moment he sincerely wishes he had the money, but he doesn't. Reluctantly he releases his grip on Lisa's pert bottom. "No can do," Dave says. "Money all gone."

Lisa quickly rises and gets into a flowery dressing gown. "You go compound bringee MPC," she demands. "I here."

Dave sits up and catches his breath. "It's late," he replies, "maybe tomorrow."

Back at Second Squad, Dave finds several guys heating ramen noodles on the oil-fired space heater. He's telling them about his encounter with Lisa when Peterson comes in the back door and overhears. There's an embarrassed silence then Peterson says: "That's OK, it's not your fault. I know what Lisa's like, she's just using me."

"Then why do you stay with her?" Smitty asks.

"I wish I knew," Peterson sighs. He has taken on the air of a long-suffering martyr.

As the men of First Platoon fall out on the frozen street the next morning, First Sergeant Williams appears in front of the formation. He never brings good news, and this time is no different. "Men, you failed the CMMI," he tells the soldiers. "The colonel says there will be no more passes, and no women will be allowed on base until we pass the re-inspection."

"You mean, we can't go to the vill?" one of the men shouts.

"That's affirmative," the first sergeant replies. "And there's more. We've had a lot of men rotate home the last couple of months, and the repo-depo is stiffing us on replacements, so now we're way understaffed. That means until further notice we will be working twenty-one and one."

"No way," someone shouts.

"How long?" another soldier asks.

"That's all I know," Williams growls. "Platoon, atten-hut. Sergeant Anthony, take charge."

Once Williams is gone, Anthony dismisses the men to go to the armory and draw their weapons. Afterward, the soldiers gather by the bus. "Twenty-one and one," Gibson says bitterly. "We might as well just move to the site and live in the fucking towers."

"So how did we fail the CMMI?" O'Reilly wonders.

"The lifers probably couldn't account for all the equipment we're supposed to have," Smitty answers.

"How's that our fault?"

"It ain't, but they got to blame somebody."

"So what's next?"

"Surprise inspection," Smitty explains. "There won't be no notice next time."

"And if we fail that?" Gibson asks.

"The battalion commander and all the company officers get relieved."

"What happens to us?"

"Nothing."

"You mean the officers catch all the shit?"

"That's right."

"So who cares if we pass or not?"

"That's one way of looking at it," Smitty admits.

Two months later, as the worst of the winter weather is coming to an end, the MPs are still working cycles of twenty-one days on with only one day off. Currently, First Platoon is on the swing shift, and Dave is in tower 14 rereading *Hawaii*. He frequently looks up from the beat-up paperback to picture himself on a surfboard with a beautiful girl. But now the light is fading and reading time is coming to a close for the day. As the sun goes behind the mountain, a full moon appears in the east. It provides some illumination but not enough to read. There are five more hours left on the shift.

Dave goes out on the catwalk and watches farmers coming in from the rice paddies. Spring is approaching, and for the last few weeks, they've been working to get ready for planting. As darkness descends, lights flicker faintly on a distant hillside and Dave wonders about the lives of the peasants there. No doubt they toil from dawn to dusk just to eke out a meager existence.

Rustling in the bushes below the tower catches Dave's lazy attention. He idly wonders if he's about to see one of the pumas that supposedly roam the site. Then the noise gets louder, and Dave snaps out of his lethargy. He darts into the tower, dons his helmet and web gear, then snatches up his M16. He goes back out just as Sergeant Wilson emerges from hiding. "I heard you up there rushing about, getting your shit together," the E-5 says. "You're supposed to have your equipment on at all times, aren't you?"

"Halt. Who is there?" Dave replies. He's following the instruction manual he studied for the CMMI.

"Cut the shit."

"Advance to be recognized."

Wilson steps closer to the fence line where the mercury vapor lamps can illuminate him. "It's me, numbnuts," he hollers. "Just look."

"That's far enough," Dave says. "What's the password?"

"Who knows?"

"Get down!" Dave commands.

"What?" Wilson says. "Oh, you got to be kidding."

"I'm not kidding."

"Well, fuck you."

Dave pulls the charging handle back on his M16 then lets the bolt slam forward. "Down," he hollers.

Wilson drops to his knees. "Motherfucker," he exclaims.

"Facedown, arms outstretched," Dave orders. "Now." After Wilson complies, Dave goes inside and cranks the handle on the field telephone.

"Sergeant of the guard," Anthony answers.

"This is Specialist Knight. I have a possible intruder up here. He claims to be Sergeant Wilson."

"Well, of course. It's Sergeant Wilson."

"I need someone to come up and vouch for him."

"Fuck that shit."

"He's lying face down in the dirt."

"Knight, this is going to be your ass," Anthony exclaims then slams down the phone.

Several minutes later, a jeep leaves the guard office and pulls up to the SAD. Anthony gets out and, once through the gate, strides angrily up the perimeter road to tower 14. "What the hell?" he shouts when he sees Dave on the catwalk with his M16.

"Halt. Who is there?" Dave inquires.

"You can goddamn well see who it is," Anthony snaps.

"State the password."

"What?"

"What is tonight's password?"

"Oh, I forget."

"Get down."

"Fuck no."

Dave swings the M16 around and points it at Sergeant Anthony. The NCO glares at him incredulously then slowly sinks to his knees.

"All the way," Dave commands.

Once Anthony has assumed the same posture as Sergeant Wilson, Dave goes back to the phone. Specialist Peterson is on the switchboard. "Guard office," he says by way of greeting.

"I've got two guys up here who claim to be friends, but they don't know the password," Dave says. "Can you come up and vouch for them?"

"I can't leave the radio."

"Then you better get someone here from the compound."

"OK."

An hour later, the first sergeant is standing at the foot of the tower. "Who is there?" Dave asks.

"Sergeant Williams."

"What's the password?"

"Rough Rider."

"Top, can you vouch for these two men?"

"Yes, that's Sergeant Anthony and Sergeant Wilson." Now the two prone NCOs rise to their feet muttering angrily.

"Read him his rights," Wilson says as he brushes off his pants. "Motherfucker locked and loaded on me. That's a court-martial offense."

"He threatened his superior," Anthony growls. "That's count two."

"I was just following SOP," Dave says innocently.

"Knight, no one ever asks for the password," Williams says. "What's got into you?"

"What's got into me? Up here in a fucking tower alone eight hours a day, day after fucking day. I'm going crazy, that's what." Dave has taken to jumping up and down to add impetus to his words.

"Knight, calm down, and get a grip on yourself," Williams orders. "We will get to the bottom of this. See me in my office at 0700 hours tomorrow." The first sergeant turns to go, but Wilson brings him up short: "Top, aren't you gonna read him his rights?"

Williams half turns to give the career E-5 a pitying look. "Next time try and remember the password," he suggests.

After Williams departs, the two sergeants look up at the troublesome tower guard. "Remember this well," Anthony says. "From now on, your ass is grass and I'm the lawnmower."

In the morning Dave goes to the company office for his meeting with Sergeant Williams. Harris is at his desk working on the morning report but pauses when Dave comes in. "I'm here for a meeting with the first sergeant," Dave says.

"Yeah, he's pissed," Harris replies. "The CQ had to roust him out of the vill last night on your account."

"That couldn't have pleased his yobo."

Harris laughs, "Guess he'll have to make it up to her on payday."

The door slams and Williams strides into the office. He spots Dave and walks over with his hand outstretched. "Give me your gate pass," he demands.

Dave gets his wallet out and does as ordered. "You are now on the weapons unauthorized list," the first sergeant continues. "The armory has been notified. Do not try to draw your M16."

"Yes, Sergeant."

"You won't pull anymore tower guard," Williams continues. "You'll be on assigned duties."

"What's that?" Dave asks. But the NCO walks away without replying.

"Assigned duties means whatever shit details they can think up for you," Harris explains quietly.

By the time Dave returns to the hut, his squadmates are back from breakfast. "Hey, we're getting up a game," Smitty says. "Are you in?"

"Sure," Dave replies and grabs a seat at the table. O'Reilly deals the cards, and the players look over their hands. "They put me on the weapons unauthorized list," Dave says.

"Just when I'm losing faith in the army, they do something smart," Smitty exclaims.

"It means I can't work in the towers."

"We didn't need you anyway," Gibson says. "How many tricks you got?"

"Two and a strong maybe."

"Guess we'll push it and try for six."

"Sounds good."

The guys play spades all morning, and afterward, they go to lunch. On the menu are pork chops, real mashed potatoes, green beans, and cornbread. It's all good. "What happened to the food?" Dave asks.

"CID caught Sergeant Milliken selling our grub on the black market," Smitty says. "He's waiting to be court-martialed, so we got a new mess sergeant."

"About time," Gibson comments.

After chow Dave walks up the street to Special Services. The gate is only a block farther, and as usual, it's closed. Soldiers line the fence talking to their yobos through the wire. More bored soldiers are inside Special Services. They pack the game room, and Dave sees no hope of getting a turn on a pool table. He goes into the library and checks out a couple of books he's been meaning to read then returns to the hooch. When he gets there, the guys are gone. They have two more nights on swings.

That evening, Dave takes a book to the mess hall then loads his plate with chicken-fried steak and all the trimmings. But he has trouble enjoying the food, thinking of the men out in the towers with their C rations. It's depressing to know that, thanks to him, they're now even more shorthanded than before. So, after dinner, Dave stops by the NCO club, hoping a beer will cheer him up. Soon there are three empties in front of him, and he's working on his fourth can of suds.

The club is full of ordnance guys who would rather be out in the vill. Onstage, a Korean band is trying to brighten the gloom. They attempt "Land of a Thousand Dances," but the lead singer cannot pronounce the names of the dances. Dave listens as the singer butchers another song then goes to the bandstand between tunes and offers to sing something. The musicians are agreeable, and like every bar band in the world, they know "Gloria." As the Koreans launch into the simple three-chord progression, Dave goes to the microphone and belts out the lyrics. It's a short song, but Dave's having too much fun onstage to stop at the conclusion. Instead he ad-libs additional verses describing various things Gloria does after she comes into the room.

The all-male crowd roars with approval as the verses get nastier. It turns out Gloria is quite the contortionist.

Dave returns to Van Morrison's original lyrics for the finale then brings the song to an end. He steps down from the stage but is thrust back into the limelight by popular acclaim. After a brief consultation, he and the band choose an encore. As the musicians play the opening chords, Dave adopts his best Eric Burdon growl. He delivers the first lines of "We Gotta Get Out of This Place," and immediately everyone in the club is singing along. At the end, Dave determinedly makes his way back to his seat. Moments later, the waitress brings him a beer, compliments of a fan from across the room. Several more follow.

At oh-dark-thirty the next morning, Dave is roughly shaken awake. Through blurred eyes he sees a master sergeant bending over him. It's Milliken, the disgraced former mess sergeant. "I'm in charge of details now," he says. "You will be reporting to me."

"I don't feel well," Dave replies, and this is the truth.

"Get up and go to chow," the sergeant orders. "After that, if you're still sick, I'll take you to the infirmary."

Dave is not hungry. At the mess hall, he nibbles on a piece of dry toast and drinks coffee. This does nothing to improve his health, but afterward, he declines a visit to the infirmary. Not only because of his lack of faith in army medicine, but because Dave knows there is no cure for a hangover.

It's a chill, gray, early spring morning, and Dave's first task is to rake the company street. Passersby gaze at him wonderingly as he works because Koreans usually do this. Later, Milliken finds other jobs for his charge, and by the end of the day Dave has figured out what assigned duties is all about.

That night Dave lies low, steers clear of the club, and is therefore ready when the crooked cook comes for him in the morning. After breakfast, Milliken gives Dave a can of primer and a brush. His mission is to paint over the rust on vehicles parked in the motor pool. He's still at it that afternoon when Smitty comes over. "Hey, you missed a spot," the acting jack says, pointing to the bumper of a jeep.

"And the horse," Dave replies.

"It's our last day of swings," Smitty says and hands Dave a wad of MPC. Then Smitty stands on his tiptoes and holds his hand up. "I want to see a stack of beer this high when we get back."

"Got it."

So, Dave goes to the canteen once he's finished working. It takes him several trips to carry all the beer back to the hooch, and he has to use some of his own money to get the stack up to the height required, but it's all there when the squaddies return a little past 1:00 a.m. After fourteen straight days of work, the soldiers are ready to bust loose, and Smitty adds fuel to the fire by cranking up some Creedence. Soon "Fortunate Son" is blasting out of his Sansui speakers, and the men are singing along at the top of their lungs.

As the party progresses, soldiers set ramen noodles to cook on the space heater, which they circle for warmth and conviviality. The din of music makes conversation difficult, so dancing is the primary mode of expression. Meanwhile, guys wander in and out from other hooches, and all are welcome including Sergeant Wilson, who has some wicked dance moves. At one point the lifer catches Dave's eye and holds up his beer as if proposing a toast. Dave returns the gesture, and now the hatchet is buried.

After several hours of partying, only the diehards remain. "Look at all this beer," Smitty hollers, trying to make himself heard over the rollicking organ on a Doors track. "We got to play the circle game."

"I'm in," Gibson shouts, but after manfully downing a few more beers, the country boy falls onto the nearest bunk, which happens to be Dave's. Smitty throws a blanket over his buddy, then opens more beer. An hour later the few remaining stalwarts call it a night. After a last visit to the latrine, Dave gets into Gibson's bunk while Smitty turns out the light. A few minutes later, Sergeant Milliken comes in and stands at the foot of the cot Dave normally occupies. "Get up," he says softly, while on the other side of the hut Dave pulls Gibson's blanket over his face.

Now, the ex-mess sergeant prods the sleeping man. "On your feet," he hisses, but the lump in the bed still fails to stir. So Milliken pulls the covers back. "Oh shit," he exclaims when he sees Gibson's ferret-like face. He turns to look inquiringly at the other sleeping forms in the dark hut, but there's no way for him to tell who is among them. Angrily, Milliken stalks out of the hooch. As the door slams, Smitty whispers, "You skating motherfucker." He and Dave giggle like naughty schoolchildren who have put one over on their teacher.

As another payday approaches, the business girls of Seoksu-dong angrily gather outside the gate demanding to see Lt. Col. Barrow, commandant of the 83rd Ordnance Battalion. When that officer is not forthcoming, they take to chanting his name. Some hold up signs or wave placards and, day by day, the demonstration grows. Soon the businessmen of the village get involved. Bar owners, pimps, bouncers, pawn shop operators, and tailors all join in. Their profits have plummeted, thanks to Barrow's closed-gate policy. They don't want to miss another payday bonanza.

Dave ignores the noise from the demonstration as he walks toward the Special Services building. Then a horn honks, and he moves to the side of the road as two staff cars belonging to the CMMI inspectors pass by. They showed up unannounced three days ago and have been snooping around ever since. Now they are done for the day and heading back to Seoul.

After killing some time at the library, Dave has dinner at the mess hall. Then he prowls around the compound looking for an empty bunk. Dave has been playing hide-and-seek with Milliken for the last month and never sleeps two nights in the same hooch.

A familiar James Brown song is blaring when Dave walks past Fourth Squad. He goes inside and finds Wilson, McGriff, Jeffrie, and several other guys playing poker. "Mind if I sit in?" Dave asks.

"Always room for another sucker," Wilson says.

"You betta watch out," Jeffrie exclaims. "He lucky."

"We're gonna fire up a bowl," McGriff says as he loads a pipe with weed. "You in?"

"Sure."

Over the next couple of hours, Dave wins enough hands to stay even. However, several other guys go bust, and the game breaks up around midnight. Wilson offers Dave the use of a bunk belonging to a guy who's away on leave. Then, once everyone is ready for bed, someone douses the lights. In the darkness, McGriff starts teasing Dave. "Hey, Knight," he says. "Did you hear about that cracker and his wife getting divorced?"

"No," Dave replies, anticipating a joke.

"Yeah, they's comin' outta the courthouse, and the women be all cryin' and such, so the cracker say, 'Woman, hush all that cryin'. Sure, we got divorced, but we're still cousins.'"

Dave has to laugh. "Yo, Knight," another man calls, "what about that cracker be livin' in a trailer with his car out front on cinder blocks. You know the man's house could move but not his car."

"Just tell me something," another soul brother asks. "How can you white guys be all the time eating pussy? I mean that's nasty."

"Are you kidding?" Dave replies. "That's true love." Moans, curses, and gagging sounds now fill the hooch, so Dave is encouraged to continue. "I had this fine girlfriend once," he exclaims, "and man I used to love to get my head between her legs."

"Shut up, Knight," McGriff orders. "No more or you can go back to those crackers in Second Squad."

"Oh, OK, man. Whatever . . ."

The next morning, Dave is in the mess hall finishing breakfast when O'Reilly comes over. "Where were you last night?" the driver asks.

"Fourth Squad," Dave replies.

"Didn't you hear? They transferred Milliken to Yongsan for his court-martial."

"Oh, so I can go back to sleeping in the hooch?"

"That's right," O'Reilly says. "And if you want to head that way now, I've got something to show you."

When the two MPs get back to Second Squad, O'Reilly opens his wall locker and pulls out a guitar case. Inside is a Yamaha six-string folk guitar. "Wow," Dave exclaims. "What a beauty."

"I got it from Mr. Lee."

"At the pawn shop?"

"Yeah."

"How much?"

"Only gave him ten cases of C rations for it."

"No shit."

"Yeah, I took them from the storage room in the guard office building. They won't notice; there are hundreds of cases in there."

"What songs do you know?" Dave asks.

"You name it," O'Reilly replies. "I just can't sing."

"How about 'House of the Rising Sun'?"

"Good one," O'Reilly says, and as he picks the tune, Dave quietly sings. Meanwhile, Smitty comes into the hut followed by Gibson. They sit at the table, and Smitty shuffles the cards. "You guys sound like shit," he says. "Now get over here."

Dave wakes up in his own bed the next morning. After he and O'Reilly visit the latrine, they go to the mess hall. As they are at a table eating breakfast, Specialist Harris comes over. "Don't forget you have CQ tonight," the company clerk tells O'Reilly.

"Yeah, I'm the runner," O'Reilly replies. "Who's going to be with me?"

"It was supposed to be Daniels," Harris says. "But he went on leave. Don't worry, though, I'll get someone." The spec 4 turns to walk away but comes to an abrupt halt. He spins around and looks at Dave. "What about you?" he asks.

"What?"

"CQ."

"Yeah," O'Reilly smiles. "Why didn't I think of that?"

Dave is trapped. Neither the charge of quarters (CQ) nor the runner is armed. There's no reason why he can't do it. "You both need to be there at five," Harris emphasizes.

"Roger that," O'Reilly says, giving a little salute.

So that evening, O'Reilly and Dave go to the company office to relieve Harris and the other cadre. Once they're alone, O'Reilly shows Dave around the office and explains the job. It turns out that there's really nothing to CQ duty. The idea is simply to have someone in the company office at night and on weekends to answer the phone and make sure the troops don't get out of hand. That's all there is to it unless an alert comes in or something unusual happens that requires disturbing the first sergeant. "The best part is that only one of us has to be in the office at any time," O'Reilly explains. "So we can take turns going to chow now, then tonight, one of us can rest while the other is here."

"OK, so why don't you go ahead and eat, and I'll go when you get back," Dave suggests.

"Sounds like a plan."

In the coming weeks, Harris uses Dave for CQ almost every other day. Dave has no other job, and as a spec 4, he has the rank to be charge of quarters. Harris can always find a PFC to be the runner.

One afternoon as Dave is coming to work, he sees O'Reilly's little truck parked in front of the company office. Then the screen door swings open and Captain Pfeiffer comes outside carrying a cardboard box. "Let me help you with that," Dave offers.

"There are more in my office," the officer replies. "Go get them."

As Dave enters the Quonset, O'Reilly comes out of the captain's office lugging a trunk. "What's going on?" Dave asks.

"We failed the CMMI again," O'Reilly whispers. "Pfeiffer's been transferred to Seoul; he's taking Williams with him."

"What's taking so long, men?" Pfeiffer asks, coming up behind them.

"Right away, sir," O'Reilly replies.

It takes another hour to clean out the captain's office. Afterward, O'Reilly drives him to Seoul. Since the first sergeant is also gone, the 260th is now rudderless. It stays that way for a week and the company functions smoothly during that time. Then one morning, as Dave is finishing up another night of CQ, a stocky master sergeant comes into the office. Dave quickly gets to his feet out of respect for the man's rank. "What can I help you with, Sergeant?" he asks.

"I'm the new first shirt," the soldier says, flashing a friendly smile. Dave responds in kind while quickly sizing up his new boss. The NCO's name tag reads "Campbell," and his strawberry-blond hair, fair complexion, and piercing blue eyes seem to come straight from the highlands. He wears a CIB over his left pocket above a pair of jump wings.

"How 'bout a cup of coffee?" Dave offers. "Just made a fresh pot."

"Sounds good."

"So where are you from?" Campbell asks between sips of java.

"Texas," Dave replies for the sake of discussion.

"What part?"

"Near Palestine."

"Where's that?"

"About ninety miles east of Waco."

"Oh."

"What about you?"

"I was born in England," the sergeant replies. "Mother was English, father American. I served a hitch with the Royal Fusiliers then switched to the US Army. Better chow," he laughs.

The door to the Quonset opens, and Harris comes in. "This is Sergeant Campbell," Dave says. "He's taking over the company."

"I'm your clerk," Harris responds. "Pleased to meet you."

Dave excuses himself and goes to get some shut-eye. However, it takes a long time to get to sleep. He suspects that significant changes are in store, and that premonition is borne out a couple of hours later when O'Reilly shakes him awake. "The gate is open," the driver exclaims. "Barrow is gone, and the new colonel has opened it. Anyone with a valid ID can enter or leave as they please."

"So what?" Dave mutters. "Not much use in opening the gate when people are working twenty-one and one." He goes back to sleep.

Notwithstanding his negativity, Dave cannot resist walking into the vill later that afternoon. Johansson is also heading out, along with a couple of his buddies, so Dave joins them. On impulse, the soldiers duck into a little hole-in-the-wall joint called the Peacock Club. It's early, and the place is nearly empty, so they have their choice of tables. At the bar, several business girls carry on a quiet conversation while a Guess Who record plays. Then a tall, slim woman comes from behind the bar to take their order. Dave studies her face as she talks to Johansson. She is Eurasian and quite pretty.

After bringing their drinks, the barkeep pulls a chair up to the table. "My name Jade," she says. "You not come here before."

"No," Dave replies, "this first time."

"We not big club."

"No."

"Now gate open, you come."

"Sure."

"You say friends, they come Peacock too," Jade asks. Then she goes back behind the bar.

"What do you think of the new first sergeant?" one of Johansson's friends asks Dave. He's a short but sturdily built PFC named Matthews.

"Sergeant Campbell's not a clown like Williams," Dave replies. "He means business. Doesn't seem like a bad guy, though."

"For a lifer," another of Johansson's friends says. His name tag reads "Kingsford." Like Johansson, he's in the rotation of MPs that guard the gate. They seem to be chosen by size.

"This little joint is a nice change from the Flamingo," Dave observes.

"Yeah, it's quiet," Matthews says. "And did you notice the chick that waited on us? She looks just like Natalie Wood."

"Don't get your hopes up there," Johansson says. "Jade was yoboing Barrow to the tune of four hundred bucks a month. With him gone she'll be looking for another sugar daddy." Johansson knows everything. He sees it all at the front gate.

Dave's precarious finances preclude serious drinking in the vill this late in the month. He excuses himself and goes back to the compound. There he finds a seat in a spades game to kill off the rest of the evening.

A week later, payday comes around. After getting their money, the guys in Second Squad congregate in the hooch waiting for lunch. Then Sergeant Anthony comes in and hands Smitty a sheet of ration stamps. Once the NCO is gone, Smitty starts tearing squares off the sheet and handing them out. "You each get four of these," he says. "One stamp allows you to buy a bottle of booze at the Class VI store in Yongsan."

"I've been here for six months and never got any stamps," Peterson complains. "Why now?"

"The lifers were keeping them," Smitty says. "Campbell has put an end to that. From now on the company's allocation will be evenly divided."

"So that fucker Anthony was hogging the entire allotment for our platoon," Peterson whines.

"That's right," Smitty retorts. "What are you gonna do about it?"

"We got to make a run to Yongsan," Gibson exclaims.

"I have to drive there on company business tomorrow," O'Reilly says. "I can go to the liquor store for you."

"Me too," Dave says.

"Looks like you were right about Campbell," Smitty tells Dave. "He's not bad for a lifer."

"He and the new captain were down at the repo-depo every day last week looking for replacements," Dave replies. "We'll be getting some new guys most riki-tik."

"What's the captain like?"

"I haven't talked to him much," Dave replies. "But he's got two things going for him that Pfeiffer never had."

"What's that?"

"A Ranger tab and a CIB."

"So he's hardcore," Smitty says. "Well, I wish him luck finding replacements. We got to get off twenty-one and one. Everyone's tower crazy."

Part of the problem in the towers now is spring fever. As the weather warms, the MPs want to get out and enjoy it, but it's hard to go far on a one-day break.

Still, the following week when First Platoon finally gets a day off, the men of Second Squad are determined to bust loose. "We're going to Myeong-dong tonight," Smitty tells Dave. "Want to go?"

Myeong-dong is a neighborhood in Seoul with first-class hotels, restaurants and nightclubs. "I'd love to," Dave says. "But I got CQ."

"You and that fucking CQ," Smitty growls.

Dave sees the guys off late that afternoon then reports for duty at the company office. His runner is a cherry from the motor pool. After they've taken turns eating dinner, Dave offers the PFC the first shift. "I'll be back at midnight," Dave tells him. "If you need me I will either be at Special Services or in my hooch."

The Second Squad hooch is empty later when Dave gets back from Special Services. He lies on his cot and opens his current book. It's a biography of Peter the Great. Soon the volume falls to his chest, and Dave drifts off to sleep. After a nice nap, he wakes refreshed and goes to relieve the runner.

Alone in the company office, Dave tries to read. But after the nap, he's full of energy. So he puts the book down and paces. In the rear of the Quonset, he comes across the officer's water cooler and tries some. It's cold, tasteless, and quite refreshing. The thought occurs to Dave that with water like this there would be no need to desecrate bourbon whiskey by mixing it with Coca-Cola.

Dave goes out the door and down to the Second Squad hooch only to return to the office moments later with the quart of Jim Beam that O'Reilly got for him. He pours a slug into a paper cup, tops it off with a splash of the excellent water, and has a sip. Then he opens the Peter the Great book and is soon reading about yet another bloody revolt of the Kremlin palace guard. Dave knows that this one will end with their defeat because he's read it before. Still, he's enthralled, and it's only with reluctance that he tears himself away from time to time to refresh his drink. Over the next few hours, as the ranks of the Russian guardsman are depleted, so too is the whiskey bottle.

Sometime after 3:00 a.m., a jeep with the markings of the 728th Military Police BN pulls up outside the office. Two white-helmeted, white-belted, fully armed MPs burst in leading Smitty, O'Reilly, and Gibson, who are singing a Creedence song about "them old cotton fields back home." Gibson has a black eye, Smitty's knuckles are skinned and bleeding, and O'Reilly's shirt is in rags. They smell like stale beer. "We got called by one of the clubs downtown with a complaint about these guys," the first MP tells Dave. He's a heavyset E-5 wearing Ray-Ban sunglasses. "Seems the manager politely asked them to leave and next thing you know chairs were flying. They aren't used to that sort of thing in Myeong-dong."

"Oh," Dave says. They are very used to that sort of thing in the vill.

"We were taking them to the Yongsan brig but come to find out they're MPs," the other cop says distastefully. He's a tall, blond PFC who would look like Troy Donahue if not for a cleft palate.

"So out of professional courtesy we brought them here," the sergeant elaborates. "Figured we would let your captain take care of 'em."

"Don't worry, Sergeant," Dave says slowly and distinctly. "I'll put these three on report and see to it that the captain has them in first thing in the morning."

"Sounds good," the MP says. "And make sure to note this in the log."

"Absolutely," Dave agrees. Then he addresses his squadmates. "Now, you men quiet down and go to your quarters," he orders.

"Who in the fuck . . ." Gibson slurs, but Smitty gives the redneck a rough shove that shuts him up.

"All right, all right, whatever you say," Smitty says with a wink. "Come on, fuckwad, let's go," he tells Gibson. O'Reilly stumbles out the door behind the other two.

"I'll make sure there's no more trouble from them," Dave tells the MPs. "And don't worry, this will all be in the log and a report will be on the captain's desk when he arrives in the morning."

"All right," the sergeant agrees.

The door slams, tires crunch on gravel, and the MPs are gone. Dave breathes a sigh of relief, but moments later the jeep returns and the PFC comes back into the office. "Just noticed we're low on gas," he says.

"Oh really?" Dave stalls. He tries to remember which drawer holds the company keys, and after looking in a couple he finds them. Dave rides to the motor pool with the guys from the seven-deuce-eight, unlocks the gate, then somehow manages the refueling process. Finally, the Seoul MPs are gone for good.

Dave greedily breathes in the fresh spring air as he walks back to the company office. Once there, he grabs what's left of the whiskey and returns the bottle to his hooch. A couple of hours later, Dave is sitting with his feet up on one of the desks when Harris comes into the office. The company clerk picks up the log book and glances at it. "Looks like another boring night," he says.

"Yeah, but I got a lot of reading done," Dave replies, getting up. "Now I'm going to chow."

Johansson is in the mess hall sitting by himself when Dave comes in. He's wearing workout clothes. "What are you doing up this early when you're off?" Dave asks.

"Went running."

"No shit?"

"Yeah, with Campbell and the captain. We went up to the monastery and back."

"Cool."

"The captain and first sergeant seem to be old friends," Johansson says. "Sometimes they call each other by their first names."

"All I know is we're getting a lot of replacements in," Dave says.

"And a lot of troublemakers are going out," Johansson adds.

That afternoon Dave is playing spades in the Third Squad hooch with Johansson, Kingsford, and Matthews when one of Campbell's recruits from the repo-depo comes in. His nametag reads Martinez, and the spec 4's three rows of ribbons include a Vietnam Service Medal, Silver Star, Bronze Star with oak leaf cluster, an Army Commendation Medal, and the Purple Heart with three oak leaf clusters. "Is this Third Squad?" Martinez asks.

"That's right," Johansson answers. "We've been expecting you. Let me show you your bunk."

"So you guys are into spades," Martinez observes after dropping his duffel bag next to his cot. "We played all the time in the 'Nam."

"Then you'll fit right in here," Matthews says.

Martinez changes into fatigues while the houseboy makes his bed and empties his duffel bag. "How did you get transferred here?" Kingsford asks him.

"Army regs," Martinez replies. "After the third heart, you get out of Vietnam but have to go to another hardship post, not back to the States."

"That sucks."

"Tell me about it," Martinez laughs. His uniform jacket is still hanging on the locker door. It has a big yellow patch on one arm in the shape of a shield. A cherry comes over and points at it.

"What unit is that?" he asks.

"It's the First Cav, numbnuts," Matthews replies.

"I'll explain it to you," Martinez offers with a twinkle in his eye. He points to the horse's head in the upper section of the emblem. "This is the horse we never rode," he says. Next, Martinez indicates the black diagonal line that divides the patch. "This is the line we never crossed." Then the newcomer puts his finger on the yellow background of the shield. "And this is the reason why." The joke elicits a good laugh and Martinez is immediately accepted. No one is going to call him a cherry.

The next evening when Dave goes to the office for CQ duty, Sergeant Campbell is there. He has come up with another idea for augmenting his force of tower guards. "I've been watching you," Campbell tells Dave. "Williams told me you're a nutjob, but I don't believe you're any crazier than everyone else around here."

"That's probably true," Dave allows.

"We need to get every swinging dick up in those towers and get the men off twenty-one and one," Campbell says. "So I'm taking you off the weapons unauthorized list."

"What about CQ?" Dave asks plaintively.

"It's against regs for you to be on permanent CQ," Campbell replies. "I've put up with it for the past month 'cause I had bigger fish to fry. But from now on the clerks and jerks can take their turn at CQ as per SOP. You're going back in the towers."

"Yes, Sergeant."

No questions are asked the next morning when Dave shows up at the armory to draw his M16. His comrades in Second Squad are equally noncommittal when Dave joins them for the familiar ride out to the site. When they get there, the MPs have to wait for an infantry platoon to file out of the main gate. Chief Thunder is among the grunts, as well as several junkies and a couple of the worst alcoholics formerly of First Squad. They will spend the day humping the ridges that border the SAD. For the infantry, life at the site is truly bleak. There's no hot chow, no canteen, and no vill. As Dave watches the dispirited men shamble off, it hits him how narrowly he escaped their fate.

After the infantry departs, First Platoon goes into the site and lines up for formation. Sergeant Anthony calls the soldiers to attention, then puts them at ease. "We're going back on nine and three," he announces. At this, a hearty cheer goes up. "We start swings tomorrow then we'll go on midnights three days later," Anthony continues once quiet is restored. "After that, you get a three-day pass."

That afternoon Dave is up in tower 6 reading when the field telephone rings. It's Gibson in tower 4. "Sergeant Wilson is coming into the SAD," the redneck announces. "Be on your toes." Dave puts on his web gear and helmet and carries his M16 out on the catwalk. Sure enough, a jeep is slowly making its way up the perimeter road toward tower 4. As Dave watches, Gibson comes out on the catwalk dressed for success and carrying his weapon. Wilson talks to him for a while then walks up to tower 5 where Jeffrie is waiting to greet him. The sergeant stays there for a few minutes then looks across the way at Dave's tower almost half a mile away. Dave waves at him and Wilson returns the gesture then goes back to the waiting jeep. The sergeant isn't going to make the hike to tower 6, let alone walk all the way over to 7.

That night, Dave goes out to the vill with some guys from Third Squad. In the pool room at the Flamingo, he gets on a roll and holds the table for three games. Then his luck runs out. He goes into the main room of the club and finds Johansson, Martinez, and Kingsford at a table with Matthews who has brought a quart of Old Grand-Dad to share. Dave orders a Coke then mixes himself a drink. As the evening progresses, the level in the whiskey bottle steadily declines, but the funny thing is Martinez won't touch it. He only drinks straight Coca-Cola, won't even sip a beer. "You need to get shitfaced like the rest of us," Kingsford tells him.

"If I had your face, I'd get drunk too," Martinez replies.

"Oh yeah? You're so ugly you'd make a maggot puke."

"Then start puking, bitch."

Kingsford gives up matching wits with Martinez and pours the last of the whiskey into his glass. Then the gate guard pulls his arm back like a quarterback and launches a spiral across the room in the direction of some artillerymen. They see the bottle coming and duck as it shatters against the wall behind them. After a quick consultation, the gunners make a beeline for the door.

"Y'all come back real soon," Kingsford crows, "ya hear?"

"Hey, let's stop by the Peacock Club," Johannsson suggests later as the men unsteadily make their way toward the compound. "We can have a quiet drink there."

The Peacock has attracted a decent little crowd this night, but the MPs have no trouble finding a table. Jade is happy to see them, so after bringing their drinks she pulls up a chair and sits between Dave and Matthews. "How's business?" Johansson asks.

"Very good," the lovely bartender replies. "Much soldiers come now gate open."

Jade is wearing a plum-colored silk blouse over a white miniskirt. Emboldened by drink, Dave rests his hand on her bare knee. Jade gently moves it away. But in a short while, Dave tries again. This time Jade simply covers his hand with her own. Dave marvels at the silky soft feel of Jade's skin. They hold hands under the table until closing time.

First Platoon is going on the swing shift, so most of the guys skip breakfast the next morning and sleep in. But by noon everyone is up and ready for lunch. On the way to the mess hall, O'Reilly falls into step beside Dave. "We've got a three-day break coming," he says. "But I don't have money to do anything."

"Me either," Dave replies.

"Well, I know how to fix that," O'Reilly says, lowering his voice conspiratorially.

"How?"

"Mr. Lee says he will buy all the C rats I can get."

"That's good for you."

"I need help," O'Reilly says. "We can split the profits fifty-fifty."

"I'm in," Dave replies.

In Second Squad that afternoon, the usual spades game starts up. Gibson, Smitty, O'Reilly, and Dave play until it's time for formation. Then the soldiers of First Platoon get into fatigues and assemble in the company street. After roll call, they draw weapons and board the bus. As usual, not much is said on the drive. The MPs prefer to endure the tedious ride alone in their thoughts.

At the duty formation, Dave draws tower 15. He's absentmindedly walking up the path to it when movement just to his right catches his eye. It's a coiled-up snake making warning strikes that come within inches of his leg. Dave hastily steps back, removes the M16 from his shoulder, and chambers a round. As he looks over the sights, the reptile stares back at him calmly. It's no longer bobbing now that Dave has backed off, and he realizes it could have bitten him if it chose. Dave lowers the rifle and steps farther away. With that, the intricately camouflaged viper uncoils and moves off.

Up in the tower, it eventually gets too dark to read. Dave goes out on the catwalk and paces to kill time. He tries to bring up some pleasant daydreams, but only ugly thoughts fill the vacuum. Dave starts singing Kingston Trio songs but exhausts his repertoire long before his relief finally shows up.

Once he's back at the compound, Dave gets a half-full whiskey bottle out of his footlocker then starts a letter to Cindy. Her last one to him was all about some guy at the Colony 7 who keeps asking her out. It seems his favorite song is "Love the One You're With."

Dave has tried to write Cindy about the towers but was never able to find the words. Now, after a few failed attempts at a letter and several swigs of Jim Beam, he tries to write a poem. Over the next hour, he rewrites it several times. Bleary-eyed, he reads over what little he has:

> *Like an empty swimming pool in winter*
> *Littered with broken twigs and withered leaves*
> *My mind's a desolate void*
> *Where happy thoughts once splashed and played*
> *But are now gone*
> *So the long season of bleak and chill*
> *Brings only harsh memories*
> *Regretful actions, omissions, words now assail me*
> *Frightening that I can't stop it.*

This is not what Dave wanted to say, and obviously he can't send it. So he crumples the paper, and it joins the pile on the floor. Then he puts the whiskey away, scrawls a bland note to his wife, and goes to bed.

Later that week, First Platoon is on midnights and it's Second Squad's turn for QRF. Dave's in the ready room sleeping when O'Reilly tiptoes in and wakes him. They go outside, and the driver leads Dave to the back of the building. O'Reilly left the window to the supply room unlocked earlier in the day, and now Dave helps his friend climb inside. Moments later, O'Reilly returns to the window with a stack of C ration cases. He lowers them down to Dave, who carries the load to the three-quarter-ton truck, which is parked nearby. Then Dave comes back to where O'Reilly is waiting with another stack. Both men are nervous, but they keep going until they have removed a hundred cases. Then Dave helps O'Reilly down, and the driver gets behind the wheel of the truck. Dave climbs into the back with their booty, and they proceed to the main gate. After a few words with the guard, O'Reilly drives to the outskirts of Seoksu-dong. He brings the truck to a halt in a lonely spot, as prearranged with Mr. Lee. No sooner do the wheels stop but a crowd of Korean women in peasant dress emerges from a nearby field. They quickly unload the truck then vanish. The next day, Dave and O'Reilly go to Mr. Lee's. Each walks out of the pawn shop with a pocket full of MPC.

The men of First Platoon are in a perimeter guarding the SAD landing pad where a Chinook helicopter is parked. They are waiting for several nuclear devices to be brought out of the site and loaded on board. The nukes are going to the DMZ as part of a readiness exercise called a bravo mission.

The helicopter came in three hours ago and shut down. Since then the MPs have been standing under the hot sun grousing among themselves. "Time sure flies when you're having a good time," Martinez observes.

"Very funny," Peterson snaps.

"It's always the same," Smitty complains. "Hurry up and wait."

"Sounds like you're bored," Dave says.

"Fuckin' A."

"If you're bored it means you lack imagination."

"Fuck you."

"It's way past time for chow," Peterson moans. "I'm hungry."

"I've got something here you can munch on," Gibson offers.

"Hey, something's up," Martinez exclaims as several crew members emerge from the helicopter. They get to work starting the engines. It's a drawn-out process, but eventually, the turbines on the massive craft fill the air with their eerie whine. As both rotors on the helicopter slowly turn, a procession of ordnance technicians exits the site. Each is pushing a hand truck. A file of MPs including Kingsford and Johansson walk alongside.

As the procession goes by, Dave and his buddies get a good look at what's on the hand trucks. The devices look like fire extinguisher canisters enclosed in protective cages. One by one they are wheeled onto the Chinook accompanied by the MPs. Then the ramp is raised and as the helicopter blades turn faster, their familiar "whup, whup, whup" sound is distinguishable over the noise of the turbines. Shuddering, the aircraft lifts into the air then pirouettes 180 degrees. The MPs watch as the pilot drops the nose and proceeds with his cargo up the valley toward North Korea.

Five days later the helicopter returns, and the nukes are taken back into the SAD. That night, at the NCO club, the guys who went on the bravo mission are the center of attention. "It's like a real war up there," Kingsford says. "Trenches, sandbags piled up everywhere, concertina wire, bunkers, pillboxes, machine-gun nests, the whole nine yards."

"You can look across and see the enemy going about their business same as us," Johansson elaborates.

"What about in the rear?" Smitty asks.

"They party hard," Kingsford replies. "The infantry up there ain't nothing but a bunch of alcoholics."

"And weed," Johansson says. "Guys pass joints around openly. You walk by a bunker and clouds of reefer smoke will be coming out."

"Officers go by but don't say nothin'," Kingsford adds. "And no one salutes."

"Man, I'd like to go on a bravo mission," Smitty declares.

"I just want to go home," Dave says. "Only fifty-nine and a wake-up."

"How can you be shorter than me?" Johansson asks.

"I was stationed at Fort Benning before I came here," Dave explains. "My two years in the army are almost up."

"Then you're the shortest one here," Johansson exclaims. "You can buy the next round."

"No problem," Dave smiles as he waves the waitress over. He still has plenty of money, thanks to the C ration caper. This late in the month the other guys are practically broke.

But eventually, another payday arrives, and once again, everyone's flush. That night, Dave is among those heading for the vill. When he gets to the Flamingo, Dave finds Matthews at the door playing bouncer. "Oh, it's you," Matthews says and allows Dave to pass. Then three men from the motor pool come around the corner and approach the club. Matthews blocks the entrance, and they look at him uncertainly. "Hey, we're trying to get a drink," one of them says.

"Too bad," Matthews replies. "This is a private party."

"What do you mean?" the soldier asks. "This is a club just like the others, right?"

"Wrong, fuckwad," Matthews says. "We don't let just anyone in. Now piss off."

The leader of the group looks at the diminutive but feisty doorman and starts to say something, but one of his comrades interrupts. "Let's go to the Cadillac Bar instead," he suggests.

"Yeah, do that, motherfucker," Matthews agrees.

Inside the club, Dave strolls toward the bar as an empty glass sails across the room at his head. He ducks then hears it break somewhere behind him. Meanwhile, Mr. Park makes a note in his little black book, no doubt assessing the glass thrower a breakage fee. Dave gets a drink and takes it to a table where Johansson, Kingsford, and Martinez are seated. Tired of playing doorman, Matthews comes over. "How can you sit there drinking straight Coca-Cola all night?" he asks Martinez. "Have a real drink, for Chrissake."

"Well, maybe I could just have a beer," Martinez concedes.

"Now you're talking," Matthews exclaims. He makes a beeline for the bar then comes back with a bottle of beer for Martinez and a whiskey Coke for himself.

"You know we're all getting short; we should do some sight-seeing before we leave," Kingsford says. "As it stands, when we get home and people ask, 'What did you see?' all we'll be able to say is, 'We visited a bunch of whorehouses.'"

"What else is there?" Martinez asks.

"Shit, I don't know," Kingsford replies.

"Special Services has brochures on points of interest," Dave says. "Like palaces, ancient ruins, and monasteries. I've ridden to some of those spots on Korean buses."

"You've got to have balls to get on one of those death traps," Johansson says.

"We could go up to the DMZ," Matthews suggests. "And take the tour."

"I don't need a tour," Johansson protests. He finishes his drink then tosses the empty glass back over his shoulder. It tumbles end over end before shattering next to a group of MPs. "Hey, watch it, you fucking lifer," one of them laughs, brushing broken glass off his feet.

"Eat me," the big Swede replies.

"I'm going to the bar. Who needs a drink?" Dave asks. Everyone's hand goes up, including Martinez who has finished his beer.

"I'll help," Johansson says and accompanies Dave to get the refreshments. When they get back to the table, the guys are still talking about sight-seeing.

"So when do you want to do this tourist bit?" Kingsford asks the group.

"It would have to be sometime when all of us are off duty," Dave ventures.

Martinez turns to Matthews with an odd little smile. "Hit me," he says, and if it were anyone else, Matthews would be happy to oblige. But by now everyone loves Martinez, so Matthews ignores the request.

"All we have to do is figure a time when you tower jocks are on break and us gate guards have a day off," Johansson says. He's seated on the other side of Martinez, who now turns to him. "Please hit me," Martinez asks politely.

"What?" Johansson replies. "Are you fucking crazy? I ain't gonna hit you."

"Oh, come on," Martinez pleads; he looks across the table at Kingsford and Dave. "Won't someone just hit me."

"Cut the crap," Kingsford says.

"Some friends you are," Martinez complains.

"Oh, all right, what the fuck," Matthews says and gives Martinez a poke on the arm.

"I mean in the face," Martinez demands.

"I ain't hitting you in the face."

"Someone's got to hit me in the face," Martinez insists, "now." He leaps to his feet, knocking his chair over. "Hit me," he screams.

Johansson springs into action. He comes up behind Martinez and embraces him in a bear hug as the smaller man twists and turns in his arms. Then Mr. Park appears. "Why you makee trouble?" he asks the group.

"Him too much drinkee," Kingsford explains.

"Betta you go compound," Mr. Park insists.

"We go most riki-tik," Kingsford tells the papa-san.

"If I let go, will you settle down and act right?" Johansson asks the still struggling Martinez. A look of cunning crosses the distraught man's face.

"Yes," he agrees, ceasing his movements.

Johansson releases Martinez, who immediately spins and takes a wild swing at him. "If you won't hit me, I'll hit you," Martinez threatens. He dances around jerkily in a boxing stance, but Kingsford grabs him from behind. "Hit me," Martinez cries.

"We've got to get him out of here," Dave says. "I'll take his legs." Martinez kicks wildly, but Dave gets both legs in his grasp. Now the others join in to lift the lunatic. They carry him out of the club and back to the compound.

In the Third Squad hooch, Martinez babbles incoherently as the other MPs hold him down. But slowly he calms, and his words start to add up. "Didn't ask to be no fire team leader," the combat veteran moans. "They could have chose Reynolds, not me. But I'm the one who threw the grenade. It hit a tree and came back; all dead, all dead."

Dave goes to the company office where a cherry from the armory is on CQ. He walks past him and gets two cups of the officer's water to take back to the hooch. "Here, drink this," he says to Martinez, but the soldier has his face buried in his hands. Johansson gently tries to pry them apart to no avail. "You guys can go to bed," the gate guard says after a while. "I'll stay with him as long as necessary."

Mercifully First Platoon is on break, and the guys can sleep in the next morning. But later Dave gets restless and decides to go for a walk. On his way through the vill, he comes across Jade outside the Peacock Club. It's the first time he's seen her in over a month. According to Johansson, she's been living in Seoul with a major.

"Where you go?" Jade asks.

"Walkee," Dave replies. "You come?"

"OK, you wait."

Jade disappears to change clothes then comes back wearing shorts, T-shirt, and sneakers. Soon she and Dave are heading up the trail that leads to the monastery. When they get to the resort area, several couples are out on the pond in rowboats. Jade suggests that they rent one and presently the two of them are on the water. It's a lovely summer day with a gentle breeze blowing down the valley. Jade sits in the stern of the little boat, and Dave mans the oars. Steep mountainsides rise on either side, and the water is crystal clear. They can see all the way to the rocky bottom, but Dave doesn't spot any fish.

"My mother bringee me here when little girl," Jade says.

"That's nice," Dave replies. "Did you live nearby?"

"Live in Seoul."

"Does your mother still live in Seoul?"

"She dead," Jade says sadly. "TB."

"So sorry."

"My father, he stateside," Jade says, brightening. She rummages around in her purse and pulls out a billfold. Then she passes a photo over to Dave. The American soldier in the picture is dressed in a 1950s-style Class A uniform.

"He handsome man," Dave offers.

"Yes, very handsome," Jade agrees. "Like movie star."

After their boating excursion, Dave walks Jade back to Seoksu-dong. They're sitting on a bench outside the Peacock when Johansson and Martinez come by. "How are you doing?" Dave asks Martinez.

"OK, so long as I don't drink," Martinez replies. "And I'm done with that."

"We're hiking up to the monastery," Johansson explains. "Nothing like exercise and fresh mountain air."

"Jade and I were just at the resort," Dave says.

"Cool. Well, catch you later."

A steady stream of GIs continues past and Dave speaks with most of them. "You know everybody," Jade exclaims during a lull in the foot traffic.

"Not everybody."

"You here long time, I think. Go stateside soon, yes?"

"Yes."

Jade reaches over and takes Dave's hand. They sit quietly for a while, then she has to go. "Me workee," Jade says.

"When no workee?"

"Tomorrow."

"We go compound," Dave suggests. "Fried chicken."

"Oh yes," Jade exclaims. Spontaneously she bends toward Dave for a kiss and their lips meet. At once, both close their eyes to better savor the sensation of free-falling. After a lingering moment, Jade tilts her head back and gazes searchingly into Dave's eyes. Then she kisses him again, gets up, and disappears into the club.

Johansson is on duty at the gate the next evening when Dave walks up with Jade. "You going to the club?" he asks.

"That's right," Dave replies.

"Well, leave some chicken for me."

"No problem, you can have the gizzards."

"I like gizzards."

"You would."

When Jade and Dave get to the NCO club, O'Reilly beckons them over to a table full of MPs. Everyone's eating the club's signature dish and washing it down with Olympia beer, so the newcomers order the same. "Good choice," O'Reilly says approvingly.

"This chicken is almost as good as back home," Gibson declares. "But what I miss is barbecue."

"Why you no like Korean barbecue?" Jade asks.

"I like to know what I'm eating," Gibson replies.

"Yeah, you don't want to find out you just ate somebody's dog," Smitty comments.

"That big lie," Jade says, pouting. "We no eat dogs."

"Since when?" Smitty asks.

There's a bustle onstage as the club's Korean band arrives and plugs in their equipment. Soon the opening chords of "Satisfaction" reverberate through the amplifiers, and several couples get up to dance. Dave takes Jade's hand and leads her onto the dance floor. When the song ends, Smitty is there to claim the next dance. Afterward he and Jade return to the table laughing. "He say you sing," Jade says to Dave, "sing bad."

"Very bad," Smitty declares.

"No, he sings good," O'Reilly protests. "Get up there, Knight. Show 'em."

"Ha-ha," Smitty laughs, "go on, prove me right."

Dave waits for the band to finish its current number then he steps onstage and asks them to play "Time Is on My Side." The song is a big hit with the GIs in the crowd, and they sing along with Dave. At the end, several men shout, "Do 'Gloria.'" But there's no way Dave's going to perform his filthy version of Van Morrison's classic with ladies present. Instead, he chooses "Play with Fire," and as the first notes of the ballad sound, several couples get up to slow dance. Afterward, Dave returns to the table.

"Smitty right," Jade tells him. "You not good singer."

"My fan club disagrees," Dave replies, pointing to several complimentary beers that have appeared in front of them. He pops the top on one as Jade gets up to dance with O'Reilly. Once the song is over, they come back to the table, but Jade has barely touched her beer before another MP asks her to dance. A little later, when the band takes a break, she is ready to go.

"Hey, we're leaving," Dave announces.

"Later, then," O'Reilly replies.

"Don't do anything I wouldn't do," Smitty smirks.

Outside the smoky NCO club, Jade and Dave pause for a breath of fresh air. Then they walk hand in hand up the gravel road, through the gate, and into the village. Just a sliver of moon is visible in the night sky as they go down an alley and up a short flight of stairs to Jade's apartment. Inside the small room, the only furniture is a wardrobe closet. Jade gets a bundle of bedding out, unties it, and soon she's created a cozy arrangement of quilts, pillows, and blankets on the floor. When she sits on the makeshift bed and undresses, Dave does the same. But then Jade turns on her side and faces the wall. "No makee love," she orders. "Only sleepee."

"OK," Dave agrees. He lies on his back, crosses his arms under his head, and loudly snores.

"You stupid," Jade giggles. She reaches for the cord that held the bedding together, tosses it to Dave then turns her bare back to him again. Dave notices that she now has both hands crossed behind her. Slowly it dawns on him what he's supposed to do with the cord.

The next morning when Dave wakes, Jade is gone. Over the next month, he often stops by the Peacock to ask about her, but the mama-san behind the bar always gives him the same response: "She go Seoul."

So with the end of his military career in sight, Dave becomes cautious, and for the most part, he now remains on the compound when not at work. One afternoon, he's in the game room at Special Services when Johansson comes in. "Did you hear about Martinez?" the gate guard asks.

"No, what happened?"

"Almost kicked the bucket last night."

"Oh no."

"We were in the vill, and Martinez thought one little beer wouldn't hurt him, but he barely got half of it down before the shit hit the fan. 'Hit me, won't you. Oh, come on, please hit me,'" Johansson mimics. "He went completely apeshit, took five of us to get him back to the compound, and then we had to strap him to his bunk. All of a sudden his eyes rolled back in his head, and he went limp. We checked his vitals and come to find he ain't breathing. So I began CPR while Matthews went for the ambulance. On the way to Seoul, Doc couldn't get a pulse. So he got out a syringe and stuck the longest needle I've ever seen straight into Martinez's heart. That did the trick, but he's still in the hospital recovering. I just got back from there, told him if he ever touches another drop of alcohol again, I'm gonna fire his ass up."

"He needs to stay out of the vill," Dave exclaims.

"Me too," Johannsson agrees. "We're all getting too short for this shit. Don't need to go home with a dose of the clap."

"Hell no."

During his next three-day break, Dave does nothing but play spades in the hooch, shoot pool at Special Services, and drink beer at the NCO club. Then it's time for his last nine-day stretch of tower guard. On the first day back at the site, Dave draws tower 7. He's happy that he'll be spending the day on top of the mountain as far away from the guard office as possible.

The hike up the Choji Trail and across the saddle to tower 7 is worth the effort once Dave is out on the catwalk taking in the view. The thatched-roof cottages and mud-walled compounds of the villages below are bathed in shadow at first, but as the sun comes over the mountain, it illuminates the scene. Dave watches farmers heading out for a day in the rice paddies. They lead water buffalo pulling two-wheeled wooden carts just as their ancestors did.

The cool air on the ridgetop gives way to a sultry breeze as the day wears on. So, after a C ration lunch, Dave decides to lie out on the catwalk and catch rays. Before stripping, he looks down at the guard office far below and sees that both the three-quarter-ton truck and the jeep are parked outside. Dave's confident his phone will ring if one of the NCOs starts making the rounds. He gets out of his uniform and lies on the catwalk wearing only skivvies.

As he stretches out, the breeze caresses Dave's bare skin. Chirping insects and melodic bird calls lull him into a drowsy state. But after a while he hears a sound that doesn't fit with the natural symphony. It's a faint crackle that comes and goes so quickly he's inclined to disregard it. However, Dave can't help trying to place the sound, and finally, it hits him. The noise was static from a not-so-distant walkie-talkie.

Dave dashes inside the tower and quickly gets into his fatigues. He pulls his combat boots over sockless feet and tucks the pants bottoms inside. Then he dons his helmet and takes his web gear and weapon back outside. He's in the process of making a few final adjustments to his uniform when Sergeant Anthony emerges from the woods. The intrepid lifer has climbed the backside of the mountain hoping to catch Specialist Knight sleeping on guard.

"Halt. Who is there?" Dave says, smiling down at the scowling face of his platoon sergeant.

"You know who it is, scumbag," Anthony replies.

"State the password."

"Red Rover," Anthony snarls.

"You may pass."

Anthony turns and starts for tower 6, so Dave rushes back into his tower, picks up the field phone, and turns the handle. A cherry is manning the PBX. "Connect me with tower 6," Dave tells him.

"Roger."

Jeffrie picks up the phone on the third ring. "Anthony is on the way over," Dave exclaims. "He climbed the mountain."

"Shit," Jeffrie says and slams down the receiver.

Dave makes a couple more calls to spread the word then goes out on the catwalk and watches Anthony approach tower 6. By now Jeffrie is on the catwalk with his rifle at port arms. Anthony takes one look and keeps going. Soon the sergeant is heading down the Choji Trail, and Dave can relax. "Idiot," he hollers at himself, and once again he resolves to lie low.

The following week, Dave goes on midnights for the last time. He draws tower 12 and, as usual, begins the shift with a plan for killing off the night. He starts by striding energetically around the catwalk, pausing occasionally to do calisthenics. After tiring of the exercise, he recites poems his father taught him as a child. Dave starts with long ones like "The Cremation of Sam McGee" and "The Highwayman" then does some shorter Kipling works. When he can't remember any more poems, he begins singing.

Dave refuses to look at his watch for the longest time. But eventually, he gives in and squints at the luminous dial. Barely two hours have passed. He starts walking laps again, but his heart isn't in it. Soon he's sitting on the footlocker as the image of a black kid he knew in grammar school comes to him. Dave's parents ordered him to stop playing with Adam, and he obeyed. Now he recalls the pained expression on his friend's face when they would pass in the hall.

Back on the catwalk, Dave strides purposefully around, trying to outrun the shame. He cannot keep his eyes off his watch now and celebrates a victory every time five more minutes tick away. Finally, false dawn signals that the real thing is coming and slowly the long night comes to an end.

After two more nights of tower guard, Dave is taken off the duty roster to begin out-processing. Over the next few days, he turns in his gear, completes all the paperwork, and receives orders for Fort Lewis, where he will be separated from the army. On the afternoon of his last day in-country, Dave's in the Second Squad hooch playing spades. He's partnered with a new guy, and they are losing. "How could you throw your queen out there without a dress?" Dave snaps.

"Sorry," the kid replies nervously.

Before the next trick is played, the CQ runner comes in. "Is Knight around?" the cherry asks.

"That's me."

"Johansson called. Your yobo is at the gate."

Dave recognizes Jade from a hundred yards away. She's standing by the fence wearing blue jeans and a T-shirt. As the crunch of gravel heralds Dave's approach, she looks up and smiles. "*Yobeoseyo*," Jade says.

"Hello."

"You OK?"

"Yes, fine."

"Me Seoul."

"I know."

"You workee?"

"No."

"So maybe you come my hoochie?"

"No can do," Dave replies. "Go stateside tomorrow."

"Oh," Jade sighs. She musters a brave smile. "You happy now, yes?"

"Yes."

A familiar feeling of self-loathing settles over Dave as he walks back to the hooch. But that night, after a few beers at the NCO club, his spirits brighten. This is his last night in Korea, and Dave's fellow soldiers are determined to give him a proper send-off. So it's rare, during the evening, when any less than two fresh beers are on the table waiting while he guzzles the current one. All are provided on a complimentary basis by his soon-to-be former comrades.

The next morning, O'Reilly takes Dave and his duffel bag up to the gate so he can catch the shuttle bus. "We should have hit the supply room again for more C rats," the driver says wistfully.

"That's for sure," Dave agrees. The two soldiers often spoke of making another raid on the supply room but never did. It was just too nerve-racking that one time.

"I'll be following you in forty-six more days," O'Reilly says.

"That's short," Dave replies. "Look me up if you're ever in DC."

"Will do."

Dave takes the shuttle to Yongsan where he catches a bus to Osan Air Base. Once there he checks his baggage then goes to a hangar that serves as the departure lounge. Inside, uniformed soldiers occupy rows of metal folding chairs while they wait for the flight. Dave has a horrible hangover, so he goes to the canteen up front and gets a cup of coffee. On the way back his hands are shaking, and he splashes java on a major's shoulder. The officer stiffens as the hot liquid penetrates the fabric of his uniform. He turns to glare daggers at Dave. "Uh, sorry," Dave says. Somehow the major controls his anger and turns back around. A couple of hours later the troops line up to board a red-tailed bird. It will make one refueling stop in Anchorage before landing at Sea-Tac. Dave will be out of the army in less than a week.

CHAPTER FIFTEEN
JOB FAIR

"This is completely bizarre," Dave says. He and Cindy are drinking beer in a rustic tavern at Annapolis Junction, Maryland.

"What's bizarre?" Cindy asks.

"One day I'm in a tower on a mountaintop in Korea and then, pow, I'm sitting here with you."

"All I know is one day you have a job and then, pow, you're unemployed."

"No, I mean it's just surreal," Dave persists. "Was the army thing only a dream? Or is this a dream?"

"You're cut off," Cindy replies. "What's wrong with you? Two beers and you start raving like a maniac. When are you going to get a job?"

"First I have to buy a motorcycle."

"What for?"

"To be a motorcycle messenger, you know, in DC."

"You'll get killed," Cindy exclaims. "And besides, don't you think you can find something better?"

"It would be cool."

"Colony 7 is looking for a salesman."

"To sell tickets?"

"No, stupid, to sell ads in the program," Cindy explains. "You've got a good line of bullshit. Why don't you apply?"

"OK."

"We'll have to get you a suit."

"Forget it."

"Tomorrow, at Hecht's," Cindy insists.

"Oh, all right."

"I'll go with you."

"No need."

One week later, Dave goes to the Colony 7 dinner theater wearing a suit he found on a closeout rack. He's shown into the office of Bruce Rawlins, the general manager. "What kind of sales experience have you had?" Rawlins asks.

"None," Dave admits.

"So what makes you think you can do this job?"

"I don't know," Dave replies. "People seem to like me, and I can often get them to do what I want."

"You have to be persistent," Rawlins says. "You can't get discouraged."

"Oh, I'm persistent!"

"Well, we love Cindy, so we'd be willing to give you a shot at this."

"Thanks."

"What questions do you have for me?"

"Well, Cindy didn't tell me what the job pays."

"We pay seven percent commission off the top."

"Any benefits?"

"We reimburse you for gas and expenses."

"Oh."

"How does that sound?"

"Great. I'll talk it over with Cindy and get back to you."

After the interview, Dave drives directly to the Maryland Employment Commission office. It's in a nondescript strip mall next to a Dart Drug. Inside, the décor is highly functional with metal desks, rows of filing cabinets, and a waiting area similar to a bus station. Dave is given a number along with several forms to fill out. An hour later, he's called into a meeting with a counselor.

"I'm Mr. Smathers," the man says without offering his hand. "Have a seat."

Smathers is a heavyset black man with a short haircut and tired eyes. "I see you were recently discharged from the army," he says with a glance at Dave's file.

"Yes, sir."

"Have you filed for unemployment yet?"

"Hadn't thought of it."

"Well, that's the first thing we need to do," Smathers declares and hands Dave a claim form. "You've got thirteen weeks coming."

"That'll please the wife," Dave smiles. He gets no reaction from the bureaucrat.

"To receive benefits, you must apply for a minimum of five jobs a week," Smathers explains. He points to a bookshelf across the way. "Those are binders full of job announcements sorted by type. What do you want to do?"

"I'm thinking maybe sales."

Smathers rises from his desk. "Come on," he says. "I'll show you."

The counselor selects a binder full of flyers for various sales jobs and hands it to Dave. He thumbs through it and sees that most of the employers want applicants to mail in a resume. "Have you got any sample resumes?" he asks.

"Sure," Smathers replies. Dave takes several with him when he goes.

That night, Cindy prepares a casserole for dinner while Dave makes a salad. After eating, they smoke a joint on the balcony. Below them, brick paths lead through the landscaped green space that separates their building from others nearby. Tennis courts and a swimming pool are tucked in among the trees.

"How did it go with Bruce?" Cindy asks after getting a last toke from the tiny roach.

"It went OK," David replies, "but it's straight commission."

"Well, you've got to start somewhere."

"I get thirteen weeks of unemployment compensation. If I can't find anything better before then, I'll take it."

"The job might not be there then," Cindy complains.

"That's the way it goes."

The next day, Dave goes out and purchases a Smith-Corona portable typewriter. It's not cheap, but with money coming from the government, he decides to splurge. When he gets home, Dave sits at the kitchen table and types up a resume. It doesn't take long since he's only had two jobs.

Over the following weeks, Dave goes to the employment office almost every day, and Smathers helps him choose openings to apply for. Then the phone begins to ring, and Dave starts going on interviews. "How did it go?" Cindy asks one evening when Dave picks her up at work.

"The interview was going fine until I spit in his face."

"Oh, come on, can't you be serious?"

"Yes. Well, it went all right, and they offered me the job, but it's a car dealer, and all they need me to do is greet customers in the lot, find out what kind of car they want, then turn them over to a sales manager. If he makes the sale, I get a spiff."

"Well, that's something."

"OK, I'll consider it."

"You've only got nine weeks left."

"I know."

At the employment office the next morning, Smathers hands Dave a flyer. It's about a sales job fair at the Ramada Inn in Landover. "You need to take a stack of resumes," the counselor says. So Dave goes to a copy shop and pays for twenty-five copies of his skimpy resume. Then on the appointed day, he rises early and gets to the Ramada while exhibitors are still setting up. With time to kill, Dave goes back outside and steers the VW to a nearby 7-Eleven. He sits in the bug for an hour reading the newspaper while sipping high-test coffee.

A line of worthies snakes through the lobby of the motel when Dave returns. He gets in the queue and a little while later the doors to the ballroom open. Inside, Dave finds rows of tables manned by impressively dressed executives for firms with instantly recognizable brands. During the next hour, he discovers that Xerox is looking for hard chargers to market copiers, IBM wants the cream of the crop to sell Selectrics, and Pitney Bowes needs closers to push postage meters. Dave is happy to be among this pantheon of household names, but after visiting several tables, he learns that not having a college degree is a killer. Also, his outdated suit fails to impress. Soon, he's wandering despondently among the tables despising himself for thinking he might belong here.

As Dave is heading for the exit, a sign on one of the tables catches his attention: *Ask About Our Veterans Outreach Program.* An attractive middle-aged lady behind it greets him with a smile. "I'm a veteran," Dave tells her.

"Thank you for your service," she replies.

"I was drafted," Dave elaborates.

"Makes no difference. Do you have a resume?"

"Yes, ma'am."

The executive quickly peruses the scant information on Dave's rap sheet. "So you haven't started college yet?" she asks.

"No, ma'am."

"Well, no matter. We can waive the college requirement for veterans. I have a little aptitude test that would only take twenty minutes. Are you interested?"

"Yes, please."

Dave is given a questionnaire, a #2 pencil, and a form to record his answers. It's a multiple-choice test, so he's confident at the outset but quickly realizes his normal approach won't work. Usually, with multiple choice, he eliminates the two ridiculous answers and then relies on intuition to discern which of the remaining two is correct. But all the questions on this test are subjective, and each of the answers is plausible. So Dave stops trying to game the test and just answers each question off the top of his head. It takes longer than expected but he finally finishes then turns in the answer sheet. "We will call you," the executive says, handing him a card. She's from the human resources department of Procter & Gamble.

On his way home, Dave goes by the Colony 7 and waits for Cindy to get off work. They go to a Giant Supermarket to get bread, milk, bananas, beer, and other necessities. At the checkout, they end up paying almost thirty dollars. "We're only getting sixty-three dollars a week from your unemployment," Cindy says when they get home. "You can see it doesn't go far."

"But that's almost as much as we got from the army," Dave replies, popping the top on a beer.

"Yes, but what happens when it runs out?"

"I'll sell drugs."

"Very funny."

"Come here and give me a kiss."

"Fuck you."

"You're a mind reader."

Cindy goes into the bedroom and slams the door. So Dave rolls a joint and turns on the TV. Later, when his wife fails to reappear, he gets a pillow, sheet, and blanket out of the hall closet, makes up the sofa, and goes to sleep.

The following Monday, Dave goes back to the employment office and finds several leads. He heads home, has a PB&J sandwich, and starts cranking out cover letters. Just before it's time for him to fetch Cindy, the phone rings.

"Hi, this is Susan Beecham. I'm calling from Cincinnati."

"Hello."

"You completed an application for us last week," Susan says. "Are you still interested in employment with Procter & Gamble?"

"Yes, I am."

"Well, we were impressed with how you did on the screener you completed at the job fair and were wondering if you might be willing to undergo a couple more assessments. We'd like to get an idea of how you might fit in with us."

"Sure," Dave replies. "I'd be happy to."

"Our regional office is near Philadelphia. Can you go there on Thursday?"

"That would be fine."

"Record your mileage and save your gas receipts so we can reimburse you."

"OK."

"If you have something to write with, I can give you directions to the office."

"Great."

It's dark, and a cold rain is falling later that week when Dave drops Cindy off at work then heads north on I-95. He stops for coffee and a pee break in Wilmington then follows directions the rest of the way to Plymouth Meeting. The address he was given turns out to be a chrome and glass building in an upscale office park. In the lobby, Dave finds the directory then rides an elevator up to the third floor, which is wholly taken up with P&G offices. "Hi, I'm Dave Knight. I have an appointment with Ms. Hightower," he tells the receptionist.

"I'll ring her," she says, and soon, a tall, dark-haired businesswoman comes up the hall. "Hi, Dave, I'm Beverly Hightower," she smiles.

"Pleased to meet you," Dave replies.

"We've got you set up in a vacant office. Come on, I'll show you."

Half-way down the hall, Beverly stops and ushers Dave into a plainly furnished office. An oversize envelope is on the otherwise bare desk. "That's the first test Cincinnati sent for you," Beverly explains. "There are three more. After each one, you get a ten-minute break."

Dave settles behind the desk and opens the envelope. Inside are several #2 pencils, a Scantron answer form, and a baffling, spatial reasoning test consisting of a series of puzzles. As Dave struggles with the questions, he breaks into a cold sweat. An hour later, he reaches the end of the ordeal and is ready to wave the white flag and head home. Instead he stays, and after a much-needed break, he begins work on a lengthy personality type indicator. The questions on it are interesting, and the answer choices require deliberation, so it takes the rest of the morning to complete. Then he's given a voucher for the cafeteria.

Once he's eaten, Dave returns to the office and wends his way through a psychological assessment. He uses his break time afterward to go outside where a yellow Porsche Carrera in the parking lot is doing its best to brighten the otherwise gray day. After admiring the beauty from every angle, Dave goes back inside where Beverly is waiting with some good news. "I hold in my hand the last envelope," she says.

"Is it hermetically sealed?" Dave inquires.

"Ha-ha."

Inside the envelope is an IQ test. Dave confidently works through the critical reasoning portion but struggles toward the end of the math section. He hasn't quite finished when time expires and Beverly comes to get his answer sheet. "We appreciate you taking the time to come in today," she says as Dave is getting ready to leave. "I work for Nick Carroll, the regional sales manager. He's out today. Otherwise, I'm sure he would have wanted to meet you."

"Maybe next time," Dave says with false bravado.

The next morning, Dave records his mileage and expenses on the form provided by P&G and mails it off with the receipts. Then he has an interview with a company he sent a resume to out of curiosity. Their opening is for a pre-need counselor with sales aptitude but no experience required. Dave finds the firm's office in a high-rise building in Bethesda. He's dying to know what pre-need is, and a sharply dressed man with a fading tan is happy to explain. He tells Dave that only the very best salespeople have what it takes to thrive in the pre-need business. They must persuade prospective customers to face unpleasant facts and still maintain rapport. The man is convinced that Dave can do it and offers him the job on straight commission. Dave promises to think about it.

On the way home, Dave stops at a convenience store, picks up a pack of Zig-Zags, and splurges on some Heineken. He's hoping to get Cindy in a cheerful mood, but it turns out he could have saved his money. She's already happy and can barely contain her joy when Dave picks her up. "I got promoted to production manager," Cindy whispers. "Drive, and I'll tell you all about it."

Cindy seems fearful that someone in the Colony 7 parking lot might hear her being overly enthusiastic about the promotion and rescind it. But once they are well away, she loses all inhibitions. "Hot damn," she yells. "Hot diggity goddamn diggity damn. I did it. They chose me. Not Gary in props. Now that loser is going to report to me. Ha." Cindy puts her arms around Dave's neck and smooches his cheek. Then she moves her lips around to his. It's promising, but first they have to make it back to the apartment alive. Somehow Dave keeps his eyes on the road despite all the distractions.

Mr. and Mrs. Knight sleep in the next morning. It's past noon when Dave goes to the door and retrieves the newspaper. He starts coffee brewing then sits at the kitchen table and reads. After a while, Cindy appears. "Did anyone get the license plate of the truck that hit me?" she asks.

"No, but I saw a Jose Cuervo logo on the side," Dave replies.

"Don't tell me we got into that," Cindy exclaims.

Dave goes to the trash bin, pulls out a bottle, turns it over, and shakes it to prove that it's empty.

"So that's why my head feels like someone used it for a piñata," Cindy moans.

"I warned you," Dave says. "But you wouldn't listen."

"Warned me what?"

"Not to eat the worm."

"Oh, shut up."

"OK, but next time . . ."

"There won't be any next time," Cindy says emphatically. "I don't know what got into me."

"You got promoted," Dave replies. "Don't you remember?"

"Oh, big deal," Cindy exclaims. "Really, what's to celebrate? Let's face it, this is the sticks, and the Colony 7 is bush. Why did I attend Bard? Certainly not to do dinner theater."

"Seems like someone told me something recently that might help you," Dave says facetiously. "Oh yeah, now I remember, she said, 'You've got to start somewhere.'"

"Just listen to yourself," Cindy replies icily. "What a snide, snarky bastard you've become."

"That's not fair," Dave protests. "I have some redeeming qualities."

"Name one."

"I can lick my eyebrows."

"That's it," Cindy replies. "I'm going shopping then to a movie, don't care what's playing. Do me a favor; don't be here when I get back."

Three weeks later, Dave's unemployment benefits run out. He's about to accept a straight commission job when Beverly calls. "Hey, good news," she exclaims. "HR says you're a go."

"Thanks, Beverly, you just made my day."

"Of course, it's going to be up to the hiring manager, but with Cincinnati in your corner, you're as good as gold."

"So what's the next step?"

"We have a lot of openings for territory managers in the region," Beverly says. "The closest to you would be Baltimore-Washington. I can arrange a meeting for you with Walt Frazier, if you like. He's the district manager."

"That would be great."

"Any idea of when you would be free to do it?"

"The only day I'm not free is next Tuesday. Other than that, I'm wide open."

The next morning, Beverly calls back, and the meeting is arranged for Monday. "Honey, I'm so proud of you," Cindy says that night after Dave gives her the news. "I can't wait to tell my mother. We both thought that since they quit calling, you must have blown those tests."

Dave is ready to let fly with a sarcastic comment but manages to stifle it. Later he hears Cindy on the bedroom phone laughing and joking with her mother. "Mom says we've got to come up for Thanksgiving," Cindy says when she comes back to the living room.

"Sure," Dave replies, "what else would we do?"

"Well, there's your father. You haven't been to Florida to see him and Perle yet."

"That's too far to go for just a few days."

"What about Melissa?" Cindy asks.

"I called her," Dave says. "We discussed the three of us getting together for lunch in Annapolis one day, but Thanksgiving is out."

"Then Princeton it is," Cindy says.

After a rainy weekend spent lolling around the apartment, Dave goes to Silver Spring on Monday for his interview with Walt Frazier. He's hopeful, but the meeting turns out to be a disaster. Clearly, the P&G sales manager is only doing it as a courtesy to Beverly. After a scant ten minutes, it's over. That night the gloom is so thick in the Knights' apartment a case of Tide wouldn't wash it away. "So now we're back to the drawing board," Cindy complains, "only this time with no unemployment benefits."

"I'll call New York Life tomorrow," Dave says, "and see if their offer is still good."

"Get real," Cindy scoffs. "Who would you sell life insurance to? You don't have any friends, don't attend a church, don't belong to any clubs. You're a recluse."

Dave returns to the employment office in the morning and throws himself on the mercy of Mr. Smathers. The counselor has had several new sales jobs come in that look interesting. Dave makes notes on each opening then he goes home and starts writing cover letters. A little later Beverly calls. "I hear things didn't go well with Walt," she says.

"That's an understatement."

"Well, he can be difficult," Beverly sympathizes. "But we have openings in several other districts. Are you willing to relocate?"

"Yes, I am," Dave replies. "Of course, it would depend on where."

"What would you think of New York?"

"That would be great."

"Let me call Paul Braxton, the DM. I'll get back to you tomorrow."

"Thanks."

The next day it's all set. Dave will fly to Newark at the end of the week and meet Paul Braxton at the Airport Marriott for lunch. "You'll like Paul," Beverly says. "He's a live wire."

So, on Friday Dave catches an early flight to New Jersey. His fellow passengers are mostly lawyers, judging by the thick files they bring out once the seat belt light goes off. Dave feels honored to be among people who are important enough to fly to work. But instead of a legal brief, he only has the newspaper to read.

Dave gets to the Marriott, an hour early for the meeting. While he waits, he works the *Jumble*. It's a tough one, and he misses the help of Sergeant Calhoun, but finally the answer dawns on him. Then Dave puts the paper away and goes to wait outside the entrance to the restaurant.

Presently a distinguished-looking gentleman approaches. He's dressed in a navy-blue suit, white shirt, and red tie. The man walks straight up to Dave and sticks out his hand. "I'm Paul," he says confidently.

"Dave Knight."

"That's what I figured," Paul grins. "Beverly described you to a T. Have you ever tried combing that hair?"

"Yes, but the comb broke."

Paul laughs easily, and Dave is glad he resisted Cindy's pleas for him to get a haircut. After the army, he's letting his frizzy hair grow back out.

Once the two men are seated, the waitress appears. "Can I get you gentlemen something to drink?" she asks.

"Definitely," Paul replies. "I'll have a Jack Daniels on the rocks, make it a double."

"Same here," Dave echoes.

"I guess that's one thing about the army," Paul says. "You learn to drink."

"Were you ever in?"

"No, I was too young for Korea and too old for Vietnam, but every army guy we've hired has had a hollow leg."

"I believe it."

When the waitress returns with the drinks, Paul orders a club sandwich and once again Dave follows his lead. Then the district manager gets a manila folder out of his slender briefcase. "You made quite a hit with HR," he says. "I have the report right here. Did they tell you anything about the position?"

"No."

"Just as well," Paul says. "I'll explain. Our job is to maximize volume sales of P&G household products through the trade. Territory managers do that by making sales calls on supermarkets with the goal of convincing store personnel to correct any issues they find that are detrimental to product movement."

"Like what?" Dave asks.

"Out-of-stocks, missing reorder tags, wrong prices, lack of display activity, poor shelf position, or inadequate shelf space. We will train you to survey the store, identify issues, then present solutions to store management."

"Do I have to go to Cincinnati for that?"

"No, all your training will be conducted in the field at the regional level."

"What does the job pay?"

"Base of nine thousand, five hundred plus bonus," Paul replies. "And you get a company car."

"Sounds good."

"So are you in?"

"Yes."

"Let's drink to it," Paul exclaims. He reaches for his glass, but it's empty. Dave is similarly embarrassed, but just then the waitress returns with their sandwiches and a solution to the drink drought is set in motion.

"To your future with Procter & Gamble," Paul toasts once the replenishments arrive.

"Hear, hear!" Dave joins his new boss in a celebratory swig of whiskey.

The two men tuck into their sandwiches and quickly polish them off. Now they can relax and tend to their beverages. "Paul, I have a question," Dave says.

"Fire away."

"It just occurred to me that you haven't asked a single interview question."

"Didn't have to," Paul replies complacently. "It's all in here." He taps the manila folder.

"So you had already made up your mind about me?"

"Right."

"What in the report caught your eye?"

"Cinci has three ratings they give prospective hires," Paul explains. "Low recommend, recommend, and high recommend. You're a high recommend. That means if I hire you and you turn out to be a dud, it's on HR, not me."

"That's just like the army," Dave says.

"How so?" Paul asks.

"CYA, baby," Dave responds.

"Damn right!" Paul holds out his glass. They clink and drink to it.

"But seriously, there was something else I liked," Paul says.

"What's that?"

"You're an ENTJ like me."

Dave has no idea what an ENTJ is and decides not to ask. "But I interviewed with Walt Frazier," he says instead. "And Mr. Frazier had the same report you have, but he turned me down."

"Did he say why?"

"Said he didn't want anyone with mental disabilities."

"That idiot," Paul exclaims. "The report says you have some learning disabilities, not mental disabilities. I called HR about it, and they said as long as you don't need to learn trigonometry for this job, you'll do fine."

"Well, that's a relief."

"They also said that you have one of the strongest sales profiles they've seen."

"Guess I better not turn out to be a dud then," Dave smiles.

The waitress comes back and takes their plates. "Ready for another?" she asks.

"Better not," Paul replies. "Just the check, please."

"My pleasure, I'll be right back."

"So how long will it take for you to move?" Paul asks.

"Not long," Dave replies. "Just have to give a month's notice where we are now, then find an apartment up here."

"You can stay at a hotel in the meantime," Paul says. "We'll cover that cost plus the moving expense once you find a place."

"Great."

"Beverly will help with all the details. She's the regional sales coordinator."

"Beverly's great," Dave says.

"Don't tell anyone I said so, but she actually runs this region, not Nick."

"I believe you."

Paul takes care of the tab, then he and Dave walk outside. Planes are taking off and landing less than a mile away. The din of jet engines fills the air, so Paul raises his voice. "Tell me something," he says. "You ain't one of them idiots that spends every spare moment out chasing that little white ball, now, are you?"

Dave intuits the correct response to this question. "'Fraid so," he admits.

Paul sighs. "Oh well, guess you'll fit right in with the rest of the mob."

After treating himself to another double whiskey on the flight home, Dave finds Cindy waiting for him at the curb outside the terminal. She's standing by the car impatiently looking this way and that but doesn't see Dave till the last minute. "I got the job," he tells her. "We're moving to New York."

"Yahoo," Cindy screams as she throws her arms around her husband. "Broadway, here I come."

The young marrieds hug and kiss excitedly, but then an airport cop pulls up in his patrol car. "You're not supposed to park here," he says through a rolled-down window.

"Don't fuckin' worry about it, officer," Dave replies with a grin.

"Yeah, right," the cop says. "Just move."

And so they do.

CPSIA information can be obtained
at www.ICGtesting.com
Printed in the USA
LVHW051720060522
717695LV00001B/9